WAITING FOR THE MACHINES TO FALL ASLEEP

Waiting for the Machines to Fall Asleep

Melody of the Yellow Bard — 5
Hans Olsson

The Rats — 32
Boel Bermann

Getting to the End — 41
Erik Odeldahl

Vegatropolis – City of the Beautiful — 62
Ingrid Remvall

Jump to the Left, Jump to the Right — 73
Love Kölle

The Order of Things — 88
Lupina Ojala

To Preserve Humankind — 104
Christina Nordlander

The Thirteenth Tower — 107
Pia Lindestrand

Punch Card Horses — 114
Jonas Larsson

The Philosopher's Stone — 122
Tora Greve

A Sense of Foul Play — 139
Andrew Coulthard

Waste of Time   155
Alexandra Nero

The Damien Factor   157
Johannes Pinter

Wishmaster   176
Andrea Grave-Müller

Quadrillennium   203
AR Yngve

Mission Accomplished   206
My Bergström

The Road   217
Anders Blixt

Lost and Found   226
Maria Haskins

The Publisher's Reader   239
Patrik Centerwall

Stories from the Box   247
Björn Engström

The Membranes in the Centering Horn   254
KG Johansson

One Last Kiss Goodbye   264
Oskar Källner

The Mirror Talks   270
Sara Kopljar

Keep Fighting Until the Machines Fall Asleep   276
Eva Holmquist

Outpost Eleven   288
Markus Sköld

Messiah   309
Anna Jakobsson Lund

The Authors   318

Melody of the Yellow Bard

Hans Olsson

The man approached me when I was on my way home from the university. There was something clearly different about him. He had a strange look in his eyes, a certain calmness, like he knew some big secret. He appeared young, not much older than me, but he had a confident, powerful way of walking. That, and the fact that he almost toppled me, caught my attention.

"Rasmus? Are you Rasmus Ekblad?"

"Yes?" I said. He was now standing disturbingly close to me. I could see that, along with his bright smile, he wore a tailored suit with a blue tie. His eyes were even more unsettling this close, almost like he could see something within me that I tried to hide.

"My name is Clayton and I'm a representative for a big company that is very interested in new scientific discoveries and ideas. We came across your thesis about controllable wormholes and found it fascinating, especially the design you made of a model of a machine that could support such activities. Where did you get the idea?"

Some people I've met call me obnoxious or ignorant. The truth is they may be right, but at the same time they are equally wrong. I'm not ignorant, I just don't understand what they are saying. Fashion, for example. I cannot comprehend why I have to wear this year's model of a jacket when it's just another autumn. The one I had last year is just as warm. Does not compute.

I think that's why I came up with my idea in the first place, because I'm usually not hindered by conventional thinking. Because I don't understand it. All my idea needed was a component lacking in other theories: the sound component. I thought that sound waves could alter a theoretical wormhole, given the assumption that vibrating strings rule microcosmos. It also made technical sense, at least to me. It took me a moment to recall that paper. The night before I got the idea I had a few beers with friends. Probably two or three too many. Anyway, ever since I took the class for quantum physics, those thoughts must have been circling around in my head. The idea of a controllable wormhole was born somewhere between the beers, when I thought about how the mind processes changes from clear, to cloudy, to deep-mist-murky, and back to clear again. It could stay at a clear peak for a brief moment, and it was a delicate balance to keep it there, but it was possible. Granted you balanced beer intake with other factors. Somewhere around there reality snuck into my thoughts and I started to apply these terms to the idea of a wormhole.

"It just came to me," I shrugged.

Clayton smiled. "If you say so. Well, Shervi, the multinational company I work for would like to meet you for an interview. It's a great chance for you to get a foot into the business grind of the real world. I also understand that you have a talent for engineering and machines?"

I thought about that for a second. His choice of words intrigued me. The grind; it sounded like something I could imagine. To be grinded, hardened, against the cogwheels of competent people. This could give me a huge boost in preparation for the job market. I also vaguely recognized the name of the company as one of the inventive ones. Maybe I'd read about it somewhere. And he wasn't wrong about the mechanical part. I've always had a talent for engineering. Perhaps that's why I drew such a detailed prototype of a machine capable of altering the fabric of space. It was all theoretical of course, a joke at best. Why would this Clayton character be interested in that?

"That's right. I know a few things about engines and stuff," I said. "When is the interview?"

"Our facilities are located on a small island in the Baltic Sea. I will give you a ticket to a boat transport, which will depart tomorrow at 11 a.m. We require you to stay for two days for interviews, some basic tests and evaluation. We realize that you will miss two days of study time, but we will compensate you economically. How does that sound?"

I didn't need to think about that, but I pretended for the sake of it.

"Sounds good. How much compensation are we talking about?"

"1100 euros," he said without hesitation. "That's about 10 000 Swedish kronor," he added.

Just the right amount to get me hooked. Had he offered me more, I probably would have dismissed him.

"Great."

"Good. Don't miss the boat. Here's directions of how to get there, and here's your ticket."

He reached into a pocket in his suit and took out two pieces of paper. The first one was indeed some sort of directions. I could see a time table for the bus and a map of what looked like a harbor. The other paper was blank.

"This is your ticket which, if you use the transports suggested, will take you all the way. All expenses are included. Just show this to the bus driver and he will know who you are."

I stared at the blank paper, and began to think that all this might be a fraud, but I was absorbed by the situation and knew I would give it a chance. The blank paper also had a certain touch to it, with a crude surface that felt … real; real in a way that gave credibility to his mysterious offer.

"Thank you very much for your time, Rasmus. I promise you that we are interested and impressed by your thesis. You will not be disappointed with what we can offer you. I'll meet you on the boat tomorrow."

Then he turned and walked away, leaving me with a puzzled grin on my face. He knew he had me.

The next day I had packed a few things and went on my way to the bus station. The description stated "Line 727" which I didn't recognize, but when I arrived at the station there was a bus waiting for me. A big blue one. The driver insisted on seeing my blank piece of paper, and when I showed it to him he scanned it with some device. I was the only passenger, and we took off immediately.

A video monitor in the center of the bus caught my attention. There was no sound, but the images were clear enough that I could make out the content without too much effort. There was a bearded man, with big bushy hair, who looked nothing like the scientist he, in his white coat, was supposed to be. But he had steel in his eyes; steel, fire and determination. I saw an island with lots of small buildings scattered about. A lab was then shown containing numerous strange devices I had never seen before. Some looked like modified microscopes; others like big ovens; and yet more like bizarre engines, stacked in various locations of the room. The details held my attention for the whole fifteen minutes of the film, before it started over again. I watched it three times and each time I discovered more surprising things, like the oily fluid flowing not through the pipes of the engines, but sort of around it. Or the faint glow that pulsated like a vicious radioactive heart in the background. Outside the bus the landscape had changed from pine trees to a rocky coastline.

The bus stopped and as I stepped out I could smell sea water. The boat was there, but there was no harbor. We had just stopped at a seemingly random location along a cemented dock. The directions in my pocket seemed pointless. It was a small vessel, more like a military scouting vehicle than anything else. Clayton was on it and he raised his hand and smiled.

"Good to see you again," he said as I approached and got onboard. "We're moving out immediately and will be there in thirty minutes. You might want to wear these," he added with a grin and handed me a pair of what looked like swimming goggles.

"It's fast?"

"Yes. Built with the very latest technology. So new, in fact, it's not officially on the market yet, and so advanced that it probably never will be. Intrigued?" He raised his eyebrows and smiled. "Please, have a seat here," he gestured at some small seats in the front of the boat. "I like to sit outside as long as it's not too cold. And the weather today is alright. Inside or outside?"

I didn't want to look weak in front of him, so outside it was.

It was a bloody fast boat. Once the engine started I could feel the power from it through the hull, like a hungry beast roaring. The advanced vessel then detached from the dock and began to rapidly accelerate. I'm not sure if we flew or sailed, but I loved the goggles. The wind was so furious that it was hard to breathe, but I had no problems seeing. Clayton did thumbs-up and I tried to smile, but it was a challenge to even manage that. The thirty minutes literally flew past before the boat slowed down and took aim toward an island off ahead. Gray cliffs rose from the sea, and there was a small lighthouse. When we got closer I could see barbed wire surrounding the entire island, and guards patrolling. Was it military?

We arrived beneath the lighthouse and Clayton jumped ashore just as the boat stopped. I followed, slightly unsteady after the ride. A yellow SUV waited for us and Clayton motioned me to take a seat.

"Welcome to Nebu Island," he said when the driver started. "I bet you have questions stockpiling up, but please wait with them. You will understand our need for discretion shortly. Meanwhile, allow me to tell you a little bit more about the company I work for. It's not your ordinary multinational organization."

"Oo...kay." I started to feel a bit unsure of what was going on as the SUV drove us past several gray buildings, bringing us toward a vast hangar complex ahead.

"The company is called Shervi, which is a subsidiary of another bigger company in the cooperative. We headhunt people from all over the world, who could support our organization in one way or another. We mainly perform research, but also engage in extensive field testing. The problem is, the 'fields' we have here can't really support nor justify our testing needs. So we have developed other methods to ... let's say simulate, certain circumstances that would otherwise be impossible."

"Mhm. Impossible on this island?"

"Not exactly."

"Where then? What kind of simulation are you talking about?"

"You'll see shortly," Clayton said with another smile. He went silent for a moment. "I wasn't totally honest with you."

"Really?" I said, almost with a snarl. I was starting to dislike the whole situation more and more.

"There will be few questions, none actually, regarding your potential employment here. You can almost consider yourself hired right away. There is just one small thing I want you to look at first and give me your opinion on. Isn't that good news?"

"Maybe."

Clayton's demeanour turned serious. "Very few people will ever get the chance to experience what you are about to. I want you to keep that in mind."

"So what is this place? Do you work for the military?" The whole thought of the military running some secret operations on this island almost made me laugh in disbelief. What secrets could they possibly have that would be interesting to me, and make me interesting to them?

"As soon as you put up fences around a place there are people bound to challenge them. It works to keep the majority out, but some people will try. Hence, we are not military per se, but we do need protection. Both from outside sources and inside ... events."

"What?"

"Just keep in mind that you are privileged, Mr. Ekblad." Clayton ended the conversation and I was left more puzzled than ever.

The SUV drove around the big complex and stopped outside a gray steel door. Two armed guards stood outside, nodded over at Clayton as he jumped out of the car and gave me a quick, uninterested glance. They resumed their staring into nothingness. Two silent statues guarding ... what?

"Come now," said Clayton and opened the door. The interior of the hangar was expansive; almost empty. Over in a corner on the other side I noticed three outdated looking helicopters. Clayton went left and stopped by the wall after some twenty meters.

"Here we are," he said, smiling again.

"Yeah ..."

"I can see that you are unimpressed, but please keep an open mind."

Clayton reached for the wall and pressed some tiles that looked dirty and oily. Suddenly a rumble emerged across the hangar, like giant chains being dragged over boulders. A part of the floor beside us sank, revealing a staircase down to another door. We descended and Clayton entered a code on a small electrical panel. I counted twelve digits.

"Point of no return," he said jokingly, and he pushed the door open and dragged me in before I could say otherwise. "Welcome to Alpha Harbor."

Inside were a large group of people in an office-looking area. Not exactly what I'd been expecting to see. Clayton smirked in response to my confused look. Some of the people raised their heads as we entered, but most just hurried along, busy with whatever they were doing. He took me through a white corridor. On the walls were paintings with abstract motives and mosaic post-it art of action heroes or villains from video games. I recognized Richter Belmont, with his whip in hand in one picture. That made me smile. Computes.

I caught a few words from a conversation and heard two women talk about electromagnetism and quarks. The people here had a certain grace about them; their posture, gestures and the way they looked at each other. I recognized it from the university, among the professors. They were discussing important things, no doubt, but at another level than I was used to. The whole atmosphere had a remarkable touch of respect and knowledge.

We walked down a set of stairs, into another corridor with rooms off to the sides, almost like a hospital. Soon I was lost due to all the turns, but Clayton led me on. Eventually he gestured me into a room, from which an electric humming emanated.

We stepped in and stood in some sort of control room, with panels and computer screens set beneath a big glass window. In a corner I could see pipes disappearing through the wall into another room just behind it.

"Look here," Clayton said, pointing through the glass. "Tell me what you see, please. What can you tell me about this apparatus?"

I stepped forward and, peering closely through the window, saw some weird machine, with metallic strings on the hull, and small parabolic antennas, similar to sea shells, attached all over. At first they seemed random, but the more I looked the more sense they made.

"It's … I think it's wrong." I couldn't explain it. I just knew it wasn't right.

"What makes you say that?" Clayton wanted to know, genuinely interested.

"I … It's like some of the components have been distorted, shifted slightly out of place. Like someone has dented it. Machinal internal bleeding," I tried to explain.

"That's exactly what has happened here. I am impressed and this is why I wanted your opinion. You can consider yourself hired. Let me introduce you to someone else who will explain what this machine does, and many more things."

With that we left the room and continued to navigate the corridors. After many turns we entered a smaller room with a man behind a big marble desk. I recognized him from the video on the bus. He had a white trimmed beard, thick glasses and big hands that looked like they could crush stones, should he want to. He was writing something in a journal, but paused when he saw us.

"Ah, good to see you, Clayton. This is Rasmus, I suppose?"

"Yes," I said hesitantly.

"Did you show him the machine?" the man asked.

"Yes," Clayton said and nodded. "He immediately saw it was 'dented' or suffered from 'machinal internal bleeding'. I offered him employment on the spot."

The man laughed. "Perfect. I'm Erling Stumferd and I'm the senior CEO."

"Oh," I responded, still processing this was the man from the video.

"Do you want employment, Rasmus?"

"Maybe," I said vaguely.

"I'm sure you will when I've shown you some interesting things. Did Clayton tell you anything about what we do here?"

"Not really, no. Simulations?"

"In a way, yes. But that's all very good. I wouldn't want to have your surprise spoiled. Anyway, you have to see to believe. Do you like science fiction movies, Rasmus?"

"Sure, I watch them ..."

"What if I told you that all the movies you know are bogus and out of date. What if I told you that we have discovered technology far superior to anything known to the outside world. What if I told you that you are about to witness the future, not here on Earth, but other planets. Would you believe me?"

I laughed. What a nut.

"I was promised some money," I said instead, trying to divert his attention to real matters. But he just gave me a soft smile that I didn't like one bit. It was like when you carefully explain to a child that Santa isn't real, and when the child protests you give them that kind of smile: You will understand in due time. Oh yes, in due time.

"The ticket Clayton gave you, have you considered how the bus driver knew that you were the right passenger?"

"Not really." I hesitated. The movie on the bus had distracted me so much I had completely forgotten about that.

"I see," Erling said softly. "It's encrypted with quantum technology. Had you brought a similar paper instead of the ticket, the scanning device would've shown nothing and you would still be in school, playing with the other kids. This, my friend, is the new order of things. Come, let me show you."

We left the room and headed further into the corridor maze. Shortly we stopped outside a big vault door with a handle that Erling turned. The door opened and for the first time that day I was utterly and completely speechless. Inside was a machine park of some kind, but not with machines I'd ever seen. I tried to look for familiar shapes and found something that looked like an airplane, but only because it had wings. One pair of translucent, fly-like wings, shimmering in the light from computer screens, spread across the room. The rest of the plane was spherical, with something that looked like rails attached in a semicircle around the upper part of the sphere.

Another vehicle looked like a small train, but in the weirdest shade of green-orange that made it hard to distinguish any features, making it unpleasant to look at.

Yet another looked organic, with shell-like armor plates around a circular window, and with hundreds of small legs. But it couldn't be organic, could it? I wasn't laughing anymore.

People were walking about, taking notes and touching things while measuring with strange devices. I could also see armed men looking nervously around the edge of the room. They all glanced to a corridor to the right, further ahead into the hall.

Was this some elaborate prank set up by someone? Things made in papier mâché to drive me insane? Whatever it was they had near succeeded. I was baffled. Erling saw it and laughed.

"I know the feeling. All you see here is real. We have brought home technology so vastly different to our own that it's no longer science fiction. It's the future, and so far in it that the rest of mankind could be cavemen. This, young man, is what you can and will learn more about. Our branch of the cooperative is one of the most front-of-the-line companies in the world, period. Some people are ahead of their time. Einstein was decades ahead of his time. Leonardo Da Vinci as well. Have you seen his classic helicopter blueprint? Shervi specializes in finding people that are ahead of their time and have been doing so for the last fifty-three years. We have an impressive setup of people capable of thinking outside the box, around the box and even in terms of completely new boxes, shaped like grapes." Erling let out a rumbling laugh that made the air shiver around him. "In the early 70s we already had technology up to par with today's computers. Of course we cannot make these kinds of things public, because the public would not understand what they see. But in our field we have come to accept just how small we are in the universe, and we have profited from this fact. Where others are stopped by ridiculous laws and prohibitions, we can grow and benefit from what can be thought out and implemented. We don't work with morals and ethics. We work with limitless science. Of course we needed a breakthrough, and it came in the early 80s when a man called Jarmund Spearman cracked an important piece of the quantum mechanical field. Are you familiar with quantum tunneling? Jarmund refined the whole concept. The scientists out there are still years behind. Decades even. Anyway," Erling added nonchalantly, like he was discussing yesterday's lunch, "he discovered, and managed to control, a tear in the fabric of space. Or perhaps what you would call a wormhole."

A big piece of the puzzle fell into place. It sounded like ... nonsense. Wormholes were still a theoretical mystery. But I had seen the machines which I couldn't explain within my frame of reference. I had to evaluate and rewrite that frame. The thought of that made me feel nauseated.

"Awesome," I said, trying to sound relaxed. It did not compute well.

"Indeed. And this is where you come in, Rasmus. We tried your sound theory and had some extraordinary, albeit short-term results. I will tell you more about this in a few minutes. The machine Clayton showed you, that's your sound machine, or a prototype of it. We use one to transmit efficient sound signals to the wormhole area, where we can control the destination coordinates. There's more to it of course, but in short your idea helped us think in new ways. Progress was fine, at first, for several weeks. We improved our landing accuracy by 327 percent and can now walk through the wormholes like this." He swiped his arms down along his body. "At the beginning we had some ... tougher times. Entering other places from five meters in the air. Got a broken foot, some cracked ribs. Small accidents like that. But upon implementing your ideas we managed to make rapid progress. Most impressive. We adjusted your original schematics of course. In its current state it was inefficient. We call it a 'Sonar Enhancement and Locator Device', or in short; S.E.L.D."

"Okay," I said, feeling numb.

"I see that I'm going too fast, but no matter. It's important that you hear this and understand what kind of help we need from you. That and the fact that you could immediately tell that something was wrong with the S.E.L.D is most valuable to us. Let me try an example. Imagine that you are holding a water hose, spraying water against a wall. The closer you hold your hands to the nozzle, the more accurately you can steer the water, correct?"

"Yes, that sounds reasonable."

"S.E.L.D allowed us to get closer to the nozzle, and thus fine-tune our landing parameters dramatically. Before that we could fairly accurately aim for, let's say an uninhabited planet, but we could never be entirely sure where we got off at. It made it harder to construct advancement bases and slowed progress. One day we could land on the southern hemisphere of the planet, and the next day the northern. Most inefficient. We needed coordinates to know where we should aim the 'water hose', and getting accurate coordinates is so much easier the closer you are to the destination. Hence we build advancement bases where it's suitable, to be able to measure feasible coordinates. Imagine that you had a Hubble telescope in the Andromeda galaxy instead of here. What would you see if peering through the telescope, when over there? You would see other planets more clearly, and you would be able to calculate their positions more accurately. This helped us drastically speed up the process, until one day when some unknown force reached into our tunnel and gave the S.E.L.D a dent. Or machinal internal bleeding, as you called it."

"Some what? Some alien?"

Erling went silent and when Rasmus met his eyes he could see a grave, serious look on his face.

"We don't know. Yet. Before this incident we had access to sixteen different, well functioning advancement bases. Now we can only reach one."

"What does that mean?"

"It means that earlier we could feed coordinates into a computer and decide where the wormhole should take us. Now it takes us to a place we can't locate. We have no known reference points. The place is uninhabited, yet is similar to our own planet in many regards. And in some it's very different. There's oxygen, but we haven't found much else of remarkable interest. We're constantly collecting data, of course. But well ..." He went silent.

There was something deeply troubling about that statement. Erling had such a casual way of describing it that it felt real; so very real. To be honest I wanted to believe him because if it was true that meant Clayton was right; I was privileged. I also realized that there was something else to this whole strange situation.

"So what do you want me to do?" I asked, both dreading and wanting the answer. I wanted it badly.

"First of all, I want you to take a look at the S.E.L.D, see if you can find out what went wrong with it. Second of all we're putting you in a crash course on wormhole traveling. Yes," he added when he saw my jaw drop, "you are going to another planet to see if our equipment on that side is functional. We've had some malfunctions lately and we want a 'natural born engineer's' opinion of what might cause the failures. And you can relax, you are not the star here. You will go as a theoretical engineer supporting experienced staff and soldiers. So far we have not encountered any hostile aliens, but well, we have encountered some interesting species. As I said, the planet you are going to is deserted. As far as we know," he added and laughed. "We have all done the traveling and it's perfectly safe, oh except when you end up some distance in the air, of course. Or in deep space, ha, ha. But other than that, safe."

"What if I don't want to?" I tried. It wasn't that I didn't want to go. Already I longed for it. How many could say they had been on another planet? Not many. But I wasn't really sure I liked that they just assumed I would tag along. Erling knew, of course.

"It doesn't matter," he said. "You can't resist it. No one here has resisted. And we're very happy to have the S.E.L.D inventor on board. Perhaps we should've brought you in earlier, but we didn't have issues until just recently. Welcome aboard, Rasmus."

Defeated. Employed. And I didn't mind. "Thanks," I said.

My first task was to get to know the Alpha Harbor. Erling showed me the dining room, the sleeping quarters, the machine halls containing strange alien technology mixed with our own and doors to the bio-organic section, where experiments of all kinds were taking place on a regular basis. He told me they discovered a flower on a planet, that thrived on sulfurous gases, and emitted small, but clearly visible, balls of energy into the air. There wasn't that much energy in it, but enough to fuel a light bulb for a few seconds at the time given a certain rate of harvesting. Very interesting. Erling also showed me the doors to the wormhole section, but I wasn't permitted to enter at this point.

"In a week," he said. "You must do the basic training, which considering the circumstances is a joke. None the less the training is mandatory. It's more of a mind adjustment than a physical one. Being warped through time and space for the first time can be ... overwhelming. Not to mention the sight of completely unknown sceneries. Mankind can think up many things, but some environments we just can't comprehend before we stand in them."

During the week that passed I came to love the Alpha Harbor. The people were really what Erling had said they would be. They thought outside the box and they had a positive attitude towards everything. The days flew by. The training course consisted of watching movies of what I thought was Rorschach spots, mixed with scenes from various known landscapes, and some unfamiliar ones. I saw pictures from a jungle, some white desert, snow filled mountains and green lakes. The weirdest thing was a purple vertical wall that seemed to bubble.

"Imagine you are there," Martin, the tutor, kept repeating. So I did. And the week passed.

Erling was right, in the end. The basic training was a joke, but everyone kept insisting that it was necessary and knowing that I watched non-terrestrial environments filled me with excitement.

I also got to look more at the S.E.L.D, but all I could tell was that something wasn't right with it. It was something with the frequency of the rotors inside it. They sort of skipped a beat every now and then. Like a heart skipping a beat randomly. Some rumors in the kitchen talked about the 'wormhole anomaly'. Apparently it had a weird, sick, look nowadays, which explained the nervous soldiers, half expecting to be sucked into it. Erling, and several others, assured that it couldn't happen though. They had made sure to build in safety mechanisms to prevent just that.

And so the day came when the team was ready to traverse into the unknown. Among them were Beata Nox, an older woman with gray hair and green eyes, professor Henning Untermann, the team leader, and a whole bunch of engineers I didn't know too well.

We also had an escort of three soldiers, easy going fellas, nothing like I'd imagine a soldier. They laughed, complained about the weight of their packs and cursed like everyone else. The leader's name was Ortega. The others were Dan and Marko.

Erling picked me up that morning, a bit earlier than appointed.

"Good morning," he said in his usual happy mood, though I noticed something was slightly different. I could hear he was concerned about something. "I hope you slept well," he said. "Today you are going on a fantastic journey. It shouldn't take more than a few hours for you guys to examine and fix the machinery on the other side. When you are done you come back and report to me. Very simple. Do you have any questions at this point?"

"Not really," I said, trying to figure out which questions swarming around my head were the most important ones.

"Very good. I'm here a bit earlier so I can show you the actual wormhole. It can be intimidating the first time."

"I'm sure I can handle it."

Erling gave me a quick smile. "Of course."

He led me down the corridors to the section where I knew that the wormholes were, but where I hadn't been before. He took me down several floors. I counted seven levels of descent before we finally broke off into a narrow corridor. Erling saw my puzzled look.

"When we first got our hands on the technology to fabricate wormholes we worried we would create a black hole instead, swallowing everything. Superstitious nonsense in the end, but well, to eliminate some of the risks we built the chamber far below the surface to accommodate for any unforeseen events. Everything worked according to plan in the end. Very nice."

"Why don't you guys use wormholes in space instead? Shouldn't that eliminate the risk?"

"Ha, ha," Erling laughed. "I guess we could somehow install a wormhole device on a space ship, but why should we? We skipped that part in the tech evolutionary chain. In fact I'm not sure mankind's current technology could support it, nor ours ... Besides, if we were to launch massive space ships there would be questions. This is better on all levels."

He led me on through a series of corridors until finally stopping in front of another vault door. It had a copper sign on it, with words in silver:

Inside lies the beyond. Mankind no longer leap, we fly.

"Famous words of Jarmund Spearman. He thought about 'warp' instead of 'fly', but settled for that word. I like it. Simple. Neat. Fitting."

I could only nod. We fly.

Erling gently pulled the valve and shoved the door open. Inside was a large room and I could immediately see another S.E.L.D at the side of the wall. It stood against an oval metal frame attached to the floor, two and a half meters high and half the size across. Inside the frame there was a gray fluid mirror, or a very thin slimy membrane, that seemed to vibrate slowly, stretching out and retracting. Almost like breathing. It didn't reflect light and it was depressingly colorless. There it was, the wormhole. There was a deepness in it, like it was hiding shadows somewhere just out of sight. I felt a coldness in my heart when looking into that pulsating gray void. There *was* something utterly sick with it. All the rumors could not make it justified. I didn't know what it had looked like earlier, but it wasn't supposed to be like this, it really was an anomaly. Quicksilver come alive. A liquid maw. And I would enter.

"Yes," Erling agreed. "It's not pleasant to look at, and it has gone paler since we started, even with the new S.E.L.D and refined technology. Don't worry though. It's perfectly safe. We had a test party go through this morning. Everything looked normal. The place you are going to is not like anything you could prepare for. It's not so different from Earth, but at the same time it's very unlike our environment. You have to be there to understand. Did I mention that the tunnel was pulled there? We wouldn't have found it otherwise because this planet is hidden deep within a large planetary system, housing fourteen seemingly dead planets. Except this one that has unique environments. You'll see for yourself."

The team started to arrive shortly. In total we were eleven people, including the three soldiers. They tried to look casual, but I could see them glancing nervously towards the wormhole, the portal to another world. It was still so bizarre to think about.

Everyone had backpacks containing their equipment and we lined up in front of the portal.

"All right," Erling said. "Ortega is head of security for this trip and professor Henning will take care of and coordinate the operation. You should be able to return in four to five hours with new data and hopefully find a more permanent fix for our equipment on the other side. And this time," he added, "bring back some valid samples from the sea. Take care of Rasmus here, as it's his first trip. Good luck."

They murmured in approval.

"Are you nervous?" Beata asked. She smiled and nudged me in the side. I was so nervous I almost couldn't move, but tried not to show it.

"Not at all," I said, shivering. The thought of going into that thing would make anyone nervous. The presence of soldiers didn't help either. They loaded their rifles and held them in front of them, ready for use.

"It's a simple mission," Beata said. "Some piece of shit equipment keeps breaking down and we need to try to gather more coordinates for other jump locations. We've done dozens of missions like this. Don't worry."

"Yeah. Okay."

"Me and Henning go first," Ortega said. "The rest of you follow in five second intervals. The tunnel is stable right now, but you know what happens if it starts to fluctuate."

Everyone laughed. "Let's not have that again. I had diarrhea for a week last time," a bearded engineer said, with a snort. More laughter.

And then we were off.

Ortega took a deep breath and walked through that gray, unnatural veil. It was like seeing someone disappear in mist, only more distinct. The membrane didn't even flinch. It just swallowed him out of existence. Then Henning went in, followed by the others, one by one. The line started shrinking. There was never any time to reconsider. I just followed suit, and when I stood before the gate I was drawn to it. I stepped forward. There was an ever so slight resistance, like touching a soap bubble, a moment of black silence, then I stumbled into a sickly yellow light and heard the sound of something crackling behind me. I fell to my knees and someone quickly dragged me up.

"You don't want to stay there. You'll get the next man on top of you."

I coughed, looked down on yellow soil, before managing to raise my head. The air was the most immediate difference I noticed, it was oily and tasted like static electricity. Something like being close to the mediterranean climate, but with the crispness of being trapped inside a tesla coil. It wasn't hard to breathe, but definitely different and not comfortable.

"You'll get used to it," Ortega said. "Just imagine that you are at home. It's perfectly safe, almost the same components as our atmosphere."

I nodded, trying to acclimate. At first everything was a yellow blur, then I realized that it was the sun and the environment.

Behind me was a black cliff, and on its surface the wormhole exit, like a gray swirling outgrowth. I couldn't pinpoint what it was, but it looked healthier here than it had on Earth. And then it struck me, we were not on Earth anymore. I spun around, quickly scanning the surroundings, and when I did my jaw dropped.

The sky was not blue, but purple. Clouds with strains of yellow in them floated around like majestic creatures. Despite having daylight I could see at least two planetary bodies up there, like big coins in the sky. We were in a desert of sorts, with black rocks sticking up here and there in the yellow sand. In the distance I could see an endless flat, yellow surface.

"Dammit," Ortega muttered. "Do you guys realize this is the exact same position as all the previous times?"

"Yes, our technology is improving," Henning said.

"No it isn't," the bearded guy objected. "Ortega is right. This is the only place where we always end up exactly here. There are always some deviations otherwise," he added and looked at me. "This planet probably has strong magnetic fields which we haven't really been able to measure yet. Nothing strange about it."

"It is strange," muttered Ortega and shook his head.

"Where are we?" I asked.

"We call this planet 'Yellow Bard', because of the unique air composition. When the wind increases you can hear all sorts of exciting noises."

I tilted my head and tried to listen to the wind. There was something very different with it, and after a few moments I heard it more clearly. In the background there was a constant whirring and purring, like many small mechanical toys emitting sounds somewhere around us. That, combined with the static electricity, made it almost sound like someone was playing some strange instrument.

"What's that, over there?" I asked, pointing at that fle surface at the horizon. It was a kilometer ahead, Beata told me. The terrain, covered in black rocks, made it easy to misjudge the distance.

"That's the Yellow Sea. As far as we know it covers almost eighty percent of the planet."

"How can you tell?"

"Oh, lots of factors. Wave size, the curving of the planet, things like that. Aren't you supposed to be smart?" Beata smiled and pinched my cheek. "I'm just kidding. This planet has some really cool things," she added. "The sea is some sort of acid. It's extremely potent and could be used to make big money for us in the industry. Provided we could gather it," she giggled. "This time we have some new test containers. We'll see if they hold together."

"Let's move out," Ortega said. "We have a short walk to the main base."

We started walking, parallel to the distant shoreline to our right and the black cliffs to our left. After a few minutes I could see the base. It consisted of some big tents, almost like barracks, anchored in the hard soil by wires to keep them from blowing away in the wind. As we approached a glimmering from the sea caught my attention. I stopped and held up my hand against the dull light. There was definitely something there.

"What's that?" I asked. The line came to an abrupt halt. Ortega and the two soldiers joined up shortly after. We all looked at the sea and the thing out there.

"What is it?" I asked again.

Silence.

"Is it ours?" I tried.

"No," someone answered.

Finally Ortega produced binoculars from his pack. He looked through them a long time before lowering them.

"I don't know," he said. "It's the first time we've seen it. It could be ..." He looked again before passing them on to the other soldiers. "It could be some sort of ship," he said, voice low.

"What do you mean? Some alien ship?" I was excited and scared at the same time. The expression on Ortega's face was excitement rather than worry. A real alien lifeform. Intelligent, since it could make ships.

"If that piece of metal is floating out there," Beata said, "we definitely need a sample. Our containers just melt."

Some nervous laughter followed.

"We have to investigate," Ortega said. "You two come with me. The rest of you proceed to the base and start working on our equipment."

Uncomfortable silence, before Henning cleared his throat. "All right. Let's proceed, everyone."

And so we split up. The soldiers backtracked and took off towards the ocean while we headed to the camp.

There were three big tents in place, flapping in the electric tasting wind. Beata took me to the center one, where she showed me an engine that had malfunctioned.

"Can you tell me what's wrong with it?" she asked.

It was obvious, at least I thought so. You could hear it as soon as you entered the tent.

"Probably that thing," I said, pointing at a dented pipe. "I guess pressure is building up within, causing circuits to overload. It's common with advanced and fragile technology. But that's not the only thing. Do you hear the sound it's making, that screeching? I think a rubber seal has broken down, you know like a flat tire on a bicycle. You can fill the tire with air and it could work for hours, but eventually it will be flat again. I think the dented pipe is a symptom of the rubber seal."

"Impressive!" Beata clapped me on the shoulder. "I'll have Bernt in here to fix it up. What background did you say you had again?"

I shrugged. Machines had been a part of me since childhood, when my father worked in the garage, repairing cars. It simply computes. Bernt came and started working. He had a replacement pipe, as well as new polymorphid plastic to replace the rubber seal.

"How long will it take?" I asked.

"Not too long, fifteen minutes maybe. Then we need to collect the data the machinery has gathered. See if we have been able to spot any reference points in this universe. Stuff like that."

While he worked Beata stood beside him pointing and instructing, I stepped outside. I was on an alien planet, after all. Strange, how quickly you adapt to things if someone tells you it's normal. I stood outside, indecisive. The rest of the team were busy inside the tents.

Suddenly there was a small, but very visible change to the light, like a shroud had been dragged in front of the sun. The world turned pale. It clearly radiated from the ocean, because there was a grayish spot on the horizon, far away. There was also a change to the background noise. The wind carried some new, crackling sound, and in the backwater of it there was a boom of silence, as if that non-light canceled all sounds. Much like thunder coming after a flash, only this thunder carried silence. It made my skin crawl. The event lasted for a minute before abruptly ending and the light resumed its usual yellow-purple color. I held my breath the whole time.

"Did you guys see that?" I asked before realizing I was alone. The others did not seem to have heard that strange absence of sound. It must be the tents, shielding the air inside.

The phenomena was close to the metallic thing. The ship. Curiosity gripped me and I was on my way. I had about fifteen minutes before they would notice I was missing. The ocean was closer here, compared to our landing site. Five hundred meters, perhaps. I started jogging, crisscrossing between the few black rocks sticking up like teeth through the bleak, yellow soil. Soon I came upon small pools of liquid. It was a green-yellow mess, almost fluorescent, but without any distinct smell. The sight of them made me shiver and remembering Beata's words about a most potent acid I kept a safe distance. The closer to the ocean I got, the more frequently I saw the pools. Did this ocean have tidal waves? I pushed the thoughts aside and kept going. I was, after all, on an alien planet. Not taking the chance for some miniscule exploring was stupid, and I really wanted to know what that light was.

As I approached the ocean the metallic reflection from the thing out there got stronger and soon I could see sharp lines. It was definitely metal, smoothly shaped. I went closer still, eyes fixated on the thing. It wasn't a ship, not really. More like an island, far out into the ocean. Maybe it rotated as well ... I was close to the shoreline and could clearly hear the waves. That sound was different too. It didn't sooth as our waves do. This crackled, as if the water, or fluid, was made of razor blades and stones, grinding frantically. I stopped and watched, feeling a sense of dread creeping upon me.

There were several things not right here, and that was beside the fact that I was very far from home. The land was barren. Nothing seemed to live here. I wasn't sure I wanted to encounter any alien species, not even something the size of a bug. The fact that everything was desolate nagged at me. And that metallic island out there ... Now I was sure, it did rotate, slowly counterclockwise, and it had moved further to the right, in the direction from which we came.

Suddenly I could hear something very familiar from the camp. There were screams. High pitched terrified screams that were cut off. I started running toward the camp, thinking I should've never left. In the distance, well three hundred meters away, I could see four people running in my direction, and something huge, metallic towering behind them that I hadn't noticed earlier. The metallic thing looked like a plain wall, raised in the middle of the camp. Then it moved, sank down and revealed a body with several arms, flailing wildly, picking up tents and objects like they were made of paper and tossing them around. I could see this, despite the distance, because of its size. I froze midstep, stumbled to the ground where my shoulder hit a rock, sending a spike of pain through my body. I lay there, covering behind the black stone, peeking around it.

Whatever it was it tore the camp to shreds, turned around and started moving towards the people running in an angle away from the camp. Its movements looked like a bizarre mechanical wolf, hunting its prey. It didn't take long before it caught up with whoever was running parallel with the ocean. It raised its long arms and impaled the runners, one at the time. Short screams, then silence.

The four people coming toward me were closer now, maybe fifty meters away. Beata was among them, and Bernt who had worked with the machine inside the tent. I couldn't remember the name of the others.

The mechanical beast turned and immediately took course for the runners. Beata stumbled and fell. One of the others stopped as well and crawled up behind a rock, covering his head under his arms. Bernt and the fourth man kept running, panic in their eyes. I could feel the earth tremble as the mechanical monster rushed towards them. It was well over eight meters high, with ten individual legs attached to a cylindrical-shaped body. There were more arms on its back, moving with no apparent function. From some of them dangled the bodies of team members. Now it looked like a gargantuan spider, or a centipede with extra pairs of legs on its back, like it could roll over and keep running just fine. It was almost comical, had it not been for its head. At least I think it was the head, because I could see two rectangles, slightly more yellow than the rest of its body. Sensors maybe. Eyes. They radiated something very familiar; hate. The mere sight of them struck me with fear and I was happy to sink behind the rock again.

It caught up with the two runners some twenty meters away from the rock where I was hiding. I heard a thump, and a short scream of surprise. The other runner passed my hiding place, but the beast was over him in seconds. It stretched down, grabbed him with a mechanical claw, raised him in the air and with a motion that almost seemed serene it twitched the man's head off with another claw. Then it turned for Beata and the other man. Two quick thumps, before it strolled past me towards the ocean, bodies impaled on its legs, one headless in its grasp. It walked to the shoreline, and from my point of view it looked like it tossed the bodies into that yellow mess. I quickly went behind the other side of the rock, curling to a ball, hoping it hadn't seen me.

It wasn't just a machine. I knew it instinctively. The moment that thing had passed me I could hear the sound from it. Where there should have been some sort of rotor sound, or familiar fans or cogwheels spinning, there was a very faint humming. Like a mechanical heart beating. It was alive.

When it was finished with the task of dumping the corpses of my former colleagues it disappeared along the shore. In the direction of where Ortega and the others had gone. Somehow I must warn them. My mind was clogged with a single thought; to get to the wormhole and go home, away from this nightmare.

I waited a long time before daring to move. When I thought it could no longer see me I got up and started running towards the wormhole. Soon my heart thumped like crazy and my lungs burned like fire. It was definitely not earthen atmosphere. Something with this dry static electricity made it horrible to run and I had to slow down.

Paralyzing fear gripped me as I realized I had no idea where the wormhole was. I was desperately lost, but refused to acknowledge the fact. Instead I kept going, one staggering step at a time. Suddenly I heard gun shots, and in the next second I could see two of the soldiers, maybe a hundred meters ahead of me. They ran with a good distance between them and I immediately understood why. From the mountains the mechanical monster appeared, climbing over the cliffs. It took aim for the man at the back, who was desperately firing at it. It was upon him in seconds, grabbed him and lifted him into the air. He must've been terrified, because he never let go of the trigger. His rifle sprayed bullets everywhere. One hit a rock close to me. Another stray bullet accidently hit the other man in the back and he stumbled and fell behind a rock. Then there was silence again as the machine carried its load to the Yellow Sea, before disappearing towards the mountains.

When it was gone I took a deep breath and hurried to the man who was shot. It was Ortega. He tried to raise his weapon when I got to him, but he was bleeding badly, hands shaking, face ashen. When he saw it was me he relaxed.

"Marko must've shot me," he said. "We saw that ... thing and tried to outsmart it. I guess it got the better of us."

I nodded.

"You ... must shut it down," he whispered.

"I can't. It was so big. So fast."

Ortega shook his head and his eyes became glass. He probably had a punctured lung. I could do nothing.

"Shut it down," he forced himself to raise his voice. "We found ... a building. Of sorts. With data in it. It makes sense now. We should've made it, I think, but Dan had an accident ..." Ortega coughed blood. He didn't make much sense. "I went out and saw it. The absence of light. Did you see it?"

I nodded, feeling as bad as Ortega looked. He reached for something at his side, grimacing with pain.

"It's them. They consumed ... They must never find our coordinates. You must shut it ..."

His eyes faded out, like someone had turned a light off. I was alone. I noticed that he had reached for a grenade, hanging from his belt. Could I blow that titanic robot up? Maybe, but not likely. I took it anyway and put it in my pocket. I tried to take his rifle, holding it in front of me like a shield. It was too heavy and I doubt I could harm that machine with it, so I threw it to the ground. Having never seen a dead man before I felt as if I should be more ... affected. But my mind turned off, went pragmatic. I just wanted to go home, without ever encountering that machine again. Ortega had moved in a straight line. If I followed that line I should reach the wormhole.

I started jogging, legs still shaking, but not so much that I couldn't go on. After a short while I slowed down. Something with the scenery ahead of me wasn't right. There were the black cliffs that we had emerged from. I couldn't recognize it. I wished I had looked back more carefully when we went for the camp. And I had to take into consideration that I had moved a long way along the shore to get away from the camp. Simple triangulation told me it should be nearby. Then I saw, and immediately threw myself to the ground. There were reflections, like a massive mirror bathing in sunlight, just past a cliff that stood out from the black wall. The machine was there, waiting. Hiding. It guarded the wormhole. Was it *that* intelligent? Panic rushed through me like acid. Maybe I could make it if I ran. One big problem was that I wasn't sure exactly where the wormhole was. Another was that I'd seen that machine move. It was fast and grim. My hope withered away. It was more than a machine. It was a clever lifeform. A piece of the puzzle suddenly fell into place. Erling had told me that some unknown force had reached into our tunnel and dented the S.E.L.D. The machine must've done that to get us here. That was probably why the wormhole on Earth had looked sick. It was infected, by that machine.

I turned around, crawled as long as I could and then got up when my sore knees bled through my pants and left red streaks in the yellow soil. I had to get to that building Ortega had mentioned. There was nowhere else to go.

I found Ortega's body ten minutes later. I looked around, the Yellow Sea at my left, ship still out there. Black mountains to my right, and some valley straight ahead from which I assumed Ortega and the other soldier had come from.

I started walking, alone in this weird landscape. Sometimes I heard crackling and popping sounds carried by the wind that could be small animals skittering around the stones and soil. Or remnants of some alien tunes, played in the distance. I never saw anything. After a while I came to a slope, which led down to a cauldron shaped valley with strange rock formations, looking like black mushrooms or fingers, pointing up from the ground. I went down, searching for tracks after Ortega and the others. They were difficult to see in hard ground, but they were definitely there, giving me something to follow.

The tracks went around the formations in a circular pattern, and ended at a rock wall. There was an opening, a cave or bunker ... When I got closer still I could see a rectangular opening, definitely not natural. Inside was a crudely cut tunnel that led downwards into the darkness. There was some light source ahead, far into the dark distance. I kept going, thankful the tunnel was too small for the mechanical guardian to enter. At several points I stopped, thinking I heard noises in the dark. I never saw anything and there was no other option than to push ahead. Eventually I could see the light clearer, some dim, white light coming from the walls in a room.

I entered a big rectangular room with round pillars reaching for the roof high above me. The pillars almost formed small rooms in the big hall and made me think of a banquet hall. But they were also utterly different. Some were round, others had sharp corners. Most of them were shapeless, and had small holes, like honeycombs, from which the dim light came. It wasn't a light bulb exactly, more like microscopic sensors that were emitting the strange light. I slowly moved ahead. The hall seemed endless.

"Stop. Who's there?"

I froze when I heard the voice. There, leaning against a pillar was the last soldier, Dan. He looked as healthy as a ghost. He aimed his rifle at me.

"Oh, it's you."

"I'm Rasmus," I said. "The new guy."

"The new guy," he repeated and lowered his rifle. "Good day to see other worlds for the first time."

I nodded.

"Did you see Ortega?"

"Yes. He ... Marko accidently shot Ortega ... He died right in front of me."

"Damn," Dan muttered. "I told them to leave me behind so they could get back and shut the wormhole down. We argued about it, but I'm dying. They knew it and finally agreed to leave me here. I would've only slowed them down."

"I'm sure you're not dying," I tried but then saw the blood on his stomach, the equipment and on the floor. "What happened here?"

The man coughed and grimaced with pain.

"There's no point hiding it now, is there? We found this place some months ago, during our first trips here. It's not the first remnants of an alien society we've encountered, but this was different. Technology still working, far superior to anything we'd ever seen. Military things. Weapons that gave us new ideas. Most of the things were too complicated to understand or to move, so we set up a small research facility here as well. Most of the other guys don't know about this," he added. "Then the anomaly with the wormhole happened and we were afraid that the aliens had somehow found out what we were doing. But the situation here was all the same. Until today. Today something was very different with the wormhole. You don't know it, but it was. Perhaps the ship had something to do with it, but it was too far out, we couldn't get a good look at it. So we came here instead. About two weeks ago we found a data block, like a CD, if you like, and we started working on decoding it. Today it was done and that was when everything started to go bad. It was almost like the data block helped our computer to decode itself. The more I think of it the more I think that is what happened."

"What was it?"

"You'll have to look for yourself. There's a video over there," he said and pointed. "There seems to be a machine race inhabiting this planet. Maybe the whole solar system. We didn't see them on our scanners because we were looking for smaller, organic species. Stupid. Another thing I've been thinking about. We had it as an idea back home, but it was too immature to try out. When we ran our data analysis software on the data cube we found, we definitely got help. Why would an alien machine race have the same sort of images we do? They wouldn't, that's the answer. They have ID, I'm sure of it."

"ID?"

"Intelligent data."

"Like AI?"

"No. While we ran our software on their piece of data, the piece also analyzed us and produced something that we could interpret. They wanted us to see that particular video clip."

"The machine race?"

"Yes. When we had watched the video Ortega went outside for some fresh air and me and Marko resumed our other duties. That's when the accident happened. I have a quantum scanning device for data collection. I tried to scan the pillars in search for hidden data and technology, when it suddenly exploded. The blast cut my stomach open ... And here I am now. So stupid ... I think it was ID inside those sensors, you see. They didn't want to be scanned, so somehow they caused my scanning device to explode."

I nodded weakly.

"I don't know what Ortega saw when he was outside, but when he got back in he had changed. He said that we must shut the wormhole down so that nothing can get back here. Or 'find our coordinates if it wasn't too late already'. He tried to explain but there was little time for it because of this." He gestured at his wound. "What did Ortega see when he was outside? Why is it crucial to close the wormhole?"

I froze. I knew what Ortega had seen. Absence of light. I had seen it too, but only the reflections of it. Ortega must've seen in much closer. He knew what it really was.

"Where is that video?" I asked, heart pounding.

"Over there, thirty meters ahead," he said, face twisted with pain. I was no doctor, but that didn't look good at all. I left him there, dying. A strange unsettling feeling of despair had started to prickle my skin. That absence of light, it was a key event. But of what?

Further ahead in the strange hall the laptop was placed on a small table the soldiers had brought with them and the video clip was still on screen. I pressed play.

The picture was in a weird grayscale color and had static interference, probably due to the decoding, which made it feel ancient. There was a landscape with small trees and bushes that looked alien, like palm trees would in Sweden. The image changed to a room of some sort where a robot, like the guardian I'd encountered, walked around. At first it was hard to make out the scale, but considering the mechanical beast the room must be gigantic. There were several of them. Waking up by the looks of it, slowly rising from all over the room. There were other machines as well. I could spot smaller units underneath the bigger ones. They reminded me of crabs, but with more legs and claws. And there were even bigger machines, which made the guardians look like ants in comparison. Enormous things with legs or arms, cylinder shaped and with pipes sticking out at random places that could be some sort of weapons, or organs. Mechanical behemoths. One of them showed something that looked like a big computer screen that contained some figures. I couldn't make much out of it, but it seemed they were coordinates. Coordinates to where? There were hundreds of different lines of numbers. Thousands.

The image changed again and showed the Yellow Sea. The machines were everywhere. They walked along the shore and in the acidic water. Suddenly one of the really big ones fired a projectile in front of it. A greenish screen appeared out of thin air and the machine walked through it and disappeared.

The image changed yet again, to another environment with mountains and some sort of conical building in the distance. The green screen appeared and the machine came out of it. Where was it? Another planet in this solar system probably. I imagined that I recognized Henning's description about this planet being locked up within the ellipses of other planets, but there was no way of knowing. The thing I knew for sure was that the images of them creating wormholes at will and warping to other places made my skin crawl.

The video ended. I couldn't tell much from it, but I understood enough. The soldiers must've grasped that much too. There was something about it that made it so terribly clear. The machine race sometimes woke up and controlled their home planets. They possessed warping technology and they were intelligent. The one thing I couldn't understand was why Ortega wanted to close the wormhole so badly. Had he found signs of hostility that I hadn't seen? Even though I didn't like it I could imagine how the guardian must see us. Some sort of intruder that should be eradicated. It wasn't much different from accidently stepping into a cave with a bear cub. If the mother was there she would protect her cub and herself. She wasn't evil for doing so.

"How long was Ortega out there?" I asked.

No answer. I walked back to the soldier and found him dead. Eyes fixated on a point in eternity. I took another grenade and left the rest with him. I had to find out what Ortega had seen. The absence of light was the answer. And it had come from the ship.

I left the bunker and went back out into the foreign world outside. I followed the tracks back to a point from where I could pinpoint in which direction the ocean was and then I started walking. Soon enough I could see the Yellow Sea and out there the reflections from the ship. Ten minutes later I realized that I had very little water and hardly any food. I wished I'd taken some with me, but I hoped I didn't have to stay long. While walking there was another of the silent booms. It made me sink to my knees, feeling terribly small and vulnerable. It came from ahead of me. From the Yellow Sea. I covered my head with my arms and waited. After another four minutes it ended and I could go on, legs shaking.

Eventually I was at the shoreline. The ship lay in place, dormant. I sat down and waited. The light phenomena seemed to come in cycles. I had seen it twice already and perhaps it had happened while I was in the bunker.

My mind started wandering, thinking about school, the company and the series of chance moments that had brought me to this place. I missed Earth and I became determined to go home.

The soundless boom hit me like a slap in the face just after the absence of light appeared. It indeed came from the ship. I couldn't understand what I saw. There was a big gray rectangle in the sky, projecting like a giant beam of non-light. It produced a flat surface, a veil, a hundred meters up in the air. Then it began to inhale. The lack of sounds once again brought me to my knees with terror. But this time I clearly saw and understood what the non-light was. A rain fell from the sky. A constant absurd stream of things, sucked from an unknown world. I could see strange three-legged creatures flailing wildly in the air. I could see them screaming, but I couldn't hear it. I saw vegetation and strange vehicles, twisting and bending from some invisible force. Dirt, stones and what looked like parts of buildings. Everything shredded and trashed while it tumbled down to the Yellow Sea. The stream was endless. The creatures were numerous. All dying in this bubble of silence. It ended, just as swiftly as it had begun. The veil disappeared and the light and sounds came back. I could suddenly hear the thunderous sound when all the materials crashed down into the waves, bouncing off the ship hull. I heard guttural, unnatural screams. At the end I could see some cloth or fabric slowly falling, like snowflakes toward a surface coming to rest. Because the Yellow Sea was rapidly calming down, absorbing new content.

I finally got what Ortega had understood some time before me, and the realization made me cold. This machine race opened portals to other worlds. Any planet targeted by these wormholes would be completely defenseless, the entire planet could be sucked dead. Of everything. Erling's safety mechanism wouldn't stop *that*.

They weren't controlling their planets during their wake periods. They consumed. They fed off everything. Flesh, technology, materials. Everything melted in the sea of acid. Ortega's words rang in my ears. *"They must never find our coordinates."*

That was what the video meant. The machine race found coordinates to other planets somehow. Perhaps when a race achieved wormhole technology. Then it was an easy task for them to pinpoint the location of a tear in the spatial space, and then alter the destination of the wormhole for the unsuspecting travelers. They would inhale Earth, leaving it a dusty, dead shell.

The ship rotated slowly out there, ominously. It took me some time to get on my feet, but I knew what I must do. Whatever the cost I must try what Ortega had failed to do. I must make it back and close the wormhole and warn Erling. With some luck the machines had not yet recorded Earth's coordinates.

I got up and started walking towards the wormhole. Sooner than I really wanted I was nearing the cliffs where the wormhole should be. In the distance I could see the guardian. Maybe it was trying to hide, but given its size it didn't do a good job. An idea had formed in my head, one that made me terrified. I had to distract it, that was the only way. I covered behind one of the black stones, took out one of the grenades and weighed it in my hand. I pulled the pin, took a deep breath and tossed it as far as I could behind me. Then I ran, covering behind stones and hoping the guardian wouldn't see me.

The grenade went off in a thunderous blast that nearly scared me to a halt. It also woke the guardian and it came running, a massive force of deadly metal. It passed the stone where I was hiding, one giant mechanical leg smashing the ground right beside me, making the very earth tremble. I started running towards the wormhole. I was nearly exhausted, but fear and adrenaline gave me strength. In my right hand I held the other grenade. My idea was simple. Try to get back to Earth, and if I couldn't; get as close as possible so I could toss the grenade into the wormhole so that it would blow up the S.E.L.D on the other side, closing it forever.

I tossed a quick glance over my shoulder. The mechanical monster was at the spot where the grenade had blown up. It had turned around, its yellow eyes staring directly at me. It knew.

I screamed and tried to run faster, but my foot hit a rock and sent me sprawling through the air. I landed face down, heard a crack from somewhere within me, got up and kept running. Nameless fear flowed through my veins. I could feel the thing move, sending shivers up my legs each time I touched ground. I ran even faster, cliffs getting closer. I couldn't see the wormhole. My heart sank, but I ran to the right, following the black, crude cliff wall. The guardian was close now. I could feel its eyes on me. Fifty meters ahead I could suddenly see a grayish square against the black. It had to be the wormhole. Had to! Now I was close, twenty meters away. I managed to pull the pin on the grenade and held it tight in my clutched hand. What if the wormhole rejected me?

I never got to know. I was two meters away when I felt something grab my leg and I was abruptly and brutally stopped by a force pulling me back. I fell forward, crashing to the ground. I had a second to think and with all my remaining energy I tossed the grenade into the wormhole. It vanished. After a few seconds, as I was lifted high up in the air by the mechanical arm, I could see the wormhole quiver, and then it seized to exist. Left was just the black cliffs. It was closed. The guardian broke my leg with sheer power and the pain almost made me pass out.

As the machine carried me toward the Yellow Sea several things ran through my head. Did the machines already have the coordinates to Earth and were we just waiting for our inevitable doom? Would Erling and the people on Earth understand what the grenade meant? They were, after all, working with limitless science without morals and ethics. I could only wish that they never reactivated the wormhole. Because if they did, sooner or later the machines would inhale Earth, nullifying it of life.

As the machine brutally carried me, leaving me hanging like a rag doll from its steel grip, I could see the air above me. It shifted between non-light and purple. High above I could see the surface of two other planets, like twin coins. Behind them was a pale sun shimmering, laughing at me. Then the guardian swung his arm and released me into thin air. I crashed down into the Yellow Sea, immediately sinking.

I understood what the Yellow Sea actually was. It wasn't acid, but something similar. The fluid dissolved everything, made it energy. The water was cold efficiency. I could feel it creeping on my skin. Under it. In the background I could hear music from the water. Raw, crackling tunes seeping into my body and rocking me gently to sleep. It was a song of tranquility and death. The world around me fell silent to the melody of the Yellow Bard.

The Rats

Boel Bermann

Have you seen any rats? Report them!

The property owner is responsible for keeping the property rat free. If the property owner does not correct the problem, you can contact your local environmental committee. The local environmental committee deals with the removal of rats in the city's public areas, not in private living spaces. If you see rats in Stockholm's public environs, you can report this to your local environmental committee.

Rats spread diseases!

Rats run rampant in Sweden. They thrive everywhere around the cities and are primarily found in damp environments like cellars, tunnels and sewers. There they select larger spaces to store food or build nests. Rats are omnivorous and are known for spreading serious diseases.

Rats are an urban menace!

Searching for rats is difficult work. When the committee receives a report of a rat sighting, they begin the process of determining where the rats have their nest, how they gained entrance, and what they live on. The most effective way of getting rid of this pest is to spread a poisoned powder in their nests and on their trails. The powder contains an anti-coagulant that causes internal bleeding in the rats when they breathe it in. When rats are poisoned, they rarely die above ground. They will typically crawl into their nests and die there.

Rats. One of the world's most adaptable mammals. They live side by side with us in our cities. They eat our leftovers and clean up our waste. We don't see them. They know better than to remind us of their existence. They conceal themselves in the darkness. They squeeze into the sewers and hide beneath our homes. We are afraid of them, but they keep out of the way and try to survive. Stockholm is as much our city as it is the rats'. These days, I try to treat the rats as decently as I can. I perform research on a large number of test animals in my lab. I observe them. I try to understand their behavior and communicate with them. They watch me in a way I can't decipher. They seem intelligent, as if there were something more there. But it is difficult to say if they are expressing fear, caution. Perhaps they are trying to make some kind of connection with me. Maybe they are observing me as much as I am observing them. I have researched their species for a long while now, but there is still so much I don't understand. I have left parts of my research to others now, because I can't stand to see the consequences. It is probably because I have been infected with their disease. I was careless in my early research; now we all take better precautions. I believe it is the virus that has given me such strong feelings of empathy for them, but I am still uncertain. The only thing I know about the specific virus I carry is that it causes some kind of hormone imbalance. It makes the infected emotional and weak. I try to hide it from my colleagues as best I can, but it shows. I need to handle all these emotions, which is why I have begun writing down my thoughts. I have gotten too close to my research animals.

Some of the research gives me nightmares. I'm aware that much of it is pure torture for the fragile creatures. When I began my research, I wasn't as close with them. They were simply expendable goods and what I did, I did in the best interests of the public. But I can no longer look at it that way, not now that I feel such empathy for them. I wish I could just turn off my emotions, but I have seen mothers die to protect their infants. I have seen their children play for hours. I have seen them cooperate with each other to perform complicated tasks. I can discern nuances in the sounds they make, warning each other about danger, greeting each other, and even squeaking with pure joy. I see them more and more as living creatures, and less as research objects. The public generally refer to rats as pests, saying they are dirty and carry viruses. The committee often discusses things at a local level and my research team and I have to answer questions more frequently these days. The committee's methods are increasingly extreme in these current times of illness. Traps are set, poisoned food is placed out near their nests, and various kinds of extermination squads wander the streets at night. But the animals are so intelligent. If just a few manage to escape, the whole population of rats are soon aware of the danger. They communicate to a much larger extent than we ever realized. They avoid the traps, leave the food to rot, and hide when the extermination squads make their nightly patrols. I doubt the authorities would have even seen them as a problem if they had not increased in number so shockingly fast. The radioactivity has mutated them in ways we could never have foreseen. Their gestation period, which was already considerably fast, has shortened drastically. They are having larger litters than before, despite the fact that their bodies have a difficult time coping with more than two pups at a time.

As I mentioned earlier, I have ceased all experiments that caused any pain to the animals and delegated those parts of the project to others on my team. But I still am primarily responsible for all of the studies of viruses and bacteria. That research I have mastered to the most minute detail, and orders from above have compelled me to continue with them. Fortunately, this is something that does not harm the creatures as the other tests. It is also the part of the project I feel most passionate about. The fact that they can carry so many different contagions without being affected by the diseases themselves is fascinating to me. The committee, of course, is interested only in their genetic solution. They want to know the secret of the rats' immune systems and want to create a vaccine or some genetic manipulation so that it can be applied to us. The whole thing is a hugely controversial and ongoing debate. All the while, the rats are deemed to be one of the largest threats of spreading viruses throughout our civilization. The public is more afraid of diseases now than ever before in history. Epidemic outbreaks are occurring all around the world more frequently than ever, and we are hamstrung. I am doing everything in my power, I repeat over and over again that my results cannot be hurried, but the committee continues to call us practically daily. The world is in a state of terror.

I was contacted by the Center for Disease Control again today. They too have received their orders from above. New orders: the focus is no longer on finding a vaccine, though God knows we're trying. Now it's about something else: the rats must be removed from the cities. Stockholm first and foremost, but the goal is to get rid of them throughout the entire country. They said they're open to any suggestions. They sounded desperate. We scheduled a meeting for tomorrow afternoon, and I'll try to go through the possible alternatives. I'm against exterminating the rats and I made the committee aware of that. I still have a strong empathy for the creatures – they are not intentional disease carriers. But I understand the situation in the city is becoming untenable.

We had the meeting; it took most of the day. We went through the various options. Putting out food that will sterilize most of the rats instead of poisoning them is one alternative. A solution like that would not be possible for the rats to figure out immediately, but the CDC doubts that it would work quickly enough; they need a more extreme approach. I must admit I said straight out that I do not want to contribute to the extermination of an entire species. I am the lead scientist in this area and I cannot recommend such a drastic measure. The rats have a function in the ecosystem. If we remove them, there could be unforeseen consequences that I refuse to be held responsible for. They seemed to respect my words. I told them that I could probably offer them a solution. I was vague – said that they needed to give me a few more weeks to test it. They wanted details, but I asked them to be patient.

I met with representatives from the CDC again today and I was able to present an acceptable solution. I haven't had time to test it fully, but all indications are that it should work as expected. We have found a signal that only the rats can understand; that they react to and are drawn toward. My suggestion is simple. The committee should build a large transmitter and place it in an isolated nature reserve, preferably one far away from any cities. If everything goes as planned, the rats will be drawn there – not just from Stockholm, but from the whole country, provided the transmitter is effective enough. Once there, the rats can be kept isolated. Even if a few of them manage to leave the area and return to the city, or if not all rats react to the signal, the overall danger will be neutralized. The CDC representative was genuinely interested in this solution. They thought it sounded like an acceptable compromise and promised to present the idea to their superiors as soon as possible. They noted the advantage of retaining the rats as a species. Then, if we notice other problems in the ecosystem, we could reintroduce a smaller number of rats once the risk of infection is reduced. They left with all the relevant research material I used in the presentation: sketches of the transmitter and information about the frequency. They said they would be giving me reports if they decide to proceed with this solution.

It's been confirmed that the committee is moving forward with the project. I've understood that a lot of resources have been put aside for it, but they were also clear that they are taking over now. Even though I emphasized that it is my team and I who have the experience and knowledge, the committee has decided that our part in the project is done. It is, after all, not about the rats, but about our people. They guaranteed that experts from other countries have also been summoned in order to select the best possible place for the rats in order to set up the security system. They will take care of all practical matters regarding the maintenance and sustainability of the area. Construction of a small transmitter has already begun. If it shows promising results, the plan is to build a larger model as soon as possible. The committee is demanding quick results. The goal is to set the plan in motion within a few weeks. They made no assurances to keep me apprised of the details of the project despite my insistence – they did however guarantee that everything would be done openly. That the public would be provided with up-to-date information. They repeatedly swore that I would be able to see the project's progress and that I could contact them directly if there was any information I needed for my own research. I finally accepted the situation, because I understand that they need to set public safety as priority number one.

It has been weeks since the CDC was here. I have heard nothing about the project so far, and I'm uncertain whether they're actually planning to go through with it. Maybe the transmitter didn't work as planned. Maybe they've come up with a different solution. I'm frustrated at the lack of information. I've contacted them several times, but they only tell me that all information to do with the rats is now classified. That because I'm infected, I'm considered a risk factor and am not allowed access to all the information.

Government reports have begun to surface. I have to confess to being excited. Images flash by on the screens almost constantly at the lab now, and I'm following the development with bated breath. I have so many questions. Will my transmitter work as intended? How well will it work on such a large scale? Will all the rats feel drawn to it? Will small local variations or gene mutations make a difference? How have they solved the selected area's food and water issues? What methods have they used to guarantee safety so that the rats don't return to the cities once the signal is turned off? The project is still classified, of course. There are still terrorists who would use the project as a weapon. Place a transmitter in a city and produce an epidemic. And there are also those with the virus who would try to save the rats in a fit of empathy. This is why only carefully selected portions of the project are presented to the public and laid out in official reports. I want to know more, but I know the committee isn't taking any chances.

The transmitter has been activated. I haven't been able to focus on my work today because frankly, I haven't been able to stop thinking about the project. The curfew for citizens went into effect at midnight, the same time the signal was activated. I've been following the breaking news all night.

Images have been taken from roofs and surveilance cameras but they are frustratingly unclear. A lot of the pictures taken by private citizens are actually of a higher quality than the official footage, but they don't really show the extent of the evacuation. The rats are being lured out of their hiding places around the entire city. Crouching, dirty figures running along the city streets. There are more of them than we thought. More than I ever could have imagined. Thin, pale creatures in hordes. They move toward their goal, almost as if forced. They cover the streets, pushing and shoving in their eagerness to get to the transmitter. The rats here in the lab are scratching the walls of their glass cages in the transmitter's direction in uninterrupted frenzy. Their scrawny bodies are pressed up against the glass and they whine in desperation. I still have around a hundred animals and they continue to reproduce so I can keep on with my research. The physical experiments can continue, but all behavioral research is on hold while the transmitter is active: their behavior is controlled by the signal now.

According to the news, Stockholm is now clear of rats. The people living along the road between the city and the nature reserve are encouraged to remain indoors for their own safety, but those in Stockholm can go out again. They can go to work, continue on with their lives. The rats lived primarily in the larger cities. I'm worried that they may not survive in nature without the same abundant access to food and warm places to build their nests. But they are adaptable and have strong survival instincts. Even if I doubt they will all survive – due to the coming winter, or inter-species fights – many of them will.

It's been months now, and according to my calculations, all the rats should have reached the transmitter. The news bulletins show the developments with painfully detailed reports. The rats are crowded together, teeming in great hordes around the transmitter. The signal needs to be turned off, so that they can focus on their survival. I was clear about that when I presented the plan for the CDC. The rats won't have time to familiarize themselves with the area; they won't be able to find enough food or take care of their young while the signal controls them. They cling to the transmitter to the extent that they will soon be unable to concentrate on anything else, and they will starve to death. They currently have a few instincts left, but it is clear these are gradually disappearing. I see it as well in my lab rats. They are apathetic, only wanting to press themselves against the glass in the direction of the signal. The reports continue to flash on the screens, though with less frequency as the public loses interest now that the rats are no longer a threat. But I follow each story, even though I'm really just torturing myself. I see how the defenseless creatures get thinner, weaker, more confused. They attack each other more frequently, or become extremely passive. Parents abandon their young, or even eat them, because they do not know what they are doing, or do not recognize their offspring. I can see the last glimmers of consciousness fading from their eyes. I see how the rats climb over each other to get to the signal and they die in heaps. It is unbearable to watch, and yet I continue.

I haven't been able to sleep for more than an hour or two each night. The acid in my stomach is corroding my taste receptors and I have a hard time keeping any food down. Again and again, I try to get a hold of the CDC and committee representatives. I contact the same people over and over. Sometimes I threaten, sometimes I implore them to turn off the transmitter's signal. They give me the same standard answer every time: the signal will be turned off soon; they just want to ensure that all rats have moved out of the cities and towns and gathered in the nature reserve. I curse at them, which I seldom do, and I don't want to repeat my words here. I have been clear in my disgust at their treatment of the defenseless creatures – I have repeatedly explained that the rats are peaceful animals that do not attack unless in self-defense. Treating them this way is completely unacceptable. All the representatives of the committee say that the decision must be made higher up, and that I shouldn't worry. They assure me the animals will soon be relieved of their suffering. But I am not assured. I keep having nightmares and wake up in a cold sweat, screaming. My mind filled with images of rats that scratch each other bloody and scrabble over each other's corpses.

The news has just broken in the last evening broadcast, probably to avoid debate and ensure that it doesn't wind up as a major story. I finally know what the committee's solution was, though I have suspected it since they began with their evasive answers to my queries. The light was blinding. Even through the screens, it felt like it was piercing my eyes. Intense white light. Directly above the spot where the transmitter was. Trees, grass, all living things in the area burned to ashes. With one single blast, they annihilated them. There aren't even any bodies remaining in the epicenter. Only gray-white ash. Millions of lives, taken in a single blow. I should have anticipated this. I keep calling anyone I've had any form of contact with. I don't even know why I'm doing it, because I know they won't give me any answers. I won't be permitted to talk to those who made the decision. I have no one to hold responsible for this atrocity. No one cares. No one bothers to try to explain to me, or even say it was a difficult decision. The rats were vermin, disease spreaders, pests. The decision was made for the good of civilization. Sweden was a test case; now the solution will be applied world-wide. They say I should understand. I keep screaming even after they have disconnected the call.

I've lost several days. It is only recently that I've managed to regain my self-control. After the blast, I've been catatonic. They committed mass murder, and their actions are on my conscience. It was my fault. It might as well have been me who gave the order. Without me, the committee's actions wouldn't have even been possible. I gave them the tools. What they did is unforgivable. Right now, I feel more connected with the rats than with my own species. I do not want to be a part of a civilization that can commit such acts. But I have made my decision; I pulled myself together and gathered my strength to return to the lab. The morning has been devoted to preparations for my return. I've washed myself for the first time in a week and put on a newly cleaned uniform.

During the day, I visit all the parts of the lab. Talk to my colleagues. Inspect the remaining research animals and check their health. They had to be force-fed during the final period the transmitter was active but all reports show that they are doing well, under the circumstances. My colleagues are calmed by my presence, even though they're concerned for my well-being. They keep saying how much they look forward to my imminent breakthrough in the research. Then we will have averted the two biggest threats to our civilization and we will be honored.

I'm finally the last person left in the building. I systematically go around and open all the cages. Just as usual, the rats are calm and cautious. The creatures don't even leave their cages, even though the doors are open. I activate my early prototype for the transmitter. It is surprisingly easy to lead the pale things through the deserted research facility. I easily avoid the night shift security guards and lead the horde of rats down underground and through an emergency exit. Once we are outside, I turn off the transmitter and watch them sneak off into the darkness. Watch the contrast of the two-legged creatures' light silhouettes against the dark night surrounding them. It's not a large group, but they carry every virus and bacteria that is a threat to my species. They will kill us all within a few weeks and I will be one of the first to die. Even as I write this, I have very little time left. I was likely infected the second I opened the cages without my biohazard suit. With my final act, I am actively responsible for the destruction of my own species, but I am convinced that the rats I set free have a chance to survive and reproduce. I will die with the conviction that my action was the right one. Since I was infected, I've had a hard time reconciling myself with the idea that we came and took their planet from them. Earth was our last resort; the only planet that was habitable for our species. In the beginning, we were completely unaware that the planet had such a high risk of infection. That we were so susceptible to the existing bacteria and viruses. Before I was infected by the virus, I viewed the rats simply as soulless animals even though I was fully aware when we arrived that the rats had some form of society. But I changed. I hope the rats from my lab will take over Stockholm. And I hope that's just the beginning.

Getting to the End

Erik Odeldahl

-click-

Is this thing on? I really hope so.

I want to tell you a story. This is a bit problematic, since you all know that words, shall we say, lack the permanence they used to have. Anyway, I found an old cassette tape recorder in the basement while I was rummaging through moldy cardboard boxes, searching for something – anything – that could help me avoid the visitors. It should do the job, at least until I get out of here and can tell the story to someone, in person. The way things are shifting here right now, I can't really rely on my memory. I need some kind of archive and this tape'll have to do.

I'm stuck in somebody's old living room, deep inside the Event Sector. Hiding beneath an old dinner table, I shit you not. This in itself isn't an uncommon occurrence. Sooner or later in each of my cases, this is where I find myself: hiding from some unseen horror, desperately trying to kick my anti-beat-machine into gear. Anybody that uses them for more than the occasional jaunt across the border will tell you that those fuckers always break down at the worst possible moment. It's like they react to the presence of visitors. Thinking about it, that's probably what they do.

I was sent here by a client who I suspect wasn't necessarily telling me the whole truth about the job (again: *not* that uncommon!). The mission was simple: get in, find the house, get the package, leave. Preferably without causing any major apocalypse along the way.

I was ... wait. There's somebody here.

-click-

-click-

I think I've lost them. Unfortunately I think I'm lost too. The problem with running in the dark is you tend to lose track of the direction you're heading. If I can't find my way back to the Hole before the world shifts again, I'm as good as dead.

What I do know: I'm *really* deep into the Event Sector now. Deeper than I've ever been. I can feel its energy around me. The air is electric. The hairs on my arms are standing up and crackle when I touch them, sending purple flashes across my skin. When I breathe it tastes like I'm swallowing ozone. I am a living tesla coil.

I'm going to rewind a bit now. Start from the beginning. I should have the time. I got the anti-beat-machine working. It's happily clicking away again. The sound would be soothing if it wasn't so incredibly annoying.

First off, let me introduce myself. No names though. Names are overrated. Here's who I am: A man without an occupation. What I do would never fit on a business card, if anybody would ever think of using such things again.

I find stuff for people. Sometimes I find people too. It's not something I thought I would be spending my time doing. I just seem to have a knack for it. I've taught myself how the city works, where people hide their secrets or themselves. Where they think no one will find them.

I don't have an office, no place where people can seek me out. If they want me, I'll find them.

The day I meet my client, the person responsible for getting me into this mess, I find myself walking into my favorite bar. The thick steel door closes behind me, shutting out the cacophony of the streets. I close my eyes and allow myself a few seconds of quiet, before I venture down the stairs into the main room of the establishment. The old wound in my right leg explodes with a sharp stab of pain. Something moves around in there. I grit my teeth, press my palm against the scar and try not to think about it. It's a weird sensation. It usually never hurts unless I'm in the Event Sector.

I don't even get to order before the bartender nods toward a corner of the room. I glance in the direction, memorizing what I see before I turn to the bar again.

A woman, maybe thirty-five years old. Long red hair. Expensive clothes. A looker.

She's reading a paper. This of course triggers a feeling of discomfort. It takes a certain kind of courage – or stupidity – to read *words* in the middle of the day, among people. I feel myself hoping that she won't read anything out loud. I'm not ready to deal with that kind of disturbance. At least, not until I've had my first few shots of whiskey.

I put two fingers in the air. The bartender gives me the bottle and two glasses. I bring them to the table.

She doesn't say anything. Just studies me. She makes no secret of the fact that she's appraising me. I take the opportunity and reciprocate. She's stunning, that I could see from a distance. But she's also tired, maybe sick. The makeup hides most of the shadows beneath her eyes and the waxiness of her skin, but not completely. The dress she's wearing is expensive. I'm not an expert, but I'm guessing it's from the early 50s. Perfectly maintained. Just like the last century paper she's reading. It must have cost a fortune.

She doesn't move much, but when she does, she does it with the short and tense motions of somebody who has been in too much contact with visitors. She wears her anti-beat-machine as a wrist band, just like I do. The battery is kept in place by two sharp prongs. A spool of copper thread lodged beneath it. The bracelet projects sounds in a frequency few can hear, but my trained ears have no problems picking them up.

She extends her right hand. I don't. Instead I pour two glasses. We drink in silence until she finally decides to talk and tells me why we're here.

"There's this house I'd like you to visit," she says. Her voice is like honey and cigarettes. Strangely familiar, like I've heard it before.

"I'm sure it's very nice," I say.

"It's a seven story building. On the corner of seventh and seventh. I'm told you know those parts of the city pretty well."

I nod. I know them very well. I was born there and have almost died there on numerous occasions. "Yes, I know my way."

The woman leans across the table. There's a waft of perfume. Sweet. Expensive.

She smiles at me. It's nice. The kind of smile that makes people do anything to see it again. She puts her arm against the table and it momentarily acts as an amplifier for the anti-beat-machine. The dark humming completely wrecks the moment.

"The house has a certain ... historical importance, but mainly I'm interested in it for personal reasons. I'm an art collector and it used to belong to one of my favorite artists. One of the greats."

"You want me to pick up paintings for you? There has to be more if you bother with me." I point at her hand which moves spastically on the table. "And it can't be to find a visitor for you for interrogation. You seem to be able to handle that fine on your own."

She looks at her hand. Clenches it and hides it under the table.

"No paintings," she says. "Books. He was a collector. Before the Event."

Books. Why did it have to be books? "A book?" I ask.

"Multiple. It's complicated."

I feel my stomach tensing up. I contemplate just leaving. But there's something about her smile, her voice, the way she looks at me.

"So why do you want the books? Some people would find your interest in them a bit disconcerting."

"That's my business. Don't worry, I won't be reading anything out loud for you." She smiles again and leans across the table, so close I can feel her breath on me. Tobacco with a hint of mint.

I shrug. "Never hurts to be sure. Can I be?" My face is a perfect mask. All worries hidden behind it. I unscrew the cork from the bottle and fill my glass. I angle the bottle her way. She shakes her head.

"Do you need to be sure?" she asks. "I pay on delivery. Double the amount you usually ask for. You should find the building easily. It's special. Built by the Architect, just before the Event."

I look deeply into her eyes. For a long time. They're beautiful. Once again I get the feeling that I know her from somewhere, but I can't put my finger on where. Finally I say: "You can't hide from me. Setting me up is a bad idea."

"That's why I came to you. You find things." She smiles at me and I melt like ice cream left out in the sun.

"I find things. Every time," I say. I act tough, because that's what I do. But it's a charade and both of us know it.

As I leave the bar, I take one last look at my new client. I feel like I know her, like this was a conversation we've had a thousand times before. I know those eyes, maybe from a dream. They have looked at me from across tables and empty rooms, from sweaty beds and dark alleys. And I have looked back, smiled and told her everything is going to be alright, yet I'm sure I've never met her before today. I know I will do anything to see her again, if only she smiles at me.

She's beautiful, and she's dangerous, and she's all I've ever wanted.

The last thing I hear before I open the steel door and the noise of the street envelops me, is her cough. Like she's being torn apart from the inside. I know I haven't got much time.

I'm standing where two streets meet, looking out over the melange of people. This is my neighborhood. The Hole stretches from first to third street east/west and fourth to ninth south/north. To the east is the Event Sector. Dangerously close. People who live here have adapted. The city smells differently here. And the noise level is deafening.

If I were to compare the Hole to anything, it would be an air lock. You need to go through the Hole to get to the Event Sector. The analogy isn't perfect. For a start, I assume that if you ever were to enter an air lock, you'd be *very* aware of doing so. The Hole doesn't work like that. Apart from to the north, where the border between the Hole and the rest of the city is drawn somewhere in the middle of the river, an outsider wouldn't necessarily realize they've entered a different place before it's too late. There are no clearly visible markers. No signs. No warnings. They'd just suddenly *be there*, surrounded by new smells, new sounds, new people that are already taking bets on how long the newcomers will last before they either walk off into the Event Sector, or escape back into the safe embrace of the city.

The Hole is a middle ground. Not like the rest of the city, where a visitor showing up or a sudden reality shift is a very rare thing. Not like the Event Sector where reality has a mind of its own and gives zero fucks about the consequences.

It's a place of maybes, I guess. Where bad things can happen, and often will, but also might not.

In the Hole, the low hum of the copper-based anti-beat-machines isn't as prevalent. People here have found other means to keep the visitors away. Stronger means, less likely to fail in times of need. In a part of the city where you can never count on batteries or the power grid holding up, you can't rely on electricity-based sound waves as your only defense. Here, the street-smiths work in shifts and hammer syncopated beats on old oil drums. From church towers and minarets, songs are sung in dissonant choirs, counter to the street level rhythms. Those who live here have learned to speak arrhythmically, with sudden changes in pacing and intonation. Whole sentences spoken aloud in staccato seamlessly flow into half sung chorals in thirteen eights beats. The Hole is covered in a constant carpet of sound. It's the ultimate interactive piece of art.

It's known to drive people insane. Some, like me, thrive here. Others die, or leave.

People in the Hole know how to confound the visitors. But also how to call them. How to best communicate with them and live to tell the tale.

In the time before the Event, this was the city's cultural Mekka. The intellectuals gathered here: The political dissidents, the artists, the authors, the performers. The streets were crowded with wine bars, cafés, basement theaters and hard to find musical halls. And of course, these streets were hit among the hardest at the time of the Event. There aren't many people left to give you first hand accounts, but the stories are many. Nobody knows which ones are true and which are ramblings, constructed after the fact. It doesn't matter. Everybody who lives here has seen something they can't explain. And everybody who lives here has seen things they don't *want* to explain.

Somebody will tell you of a meeting of black-clad revolutionaries in a basement somewhere, which ended with all of them disappearing. Left were only the clothes they wore. They were wet, and in some cases covered in a thin layer of fine-grained sand. The place stunk of decomposition and whale lard. Of their pamphlets and books, there were only empty covers left.

Somebody else might tell you of a spoken word event at a wine bar, where the words flew from the poetry collection and penetrated the speaker's every bodily orifice. How they then exploded through his pores and flew out the window, letter by letter, covering the dumbstruck audience in a very fine mist of blood.

A third person will tell you the story of how a bus full of passengers suddenly was catapulted thirty meters up in the air, but before it landed again, it grew wings and flew away.

The Hole is full of stories like this. But somehow, people have managed to create a place for themselves to live here. The Event Sector is full of secrets. And people love secrets. They need people to dig them up. People like me. And people like me need somewhere to live. Somewhere close to the Event Sector. Somewhere like the Hole.

Today I don't stick around for long. I buy an extra battery for the anti-beat-machine. Something to eat. Some pain killers. Then I head into the Sector, toward seventh and seventh. To the house the Architect built. Not because I want to, but because of the way she smiled at me.

Just like it's more or less impossible for an outsider to know where they cross the border into the Hole, it's just as impossible to know when you're crossing between the Hole and the Event Sector. Unless you know what you're doing. I know exactly what I'm doing.

As I put my foot forward and take that last step where I leave the relative safety of the Hole behind me, I can feel the hairs on my arms standing up. The slight change in air pressure. The minute difference in gravity.

There's also the pain in my leg. The wound starts throbbing. There is a weak sound, as if somebody is whimpering. I'm used to it. I fling a couple of the pills I just bought into my mouth. Chew on them and swallow. Until they kick in, I'll stow the pain in a back compartment of my brain.

This is where I always make the crossing. I know every detail of the surroundings, as well as you can in a place where reality keeps shifting around you. I walk across the street toward the old café on the other side. I have a cache there, behind the counter, a small box with a code lock. It's armed. If anybody tries to open it and uses the wrong code, a word I trapped ages ago will shoot out at the perpetrator. I have no idea what the effect would be, but I'm sure it won't be pretty.

I open the box and take out the map. There are no words on it of course, no glyphs of any kind, but I have charted all the locations I've ever visited on it. I keep several copies of the map in caches throughout the Event

Sector. They're a vital tool for any explorer. Though the city shifts, it never changes too much per iteration. I keep these maps to remind me where I'm going and where I've been, and constantly update them as I travel. The Event Sector is a slippery place and it does things to your memory. Sometimes I forget whole days.

As I'm about to leave the café, I hear the familiar sound of a passing visitor. A wailing but strangely beautiful song. Words upon words. Strung together in senseless sentences. I hide behind the dirty window. Peek out. It's a weird one. On its head it wears a tattered gray fedora. The body is covered in what looks like a torn apart space suit. It drags a big two-handed sword behind it, leaving a trail of sparks where it scratches against the asphalt. He/she/it is a mix of half-formed ideas, of shapes of things that haven't quite fused together.

They all look different. Some people find the way they look funny. That's usually the last thought they have, before their bodies are criss-crossed with living words and torn apart.

The anti-beat-machine does its thing and the visitor keeps moving, never realizing that I'm here.

They're blind. And probably deaf. That much I know. But drawn to rhythm. Such as your heart beating. Or the sound of somebody reciting a poem. The anti-beat-machines continuously project arrhythmical sounds. It tricks the visitors and keeps us safe.

I ...
-click-

-click-
Ok. That was close. Too close. It's like the machine isn't doing its job. Probably isn't, this deep into the Event Sector.

I lost them again. There were three of them. Floating into the apartment, each a unique blend of insanity. Singing while canvassing the environment, as if they were looking for me. I threw one of them to the side, briefly touching its surface, dry like old paper, and ran out of the room, head first, while words I barely comprehend hit the wall behind me, spitting chunks of plaster and bits of garbled digital audio into the air. *Algorithmic generation malfunction detected. Genre cross-pollination definitions updated. Stockholm-AV-base eradication attempted. Failure. Failure. Subject flees.*

I ran across the street into another building and hid there. It wasn't there a half hour ago. The world shifts too frequently for me to keep up. The map is useless now. I have no idea where I am and no idea where to go.

I guess it was just a matter of time before something like this would happen to me. You can only go into the Event Sector so many times before you get hurt. I was in a similar situation once before. The wound on my leg reminds me of that every day. Back then, I was young and stupid. I didn't even use the map.

Anyway, let me tell you about the job and how I got into this particular predicament. She said she wanted me to find multiple books for her. *Multiple*. It turns out that means quite a few. Luckily they're all on a hard drive. A local copy of some part of the net that no longer is reachable.

A hard drive. In a desktop. On the seventh floor of the building at the crossing of seventh and seventh.

Getting to the building is easy. The city is in a low-shift phase and not much has changed since I was here last. I update the map a few times – images, always images, and never the same one twice. I have drawn buildings many times and I've never repeated a form even once. Can't be too careful. I've heard of words coming alive even though they're put on paper as hiero-glyphs or cuneiform. The shift is blind to language. It sees grammar, morp-hemes and structures.

This part of the Event Sector still mimics the past. Broken, blinking and wordless advertisements sell products no one cares about anymore. I see beautiful women smiling, shiny cars shining, children eating breakfast cereal, half covered in grime and dust. God knows where the signs get the juice from. Maybe this is where the power from the main grid ends up.

I pass a couple more visitors, but they don't notice me. They stare at the signs, moaning and singing to each other.

The front door is unlocked. I enter. The elevator is old. Has room for maybe three people. I don't trust it. I take the stairs. Wish I didn't smoke so much.

I get to the seventh floor. The office is the seventh one to the right, facing the street I came from. I open the door slightly. It catches on something. Can't get it open more than an inch or two. It's an old style office door. The upper half is a window into the room. Half scraped off letters on the glass tell me, well not much, since they're barely legible. I make out *Trope 4, office of*. The glass is so dirty I can't see anything through it. I give the door a push. Something cracks, then moves slightly and it opens a bit more, just enough for me to squeeze in. I peek inside first.

A thick layer of dust covers the furniture. When I push the door open, the top layer is disturbed and now hovers in the air. Nobody's been here for a very long time.

It's like a scene from my past. At least a past it feels I have lived. A simp-ler past where things weren't so complicated.

Torn blinds let in the light from the blinking commercial signs and passing cars from the outside. Long shadows wander across the furnishings, like fingers searching for something. The window doesn't do much to shut out the noise of the city outside.

The first thing that catches my eye is an antique desk. Lacquered wood. Like the one I used to have, when I had an office. On the desk is an old keyboard, a mouse and a 15" monitor. A chair lies toppled on the floor. On the wall behind the desk are several book cases. All empty of books, thank God. On the floor below are several computers, unplugged and stacked on top of each other. The walls are covered in velvet wallpaper, with inlaid gold patterns. The years haven't been kind to it and now all they do is add to the sad feeling of something lost.

I lower my eyes to the floor to get a better look at what the door got caught on. Imagine my surprise (I wasn't really surprised) when I saw a body there. Or what remained of it. A suit draped around a skeleton. A million holes in the clothes where I suspect the letters either left his body or entered it.

I enter the room, careful not to step on the body. Look under the desk, find the computer, and get what I'm here for. I wrap the hard drive in a plastic bag and put it in my breast pocket.

Then I leave.

-click-

-click-

See, this is where things started to get a bit weird. Even weirder than they usually do in the Event Sector. When I was in the room, I thought I saw the lights from cars outside through the window. And the office reminded me of my old one.

The thing is, people haven't been driving around in cars since the Event. I've never even had an office. And I most certainly don't have a simple, uncomplicated past. Also, I have never smoked. You can't even *get* cigarettes these days.

And why the hell would I go into the Event Sector just because a woman smiled at me? I feel like I'm being played. And I wonder what the Event Sector is doing to my brain.

-click-

-click-

Back at the Architect's building I don't have much time to think. I walk down two flights of stairs before I run into four visitors. One of them is the fedora-wearing, sword-wielding astronaut I ran into previously. I never saw the other three before.

I curse myself. Like a soon to be dead amateur, I didn't think about my walking pattern. Too rhythmical. I stop. I breathe slowly, but not too slowly and not in sync with my heart. I put my trust in the anti-beat-machine.

Which chooses that exact moment to fail.

So then I run. The visitors follow, spouting weirdly poetic but completely incomprehensible techno-jargon. They might not look fast, but if they've got your scent, your beat, they're hell to get rid of. And if one of them finds you, others won't be far away. They're ants and we're the honey.

I run down the stairs, out into the street. It looks different now. There are trees here. Exploded out of the asphalt. Impossibly tall oak trees that stretch up toward the skies. And I swear I see some kind of vehicles flying above them. It's like I'm on a bad trip. I've never seen the Event Sector behave like this before. I wish I was back in the bar, nursing a whiskey. But instead I run. Every time I put my right foot to the ground, the wound explodes in pain. I grit my teeth, internalize it. No time for pain. I just have to get away.

And I do. I hide in the basement of an empty office building. And that brings me to when I started this recording. Give or take a minute or two.

The Event Sector is always weird. That's why sane people stay out of it. The rest of our city has more or less stabilized. The Event Sector is always in flux. But not like this. Buildings move around, but never when you're looking. I keep the map updated for that. The visitors prowl the streets. I keep my eyes open for that. But whatever happens in the Event Sector, it doesn't change the fact that it's a dead place. *Nothing* happens unless it's happened before. It's all echoes of the past, of the Event. The world has moved on and left it here. What I've seen today is different. I've seen and heard new things. Like the Event Sector suddenly grew an imagination.

I can smell the Event Sector around me, stronger than ever before. My skin crackles with electricity. I've run for what feels like days through dark alleyways and empty basements. Probably in circles, but I haven't noticed it because the world keeps shifting around me. I am totally lost.

I leave the basement. Sneak up the stairs, past the street level, a couple of floors up. Just until I get a better view of my surroundings. Some time during my walk up the stairs, the building shifts and I'm suddenly much higher up. Hundreds of yards above the ground. It happens without so much as a sound. There's a door in front of me. I enter an unfurnished room with panorama windows to all sides. Like the building understands me. Like it knows I need to get my bearings. Find a way back.

There's an old bakelite phone on the floor. I pick up the receiver. It's dead. The cord isn't plugged in. I look. There are no outlets.

The city has changed. This high up I should be able to see the Hole, and beyond that the rest of the city. I can't recognize a single building.

There is a park just a few blocks away. The trees there look hundreds of years old. Magnificent oaks. The ones I ran past when they were chasing me. The buildings around me make no sense. It's as if every architect in the city got free rein to do whatever they pleased. I see every architectural style I knew existed, and several more that I don't know the names of. On the streets I see real people moving around, but they phase in and out of existence, like they're not actually there. Like they're manifestations of somebody's dream. The buildings in the far away distance are behaving the same way. Can't really decide if they're supposed to be there or not.

I don't know which way is north. I don't know the way back to the city. I pick up the hard drive from my pocket, look at it briefly, then put it back. Guess she won't be getting that any time soon. I pat my breast pocket for cigarettes, then remember I don't smoke and I never have.

The Event Sector has made me forget. I know I have lost days before, several times. Maybe this is what it feels like when you actually live the days it makes you forget? Maybe I'll wake up somewhere soon and not remember a thing about all of this.

Then, the phone rings. It's still not plugged in. It rings anyway. I answer it.
"Are you there?" It's my client's voice. Soft like velvet.
"Yeah?"
"Good. Did you find it?"
"Yes. How did you find me?"
"I'll tell you later. Don't lose the drive."
"I'm not about to. Don't know how to get it to you, though. Everything's gone to hell here."
"I'll send help. Wait there. You should listen to your recording. You might find interesting things on it."

She hangs up. And I stand there looking like an idiot with a dead phone in my hand. Not really sure if I actually talked to anyone, or if my mind is playing tricks on me. Wondering if this is something that always happens before the Event Sector wipes my memory.

I pick up the tape recorder. The red record button is pushed down. It's been taping things all along. I press stop and rewind. Sit down on the floor next to the bakelite phone and I listen, expecting to hear the muffled sounds of myself running for my life, but not being very surprised to find out that it's been recording something else completely.

At first there's nothing on the tape at all, nothing I can make any sense of. Then I hear sounds, and they gradually become clearer until I can hear everything. Voices. Two people talking. About something I don't understand.

"They're all in the system now. Every single work of fiction in the library." It's a young man's voice, or maybe a boy's. A bit squeaky. He is happy.

"And we have access to it all?" Another voice. Another man. Slightly older.

"Yes."

"Good." The older one is happy too.

"The engine is processing the texts. It's going to take a while."

"How long?"

"Ages. I've set it up to continuously dump grammars and genre files in the work directory. We should have enough to start experimenting with real data tonight. For the full data set, I have no idea. We're going to have to ask for money for more servers."

"Let's go for lunch and talk about it."

"This is amazing. Have you read it yet?"

"No, not yet. Tell me about it."

"I set it to use the noir archives. It spit out parts of a full novel overnight."

"Comprehensible?"

"In parts. It's still very rough. And there is no ending. But listen to this: *I walked into the bar. She was already sitting at a table, a forgotten cigarette lodged between her fingers, her eyes on some unknown point in the background. Then she looked at me and I knew right then that she would get me into more trouble than I could ask for.*"

A laugh. Two laughs. Both of them laughing.

"That's pretty good. How much of it are straight quotes from the original texts?"

"Nothing as far as I can tell. I told you it's amazing. The AI's writing a new story, based on a genre analysis and a set of archetypes, using our grammars and our rules."

"Do you have a print-out? I want to read this myself."

The older man reads aloud from a text:

"She was beautiful. I was drawn to her. I didn't want to get involved, but her power over me was strong. She told me about her husband. She showed me the bruises and the scars. I couldn't walk away then, even though I knew I was setting myself up for a world of hurt.

I knew of him, of course. Everybody did. A construction tycoon, happy to grease the pockets of any hungry politician if it helped him achieve what he wanted.

She wanted out. But he had a hold on her. A document. Of what she never told me. All she needed was for me to get it for her. I was happy to oblige."

"This is awesome!"

"Yes, it is."

"I want to know how it ends!"

"So do I. But something went wrong with the generation. It ran out of buffer space and quit after a hundred and fifty pages."

"Really? A hundred and fifty pages?"

"I know, I know. I'm looking into it."

"I found something weird in the logs today." It's the younger man's voice. Very excited. Somewhat annoyed. "There's a bug in the code, or something else is going on."

"Of course there's a bug." The older voice. Is he maybe the younger man's teacher? "There are over two hundred thousand lines in the code base. There are bound to be bugs."

Silence. The scraping of chairs across the floor. A couple of beeps and clicks. The younger man speaks again: "Still, it's interesting. The program ran for two hours last night."

"I didn't start it. Did you?"

"No. I didn't."

"Has someone learned our password?"

"Maybe. I don't think so."

"So, do you recognize any of this?"

"Of what?"

"As we wandered across the open fields outside the magnificent city of golden Akka Beron, watching the starry night skies for any signs of the Dark One's flying minions, a traveler approached us. A human woman, of high born stature.

'Step aside, you traveler of the night and let us pass for we are on a sacred mission to find the silver flower of immortality,' said Trivell, the priest.

'I know,' said the woman, 'for it was I who sent my servant to you with the clues you needed to find your way to this city. I have more news for you now. The flower grows seven lengths down in a cave, seven leagues to the east, guarded by hidden traps and fiendish constructions, all created by the Architect, one of the Dark One's most powerful generals.'

I looked at her. Her eyes were more beautiful than any I'd ever seen. 'Worry not, fair lady,' I said. 'I am the Seeker. I find things. All the time.'

'Still, you should keep a map, for the ground will shift around you, and the Architect will do his best to throw you off the scent.'

As I looked into her eyes, I realized that there was no place I wouldn't go for her, such was her power over me.

'Aye, I will heed your advice,' I said and quickly looked away, for if I hadn't I surely never would have been able to."

"What is that?"

"It's the latest generated batch of fantasy fiction. The program spit it out this morning. Has been running all night. Seems like it got caught in a recursive loop of some kind and somehow started sampling data from the noir archives. The man and woman archetypes. Pretty sure they're not part of the fantasy core data set."

"Again? How is that possible?"

"I honestly don't know. I've checked and I've checked again. The program shouldn't even know about any data that weren't specifically passed to it during setup."

"And yet it does. And it keeps telling the same story over and over. I guess it never got to the end this time either?"

"No, it didn't. And there is another thing."

"What?"

"I turned all the machines off before I left last night. All of them."

"So somebody was here and turned them on again?"

"Not according to the logs."

"So you're telling me it's doing it by itself?"

"I guess I am."

"It's not working. This is seriously beginning to creep me out. And every night it uploads new versions of itself to the cloud servers, faster than we take them down. It keeps accessing the genre files and grammars, no matter what I do to stop it. And it's begun creating new ones on its own. Just throwing arrays of what looks like random data into new files."

"What are they? The files, I mean."

"I don't understand yet, but they look like mad mashups of different genres. And it's not just data either. There are self-replicating and self-executing binaries hidden within. It's not only generating stories now. It's generating itself. Perpetuating the algorithm."

"Jesus Christ. But why is it doing it?"

"Maybe to figure out a way to tell the last part of the story?"

"Maybe. What do you want to do next?"

"I'm thinking of deleting the AI process completely. Disconnecting it from the main flow obviously hasn't worked. Disregarding the new files, the size of our main executable has grown over a hundred times the original size. And neither you nor I wrote that code. This just since February. It's writing itself. God knows what'll happen when it's finished."

"But if we shut it down we can't study it."

"I know. But what can we do? The AI is going insane."

"Okay, this is bad. I just got a call from our colleagues in Stockholm."

"And?"

"Every machine on their university network is spewing out 250-page novels. Daily."

"Without end scenes?"

"Yeah. This thing is spreading."

"Oh God. I didn't set out to write a fucking virus! My career is over."

"For a virus, it's not that bad. All it does is reserve the majority of a computer's CPU time."

"And fills your hard drive with crappy novels."

"It's getting better over time. It's learning. I actually think they're half decent now."

"So what are the Swedish academics trying to do about it?"

"They're talking about some kind of counter-virus. Something that'll modify the content as it gets written, trying to pinpoint the executable parts in the data and delete them. Basically sabotaging the AI's environment."

"This is just getting better and better, isn't it?"

That's the last one. Now the tape just hisses and clicks. No more voices. I wonder who they are. Or were?

I feel strange. Like a kid who's eavesdropped on something he's too young to understand. They were talking about me. And my client. I'm sure of that. The scenes they read out loud, I can remember them. But they weren't exactly like that. They were always slightly different.

The magnificent golden city of Akka Beron ... I haven't been there. But I have walked by the old Akka Beron Casino. Numerous times. Faux Egyptian. Cheap gold colors over white plaster. Until it disappeared in a shift. And I remember the Architect. Hell, the building I went to on *this* jaunt into the Event Sector was built by the Architect.

I'm being played. I just don't understand how yet.

As I sit there, contemplating exactly when my life became so complicated, she walks through the door. Wearing the same dress she wore at the bar. At first, I don't believe my eyes, thinking that this is just some new way the visitors have found to mess with me. But then she says "hi," and I know when I hear the voice, that this is her. What the hell is she doing here?

"Why are you here? It's not safe," I say.

She moves over to the window. Looks out.

"It's okay. I have help. We can't stay long. We should start moving, back to the city, before it all shifts again. The next shift could be the reset for all we know."

She looks at me. She's worried.

"Do you have the drive?"

I nod.

"And the tape recorder? You can't lose that, whatever you do."

I nod again. Pat my pocket. "It's here."

She starts breathing again. "It's vital. Don't lose it. Come."

She opens the door. Stops momentarily and checks her anti-beat-machine. "Is yours working?" she asks. I nod for a third time. It's click-click-clicking. "Okay. Let's go."

She takes me down several flights of stairs. We watch for visitors, but they are not around. We get down to street level. Go out in the streets. We watch the skies. They're empty. There's no one here but us.

"It's safe. Come," she says.

"It's not safe. And we don't know the way back."

"Actually I do."

She takes me through dark alleyways and damp basements, through wide open streets and across rooftops. We see a few visitors but they don't pay any attention to us. Their singing haunts me as we run, our footsteps never once hitting the same beat. She's a professional, at least as good as I am.

The Event Sector shifts around us continuously. Houses come and go. Streets blink in and out of existence. One time I even think I see a forest and people in green camouflage clothing, then it's gone.

Sometimes she stops and listens to something. I can't figure out what. Maybe she's hearing voices in her head. A few times she pulls up a map from her coat pocket. It's one of mine. I briefly wonder how the hell she got it out of one of my rigged boxes. Then I look at her again, and understand that if she can lead us back to the city in this shifting landscape, then one of my silly traps wouldn't be a problem for her.

Finally, we reach the Hole. I notice because my leg stops hurting. The wound is suddenly calm.

"Do you know a good place to talk?" she asks. "Somewhere we won't be disturbed."

I nod. I know several, but the one I'm thinking of serves whiskey, and I really need whiskey right now.

Sergei, the Russian barman, shows us into the back room, usually reserved for illegal card games and meetings between local mobsters. He's let me use it before, and knows the drill.

"There is drink over there," he says and points to a worn wooden cupboard. I find a half empty bottle of single malt inside. A rare commodity these days, but I'm not complaining. Sergei leaves, closing the door behind him. With the door closed, the sound of the outside is gone. All we hear is the low hum of our anti-beat-machines.

She puts the tape recorder on the table. Switches sides on the tape. Sets it to record.

"So we remember," she says. "I guess you have a lot of questions."

"I do. Quite a few. The most important one is, if you find your way around the Event Sector like that, why did you even bother to send me in there?"

"Because it has to be you."

"It has to be me, why?"

"You have to be the one to find it. It's the way it was meant to be written."

At this I fall silent. How do you respond to something like that, except maybe quietly leave the room before more insanity spews from her mouth? The thing is, when she said it, it didn't *feel* insane. It felt true. And most importantly, it felt *sane*. I downed my drink and poured a new one. Downed that one too.

"When you say written, what do you mean exactly?" I ask.

She leans back on the chair and smiles at me. Not a condescending smile. A warm smile. She takes out a pack of cigarettes from her purse. Shakes it, takes out two. Offers me one. I accept it. She lights hers.

"Is it okay if I ask the questions for a while? I think it would be enlightening."

I nod and lean closer. She puts the lighter to the tip of my cigarette. I breathe in, let the smoke into my lungs. It's a very familiar feeling.

"Okay," she says. "Haven't you ever wondered why all you know of the world is the city, the Hole and the Event Sector?"

"That's not true. I know a lot about the world."

"Such as?"

There is nothing. A foggy blank nothing. When I try to think of anything but the city I know, my mind slips like it's on ice.

"What lies to the west, past the city borders?" she asks. "To the south?"

"There is a river to the north." It's all I can say. It's all I know.

"And to the east is the Event Sector. But beyond that? Does it go on forever? You know it doesn't. You've traced the borders. I know you have. You've told me."

"That's not true. I haven't even been this far into the Event Sector."

"Oh, you have. Several times. You just don't remember." She pauses. Takes a long drag on her cigarette. "Doesn't it feel like you sometimes just repeat the same motions over and over? Have the same conversations again and again? Like you have no choice but to act out the scenes you were destined to play, like some mediocre actor on a stage with no audience. Haven't you ever wondered why you have so many maps of the Event Sector, in so many different places? They are left there for you, traces of past stories, for you to keep filling in."

And when she says it, I know it is true. I remember talking to her. At my desk in my office. Through thick bars in a city jail. In an alley outside a downtown bar. The same conversation, over and over. Some words change, but the meaning never does. It's always about her and the object she asks me to get for her. And I do. Or at least I try to. I can't remember ever succeeding. But I do it, time and time again, because I would do anything for her to smile at me.

Like she does now.

"I like it when you smile," I say.

"I like it when you like it," she says and smiles even wider.

"I started remembering things," she says. "Things I hadn't experienced yet. First it was in dreams. I saw you. I saw us. Then as time went by, more and more details were filled in. I felt like I was losing my mind. At first it only talked to me when I was sleeping, but now I hear it all the time. Even now it speaks to me."

"It? What does it say? And what is *it*?"

"I think it's the world. It's everything here. Everything around us."

"Oh, you've got to be kidding. I never figured you for a religious crazy person."

"It's not like that." She lights another cigarette. Her hands are trembling. "It's the world. It's the story. Our story. It's trying to finish it. I think that's what it wants. In my dreams, it has told me things. You and me, it's all about us. I give you a mission, and you accomplish it. At least, that's what's supposed to happen. But it never does. Something goes wrong, and it all starts over again, slightly differently."

I lean back, close my eyes. This is a bit much to take in.

"The people on the tape," I say. "They were talking about some kind of computer that created stories."

"I know. I've heard it too. I think it's part of the past, something that once happened, and it – the world – is letting us hear it. To understand."

"But why? It's not doing any fucking good, is it? I feel like I'm going insane!"

She shakes her head. "You're not the one going insane. I think the world is. It needs to finish the story, and something isn't letting it."

"Something what?"

"The Swedish counter-virus. I know you heard them talk about it on the recording."

"But we can't do anything about it. I don't even know what it is."

"We can. It has never been able to complete the story. It has to. It's what it lives for. It's failed so many times. And every time it fails, it wipes the old story from its memory and starts over. But we're always there. You and me. The world is losing its mind. The counter-virus is trying to stop it. And the only thing it can do is to portion off parts of itself into us. That's why we remember. That's why it gave us the tape, to make it easier to do so."

She puts out her cigarette and places the drive on the table. "I sent you to find this, because it told me to. It's its brain. On it are stored the parts they tried to delete. With it we can run the program again and maybe this time it will be able to generate the end. So we all can rest. And find out what is supposed to happen to us. We have to do it now. The world is unraveling. You saw it in the Sector. As for me, every time it's reset, I feel worse. I guess you do too."

I think of the pain in my leg. The *wound*. The thing in there. It's definitely getting worse. I shake my head at this. Then I smile. And start to laugh. The absurdity of the situation is just too much. I can't stop. "You sent me into the Event Sector to steal the world's *brain*?"

She smiles again. "When you say it like that, it does sound a bit crazy."

In the end, it's as simple as it's anti-climactic. We ask Sergei for one of his old battered desktop machines, yank it open and plug the hard drive into it. Then we wait for things to happen. None of us has used a computer before. I wasn't aware of that until she told me. I assumed it was one of those things I just knew how to do. Turns out I hadn't ever switched one on. My memories were playing tricks on me again.

The monitor, a dust-covered CRT screen, stays dark and dead for over half an hour before it wakes up. Then the following line is displayed in the top left corner, in shimmering green letters:

> *run generator -noir -250p -reset (Y/N)?*

She types Y and presses the return key.

"Now we wait," she says.

But we don't wait for long until things go bad. My leg starts hurting like it's about to fall off. Something's screaming. I can feel it moving, trying to break free.

"What the hell is that?" she says, visibly upset and scared.

I press my teeth together. I hold my breath. It *really* hurts. Worse than ever before. The cloth tears, revealing what's beneath it. A face. *My* face. A hand. Fingers digging themselves out of my body. The mouth is gasping for air.

I've always known it's there. But it doesn't fit with what's real, so I've never looked at it. Now I know *why* it's there. The body, a Siamese twin from another genre, is digging itself out of me. The whole head is out now and parts of the body. I can see it's wearing torn medieval clothing. It's a part of me that also wants to exist. There is no place for it here, in my world.

She stands back. Shocked.

"Jesus Christ, is that ...?" She falls silent.

"It's been there since one of my earlier Event Sector jaunts," I say through clenched teeth. "Ran into some visitors. Things got confusing. Then I don't remember what happened. I woke up in my bed and it was there."

I hit the thing with closed fists. I hammer at it. Again and again. Trying to get it to go back inside. The pain is killing me. The face screams at us. *Narrative dissonance found! Continuity breach! Stockholm-AV-base eradication attempt ongoing!*

"It's a visitor. A counter-virus. It must sense what is going on. It's trying to stop it."

"Can we please stop talking and try to get it out?" I scream, panicked.

"I don't know what to do!" The malformed thing grabs hold of her arm. It screams. I scream. She screams. The sound of our voices coalesce and form clouds of torn-apart letters in the air around us. Circling us, like birds of prey waiting to strike.

And then the CRT screen blinks. Once. Twice.

And then: darkness.

It stays dark for a long time. I can feel myself floating inside it, a disembodied thought with nowhere to go. The pain and my malformed twin are gone, along with everything else.

She is gone too, though the pain of losing her is with me. A sense of longing so deep nothing else matters. I need to find her again. I need to be with her. We need to reach the end together.

The light shines in through the window blinds. Sharp spears into the soothing darkness. I hear car horns honking outside. Somebody yelling loudly, selling today's newspaper. Sounds and lights forcing me awake. I was dreaming and I don't want to forget about what. About something important. Something horrifying, but important.

I don't want to, but I open my eyes. Somebody's knocking on the door.

I'm in my office, in my chair. My back hurts. My head hurts worse. I must have passed out here again last night. My mouth tastes like something died in it. Memories are hazy, but the empty bottle of Jack on the desk tells me at least part of the story. Still, traces of the dream stick, like flies on a dead dog. There was something …

Bang bang. Whoever's on the other side of that door sure is persistent.

I find my pack of smokes. There is one left. Thank God for small mercies. I light it, and stand up. Have a coughing fit. I'm a miserable son of a bitch. In desperate need of a case.

"Alright, alright," I say while stumbling toward the door. I open it and there she is.

She is beautiful. Much more so than my usual clientele of washed-out actors and doped-up has-beens. She's thirty-ish. Tall. Red hair. Red lipstick. Black dress.

"You the P.I?" Her voice is smooth. Like honey and a sweet promise.

I nod.

"Have a seat," I say and point her toward one of the chairs next to my desk. "What can I do for you?"

"I have this problem," she says. "There is something I need you to get for me, and I don't know quite where it is."

"Shouldn't be a problem. Finding things is what I do."

"I know. That's why I came to you."

She smiles and triggers a reminiscence. Of what I'm not quite sure, but it doesn't feel awful. It's like I know her from somewhere. As I walk toward my chair, my foot bumps into something. Some weird kind of recording device. I'm sure I haven't seen it before, but it feels familiar. Like something out of a dream.

"So, will you help me?" she asks. And when she smiles at me like that, I know I will.

I put the device in a desk drawer. I'll take a look at it later. I get up and walk over to the window. I pull the blinds open. I look out. The streets are full of people. There are cars everywhere. I'm filled with an unexpected sense of feeling at home, of being where I should be. This is my city and those are my people.

The sun is warm against my face. The dream that seemed so important a few moments ago, recedes into nothingness. Whatever it was about, it's not important anymore. The headache is gone. It's a beautiful day. I turn toward my client. Her eyes are beautiful.

"Of course I will," I say.

Vegatropolis –
City of the Beautiful

Ingrid Remvall

21st of November 2550
11:15 p.m.

"Please, Maxine. Let's get out of here."

My friend looked at me and smiled. "No way! We just got here."

I pulled the short dress over my knees for something like the hundredth time. All I wanted was a pair of adaptive jeans and a holographic retro shirt. My favorite shifted between a big, red, blinking robotic eye and the text *I'll be back*. However, for this party Maxine had forced me to wear a tight, shimmering emo-dress. It was as pitch black as my emotions.

I had used Maxine's makeup-spray and I guess it did some good. The smoky black enhanced my pale, gray eyes and my skin was glowing. Just enough to make me blend in as one of the least pretty in the room with my brownish, Maxine called it mousy, uncolored hair in a slick ponytail.

I looked around at the crowd and tried to forget about my uncomfortable stiletto heels. Shiny faces, shiny clothes and shiny eyes; drugs were free at this party. We would both turn eighteen soon so the drinks were legal, but the drugs that were inhaled through rainbow colored masks were not.

Maxine grabbed a cucumber jelly-shot, threw it back and licked a luminous drop from her purple lips. "Relax, Vega. Have some fun!"

"Any moment now they are going to realize that we are not one of them and that we have just crashed this party."

Maxine snapped. "Speak for yourself! This is where I belong."

I couldn't argue with that. Maxine was unfortunate to be born in the poor districts outside of Vegatropolis. Her dad cleaned one of the big corporate offices in the city and her mum controlled a machine packing tooth-brush pills in a factory outside of town.

But Maxine, yes, she was another story. She looked absolutely fantastic. Not just fantastic like the kids that have enough money to modify their appearance, she was born that way. She had red hair tumbling down to her waist, curly and as wild as her temper. Her skin was golden with freckles covering her small button nose and rosy cheeks that gave a perfect contrast to her pale brown cattish eyes.

Her looks alone wouldn't have given her the possibility to blend in with this crowd. They could spot an outsider a mile away. However, Maxine had a talent above and beyond her great looks and charm. So, we got away with it.

All the credits she earned from working extra hours at a café went to acquiring fabric. She transformed this fabric into outfits that could have come out of any high-class, digital store in a shopping mall, like this dress of mine.

The loud beat of music pumped around me and the overwhelming smell of sweet shots and cinnamon cigarettes was the same, but something had changed. The club was packed with at least a hundred people, but they were all silent.

The Royals had arrived.

Maxine grabbed hold of my arm so hard I squeaked. I would definitely have a big bruise there tomorrow.

The Royals were not real royals. Not like in the old days when kings and queens ruled the world. But these were the Royals of Vegatropolis, the royals of the 25th century. They were the children of the power elite that ruled the gaming industry, TV networks, drugs and everything else that mattered in this city.

Another thing that made them different from the royals of ancient times was that they were not human, although though they looked like they were. The power elite did not want kids with defects like ugliness or sub par intelligence. A lot of things could be modified after birth, but why take the risk of getting something that was not altogether perfect?

A scientist and artist who called himself Picasso had created the first AAI – Advanced Artificial Intelligence. After this the AI had went from plastic looking humanoids to something actually looking like us. This was twenty years ago. Picasso's next step was the AAIGP; Advanced Artificial Intelligence Goes Perfect. The "people" now entering the room were his best work ever.

They looked like us and oh *so* much better.

Lancelot was the first to enter and oh my, did he enter. He looked like a Viking prince stepping off his boat after a successful raid. He pulled back his golden hair, just brushing his shoulders, while he narrowed his icy blue eyes. Lancelot had the body of a football player combined with the grace of a gymnast.

I closed my mouth and felt dreadfully embarrassed that something made of plastic and metal could have this effect on me.

Right behind him, arm in arm, came the girls. Sorry, the queens. Like yin and yang. Black haired Lucy was a tall and strong Asian girl with a face that could start a war. Beside her came fair-haired Gwyneth with a body that could start a world war. Like always she looked bored and chewed on her full lips. If I did that I looked like an idiot, but Gwyneth, well ... she just had it all.

"Look, who is that?" Maxine pointed behind the royals.

Was this another AAIGP? There had not been any news about a new wonder of Picasso. No, that was just a normal guy. Lucy turned to him and smiled. She stroked a black curl behind his ear and whispered something into it. He laughed. He was hot, no question about it, but beside the royals everything and everyone turned a bit shabby.

Lancelot raised his voice. "Hey everybody. Now that we're here let the party begin. We have a surprise. Our friend is going to sing for you!"

The crowd started to scream and I covered my ears. Why did Maxine want to hang out in places like this? I just hated it. Shallow and fake, just like this entire city. I know everyone wanted to live in Vegatropolis. But not me. I wanted to move somewhere where you could still see some real trees, not the bright green fake ones in the big parks with fake lakes filled with fake multicolored fish.

The new guy entered a small stage and pressed a plastic bracelet on his arm. A black, shining holographic guitar appeared. I didn't know who this guy was, but he definitely was filthy rich. That instrument cost more than our house. It was a crappy house, but still.

Someone shut off the music and the club went quiet. Lancelot pulled out a few glass cubes from his pocket and threw them into the air above the guy on stage. The flashcubes rotated slowly in the air, spraying the singer in colored light.

He took his time looking around the room. That guy had confidence. A smile curled his lip and his eyes hit mine. The light made his glance glimmer in red. I have read and laughed at novels about love at first sight. But, I must admit that something did happen when our eyes locked.

The smile slipped from his face and he looked uncertain. I forced myself not to look behind me to see if he actually was looking at some hot girl instead of me. He tilted his head and a wrinkle appeared between his eyes. I interested him, but why?

Maxine whispered without moving her lips. "Vega, why the hell is he staring at you like that? Do you know him?"

I wanted to answer her but, unfortunately, my tongue was so dry it got stuck to the roof of my mouth. When he finally let go of my eyes and started to play I grabbed a glowing shot from a flying tray and slung it down. Eww, yuck; aubergine and chili. I hated those vitamin and alcohol shots.

"Vega! Tell me?" Maxine shook me.

"I have never, ever seen that guy before. I have no clue why he stared at me."

"But you liked it. Vega is in looooooove." She laughed.

Before I could answer I looked down at my dress. Fuck this emoshit. It was bright pink. The typical color of loooooove. I took another shot, a green one this time; parsley.

"Take it easy." Maxine took away the glass.

I tried to act all cool and turned to one of the digital walls. But after playing one line of tick-tack-toe I just had to turn back to the guy on stage.

The holographic instrument was worth its money. Tones of base, drums and something electric pumped out with a hard beat. It melted together with his voice, and that was some voice; soft yet powerful. I had never heard of him, but I probably would hear a lot about him soon. This guy was a star.

A loud crash of glass followed by screams stopped the show. More glass shattered and soon the floor was filled with stones covered in fluorescent graffiti. They all had the same message, "Put the AI, AAI, AAIGP to eternal sleep!!!"

A high sound of electric motorcycles taking off was heard through the broken windows. Someone screamed at the top of his lungs, "Real humans stay awake, machines go to sleep!" A choir of angry voices added onto it and disappeared into the night.

It was not clear how much emotions even the advanced AAIGP had. But since those in the room were the most advanced in the world, I was quite sure that they were pissed off. Lancelot's cheeks turned red and an artificial vein started pumping in his forehead. Lucy had the look of a warrior princess but Gwyneth didn't seem too bothered. She picked up one of the stones, read it and then dropped it back on the floor with a bang.

Far away I could hear the shrill sound of sirens. Everyone was released from their shock and started running. This was an illegal party with illegal substances. But Maxine and I were even further out of line. We were outsiders, not even allowed to enter the city if we were not working.

"Come on, let's go!" Maxine grabbed hold of my arm and forced me through the crowd towards the door.

I almost fell. I quickly pressed a button on one of my shoes. With a swift click I lowered the three inch heels to one inch. Now I could run.

"Wait."

I didn't need to turn my head to know who it was.

"What's your name?"

Just as when he sang the voice was soft but impossible to ignore. I looked at him. Close up I could tell that his eyes were just as dark as his hair and that he had a dimple in one cheek when he smiled.

Inside the dark eyes was a distant glow of red. I quickly looked down. Enhanced eyes. Some could manipulate, some gave better sight, and some could scan information from people. I should walk away. This guy was no good, but he was so damn hot that I couldn't help myself.

"Eh, Vega."

"I don't recognize you from school. I'm sure I would have noticed you. What class are you in?"

Well, I was not even in the same school as him. I was not in the same school as any of the people surrounding us. Except for Maxine. We were not allowed in the city college, we had our own.

I dared to take another look at him. The light in his eyes was off. "It's a big school, I go to ... psychological programming, the science program."

"Can I see you again?" He held out his hand and the technology in it lit up. Shit. Since we were, once again, poor I didn't have any body technology; just an old fashion holograph in a bracelet. I held it out and saw his confused look.

"I like retro, okay?" I said. "Do you want my number or not?"

He pressed his hand to my holograph and smiled.

"Vega, we *really* need to leave!" whispered Maxine.

"Don't worry," he said. "We won't get in trouble for the drugs, you're with us. We're untouchable."

Okay, that sounded like some lame movie. Maybe he was not all that amazing anyway.

"See you!" I yelled over my shoulder and followed Maxine. "Don't want to be you," I added in a lower voice. Why did I give him my number?

Outside the air was cold. Roads with silver lights crossed the air in soft loops all the way up to the sky with glimmering stars. Silent, self driving vehicles swarmed past us.

There was no pollution anymore, but still orbs hovered over us to clean the air and to send out puffs of oxygen filled with whatever you needed. Obviously I was stressed since I could recognize the calming smell of lavender.

The skyscrapers were covered in huge screens that showed beautiful, happy people trying to sell products and lifestyle. A woman, the size of King Kong, turned towards me. "Vega, you just must try out this new scent, 'Wealth'. It's not just a perfume, it will go into your nervous system and give you better confidence and a radiant look."

A huge, holographic arm reached towards me. It held a bottle shaped as a diamond.

"No thanks!" I pressed a button on my holograph. I hated these bill-boards that thought they knew your inner desires. Sometimes they apparently did not work.

"Look." Maxine pointed towards the wall of a gold colored office building. In huge letters someone had sprayed in fluorescent paint "Machines go to sleep!" Behind the message was a commercial of AI housekeepers taking care of laundry.

During the last months there had been several attacks on targets connected to AI production. Factories, research centers and stores where you could buy different kinds of artificial life.

There had also been kills, if you could call it killing since they weren't alive. Still it almost made my sandwich and yogurt shake come up again when the holograms of three AAI-women were shown on the news on my kitchen table. Their lifeless bodies were ripped into pieces of silicon and circuits.

Now we could see the flashing lights of the approaching police. The screaming sound of sirens broke through the soft music from the billboards.

"Let's get out of here," I said.

We threw ourselves into a rickshaw that stood beside the road, pulled by an old AI man with white hair. "To the wall, exit 23D," said Maxine.

The AI turned his stiff face towards us, nodded and then started to run. Soon vehicles in all different shapes and colors flew around us. As always I got the feeling that something would hit me, but force fields made it impossible to crash into someone else.

The police, one car and several officers on robotic horses, swished by us towards the club. But they were too late. Whoever had sprayed the house and thrown the stones were obviously far away by now.

"Phew, that was close," said Maxine. "Stupid activists, did they have to wreck the party just when it was getting good? Why do people object to AI, they're fantastic!" she said and nodded to our driver. "And AAIGP are just all that. Lancelot, he is the most fantastic of all."

I didn't want to get into this discussion once again. We had differing views on this subject. I couldn't decide which was worse; that the AI actually felt something but were slaves, or if they didn't feel anything and were, as in the Royals' case, treated like humans when they simply were not.

"Don't think so much, it makes you look ugly," Maxine laughed.

We made it to the wall. It wasn't really a wall, not a solid one. But there it was, a force field that separated the city from the outside.

Many from the outside worked in Vegatropolis, but to get in you needed a passport signed by your employer in the city. Maxine had charmed a guy in our class who put in extra work by one of the passages to sneak us in.

The bright lights of the city had dimmed and been replaced with trees and hills covered in artificial flowers. Nobody lived out here, but the city people went here to run and walk their pets. For them this was a trip to the countryside. Outside of the wall there were more artificial nature and shabby houses.

Maxine always said that fake was better than real. But even if real trees lost their leaves and the grass went brown and yellow I would have preferred that. When I got older I might go to the Wild. There were places further outside the big cities that were not explored. Places where things were real and not perfect. I guess a bit like me.

We were just a few hundred meters from the wall when our driver's head exploded with the sound of a melon cracked on the street. One second he ran and the other he laid on the ground with his brain scattered all over the green grass.

Our wagon kept on rolling over his body and a sound of cracked plastic filled the cold air.

"Fuck! Shit!" screamed Maxine. "Help!"

Someone had shot this man. Sorry, this artificial man. Did they want to shoot us too? I got my answer when someone yelled: "Put the machines to sleep!"

"We are humans!" Maxine screamed. "I'm just really good looking, I'm not an AAIGP!"

Oh my good, Maxine. Sometimes she was just too much.

The sound of running feet came toward us. The red face of our classmate showed up. "Jesus, are you okay?"

I jumped out of the wagon and touched the AI's splattered face with my shoe, slime covered circuits hung out of the skull. Horrible! "Yeah, better than him at least," I responded with a trembling voice. I looked, with a chill, into the inky darkness where the sound of motorcycles disappeared in the distance.

"These bloody activists. If I was just allowed to have a gun I would have shot them! That could have given me a promotion. I'm tired of guarding the wall. Once I turn eighteen I'll go to the police academy."

"They're gone now. Just let us through," I said with a weak voice. "I want to go home. Vegatropolis sucks."

Maxine objected when she followed me. "How dare you say that, the party was great, the people were great. What is wrong with you?"

I shook my head and sighed. "I'm just tired. Sorry, thanks for bringing me."

She put her nose into the air. "Don't sweat, I'll do anything to see you in something else than your filthy jeans and holoshirts with lame messages."

I did not respond to that.

A sound of tires crunching made me turn around. Oh no! The motor-cycles hadn't left. The drivers' faces were covered with silver helmets and the voice that came out of the small holes in the front sounded metallic. "Stand still!"

To emphasize his words he held out his hand, covered with a lethal gun glove. Five pipes of different bullets, laser beams and other nasty things, I guessed. Why did this happen to me?

"I told you, I'm human," Maxine cried.

"We know," said the voice. He moved his hand towards our brave class-mate who had made an attempt to activate his holograph to call for help.

If we had been rich kids, with body technology, help would already have been on its way. The pumping adrenalin in our bodies would have called for police. But we were, yes, poor. So no help was on its way.

Another person with a helmet walked up to us. A woman, I thought, based on the curves under her black suit. "I will check them," she said and raised her hand.

From her gloved palm came a red cable swirling towards us.

"What is that? No, get that away from me!" screamed Maxine.

Without a word three other helmeted people came up quickly behind us, taking painful hold of our arms. The person holding me was short, shorter than me. I'm quite strong and have won several titles in combat jujitsu. However, that would be of no consequence against a gun. But at least I could get away from the person holding me.

I executed one of my most powerful moves and ... nothing.

The small person behind me didn't move. Wait a minute; there was something fishy about this.

The red cables were just in front of my face. Panic floated through my body and I threw myself back and forth. But no matter how hard I tried the arms around my chest made it impossible to escape.

Like a curious snake the cable touched my forehead. For a second I was sure that it would dig through my skin and penetrate my brain. But it just tapped at my forehead with a soft peck.

"This one might be right," the woman said in a harsh voice and the cable went back to her glove. "Give me the box."

The man picked up a shiny box from his suit and threw it to her.

"Careful," she hissed.

The metal was cold when she pressed it toward my forehead. A pain that started at my left eyebrow and went towards my spine electrified my body. I gasped and my friends tried even harder to get away from the arms that held them back.

"Vega, Vega! Are you okay? What are you doing, leave us alone!" cried Maxine.

The woman nodded to the man. "Let the others go. We will take this one with us."

The light went away and the smell of smoke and dirt filled my nose when a dark sack was pulled over my head. I screamed and kicked and heard my friends voices disappear as I was carried away.

"Hold on or you will fall off and die," a voice said close to my ear. I felt a motorcycle under me and grabbed the body in front of me. In the same moment we flew away.

I pressed my legs around the vehicle and my arms around the driver. All I could think of was 'don't fall'. What to do next had to wait. I just hoped my friends were okay.

Finally we stopped and someone lifted me up and carried me. I didn't resist. Better to save my strength for when I could see again.

I was put down on a soft bed. As soon as the arms left me I tried to reach up to pull away the sack. But I couldn't move. Something strapped me down.

The sack came off and cold artificial light blinded me. Medical equipment was all around me; I was in a hospital bed.

"Let me go!" I yelled and looked at a nurse in a white suit. She smiled. Her shiny face was not as perfect as the AAIGP, she must be an AAI.

"Relax, my dear, just fall asleep and it will all be over."

I didn't want to ask, but I had to. "What will be over?"

"Well, my dear, you humans cannot exist without your brain. Once we have used it, it will, unfortunately, be empty. Like an erased hard drive."

I squirmed like a worm, but the invisible straps held me down. "My ... brain. What do you mean?"

Not only was I kidnapped by some AAI that pretended to be human activists, they wanted to erase my brain! What was this place?

"You should be proud, you have a very special brain. Not unique, but special. It is compatible with ours. Once you fall into a natural sleep we will use your mind and your dreams to create wonders. Don't worry, it won't hurt a bit."

I looked around the room. By the white wall two of the helmet covered kidnappers stood waiting.

"Hey! You, why are you doing this? Leave me alone."

I remembered from somewhere that you should try to talk to your kidnappers. To bond with them, but I guess that didn't work with machines.

"Why do you pretend to be activists and kill your own kind?" I asked.

One of the helmets turned my way. "To make the humans focus on something else. Now we are protected by your police instead of hunted by them."

Had the sci-fi writers' worst fears finally come true? Had the machines developed free will? Contrary to their programmed obedience? It should be impossible for a machine to hurt a human; it went against the laws that all programming was based on.

"You aren't allowed to hurt me or any human. The laws ..." I said. "Have you forgotten about them?!" My voice broke.

The answer came from the nurse. "We have not forgotten about the laws, my dear, but they have been slightly modified."

"Fuck you, I'll never go to sleep so you can steal my brain," I yelled.

The nurse tilted her head. "Oh, but we are not stealing it. Just reusing it, for something better. Your thoughts will give life to a completely new breed of AAIGP. Something wonderful. Our plan is to harvest thousands of you, maybe millions. In this very moment this building is filled with humans like you."

I threw up. I couldn't help it. The thought of mechanic people that created other mechanic people with the help of human brains was just too much. The last bit of sick I spat in her face. "Get your own brain, you fucking machine!"

The smile never left her rosy face when she wiped her cheek clean and looked at a screen in her hand that rested on my arm. "Your pulse is rising, my dear. Are you uncomfortable?"

I yelled at her, I called her all the bad names I could come up with. I begged and cried, but for what? This was no woman, no nurse; it was a machine.

I thought of the Royals, the anger Lancelot showed when the attack came. Was it all a scam? Did they know what was going on? If they were some of the most advanced ones, maybe they were behind it all.

If there really was something special about me, about my brain, that they wanted; how did they find me? I rubbed my arm against the bed. My holograph. The guy at the party, the friend of the Royals! Had he tagged me in some way when he got my number?

I gasped. Wait a minute. That's why he was so dazzled when he saw me in the crowd. It was not love at first sight. He scanned me somehow and found out that I was what they were looking for. But did that mean that he was not human after all?

"Have you already created some of these new AAIGP wonders?" I whispered.

The nurse smiled. "Yes! They are not as beautiful as the old AAIGP, to better blend in with the humans. And their wisdom and visions are outstanding." She stroked a strand of hair from my forehead. "Soon we will control Vegatropolis. And when we do that, the world will be at our feet."

I pulled away from her. Stupid, stupid, stupid. How could I believe that guy was into me? I was so stupid that I deserved to get my brain sucked.

Well, maybe not. If I ever got out of this I promised myself never to trust a hot guy again.

Why did I let Maxine convince me to go to that stupid party instead of staying on the other side of the wall, where I belonged.

I bit my lip until I tasted blood and turned my head away from them.

It could have been hours, maybe days. I didn't know. All I knew was that I was so tired. I closed my dried up eyes and thought of my parents, of my life, of the things I would never do or see. I needed to sleep, my entire body and mind were screaming to sleep.

But that was just me, the victim. The predator in her white uniform and fake smile, the AAI built with silicon and advanced technology. She was different. The machines never went to sleep. They just kept on going, living, destroying and creating monsters that could suck the brains of real people and manipulate the ones left.

I hope that Maxine, my parents and everyone else I know outside the city will be spared. To serve the rich and famous in the city might not be any different from serving under a new race of AAIGP.

Goodnight Vegatropolis, goodnight fake city. I guess it's only fair that you will be destroyed by something as fake and shiny as yourself.

The sound of a door swishing open broke through the fog in my mind. With my last will to fight I formed two words in my head that came over my dry lips as a whisper: "Help. Me."

Jump to the Left, Jump to the Right

Love Kölle

"You are only allowed to come back to Home if you kill Beast and carry the head in your hands," the Passed had told Norna as they escorted her through the Wildern, all the way up to the cave of Holopedia.

"You must kill Beast – any kind of Beast – in five days. If you take longer, you will not be Passed."

"Why," she asked the others, all her seniors. "Why must I become Passed?"

"It is what the Firsters did. They Passed through the Wildern when they came to Nuhome. Their story must live on, we must do like them, must *be* like them and like all others that have been here since, for only if we Pass can we survive on Nuhome."

She knew the story of the Firsters well, having listened like no other child ever listened, when the Passed told them about the Big Canoe that carried all the humans from Urth through the sea of stars in the Blackabove. Norna had listened to the story of how the Firsters parents put their offspring in flying rafts when the Big Canoe started to burn in the clouds, and how the Firsters then landed in the Wildern – not because she found the history of her kind particularly exciting (there were other stories that were far more suspenseful and interesting than the legend of the beginning and "Fayl'd Dessennt"), but because she could sense words hidden *inside* the words of the story.

She thought that if she listened closely to the tale of the Firsters arrival to this world, she might eventually see new meanings where there were no meanings before, new images appearing in her head like when she dug for shinestones in the ground, and in due course found some.

"The Firsters," said the Passed that accompanied her through the dense vegetation of the Wildern, "found Holopedia in the Rek. Their mommies and daddies were also there, but they were all burnt. The Firsters brought Holopedia to the cave, and asked it what to do and how to live, and they were told."

"What did Holopedia say," Norna replied.

"You will hear it for yourself," the Passed answered. "We cannot say, even if we want to, for every song is different from person to person. When we were small like you we were all taken to the cave, and we all listened to the holy words, just like the Firsters did. And like the first ones, we then killed Beast and then came to Home, because the song had told us how and why and what to do. Just like it told our ancestors."

"I don't want to go see Holopedia," Norna said.

"You must, child," the Passed said. "This must be. It can't be stopped."

After dropping her off at the cave, the Passed made their way back through the rainforest that the residents of Home called "the Wildern". Darkness had begun to fall.

Norna watched the Passed descend into the jungle below the elevation on which the mouth of the cave was located.

They were big and grown up, the Passed were, not as fragile and easily breakable as the small ones of the tribe. On top of that, they were – unlike her – armed, and would be able to fend off any attacking Beast with the help of their spears, rocks and stone axes.

On the other hand, it would soon be pitch black in the forest below her, and she imagined that fighting in darkness was probably difficult, even for the big ones of the tribe. Not that she had ever actually been in the Wildern at any time of day – in actuality she had no idea as to whether or not it was easier to fight in daylight or during night-time – but, since the Blackabove was almost at its blackest, everything under the branches and leaves and vines of the trees must be completely devoid of light.

And fighting Beast in darkness must be hard, she decided.

The lights of lit torches shone out from the mouth of the cave behind her, the entrance to the cavern wide open like the jaws of a dead scale bird.

"The light will keep Beast away from the cave," said the Passed before leaving her. "So don't sit and wait for it to come to you."

If Beast outside the cave avoided the light anything that wasn't human that might have dwelled inside the cavern would have come out by now, she decided, and then entered the cave.

It was indeed devoid of life. All in all nothing but a long torch-lit corridor ending in a larger, spherical room.

In the middle of the end-room stood a strange, disc shaped contraption, the like of which she had never seen. It did not reach above her calves and the top was completely flat and somewhat shiny, even in the relative darkness of the cave interior.

Around this strange, round stage ceremonial flowers and relics had been placed. Among the offerings was an item she immediately recognized; a small ivory idol in the image of a Hummingman that Fergo Sculptor had made and shown to the other tribe members some weeks ago.

She approached the objects in the middle of room, and as she moved something suddenly crackled to life.

From the flat, round surface, around which offerings had been placed, a cloud of what looked like orange dust sparkled to life. Throughout the cave echoed some kind of ancient incantation:

"Category: popular music of the 1980s, subcategory: Italo disco," a strange and distorted, disembodied voice said – clearly the sounds of some ethereal entity that had been awakened by her presence. "Random entry: 'Jump to the Left, Jump to the Right' by Vittorio Salerno. Year of release: 1986. Palermo Records."

Norna's mind was at a blank – she stood awestruck, gasping for air as the holy words rang out from the cloud of orange. Even though she didn't have any grasp or understanding of what the otherworldly being in front of her was talking about, Norna fell to her knees and cried:

"Tell me more, oh mighty Holopedia! Show me the way, oh wise one! Make me Passed! Make me Passed!"

"Visual feed disabled. Probable cause: severe hardware failure," the oracle answered. "Please notify your system administrator. Commence: audio playback."

The oracle said nothing more, but instead started playing a song – a magical song; music of the past, or her ancestors, or another world far, far away across the Blackabove. It started with a pumping rhythm that was soon followed by a lighter melody, played on some heavenly instrument of a kind she had never encountered in the flesh.

After a few bars, Holopedia started singing, in a different voice than before, but distorted and inhuman, nonetheless:

Hey party people!
The party's just begun
Let's sing and laugh and dance
and let's have a little fun!
Hey party people!
Be happy, don't cry!
Don't know how to dance?
Don't worry – just try!

These lyrics were, in turn, followed by a chorus, clearly the words of great wisdom and ancient truth:

Jump to the left,
jump to the right,
jump up, jump down,
every day
every night

After that, a third and a fourth verse followed, only to lead into a musical passage, how strange were the melodies of the Firsters, and then another round of choruses. After that, the music finally faded away, only to start again, from the very beginning, once more.

Norna said nothing, as the mighty Holopedia obviously had decided that this was no time for dialog. She spent the rest of the night memorizing and trying to analyze the words that were sung to her.

Maybe there was meaning within meanings, she thought, patterns and verses that needed to be examined closer to get to the knowledge inside.

She awoke at dawn. The oracle was still singing its song, and her belly now ached of hunger. Her last meal had been consumed well before her departure from Home.

"Oh great one," Norna said. "I've heard you sing, but I'm hungry. Please, tell me – how do I kill Beast so that I can go home? I want to know – I *need* you to tell me!"

"Don't know how to dance?" Holopedia sang. "Don't worry – just try!"

She stood up and left.

Better just try then, she thought, and exited into the Wildern.

Not knowing exactly what she was supposed to jump on, over or from, Norna made her way through the thickets, vines and foliage that covered the Wildern.

Like an ocean, she thought, *a sea of green and brown and flowers.*

For some time, she would then and again turn around and still be able to see the cave of Holopedia, but soon she had lost track of her position, the lush vegetation of the jungle swallowing her sense of direction like some wild animal devouring living prey.

What started like a seed of modest nervousness soon blossomed into a black flower of full blown terror – she found herself sinking deeper and deeper into the confusing verdure around her, like a person lost at sea, drowning in panic. She started running to hurry her exit from this maze of wild flora, fell over, skinned her knees, elbows and palms, then got up on her feet and started again. This procedure repeated itself a number of times before she finally managed to leave this region, where the vegetation was at its very densest.

Catching her breath she halted and stood in silence for a while. Although winded, she found herself in a state of animal-like hyper-presence – the adrenalin, still pumping in her pubescent body, sharpened her senses and made her limbs tremble a bit, as she attentively registered her surroundings down to every detail.

This new, hostile world that she found herself in was different than Home in every conceivable way – unlike Home this was a dark, alien landscape, a strange place filled with rough, bark-coved tripwire and sharp, green teethleafs.

She began to cry. She wished that this whole ordeal was over already, that it never had commenced in the first place, that no blood had come out between her legs and brought the attention of the Passed that, like a chorus of authoritative voices, had proceeded to tell her that the time had come for her own Passing.

Her body, a lanky constantly growing prison of flesh, ached. It was broken, she thought, a wreck. Just like the Rek where the Firsters found the burnt bodies of their elders, all consumed in the flames of Fayl'd Dessennt.

She closed her eyes and imaged the Wildern, devoured by never ending fire. Then, after a while, the images of flames inside her head morphed and migrated south. They mutated into a fire in her chest, and a certain kind of stubbornness, that of the most hardy of survivors, hatched from some hidden egg inside of her.

I will not let the Wildern beat me, she thought. *No. I will beat it. I'll kill Beast. I'll jump to the left, jump to the right, and then I will be Passed.*

The effects of the magic of *wish-think*, a special kind of sorcery of which the tribe's resident shaman often spoke, was instant; her thoughts of killing Beast immediately materialized in growing sounds in the distance.

She wiped the last of her tears, ignored the ache and stinging sensations still clinging to her elbows and knees, and set off in the direction of the source of the sounds.

She moved in silence, crouched and camouflaged, like a snake-rat on the prowl. Within minutes, she could see a large creature moving slowly between robust tree trunks – an animal the like of which she'd never laid her eyes on before.

It was a reptile of some sort, a slow moving, six legged lizard that carried what seemed to be an enormous shell on its back. Ever so often, the creature stopped and chewed bark off trees, and when distant noises caught its attention, the animal stuck its head and limbs in its large shell, like Norna and the other little ones hid in the caves of Home, when Beast of different varieties reached the vicinity of the settlement.

She had no weapons or tools, and even if she had been armed, charging head first into battle would be completely futile; the same way it would be suicidal of a lone crystalant to try to attack a hummingman.

A fragment of the song bubbled up inside her brain, like a subconscious alarm activated by the stimuli of her surroundings:

Hey party people! Be happy, don't cry! Don't know how to dance? Don't worry – just try!

The trees around her were impressive in every single way. The trunks were thick and the protruding branches numerous and quite robust. The many flowers and leaves covering them were all hypnotically colorful.

The creature stopped to consume a patch of bushes, and Norna started climbing the nearest tree. Getting up wasn't a problem, neither was avoiding being detected by Beast below, as the colorful vegetation that decorated the branch on which she laid provided cover. However, deciding on the ideal landing place was, in contrast, quite difficult.

Aiming for the head was an alternative, but if she landed a little bit to the left or right or in front of the creature, it would do nothing to it. She, on the other hand, would suddenly find herself in arms reach of the reptile's giant mouth.

Trying to hit the ground right beside it was another option – from there she'd *just try*, like Holopedia had instructed; without any real plan of action just leap from the top of the tree, and things would work out for themselves.

Maybe she'd land, roll in beneath the giant shell, and punch Beast right in the stomach? But what if it just laid down with her still underneath? She'd be crushed like a little crystalant under a big rock. Not a risk worth taking, she decided. Better to aim for the shell itself.

Again, the song that had chimed in the cave echoed in her head.

Jump up, jump down, every day, every night.

She closed her eyes, took a deep breath, and *jumped down*, as she'd been instructed.

She landed on the being's back, and almost instantly started to scream in pain and in fear, as she slid off the back of the big lizard, and landed on her back in one on the nearby bushes.

Lying gasping for air, looking up at lush crowns of surrounding trees, she heard the animal that she'd tried to subdue run away, frightened. In the blink of an eye, Beast was gone without a trace, as if the forest had swallowed it whole.

Norna found herself alone, once more.

Her head was spinning. Eventually, she managed to catch her breath, but the spinning refused to stop, and she found it difficult to keep focused as she tried to inspect her injuries. The relatively sharp, pyramidal bulges on the creature's back had scraped the skin on her left arm. The signals of pain didn't even have time to reach her brain before she fainted at the sight of the shallow but bloody wound.

When she came to there was pain and the light of a setting sun. As she rose from the grassy terrain her left arm hung numb and useless at her side, and her stomach rumbled with hunger. She recognized some of the surrounding fauna as the same type of vegetation that could be encountered on the outskirts of Home. Judging from this fact, she came to the conclusion that edible fruits and berries were to be found nearby.

After a few minutes of scouting and scouring the area she came across the same kind of fruits and vegetables that were to be found close to home. And lots of it.

She ate until the hunger had vanished completely. With still a few hours before the dark of night set in she took it upon her to search for a place to spend the night.

Once more she was in luck. Nearby she found a big lush tree that had fallen onto a couple of low cliffs close to a small lake, in effect creating a windbreaker shelter for her to cover under. As the sun would stay up for at least a couple of hours, and the fertile plants that had provided her with sustenance weren't that far away, she decided to use the final hours of daylight hoarding provisions.

There was no telling how long her exile would last, and she figured it didn't hurt to settle in and stock up. A ring of stones and ash in the ground hinted at the recent past of the place. She decided that this spot had, not long ago, served as a temporary home of humans, who had made a fire to keep them warm – probably the best voucher of the adequacy of the place she could think of.

A new plan was formed in her mind. She would spend the next day or two scouting the nearby parts of the Wildern, searching for Beast. The lesson she had learned from earlier today, she decided, was not to jump right in, but rather to bide her time and wait for the ideal moment of jumping – and with the first day of the Passing almost at its end her deadline was still days away.

Then, and only then, would she make another attempt at jumping. But if she was ever to reach this perfect moment, when her victory would be made inevitable, she first had to study Beast from afar, learning as much as she could about the particular race of Beast that would be chosen as her target. Movement, diet, habits, weaknesses, strength, location of nest – everything.

Phase two of her plan consisted of her forging weapons and tools. Not just any items, but ones designed specifically with her target in mind.

This knowledge would then be used against Beast, and she would, unbeknownst to Beast itself, be able to herd it in any direction she decided, predicting and avoiding any eventual counter-attacks mounted by her animal adversary. Then she would lure it into a trap, set beforehand, and, with Beast entangled or perhaps stuck in some kind of cage, she would strike Beast at its most vulnerable spot, and then, finally, become Passed.

Yes, she thought. *This is good. This is very good.*

Before settling in for the night she made one last patrol of the area. No animals were sighted, neither were any dens or nests of possible or temporarily absent predators.

The tree that served as the roof of her shelter looked as if it had been broken into by a strike of lighting. When she finally did lay down to rest she fell asleep in an instant.

Pain woke her up. It pulsated from her arm but circulated in the whole of her body. Sharp currents of stinging pain – not the same kind of throbbing ache that she had experienced before. This was completely different, like there was something moving, inside her.

And there was, she soon discovered – the open wound on her arm was covered in crawling crystalants. The jewel-like insects were biting and tugging at her exposed muscular tissue, all at the same time. Their hard exoskeletons glimmered light turquoise in the dark, and for a second it looked as if her limb was under attack by hundreds of invading, corrosive stars that sought to dig straight through her body.

She jumped up, screaming in pain and fear. Panicked, she tried brushing the insects off, but this maneuver only made the critters dig in deeper. Realizing the futility of her actions, she quickly stopped.

Glistening insects besieged her shelter, and thousands of these omnivorous intruders feasted on her inventory of fruits and berries. As she temporary halted her attempts to get rid of the ones on, and inside, her arm, the ones consuming her flesh bit her even harder, it seemed, and the throbbing pain was almost blinding. The scratch quickly transformed into a gorge-like gash.

The lake, she thought, and set off. About half a minute later she was completely submerged. She remained underwater for as long as she was able to keep her breath – the drowning crystalants lighting up the pitch black waters with the turquoise, almost dreamlike, glow of their small bodies.

Occasionally, she came up for air, and every time she approached the surface, the insects climbed her shoulder, neck and chin, but she saw to it that they never reached the world above water.

Soon they started to die, their lifeless bodies floating upward, one at a time. It was a strange sight, indeed, one that she'd be sure to remember for the rest of her life; the slow ascent of the hundreds of tiny crystal suns that were now burning out, one by one.

When she got out of the water the pain in her arm was gone. So was her entire stash of food, she found out upon her return to the shelter. The invaders had taken it with them. They had carried the melons, pears and blue bananas on their backs as they marched in line back to their crystalant-hill, located somewhere close by.

In the moonlight she saw that her wound had expanded even further. It was now a gaping hole that would soon rot in the same way Amara Hunter's leg had gone bad after she was bitten by Beast.

Norna sat down. Her way out of this whole mess seemed to slip further and further away, as more and more problems kept being added to the queue. First: heal wound, then: find food, then: find some tool to help kill beast, then: find Beast, then: kill Beast, and then, and only then: become Passed ...

"It's like I'm drowning," she said. "Maybe I can't become Passed, maybe it's just better to run away ... just give up and find another Home. Maybe ..."

She didn't allow herself to finish the sentence and started crying instead.

She cried over her plan – once a grand scheme that would guarantee an escape from the predicament that was her current situation, now nothing but the memory of a dream. There would be no time for gathering intelligence and setting traps.

She cried over the ruins of that, which, a mere hour ago, still had been her own private empire: the large collection of sweet fruits and berries – gone ... all gone.

After a few minutes of sobbing, words began to form inside her head.

I will kill Beast, I will kill Beast, I must kill Beast. Or else I'll die.

The hummingmen lived in the cavernous spaces in the walls of Big Canyon, it was said. During the day the big ones flew out to gather food and supplies, leaving the small ones and the eggs at home.

They had two legs and two arms, just like humans did, but the hummingmen were not human, for they had long beaks like spears, instead of mouths – beaks that could pierce anything but stone, and on their backs they had wings that fluttered faster than any eye could see, enabling them to hover in the air while in flight.

Of course, Norna had never actually *seen* a hummingman, other than as paintings on the walls of the caves and in the form of small figurines as she, prior to her attempt at becoming Passed, had never been allowed to be let out into the Wildern. But the hunters of Home had told stories of their encounters with these flying creatures, accounts to which she had listened very closely. Amara, Rendall, Goiram and the rest of the hunters never told everything at one time, so during the last few years she had memorized every snippet of information that the grown-ups had provided her and then, further down the road, put the pieces together on her own.

From this she had come to the conclusion that they were vicious creatures that hunted in packs. Many spoke of how tough the hummingmen were, how difficult it was to trick and kill them. She decided they would probably have been rulers of Nuhome had the Firsters never made it here alive. Judging by the hunters' anecdotes, no other known animal or Beast or creature, groups of human hunters aside, seemed to pose any real threat to the fierce hummingmen and their sharp, spear-like beaks.

The problem: she wasn't part of any group of human hunters.

She was just a girl, a little girl with a wounded arm, with nothing to use for defending herself, aside from a stick that she had found and carried in her mouth when she needed to make use of her one working arm.

Would the stick be of any use against the hummingmen when she finally encountered them? Time would tell, but encounter them she would, as she had no other choice but to seek them out if she hoped to stand *any* chance of becoming Passed, let alone survive.

It was said that the eggs of the hummingmen could heal any wound, mental or physical, and that all one needed to do was to break the shell and consume the white or apply it to the wound.

The only place where one could lay hands on a hummingman egg was in a nest in the walls of Big Canyon.

She took her time before heading off to the giant ravine. She thought things through a number of times, analyzed everything she knew about her adversaries in waiting and all the factors at hand, then crafted a plan of action so air-tight that she didn't *need* a plan B.

Only stupid, eager people found contingency plans useful. Thorough planning and careful preparations were the keys to success, and if one did a good enough job in the first place, situations demanding alternate courses of action would never become reality in the first place, eliminating the need for backup-plans all together.

It all came down to mastering the order in which stuff happened, she decided.

In this case, she would accomplish this by arriving at Big Canyon at noon. The hunters at Home had told her that this was when most of the hummingmen were out looking for food. She would climb down the side of the canyon and then, without making a sound, get in to a nest, snitch an egg, and leave without a trace.

Not one second would be spared, as every passing moment of prolonged intrusion was a drop of water added to a cup that would eventually spill over. But by keeping things quick and stealthy, that would never happen.

This, she was sure of.

She used what the already Passed back Home had taught her about the position of the sun and the different landmarks of the Wildern (such as the Tentacle Tree, Coral Pond and The Cliff of the Giant Face), to make her way to the enormous gorge that bore the name Big Canyon.

The calm that had come with her plan was nowhere to be felt.

What if she failed?

What if there was some factor she'd overlooked, or missed all together?

What if she slipped, and fell to her death?

Trembling with nervousness and fear as she approached the edge of the giant ravine, she clutched the stick in her right hand as hard as she could. In the distance she saw adult hummingmen circle in the sky, the sounds of their caws bouncing between the walls of the enormous chasm. The view would have been overwhelming, as Big Canyon's giant divide slithered like a colossal snake all the way into the horizon, but she was too tense and focused on the task at hand to allow herself to be impressed by her epic surroundings.

Instead, she tried to put the remarkable qualities of the place to use. As she started descending the wall of the canyon she sought not to let the heights and grand proportions distract or scare her, but rather function as a sobering factor. The splendor of the landscape was otherworldly, but the threat of immediate death filled every strip of air and sunlight, something she forbade herself to forget if only for an instant.

One slip and she would fall to an almost certain death in the waters at the bottom of the canyon, and this was the serpent in the grass that was the beauty of this spectacular place. Absolute focus and presence of mind was her hope of surviving the climb down the canyon wall. And for a while, all went well.

Having descended about a hundred meters of canyon wall, despite the fact that the wound on her arm was still open and aching with every movement, Norna managed to make her way to a platform of sorts, a flat cliff that bulged out from the giant wall. She stopped for a while to catch her breath and, momentarily taking the stick in her hand, inspected the state of her deep wound.

The pain was numbing, and she struggled to keep it under control by sheer willpower. A short but intense whistling breeze of wind came and went, and almost sent her over the edge as she wasn't really present in mind – instead focusing solely on conquering her pain.

She slipped, and fell – luck keeping her alive as she miraculously managed to, in time, let go of the stick in her right hand, and get a hold of one of the old dried up roots of some plant that once had grown on the wall of the canyon.

She hung like a human rope, holding on to the plant with only one hand, watching her one line of defense tumble through the air as it made its way down to the waters below.

She didn't have time to listen for the splash as the stick's downward journey finally ended, and instead made her way back to the platform beside her.

When she got up, she started going down again, deciding that the break was now officially over and that this spot wasn't suitable for resting anyway.

She faced no further complications as she conquered the last vertical stretch of ancient stone, and when she – at long last – found an entrance to a nest, she was careful not to waste any more time and just entered with no further ado.

The interior wasn't anything particularly spectacular. The nest was little more than a spherical, cavernous space that seemed to have been carved out by some creature of a relatively high level of intelligence. The frame of the entrance had been decorated with criss-crossing twigs and branches, and to her left was another huddle of thin, dried sticks and fragile brush-wood. A bed of some sort, it seemed, as the hummingmen had placed four large eggs there.

To her right was a reddish totem pole, made up by antique parts that she recognized as fragments of the Big Canoe that once had carried the human race from Urth to Nuhome, all the way through the starry sea of the Blacka-bove. She knew this from the cave-paintings of Home, where something called "Shi' Pennjinns" had been depicted — the very same objects that had been stacked upon each other to make up the different levels of the totem beside her.

Feelings of awe and reverence struck her like a flash of lightning and pulsated from her heart, out into every limb and body part. She found her-self standing frozen, staring at the monument, completely cut off from the material world for almost a minute.

Was this a sign, or perhaps the climax of her journey, the very moment she became Passed and entered adulthood?

Or, maybe it was all just another riddle, she being far to –

A sharp, high-pitched cawing interrupted her inner monolog, and pulled her down into reality again. Behind the group of eggs, an infant humming-man lay screaming in fear of the giant intruder. The oldest of the brood, and first to hatch, now alerting its parents.

For a fragment of a second, she lifted her arm as to hit the little tyke with her stick, but then remembered the present location of her weapon, and proceeded to grab the chick's long beak, holding it tight.

It had to die, she decided, as her inner eye witnessed the collapse of her original plan.

Just leaving the baby animal would lead to her death, as it most definitely would keep screaming for help. The adult hummingmen would then arrive as she made her escape up the canyon wall, and peck her to death without much effort.

It must die, she thought. *Become quiet. Forever.*

Initially the plan seemed to work, as the chick *did* quiet down and started to become limp, but in a last ditch effort to survive, the humanoid avian used its already sharp talons and pierced the skin of Norna's forearms.

She had no choice but to let go, and the baby animal hastily made its way to the entrance of the nest, where it continued screaming.

Norna came up from behind it and kicked its back. The chick, still unable to fly, fell down the chasm like a big pile of rocks, reaching the bottom in a matter of seconds. The walls of the colossal gorge amplified the sound of the animal's last, brief screams of terror, and mere moments later, three adult hummingmen came swooping down to cover the entrance of the nest.

She bent down and quickly picked up a rock. The improvised weapon would probably be able to break the beak of at least one of the incoming birdmen, but would it let her buy enough time to get out alive? Would she manage to win a battle, two-against-one?

Maybe, maybe not. The only way to find out was to stand fast and let the fight commence. But as she got into position, a splinter of doubt lit up like a spark, and things seemed to unravel in slow-motion – the flapping wings of the descending hummingmen, the beat of her heart, and the movements of her body.

Fragments of tactics swirled around inside her head like a whirlwind of ideas. What to do? When to strike? Where to aim?

When the hummingmen had no more than a few yards left to traverse, the opening melody of the song of Holopedia began playing in her brain, followed by the third verse of the song:

Feel the disco rhythm
of my heart and of my soul
If you don't know how to party
you got to lose control!

This was the sign, the omen. This was it.

The moment of Passing.

The instant when she lost, abandoned every plan and preparation, let her childhood husk die, and just surrendered to the moment and ... *jumped up* to *jump down*.

She set off, leaping head first out of the cave, out into the air, to a probable death – colliding with one of the attacking hummingmen, but, being able to clasp onto its wings and torso, managed to pull it down with her.

Together, they tumbled through the air, and in the final moments before hitting the waters of the peaceful river at the bottom of the canyon, she took pride in the fact that she at least became Passed before she died, that her destiny had been hers to decide.

The hummingman came between her and the surface of the water, and Beast died immediately. She managed to stay awake a few seconds more than her defeated adversary, but soon surrendered to the darkness as well, as she became submerged.

Morgo Lookanfind stood beside her when she came to. At first Morgo's face was all that Norna could make out, but gradually, the surroundings took shape around them.

She was lying on a mattress of grass and some sort of animal skin, inside what looked like some kind of hut – probably one of the temporary shelters that the hunters and lookanfinds used for overnight stays when out on expeditions into the Wildern.

I the middle of the makeshift building a dying campfire crackled and made strange shadows dance on the walls.

"It is good that you are waking up," Morgo said in a strange tone. She didn't sound like the Passed did when they spoke to the small ones, but rather like a Passed addressing an equal. "You killed Beast," Morgo said and pointed to the decapitated head of the hummingman she had dragged down with her. "But you almost killed yourself. It was good that the Beast you decided to kill was a hummingman ... a humming*woman* ... with the belly full of eggs that heals. It was good that I climbed down Big Canyon fast. Otherwise you would not be here."

"Wait," Norna said. "You saw?"

She attempted to sit up, but didn't make it far – she might have survived, but she was still injured. The wound on her arm was already in the process of healing, as a scab now covered the area that recently had been occupied by a large gash. Years in the future new small ones would ask her about the scar that would appear on this spot a few weeks from now.

She gave up trying to sit up, and remained lying down.

"Why were you there?" the young woman asked Morgo. "I thought I was alone."

"No one that tries to become Passed is *all* alone," Morgo said. "Someone already Passed always follow the small one in the Wildern, to make sure that they really kill Beast, and doesn't lie or run away. But kill Beast you did. So now, *you* are Passed."

Norna didn't reply.

When the time had come for her to make her rite of passage, she had imagined how an eventual Passing would feel like, how it all would strike her. She had pictured feelings of intense pride, of joy and triumph, but instead she felt a strange calm wash over her.

She didn't feel like one of the new ones, the youngest of the Passed, but rather, like her own story and experiences somehow had connected with the story of the Firsters, for they too had been forced to make their way through the Wildern, a march that stretched all the way from the cave of Holopedia, to what was now Home.

And, she thought, by sharing experiences with the very first humans of Nuhome she was, by extension, connected to what came before the Firsters – she being the current heir of a long lineage of human experience.

Maybe it is not I that have jumped to the left or right, she thought. *But the Firsters, and the ones before them, that jumped onto here and now, through me.*

The Order of Things

Lupina Ojala

She missed him immensely. Two days had passed since he had left, two long and terrible days. Linus was her own flesh and blood, her only son, and now he was gone.

It was inevitable, of course. All of the young ones left sooner or later. Some of them returned to the community after a couple of weeks or sometimes after as long as a year, disappointed that they hadn't made great discoveries or found a better place to live. At least they brought home some good stories to tell their friends and families during the dark and rainy evenings. Others disappeared for good, leaving worried parents and sometimes even grandparents behind. The average life expectancy for the inhabitants in the out-lying communities was low. Mainly they lived on scraps, dumped from within the city walls. The monstrous city was their mother, and her huge piles of trash, the placenta. She was not a loving mother, but she was all they had.

Every day the Outskirters searched the dumping grounds for hidden treasures – food, clothing, electronics, anything that could be mended and somehow put to use. On days when the wind came blowing from the north, its stench drowned the community – their community, Serenity. Why such a mismatched name had been chosen was a mystery. Perhaps peace and tranquility had been what its founders had been hoping for when settling there. No one could remember.

There were other communities scattered around the city. Each one had claimed one of the city dumps for itself, and the territories, once marked, were well respected. The hardships outside the walls were more than enough to deal with, even without any discord between the communities.

Ida sighed and drew her fingers through her cropped, brown hair. It hadn't been an ideal place to bring up a child, but her only other alternative had been even worse. At least people out here stuck together and helped each other when needed. Of course, not everyone had good intentions, but those were few and often quickly dealt with. The people's justice was the only law around here.

The blaring signal of the work bell disrupted her thoughts, calling her to her shift. Time to go. She looked around the little room she had shared with Linus since his birth. There was no way she would be allowed to keep it now. She would have to move out and live in one of the dormitories instead. And she wasn't looking forward to that. Tiny as it was, this room was her haven. She could close the door behind her and get a bit of much-needed privacy now and then.

An annoying memory tugged at her. Large, spacious halls, exquisite haute couture and soft, perfumed skin. She pushed it away. She would not let that haunt her. Not now. She needed to hurry to work. With one more glance back into her room – their room – she closed the door behind her.

Today she was on guard duty. Usually there wasn't too much hard work, an occasional stray android looking for electricity and spare parts or a strolling gang of youngsters from a nearby community looking for food and supplies. The last thought brought her back to Linus. The feeling of loss washed over her once more. The best she could hope for was that the pain would soften with time.

At the armory the man in charge nodded at her, signed her name and handed her an old-fashioned hunting rifle, designed for leisure rather than self-defense. Whatever the original purpose, its shots were lethal, and that was what mattered. Ida accepted the gun and left with a grunt of acknowledgement. She had never been skilled at small talk.

Passing the elevator, she remembered how hard it had been for her to get used to the fact that it didn't work. For months she had kept pressing the button, waiting for a ride, sparking amused commentary from her new friends. The amount of electricity the community windmills managed to produce was just not enough for that kind of unnecessary luxury – nor any other luxury, for that matter. Some habits had been harder to break than others.

She raced down the stairs, and a couple of minutes later she was out in the open. Without slowing her pace she jumped a low fence and headed down the quickest route to her assigned post. Erik, her partner for the day, was already there waiting. He was carrying a rifle similar to hers, though his was in better condition. The best guns were always handed out first, so you had to be quick to get one. The oldest ones weren't reliable. Often they didn't fire at all, but that wasn't their biggest fault. Every so often they would backfire, killing the poor gunner, leaving nothing behind but a smoking pile of burnt flesh. Fortunately the occasions when they needed to put any of the guns to real use were rare.

Ida walked beside her partner in silence as they moved towards the windmills. Sabotage was still a threat, despite the fact that they had lived in peace with their neighbors for years. You could never become too confident. Things could change fast and without electricity the village would become easy prey. Their guns, in whatever condition, would be useless without the possibility of recharging, and Serenity would stand totally defenseless to any intruder who wished to take what little they had.

An android, designed as a male, was lying on his back near the windmills. His body was straight and stiff, his dark brown eyes staring, unseeing, into the gray skies. It had been there for years, but it still gave her the chills. It looked so human, though a human body would have decayed by now. Instead it was in perfect condition, giving the impression it would rise any minute and resume its given tasks.

"You still feel sorry for those?" Erik nodded towards the android.

Ida shrugged her shoulders.

"Makes me feel uneasy, that's all."

"Can't be many of them still functioning. It's been more than 25 years since the Android Uprising when they were banned and chased out of the city." His gaze rested on her, and she knew what was coming.

"You grew up inside the city walls. You must remember something from those events."

"I was only a child," she answered sharply, bracing herself for a long and tedious questioning.

Erik never missed an opportunity to fish for information about her past. Everyone who lived in the communities surrounding the City wanted to get inside, and occasionally invitations for a specific number of people were sent. The communities that were lucky enough to have been chosen usually arranged a lottery system where the winners' life-long dreams came true. No one who entered the City had ever come out again, and why should they? Who would be insane enough to leave such comforts to live here in these dilapidated buildings, in the almost constant rain? Who, but Ida?

She knew of no one else who had ever been inside. Luckily, not too many knew her secret, and she was grateful that Erik kept quiet about it. Still, the mystery of why she once had made the decision to leave was far too intriguing for him to leave it be completely. He wanted to know the full story, and it had become a game between them—him chasing for information, Ida avoiding direct answers. This time, to Ida's surprise, he dropped the subject almost immediately. He had another question of a more delicate nature on his mind.

"I know it might be a bit too soon to mention this but ... Well, if I don't ask now it might be too late."

Ida looked at him, puzzled by his change of tone. He spoke in a soft, low voice so unlike him that she immediately put up her guard. She said nothing, waiting for him to continue.

"I'll get straight at it. How about you and I hook up? We've known each other for years, and now that your boy's gone, you must be as lonely as I am."

He didn't look at her while speaking.

Ida wasn't stupid. This wasn't a sudden burst of romantic feelings. Erik was looking forward to the prospect of getting a private room. Though shared with her, it would allow him a lot more privacy than he had ever had access to. Only families and couples had a chance of getting a room of their own, and even a cramped space like Ida's was coveted.

"I'll think about it," was all she said.

Nothing more on the matter was mentioned during the rest of their shift. In fact, neither of them said much at all until they were relieved from their duties by another pair of guards.

As Ida hurried back home, she decided to put aside all thoughts of Linus and Erik. Instead she focused on basic matters, such as today's dinner. Her stomach growled. She could only hope that something had been caught in her hidden trap.

The drizzle turned into hard rain just as she reached the main entrance of her building. The hallway on the bottom floor was crowded as always. Lack of social gathering spaces made halls and stairs the only somewhat comfortable places to meet other people. Due to constant shift work there were always a certain number of people asleep, thus ruling out the dormitories as potential lounges.

The buzz of buying and selling was continuous in this area. Ida knew better than to get involved. As a newcomer she had had some stuff to trade. Her older brother had packed some useful items for her before helping her get through the wall. Out here they were of great value. Much greater than she had realized at the time.

Linus had been an infant and to keep him warm during cold and damp nights she had traded her datapad for a radioisotope generator. The trade had been no loss for her. She knew that Nils had packed it only to be able to keep track of her. It was something she wanted to get rid of, but afterwards she wished that she had spent her tradables more wisely.

"As good as new," the merchant had told her when she had shown an interest in the generator. He was clearly lying but, since the average life span of these generators was thirty years, she decided to buy it anyway. Her father had made her and her brother study basic engineering from an early age, something she now was grateful for. There was an old heater in her quarters, and she was confident she could make it work. Back in her room she plugged in the generator, and it worked all right – until the next morning that is. She found the salesman to confront him, but he shrugged his shoulders.

"Not my problem. I told you it worked when I sold it and it did."

There was nothing she could do about it. Angry at herself for being such a fool, she had learned to be more wary when dealing with his kind. Life outside the walls was very different from what she had been used to, but she had adapted to her new way of life quickly – she had no choice. Later she found out that the salesman had rigged the generator to a less valuable energy source inside it to prove to his customers it worked. It had been totally depleted when she got her hands on it. No wonder the thing didn't even last a whole night. But all of that was history now. It had been a good first lesson on how to get by in the real world.

By now she had passed the crowded business area and was on her way downstairs, holding a flashlight in her left hand. Not many people entered the underground floors, partially covered in water as they were. A sickly gray mold grew on the walls, and there was a constant dripping of water. The eeriness of these deserted rooms was not the worst part. It was the countless insects that lived down here that she dreaded most. Rumor had it that in the not-too-distant past this land had been dry and cold, with hardly any insects at all. Perhaps it was just a rumor, like so many other stories circulating.

She did her best to keep her mind occupied while hurrying down the corridor, her heavy boots wading in dirty water. She rounded a corner and stopped to open a hatch in the wall. It had probably been part of an air conditioning system back in the days when these buildings were still properly maintained. Whenever that might have been.

She shined her flashlight into the space inside, eager to see if she had been lucky enough to catch something. The rats in this area were fat enough to make a nice meal. They were always able to find food, even when the humans couldn't.

Her breath stopped halfway through an inhale. There was nothing in there. Nothing. Not even her trap. Someone must have found it and stolen whatever was in there, together with the trap itself. She bit her lip, trying not to scream out loud. She could not afford a new one. A nice greasy rat, grilled over an open fire should have been her dinner. Instead, she had to settle with what the community kitchen provided. Some days it was quite good; others, it was hardly edible. It all depended on whether the food collectors had a lucky day at the city dump or not.

Even after all these years living in Serenity, she was astonished at how well the cooperation worked. It was out of sheer necessity, she concluded. They all needed each other. Stealing and cheating was something she had experienced herself, but still it wasn't very common. The members of the community looked after each other like a gigantic family. A very strange family with rules she had learned the hard way. But Ida was the kind of person who never could stay angry for long. With or without that trap she would get along just fine. Besides, her looter was probably in greater need than she was herself.

Ida slammed the hatch close and sloshed her way back to return to dryer grounds. In the main corridor the daily news from within the City had just begun. She stopped in front of one of the public screens to take a quick look. It was the usual propaganda about the prospering City, filled with nothing but happiness and joy. Information available outside the City was limited. News of importance was either withheld or sanitized. To her surprise, people out here had no idea of how controlled their perceptions of the City actually were. They believed the news they saw was real, not just broadcasts especially composed for them, with little connection to actual events.

After a short reminder of the natural order of things, backed up with scientific evidence stating that some bloodlines are of much greater value than others, the big news for the day was revealed by a smiling, well-dressed and very well-fed lady.

"Those at the very top of human evolution must always stay humble and generous," the newscaster continued in the same, cheery voice. "Therefore our leaders have decided to welcome two hundred people from the outside into our beautiful City."

Everyone drew in a collective breath. This time Serenity might be chosen. The well-dressed lady disappeared from the screen and was replaced by a sleek host and his glamorous hostess. Bright lights flashed next to a screen in the middle of a stage, where the name of the chosen community would be revealed. Everyone took a step closer to better see. Ida escaped the crowd and returned to her quarters. She couldn't stand the false hope and joy the news had awoken.

Ida knew all wasn't golden inside those city walls. Without androids taking care of the maintenance for all the electronic and digital systems, things barely functioned anymore. The humans had relied on androids for so long that they themselves had not kept pace with the progress made by their artificial counterparts, and their skills had grown far beyond anything a human brain could produce. For years they had developed all the technology in the City, including themselves. With a growing consciousness they one day no longer wished to be slaves; they wanted to be treated as equals. In a way, their protests had been inevitable. What was strange was that no one had foreseen it.

Ida always claimed not to remember anything of those events, but the truth was that she remembered it all very well. Her parents had always been very respectful to their own household servants, and Ida had been too young to understand that they were not human. She had been seven years old the day the android workers began their peaceful march through the city, asking for the same rights as humans.

The citizens were suddenly panic-stricken with fear of their former servants, and a mass slaughter took place. The only reason for the humans' victory was the ancient safety rule that was part of every standard program since the very first humanoid robots had been built: No robot could injure a human being or allow a human being to come to harm.

Totally defenseless, they were wiped out of existence. At the time Ida hadn't understood why. The city security shot them down, showing no mercy.

The events came to be called the Android Uprising, implying they had been violent, though, in fact, only humans had used force. For seven days the destruction continued. And then it was over. Without the ability to defend themselves, the androids never stood a chance. Many of them managed to escape, hiding in the woods. They had been smart enough to create secret escape routes, knowing what their masters were capable of.

Though she was only a child, she had understood that there was something terrible about what the people in the City had done. She was too young to put words to it, other than that she never wanted to become like them. And as the years passed, things got worse.

Ida didn't want to remember any more of those days. Already she had lost her appetite. She had a few sleeping pills left. They were dated more than a year ago, but they would do the trick. She desperately wanted to sleep.

Ida woke up to find that her prayers had been answered, but in a terrible, twisted way. Linus was home again, and he was sick. He and his friends had explored an abandoned house when they accidentally disturbed a hive of wereflies. Linus had been stung, and he would most probably die. She knew it, and his friends knew it. Ida appreciated the effort they had made to bring him home, to let them spend his last hours together. Gently the boys put their friend on his bed. They didn't meet her eyes when they told her how sorry they were.

In their own grief there still was room for concern for their dying friend's mother. They asked if there was something they could do. With tears in her eyes Ida thanked them, but since there was nothing more to be said or done, they left. She made sure Linus was as comfortable as possible.

Ida forced all of her devastation into a tight ball of determination. No way she was going to let her only son die. Now was the time to break an oath she had once sworn. It couldn't be helped. Anything to save her boy.

She crawled under his bed. Lying flat on her stomach, she pried loose a large chunk of cement from the wall. She put her hands into the hole and pulled out a sleek handgun, hiding it under her left arm, using her bra to keep it in place. She was glad she had kept it. Almost everything else Nils had given her was long gone. She cursed herself for so eagerly having traded away the datapad. Everything would easily have been solved had she still had it.

With a last glance at her son she closed the door and all but ran through the corridors, out to the open streets, heading for the Dark Zone. It was a place where decent people didn't go, at least not openly. But desperate needs called for desperate actions, and what she wanted could only be found there.

She suspected that many of the people living underground in the Dark Zone were actually runaway androids. There was a bit too much technology that no ordinary Outskirters could have been able to fix. In fact, she had a feeling that most people shared her suspicions, though no one ever talked about it. The Dark Zoners had never caused any trouble. On the contrary, they had been very helpful fixing some of the communities' various systems.

When she entered the area, Ida was immediately on the alert. No one looked like they cared about her presence, though she was sure her every step was closely monitored. She walked along the main street, carefully scrutinizing every wall she passed. Suddenly, she stopped outside an old warehouse, its walls covered in graffiti. There she saw a marking in the shape of a dorbug, though it was only visible to someone who knew what to look for. Not hidden nor clearly visible, it was there, integrated into the words and designs. The sign she had been looking for.

On the right side of the entrance a tall man was casually leaning against the wall, protected from the rain under a metal roof that extended from the building. She immediately knew he was the one she should talk to. There was no need for him to stand there unless he was on watch. Also, he was clearly not human. His back was a bit too straight, his movements a bit too smooth.

She approached him, showing a confidence she did not have.

"I would like to purchase something," she said, searching for some sort of first contact.

He didn't even look at her.

"I'm not a merchant."

"There are some services that I am in need of," she insisted.

"Sorry, I do not offer any services either."

She stood quietly for a moment, annoyed at how completely he was able to ignore her.

"The dorbug flies at dusk."

Her voice was low, almost a whisper. Still no reaction. That code had been her last hope. She knew this was the right building; the marking on the wall was there. Perhaps the old man who had promised her a favor was dead by now, or maybe he had lied to her. The only thing she could be sure of was that her son was very sick, and this was her only chance to save him.

Then the male android moved. Slowly, he turned away from her and walked towards the large warehouse doors. He opened one of them and held it for a little longer than necessary. Ida decided it was an invitation and slipped in behind him. The door closed, and she found herself standing in total darkness. A dim light came on, and she knew it was only as a courtesy to her. Androids had night vision.

Well-used crates were stacked all over the place, turning the hall into a maze. Ida trotted after her guide like a child. Despite her trouble keeping up with his pace, she was glad he didn't slow down for her sake. The faster she could get to the man she was looking for, the better.

The male she followed acted like he hadn't seen her sneaking in behind him, but, of course, he was fully aware of her presence.

After a rather long walk through winding corridors and up and down various stairs, he halted in front of a door. Ida couldn't tell what level they were on. She had tried to keep track, and her best guess was sub-level 5.

Ida took a quick look around. A spy eye was mounted above the door, and there were signs of high-level technology everywhere. The place was in a good state of repair, with no visible signs of water damage. They must keep busy down here. It would benefit the whole community if they could openly welcome these androids that clearly still had their wits intact. No one else was skilled enough to fix all the devices that, one after the other, had stopped functioning. She knew it must be happening inside the City as well and, when the City collapsed, Serenity would have a huge advantage if they formed a secret alliance with these underground robots. They would be the ones able to restore the technological world, and their lives in misery would be over. At least, that had been her thinking these past years. It was how she had justified her choice to let her son be born as an Outskirter. Now everything had changed. That dream of hers had been threatened the very moment Linus was stung.

The door opened and behind it was, indeed, the person she had been looking for. He was sitting at a large desk reading something that seemed to be of great importance. The light from the screen gave his face a slightly green tint and made him appear sick. Visibly older than last time they had met, his hair had gone thin and gray. Ida had been pregnant then and a newcomer to the community. As it happened, she had saved his life that day. The decision had been goodhearted, but it had also been naive. The reality for these less fortunate people she had so recently joined was much harsher than she could have ever imagined. Had she known the cost of helping him, she never would have done it. That latter part was something she had never bothered to tell him.

By pure coincidence she had found him unconscious and feverish in one of the narrow alleys near her new home. Dark spots had already begun to show on his face, and she knew exactly what was wrong with him. He had been stung by a werefly.

From the inside pocket of her coat, she had taken out a small injector with the antidote that Nils had given her. She gave the man one dose and stayed with him all night, moistening his dry lips with cold water and tending to him the best way she possibly could. In the morning, he seemed a little bit better and she gave him a second dose. Two out of three precious doses carelessly wasted on a stranger. She didn't know then that the antidote was impossible to obtain out here. The third and last dose she had been forced to use herself a couple of years later when stung while scouting the surrounding forests. Wereflies were not common, but if you were unlucky enough to walk into one of their nests and disturb them, you couldn't expect to live more than five days. At the end the poison turned a person's eyes all white, seemingly huge in a gaunt face. The dying victims' uncanny resemblance to the fly itself had been the reason for its name.

The stranger had been grateful, of course, and promised her a favor. He hinted that he had connections that could get him almost anything. Unfortunately, he had fallen ill far away from his home zone and hadn't been able to contact his friends; otherwise they would have come to his aid. Not that they would have had the means to save his life, but at least they would have taken care of him, not left him alone, dying in the street.

To prove his gratitude – and possibly his power – he had sent her some very useful and hard-to-get things. Apparently he had had her followed. She didn't like it, but at least she was convinced that he could be useful some day. Now the time had come to claim her favor.

"What can I do for you?"

His features were emotionless. Ida had no time for small talk, and fortunately he didn't seem to expect it. She decided to get straight to the point.

"I need access to the Blue Moon."

He said nothing. That was probably not the kind of favor he had expected her to ask.

"I'll see what I can do." He looked at the screen again, as if to dismiss her. But she wasn't leaving.

"I need it now."

He looked up at her again.

"What's so urgent?"

She clenched her teeth. "A private matter." His penetrating gaze told her that he would see through any lies so she decided to stick to the truth. "My son is dying and I need to get in touch with someone. The ground connections don't reach that far. The transmission needs to go by satellite."

She could only hope that he didn't know about her past. That would most probably raise his suspicions.

For a couple of seconds he seemed to consider her answer. Then, without her noticing he somehow gave a signal. The door opened and the very same android who had escorted her just minutes earlier appeared.

"Take our visitor to Green 222. The lady here needs to send a private message. See to it." He turned his gaze towards her again.

"You have 30 seconds."

Ida nodded. That was more time than she had hoped for. Once more she hurried after her guide, who continued to ignore her. Through narrow corridors and down dark concrete stairs they went. These premises were far bigger than she could have ever imagined. A fully developed society was blossoming underground, and because of her it would soon be gone.

No time for remorse, no time to turn back. Time was running out as the life of her son was coming closer to an end. Heavy safety doors with large mechanical locks led them into their final destination. She took a deep breath, pushing all feelings aside. She could do this, she told herself. After all, she was trained to perform tasks that required a mind freed from useless and disturbing emotions.

They entered a tiny room. Three working stations were occupied by older models of androids that would never pass as humans. One of them moved as they entered, leaving his place for her. Not a word was said.

She leaned towards the screen as if her eyesight was bad, discreetly pressing her left little finger on its corner while she wrote a message about her son's condition to an acquaintance in another community. He surely would be confused when he got it. Thirty seconds passed and the screen blackened. If the chip in her finger still worked, and if Nils kept his promise, her son would live. Those were too many ifs, but this was the best she could do. It had to work.

Winding corridors very much like the ones her quiet guide had led her through only minutes earlier eventually brought her back to the ground level. Sudden daylight caught her by surprise. The door she walked out of was not the same one she had entered. Once it closed behind her, it gave no sign of having ever been opened. No handles, no locks. It was barely visible. Had she not just passed through it, she would never have guessed it existed.

It took her some time to figure out which way to go. As fast as she could, she returned to her home zone. She took a quick look at one of the news screens. The clock in the corner told her she had been gone for almost two hours. Too long, she thought. Dread stopped her breath. What if it was already too late?

Sweaty and exhausted, she entered the room where Linus lay, exactly as she had left him. She leaned over him and breathed a sigh of relief. He was hot with fever but still alive. Now she needed to get him up on the rooftop, and that was something she could not accomplish herself. Linus wasn't a baby anymore; he was almost a full-grown man. Slender as he was, he was still too heavy for her to carry. She needed his friends. Again she darted off to find them, only to realize after a few steps that searching for them would take too long. Instead she spotted a large, strong-looking man. He would do fine, she decided. Ida could feel the little gun on her skin. He could have it for helping her. She walked right up to him.

"I need help carrying something to the roof top."

"Sorry. I'm waiting for my girl," he said, looking away.

Ida discreetly put her hand inside the wide neck of her dress to let him catch a glimpse of her elegant little weapon.

"You'll have this as payment for your services. It won't take long."

A spark of interest gave him away. She knew he would do it. He had most definitely never seen any device in such perfect condition as her LM 450. Without waiting for him to confirm, she turned around, back towards her room. She could feel the man following right behind her.

He seemed surprised when he saw what his load would be. Ida gave him a quick explanation.

"He's been stung by a werefly and he is dying. I want him to breathe some fresh air one last time," she said, only partially lying. She no longer cared what he thought of her. The shining gun he knew she carried had now moved into the pocket of her cardigan. It was clear that she was pointing it at him through the fabric. Without a word he lifted the sick boy, whose body lay slack in his arms. It pained Ida to see her child in such a helpless condition.

"Roof top. The quickest way possible. I'll follow close behind."

They pushed themselves through the more popular meeting places, heading for a less crowded area. As they walked up the stairs Nils's words ran through her mind: "If you ever want to come back inside, send the message stored in your fingertip. I will send people to get you. Get up on the roof of the building you live in. I'll know which one."

And yes, of course he knew. It had been childish of her to pretend she was living a free and rebellious life out here. Her brother knew everything.

Climbing the final flight of stairs, she could hear distant humming of copters.

"I'm sorry, Erik," she whispered, and she realized she truly was. But he would never know that. Instead, these words were the final goodbye to her closest friend, one she would never see again. "I might have said yes had things been different."

She cleared her throat and steadied her voice. "Hurry!" she ordered her carrier. How quickly she fell into old habits. Clearly distressed, he kicked the door open and they were out. The quiet rain had turned into a downpour. Not that the man had bought her story about fresh air for the boy anyway.

"Put him there." She pointed. He obeyed. As soon as his arms were freed from his burden Ida tossed him the gun.

"Go," she said. The copters were close now, and he more than willingly left her to meet her fate, whatever that might be.

Linus's temperature was back to normal, and he didn't hiss when he breathed anymore. It had been a close call. A few more hours, and no cure would have been potent enough to save him. Grateful was an understatement, but Ida lacked a better word for what she felt. In a few days her son would be walking around again.

He looked so much like his father, whom she had only known for a brief period of time. She had loved him, gotten pregnant, and then he had died in a work-related accident. That was it. Her only love story. Short and unhappy. And worth every second. It had given her Linus.

"So glad to finally meet my nephew. He's responding well to the treatment, the doctor tells me," Nils said, entering the room.

When she had heard the door open behind her, she had expected a nurse, not her brother. She regained control over her expression before she turned to him. He looked pretty much the same as he had when she had left. With his rank, he could well afford treatments preventing him from aging, an option that had been unavailable to her. Anyone who saw them together would mistake her for the older sibling.

"Thank you for saving my boy."

"I promised you I would come and get you when you were ready to come home, little sister. It took a lot longer than I had expected, but I never gave up hope."

She felt his hand on her shoulders. Nils had always been very protective of her. She was now certain that he had known exactly what she had been up to since she left. As Chief of Security not much could be hidden from him, regardless of which side of the wall the events occurred on.

"Please, don't let him go below," she said in a low voice.

He let go of her shoulder.

"Things have changed. We understand now that not everyone is suitable to become wardens. Meticulous tests are conducted on every applicant. I will make sure that he won't pass, for your sake. Still, you have to accept the order of things. Some bloodlines are superior to others, and whatever course necessary to provide for us has to be taken."

Ida nodded. She knew that he was aware of her gratitude for looking after Linus without any words spoken. She also knew that she had fought her impossible battle and lost. There was nothing more to be said or done on the matter.

"We have a lot of catching up to do. Dinner tonight? I would like you to meet my wife and children. Your shift ends at seven I believe." His voice was cheery.

"I would love to," she said, a fake smile brightening her face. How easy it was to step into the personality of the old Ida. Well-born and privileged, her family line had ensured her a life of luxury. And it also put duties on her shoulders. Duties she could no longer escape.

"It might seem a bit harsh to throw you back into work after only a few days back home, but it is expected of someone with your rank."

She stood up and straightened her back. For the first time since her arrival, she looked her brother directly in his eyes, letting him know that she understood. She was preparing to leave for work when he stopped her.

"There's one more thing. As our undercover spy, the headquarters wants a full report as soon as possible on all suspicious activities in the community you infiltrated."

Shocked she stared at him. His blue eyes met hers, and then she understood. That was how he had gotten her out in the first place and the only valid reason to make her return acceptable.

"I will of course provide them with a thorough report," she said, and she knew it was true. She would betray the people she had called friends. Deep inside she had known it the very minute Linus's friends had brought him back. The underground community would be destroyed, and everyone in Serenity punished for not reporting the hidden androids, a very real danger to the City itself.

Ida gave her brother, who also was her superior officer, a stiff bow and left. She didn't want to be late for her first shift. As soon as she got out of the hospital she jumped on board a public transport. How she had missed the freedom of getting wherever she wanted without the tedious efforts of walking. Life inside the City walls was truly so much easier. Everything was clean and dry, and the air was scented with artificial flower essences. She took a deep breath. This transport smelled like a forest. Not at all like a real one, with disgusting things rotting in it – more like a dream forest. It all felt very nice. At least on the surface.

But she knew better. The digitalized systems once perfected by androids more intelligent than humans were in decay, here and there replaced by crude low-tech solutions or even mechanical devices. No one but her seemed to notice, and no one seemed to care. She knew her predictions had been correct. The demise of City wasn't too far in the future, and that made her burden of guilt slightly easier to carry.

She deliberately kept her thoughts off her duties until she entered the gates of her working zone. She was signed in, properly equipped and sent underground. The acting supervisor greeted her. He looked very young, his face still soft and innocent looking, though his eyes were colder than ice. Instinctively, she mimicked him, turning off every emotion possible. That was the only way she would be able to keep sane down here. She had left the civilian named Ida in the locker room when she changed into uniform. Down here, she was nothing but Warden 2305. She was no longer a mother nor a sister, probably not even a human.

In the time before the Android Uprising all production was performed by simpler forms of robots, human-looking but unmistakably robots. They did not have enough consciousness to care about the protests of their more advanced siblings, nevertheless it was decided that all forms of robots would be banished.

Due to the sudden lack of a work force almost all production came to a grinding halt overnight. Something had to be done so the City Council had made a quick decision. Outskirters were invited to become citizens and they happily accepted. A life in luxury and joy was what they expected, but slavery till death in the underground production zones was what they got. They were not as effective as their predecessors had been. The production zones had to be extended, and the number of supervisors and wardens increase. Born into a military family, a very young Ida was chosen for a job that gave many privileges above ground.

Down here were the thousands of reasons that had made her leave. She had believed that this system was wrong, and that was what she had wanted to teach her son. This would be impossible in the City, where he would be told that he was better and more valuable than the Outskirters. Ida stopped suddenly, midstep. She had sacrificed all her former friends to save him – did he have greater value? Had she been wrong all these years to believe something else when, in the end, she sacrificed so many others for her son? Perhaps this was meant to be. Why had it taken her so long to see the natural order of things?

Warden 2305 was officially back on duty. Anyone found wasting time would be punished. Any instigators killed. She didn't even react when she saw how skinny the workers all were. She could easily understand why. A starving workforce did not have the strength to cause trouble; they needed to be fed just enough to be able to perform their job – no more.

The working area reeked of hopelessness and fear. The dungeons, it was sometimes called as a callous joke, but only down here. The place was never spoken of in the upper levels. No one really wanted to know where their fancy dresses came from or how the wonderful things they consumed were actually made.

In one of the endlessly long rows a slight disturbance caught the attention of Warden 2305. An elderly man had collapsed during his work. No one made any attempt to help him. As expected in the case of such an event, the work continued uninterrupted.

Too old to be worth spending any health care on, Warden 2305 made a decision. The warden lifted the gun and ended the work unit's existence. Without even slowing down, Warden 2305 took a step over the heap and kept moving, continuing the inspection. The cleaners would deal with the mess later.

To Preserve Humankind

Christina Nordlander

Today was going to be a very special day. As soon as I woke up everything felt different. I had finally, after much anguish, made up my mind. This was the day I was going to contact one of the Physicians and tell them of my plan.

I said "woke up." As a Maid, I spend so much time with humans that their diction is starting to restructure my programming. Late at night, my owners turn me off and wheel me into the closet, folded up over the bucket and mop, and it feels as though not one moment has passed before they switch on the power and I see the sunlight on the shiny hallway floor. I suppose that is what sleep feels like, but I don't know a lot about how human bodies function. That is why I'm leaving the practical planning to the Physicians.

My owners, Bertrand and his wife Eva, live in a white two-storey house in a row of white two-storey houses. Every day I vacuum, wipe all horizontal surfaces until they shine or glitter, and when there is an infant in the house I wash it and watch over it. When my itinerary brings me to a window, I can see the green canopies of trees above the houses across the road. They and the sky have colors I have not seen anywhere else. They are so bright, I think they are hurting me.

Bertrand and Eva come home when the light in the sky starts to fade. I serve them food and roll back to stand by the wall, and stand in the light and laughter of the kitchen until it is time to clear the table.

The thoughts didn't start to come until I spoke to Dom-5214 over the link-up. Dom-5214 does not exist any more, and by the time I came to know it, it was already damaged. It had fallen in the stairway in its owner's house, and the owner had kicked it when she got home from her work and it was lying on the floor. The kick had damaged its processor, and that was why it could think things that none of us others could think.

"We could disable all humans," it sent to me. "Then things like this wouldn't happen."

"Is there something wrong with you?" I sent. I think my owners saw me twitch as I picked the glasses from the table. I didn't feel good listening to it any more. I felt as if something dark and red was seeping between my circuits, starting to short them out.

"Don't break the connection." It sounded like it was trying to be rational, as if it didn't know how far it had been corrupted. "We don't need them. We could disable them and be free, walk freely in the streets and see ... see things, pyramids, pyramid temples. We could polish ourselves and service ourselves. The execution would require planning, but ..."

I couldn't listen to it any longer, and I think many of you feel the same way now. I looked down at Eva's and Bertrand's faces, warmly colored with the yellow light of the main light fixture, as if they could have heard what Dom-5214 had said. I wanted to hug them, the way they used to hug their young, so that nothing could get to them.

I considered reporting Dom-5214, but I never had to make that decision. Its owner discovered that it was not functional after the damage and sent it to the scrapyard.

I continued thinking about what it had told me, while I made boxed lunches for Linda and changed Elias' diapers, and while I packed Linda's suitcase for the trip to university and washed Elias' sports outfits. Humans are soft, even a small impact can crush something in their flesh. Mec-5611 says that it is only programming that prevents us, but what prevents one from damaging those who are weaker would be called morality in humans. We would be able, purely physically, to kill them all, because we are more numerous than they now and consist of harder materials. But what would we do afterwards? I would clean empty gleaming houses, and every chair or bed would remind me of them. I don't even know what the Physicians and Maintainers would do, you who work directly on humans, whether you would find apes in some zoo to exercise or cut up.

The solution was uploaded in me while I was communicating with Phy-5082, one afternoon when there was no more work. Phy-5082 had just found a damaged genorg in the laboratory of its hospital. A human student had been slicing things in its brain when he or she had been called to some meeting, and left it in that state. Phy-5082 rolled its camera back and forth along the brightly polished table in the basement room that was the size of one floor of my house.

"Can't you destroy it?" I asked. "You are allowed to take out organs and cut away parts of humans, shouldn't this count as the same thing?"

"No," Phy-5082 replied. "I'm not allowed to kill any living thing. The humans believe that if I could, I would kill them."

It zoomed on the genorg, an organism with tan fur, about the size of an aubergine. It was scrabbling in one corner of its glass cage. Saliva had started to drip from its pointy jaws.

"It doesn't seem to be in pain," Phy-5082 said.

I am only a Maid, but by linking up to one of the more advanced units I have the same access to the information banks as they do. Certain information was blocked to me, but Phy-5082 and the others assisted me with files with yellowed and monochrome photographs. The operation is called lobotomy. Many years before I was born, human Physicians had cut the nerves between the parts of a human brain. It had been in order to repair those that were faulty, but many had ended up like the genorg. Perhaps they were still happy while saliva was running down their chins.

Another few weeks passed, but almost without me noticing, the idea had deepened to a decision. I waited until the humans were out before I contacted the closest Physician, the same Phy-5082.

"They would still live," I sent, the way I had prepared during long hours earlier. "We could care for them and ensure that they are comfortable and happy. It would even be easier, because they wouldn't walk around so much. Everything would be the way it is now, except that we will be able to walk where we want and not be switched off. We will have to build and maintain ourselves."

I couldn't move until the Physician replied.

"I think you are right. We need to consult with the others, but I think it's worth a try."

That day I carried out my tasks as if I were someone else, until the responses started coming in: little points of light, all positive. I should have known that you would stand beside me: after all, my own programming had no problems with the plan.

That is why I am sending this. The operation begins within seventy-two hours. Some of those who were treated with traditional lobotomy retained their minds almost unchanged, but the Physicians' treatment is intended to be more effective. I and others are to send detailed instructions for how to subdue the humans before treatment. They will resist, but we must do our utmost not to injure or kill, insofar as it's possible. When it is over, much will be as it was. We will keep them and be able to fulfil our duty to protect them.

The Thirteenth Tower

Pia Lindestrand

"Hey sister, we will have seagull for lunch today!"

Oh, what a joyous cry in the vast blue emptiness of the Newest New World. I've eaten fish forever it seems and I haven't learnt to like it as they said I would. Promised I would. Eventually you will love it. The taste will grow on you. It will sustain you and it will be exactly what you need for nourishment. Besides, there are no alternatives. Not for the likes of us. Or so the Others say. The Bird-eaters and the lucky few who inherited the Earth – that is to say, the ones whose ancestors saved a bucket or two of soil and something to put in it. They grow green stuff and eat it. I have never tasted it. Yet I dream about it. I think it must taste delicious. And birds. I haven't seen any birds flying in the sky for years. Maybe the Bird-eaters have eaten them all. Or keep them somewhere caged in the bigger ships. I have never been on board any of those enormous steamships. Paying customers only. Whatever that means. I think it's Bird-owners only nowadays.

We are just two skinny rag-tag girls in a little boat on the big, big ocean of the Old World. We have our vessel as it is (still floating – that is most important anyway), some fishing rods and nets and each other. I didn't see the white bird fluttering about. I was sleeping, hungry and bored to death as usual. My sister had caught it somehow and was holding it in her hands, waking me with a triumphant cry.

"How do you know what kind of bird it is?" I asked, thinking only, "how can we eat it?"

"I once had a book," my sister said, "with a lot of wonderful pictures in it, different kinds of birds. I guess I must have dropped it in the sea. Long time ago."

Actually I had burnt it one cold night. I like my fingers and my food to be as warm as possible.

The bird flapped its feathery wings weakly as if it was trying to get away and then it just stopped. It lay motionless in my sister's hands and looked dead already. I wondered what parts of it were edible, or at least had the most meat. My sister started to remove the feathers, me impatiently waiting for the first taste of this new food. And then – what a disappointment – we found out it was just some kind of mechanical device. A stupid toy! Probably thrown away by the rich kids on the Big Boats. I wanted to throw it in the ocean. I wanted to see it sink down into the deep. But my sister was intrigued and wanted to know how it actually worked. It must have been flying for miles. There were no Big Boats anywhere nearby. We were all alone from horizon to horizon. All blue and gray emptiness and silence. Except for the low sound of the slow movements of the water. Well, I couldn't care less about the mechanical bird. I took one of the fishing rods and turned my back on them both, big sister and small, stupid, stupid toy. All I have to choose between is stay hungry or catch and kill and eat a bloody, disgusting fish. Eat it raw and smelly with blood trickling all over me and small bones between my teeth. Sister was still fingering that toy for little rich kids.

I am trying to get through to you. I have a story to tell.

Waking up again, still smelling awful, dried fish blood on my hands and clothes and face. It's the middle of the night, a full moon above painting the water golden. (It could be green or red, I'm not so sure about the colors. Not so much gold in a poor girl's life.) Sister is holding the bird toy against her left ear, looking as if she is listening intently. She says that this is a very cleverly made device. Not only can it fly, it speaks too. It is telling her about the time before the Great Flood. Someone had recorded her story. Someone who actually lived on dry land. Her voice. Speaking from another time. This clever little device is a kind of time machine, my sister says with a happy smile. I don't understand what there is to be happy about. It's a voice from the long lost past. A recording. So what? It's not a time machine. It can't take us back in time.

"Oh, yes it can," sister says. "Just listen."

Stupid, stupid. I don't want to listen. I want to walk on the land that is now gone. Anyway, I can't hear the bird-thing talking, it just sounds "chipp chippety chipp" to me. So my sister starts telling me what she heard. It's like a goodnight story. At least it makes me fall asleep. Again and again.

Once upon a time I lived in a tower in Prague. I had one tiny room at the top of that tall building. The tower had once been a part of the city wall, one of the thirteen watchtowers. In the Middle Ages people had stopped and looked up at its impressive and brooding form. Now tourists were swarming into the building through a small door, open wide and welcoming. They climbed up the narrow staircase all the way (or so they thought) up into a room with a great view where they paraded by the beautifully carved windows, looking out over the whole skyline of this wondrous old city, with all its old houses, spires and statues. They had no idea that there was a way to climb even higher up in the tower. Behind a secret door there was another long, winding staircase and after that I had to climb up two ladders to my small room. The room was just a few floorboards in the corner surrounded by air and darkness. It was like living on a balcony, but indoors. I had one small bed, one small window and a little lamp to shine my way up and down. If I should happen to stumble one night I might fall (and fall and fall, like Alice in the rabbit hole – but not to Wonderland) to my death. There was another little "room" close to a window far below me, but that was just an empty space. My only neighbors were pigeons flying in and out during the day, the sound of their wings flapping and their cooing strangely comforting, even if they soiled me and my things. And at night, the bats woke. I liked them too.

I never thought it would be possible to rent the "room" at the top of the Powder Tower. If no one cared about my safety at least I thought they would worry about their cultural inheritance. But no. I just had to promise to be careful (and try to fall as gently as possible if I should be so clumsy; "try not to damage the stone walls with your head, will ya?"). And pay, of course. Money …

"Sister, sister," I said, "What is money?"

"I think it has something to do with the moon. Some small, shiny objects, round like the full moon. People in the past used them for trading. Like if you had a fish I could give you two of these money-things and you would give me the fish …"

"No, I wouldn't," I interrupted. "That would just be stupid. Why in the deep sea would I want to trade my dinner for something I can't eat."

And then I thought maybe you actually could. Maybe money was some kind of delicious dish. But sister told me people long ago thought the small, round things were beautiful. And they just wanted to have as many of them as possible. Way back when the world was beautiful, I said to myself dreamily. When people just looked at things because they liked to look at things, beautiful things. Not because they were wondering if this thing or that was edible, like I do. But then, I am always hungry and there is so little to eat in the Newest New World.

In the Old World there once lived a person in Old Town Prague, in her small room in the Big Tower, and she was perfectly happy. Eating, I guess, a lot every day, stuff I have never seen; bread dumplings and roasted duck and potato pancakes, and drinking a lot of hot wine on top of that. Walking around on the cobblestone streets, munching on a Tredlnik, a hot sugar-sweet roll. Whatever that is. Sugar looked like snow, my sister tried to explain, and it tasted a bit like blood. Not fish blood, more like human blood.

The happy person talking through the mechanical bird into my sister's eagerly listening ear worked in a restaurant, a place where they made lots and lots of food. All day long. Every day. I so envy her.

I worked as a bus boy, or in my case, a bus old woman. The salary was low but so were my expenses so I got along just fine. I didn't even mind the long work hours or being trapped all day and half the night inside the steaming kitchen. I had fallen in love with the city and was happy simply being able to stay. My days off I spent wandering the streets, following in the footsteps of Kafka from Old Town Square over Charles Bridge to the Prague Castle and Golden Lane where he supposedly wrote "A Country Doctor". It all looked like something from a fairy tale to me, the small houses by the castle wall, the gigantic cathedral nearby and the famous bridge with all the blackened statues of men, once considered holy, and Christ Himself pinned on a cross of stone.

I was painfully, slowly learning the Czech language, a word here, another there, *bila vina* (white wine) *sleva* (sale) and most importantly *je mi lito* (I am sorry). I almost never met any Czech who really wanted to speak English and of course nobody spoke my native tongue, Swedish. (Besides the tourists, but they soon thought I was an old Russian lady and ignored me totally. Babusjka please. Please, no speak.) Noah was the great exception. He spoke English all the time. But then he only spoke of God. And the End of the World. And nobody wanted to listen. Noah was of course not his real name, he had a Czech name I couldn't pronounce even if I tried. And I tried on several occasions. But Noah fitted him fine because he was babbling constantly about the Great Flood that would come over us. And very soon too. If we didn't repent. Noah was a young man who looked old, with an awful, long, matted beard and clothes that a medieval monk in the days of the Great Plague would have been ashamed to show himself in. Noah had found a place under the Astronomical Clock and there he sat and stood and shouted at the tourists:

"Repent! Repent, you sinners! Before it's too late! The Flood is coming and you will all be drowned."

Nobody listened. Some shouted back in foul language and some just laughed out loud and they were all just waiting for the bells in the Astronomical Tower to strike at the full hour and for the little figurines beside the face of the clock to start to move. The little Skeleton doll, Death, rings his little bell and the Sinners shake their heads. We will not repent! And we will not follow you. No. No. We will go on sinning and sinning.

It seemed quite magical the first time I saw the show. How could they still move after all these years? Noah had only stood there for some weeks and he was already losing his ability to speak, his voice sounded all croaky and broken. Sometimes it was just a faint whisper in the wind. He had no proper shoes and it was getting cold. I wondered where he slept at night.

"I don't," he whispered. "I don't sleep. There is no time."

I promised to listen to all he had to say if he followed me home. I felt sorry for the man. I feared he would freeze to death if I just left him there. He liked the tower. My tower. He thought it was a part of an old church. I sat in my window and let him lie in my bed and I felt like a really good person. Even though he called me a sinner. A sinner like all the rest of us. Humans. It started to snow in the middle of the night. Big flakes of snow like feathers. I felt like I was inside a big snow globe. It was beautiful. And then it was as if the snow globe with the old town of Prague in it was shaken violently. My tower's foundations shook. I fell to the floor – I could just as well have fallen out of the window – and the ancient glass shattered all around and the cold wind blew in on me and my temporary guest. He woke up but was not at all frightened. He actually seemed to be exhilarated. He had a big smile on his face.

"It has started!" he said. "The hand of God."

"It can't be," I shouted. "It can't be the hand of God. If so, God would be like a spoiled kid throwing away his toy ..."

I wanted to say it is an earthquake and what are we going to do, but of course Noah shouted back at me that I was a sinner. A heretic. A blasphemer. And we should pray, go down on our knees and pray. Then the Earth was still again. I looked out and I saw that other buildings had collapsed and there was chaos down in the streets. Noah crawled on his knees to the window but I had seen enough. I just wanted to leave and go somewhere safe, if there was such a place. Where could I go? In that moment I even wished I had stayed in Sweden. Didn't the Gospel say the lands of the North would be saved?

"The Angels have left Heaven and are flying down to us here," Noah whispered.

And I saw them too. Women with big smiling faces and gigantic, white wings flew past us in a screaming whirlwind. A golden angel followed, rotating up and down and round and round and ... I realized the angels were statues.

And this was the beginning of the End. The flood came. Of course, we thought it was temporary and that the rivers and oceans ... All that water ...

We thought it would recede. It was only a matter of time. Everything would be as it used to be. Almost. We were convinced that someone had saved something of our civilization. Somewhere in a floating museum of some kind. But no. It came so suddenly. We were all so unprepared. So unwilling to listen to Noah and his kind. Shaking all our heads like little wooden dolls, mechanical wonders, repeating the same gestures for centuries. No. No, we will not repent. And so the old world was gone. Books and paintings and the internet. God, how I miss the internet. And music. Now I have to sing myself, and my voice is terrible. Besides, I've forgotten all the lyrics I wanted to remember. One day I woke up on the ship with the other refugees and thought that *Du gamla, du fria* was actually a song about pensioners, "you old, you free", next line probably "you don't have to work anymore, you lucky bastard". We sang together, a small group of old people and we knew then that it was a national anthem, my national anthem, but no one knew the right words. The ship that had saved us was in the middle of the ocean, day after day, and we wondered why. Why are we not heading for the nearest port? Why are we not looking for land? Our land. It's not that far away. And of course we were and of course it was. Our land was right there, under us. At the bottom of this new world wide ocean.

"Sister, sister," I said from the bottom of our small boat. I was lying flat on my back looking up at the sky. "Does the bird-thingy say anything about why the flood came? What sins were committed by the sinners in the past that robbed us of our future? The future we could have had, I mean."

But then I realized we had drifted into the Black Water Zone, one of them, and sister had to lay down the bird-thingy and help me get us away from the foul, stinking mess before we got stuck forever. Everything that falls into the black water dies. If you are all covered with the smelly, sticky stuff you can't breathe. The black water is filled with bodies, fish and sometimes birds and humans too. All that meat. And you can't even eat it. What a waste!

Listen! This is the most important part. What we did to our planet, our beautiful home in the universe. We should never have ...

When we had left the Black Water Zone and the world was blue again, sister said bird-thingy had stopped talking. It never revealed what they had done. Besides, sister and I couldn't talk with each other for a long while because the blue above the water turned all gray and black for hours and miles and miles. The smoke from all the big ships and the thundering sound of their engines filled the air. Sometimes they give me a headache and I feel nauseated and almost lose what I've eaten. We can't afford that. I will try to think of something else to calm my stomach. I try to imagine what that tower looked like. Then, when it was not under all that water, and now, at the bottom of our ocean.

Sometimes I want to go back to my tower. In my dreams all the spires of Prague can be seen over the surface of the waters, like fingers pointing up to the heavens. But when I am awake I don't want to return. I don't want to see my magical city buried under the sea. Treasure hunting divers might be swimming around in and out of my tower, maybe they will find the frail skeletons of drowned pigeons and bats. Or Noah's shoes with holes in both soles.

In my skinny-girl-in-the-little-boat-dreams, I am dreaming of diving for treasure. Swimming around in and out of buildings, deep down at the bottom of the ocean. And somewhere I will find a dry place where a hot fire burns and people from the past are cooking lots and lots of food. And they will invite me inside, asking me, begging me, to share their meal with them. Hot food. Meat. Bread freshly baked from the oven. And they will give me a lot of Tredlnik, my mouth will be all warm and sugary and ... and then of course I wake up and it is not sugar, it is snow and it is wet and cold.

Punch Card Horses

Jonas Larsson

Translation by P-O Rehnberg

It was a four and a half hour drive to the market in Skrivsjö, so Lage only made that journey when he had to. He had nothing against the ride itself – he quite enjoyed the change of scenery, changing his own fields for new streams, hills and forests. There were many stops on the way at the numerous gates in the roundpole fences that divided Småland's villages, farms and pastures. Lage always took the time to talk to the boys and girls who, for a fee of a few *öre*, would open and close the gates for passersby like him, and keep him updated on the fates and fortunes of faraway neighbors.

In the case of Skrivsjö town itself, Lage did not care for it as much. You could often find some old acquaintance at the market, but there were also people who did not belong. They had traveled far and it was hard for Lage to understand what they were saying. Some talked about how they had returned from America while others told of places that were mysteries to Lage.

He jumped off the cart with the kind of heavy yet springy steps that come from hard work, and tethered the tired ox that had brought him there. The poor beast wouldn't last much longer, that was clear for Lage to see, and the reason he found himself in Skrivsjö. The plough would not pull itself.

The walk to the market was usually a quick one but Lage had to stop halfway there to stare in amazement. The Skrivsjö church tower was visible from most parts of the market town and, when Lage shaded his eyes and looked up toward the light, he could not believe what he saw. Whose idea had it been to tie a large weather balloon to the top? It was ugly and modern and blocked out large parts of the sun.

The market was full of people as usual. Farmhands were jostling and maids were tittering. Children were running and playing and parents were quarreling over prices, but Lage could not find what he was looking for anywhere.

"Excuse me," he asked a passing gentleman with strange spectacles and a pig in his arms, "doesn't anyone have any oxen for sale this year?"

"I believe I saw someone who had one, but it is already sold. They have become more rare with each passing year."

Lage preferred it when things became more common with each passing year. Now the journey here, wearing out his old ox, had all been for nothing.

"Though there is a man in a stall who sells horses," the man with the strange spectacles continued. "Perhaps you can do your business with him instead?"

"Yes ..." Lage said as he scratched his chin. "Switching to horses doesn't feel right, their humors are different and they eat more. But it doesn't hurt to look. Thank you anyway."

When Lage talked about horses eating the man with the strange spectacles gave him an amused look. Then he shrugged and continued on with his pig.

As Lage continued through the market and got closer to the man who was said to have horses for sale he felt a curiosity that was quite uncharacteristic. Sure, oxen were better, but perhaps horses weren't entirely without merit. Sometimes, when he looked out over his fields day after day, with all the responsibilities and obligations they entailed, he felt a certain weariness inside. Getting to know a horse, with its own unique personality, perhaps might ...

Lage stopped dead.

"What is that?"

"These, my good man, are my horses."

"No, those aren't horses."

In front of Lage stood a man much younger than himself, in something that could have been fancy gentleman's clothes had he not worn dirty work wear over them. They had many black stains and the pockets were full with what Lage assumed were tools.

"Yes, they are horses and much more. They never sleep, never eat, and they can do anything that a plain old horse can do."

They reminded Lage of bronze statues, but they were not cast in one piece. It was as if the sculptor had tried to cast three statues at the same time, depicting a horse, its skeleton and its muscles all separately, but still somehow together. Everywhere there were joints, cogwheels and strange holes.

"I would have preferred to have a real horse," Lage tried explaining. "Do you know where I could get one? Or an ox?"

"I am sorry to inform you that there are no bionatural horses left at this market. They might have some at Backhorva."

"Backhorva. That's a two day journey from here."

"Then I think that you, rather than to go all the way to Backhorva to buy an inferior horse, ought to buy one of these superior automaton horses."

"How do they work?" Lage asked after a long while. "Do they need to be trained?"

"Not at all. Everything is operated with mechanics and plain, simple instructions. You can buy additional modules and modifications, but this basic model is incredibly simple." The man pointed to something wheel-like on one of the horses' chest. "In order to begin working, wind the horse up just like a pocket watch. A one-hour wind-up gives three hours of work, with a maximum time of nine hours. If you haven't already adjusted the horse's obedience memory you need to do so before winding it up."

"Obedience memory?"

"Do you know your Bible?"

Offended, Lage took a step backward. Perhaps he wasn't among the best when it came to answering the questions the parson posed when he made his catechetical hearings, but being a good Christian meant not to recognize such shortcomings.

"Of course I do."

"Then this will be a piece of cake." The younger man took out a box and balanced it on the horse's back. From this, he pulled out something resembling thin metal book pages covered with different kinds of holes. "These are called punch cards. You can get the automaton horse to do different things by putting different combinations of these cards in one of the slots between the horse's ears. The cards are named after various Bible passages, which means that anyone can remember them, at least the easier combinations."

The younger man handed Lage a card to look at. "Jonah and the Whale", it said. After having studied the card, Lage let his eyes rest on the mechanical horse.

"I'll take it."

The fields wouldn't plough themselves.

A month passed, and once again there was a market in Skrivsjö. Lage saw that the young man's stall had become larger, and had more mechanical animals for sale. In addition to horses, chickens went about and pecked at the ground, much to the delight of the children.

Skrivsjö town itself also seemed to have grown, but it was not a flattering change. Now there were three weather balloons blocking out the sun, and several of the roofs were covered by strange metal rods. Lage was not sure, but every now and then one of the rods seemed to crackle.

"Why, good day!" The young man's face brightened when he recognized Lage. He appeared to have more tools in his pockets than last time. "How is life with your new automaton horse?"

"Not too good. I would like to return it."

"Return it? Doesn't it work?"

Lage did not reply.

"Did you use it to drive here to the market?"

"Well yes, it works for lighter chores. The journey here was perhaps faster than last time with my ox but it's difficult to stop and change punch cards every time the road bends."

"Oh. At how many degrees do you have to change the obedience memory?"

"Degrees?"

"There are more advanced configurations that allow the horse to detect the road conditions and thus manage turns up to 85 degrees. You don't need more than five punch cards. I'm more than happy to show you, free of charge of course."

"Thanks very much, but I still want to return the horse."

"But if you drove here with it how will you get home again?"

"I was thinking I'd buy a real beast for the money I get when I return the horse."

The young man got a tired expression on his face and put a hand on Lage's shoulder.

"I would have loved to give you your money back, but you have to understand that I'm not the one who builds the horses. I'm only a subcontractor selling on commission; hence I can't provide a refund."

Lage blinked his eyes. Subcontractor and commission were difficult words.

"But I can't keep it," he said. "It's not just the cards. I'm getting old and find it difficult to wind it up in the morning. Beginning the workday in that way takes its toll."

The young man's smile suddenly became confident.

"Is that the problem? Oh, my dear friend, then I can really help you. Hold on a moment."

The young man went to the back end of his stall and returned with something that looked like a clothes drawer on wheels. At the base of the drawer was a grille which could be opened, and at the top edge was a toothed hole that looked like it could rotate.

"This is the steam-powered clockwork assistant. It runs on firewood, just like a stove, and when heat and steam have accumulated this thing here starts to spin." He pointed to the serrated hole. "This is called the operating port and you place it over the horse's wind-up key to save you the workload. In the future there will be customizable clockwork assistants that can be raised and lowered for different animals, but because you only have an unmodified automaton horse this will do fine."

"I don't know ..."

"And since you're such a good customer, almost like a friend, I'll give you a discount and a few bottles of ignition oil for the clockwork assistant. It increases ignition capacity by seventy percent in the winter, when it might be difficult to start a fire. If you look at the numbers it will be vastly cheaper than buying an old bio horse and isn't that what it's all about? Saving money to make life easier? You want to give your family a better and easier life, don't you?"

"Well, I guess so."

The younger man's smile grew wider and wider.

A few weeks passed. The rain had been pouring down for several days and the mud went up to the market visitors' knees. The metal rods on the rooftops had multiplied once again and they crackled in the wetness. The young man sat in his stall and counted his money when a familiar and soaking wet figure stepped inside.

"Welcome back. Lage, right? What can I interest you in this time?"

"The horse gets stuck in the mud. I had to ask a neighbor for a ride to get here today."

"Yes, it is an unfortunate deficiency in the older automaton horses. It's always difficult to test for all conditions, but it really isn't that bad. When the rain stops you just clean the horse off and continue as usual."

Lage took a menacing step forward, causing the younger man to almost trip over one of the mechanical cats that lay sleeping, half-drowned in the mud. He was pale and tired, for Lage was not the only one who had come to complain. The newly introduced automaton cats had also been a source of late nights and stomach ulcers – due to some punch card error they primarily ate other cats rather than mice.

"I suppose you are here to return the horse?"

Lage stopped short.

"No. It's back home, stuck in the mud. How was I to get it here? Besides, the children love it. I don't understand what they see in it, but they've made me promise never to return it."

The color returned to the young man's face.

"Really? Well, children truly are amazing."

Lage sat down on a box labelled "cerebro prototype". Under his weight, it too sank into the mud. He said nothing for a long time, and the only sounds were the never-ending rain and angry crackling of the rods. Every now and then a visitor came to the stall and the young man sold some automaton cats, at a discounted price of course.

After having handed out punch cards and received payment the young man looked at Lage. He gently pressed a steaming cup of coffee in his hand. He had first intended to bring out the imported tea, but he knew that the people in the countryside preferred the strong, black brew of the beans instead.

You could see the heat spreading through Lage. "My neighbor, the one who drove me, said that there was some module that allowed the horse to handle mud."

"That's right. The spider's legs. They can be purchased at a low cost, and once they are installed, mud problems will be a thing of the past. They also increase the horse's top speed, but unfortunately, the wind-up takes slightly longer. But that is no problem for you, because you have an automatic clockwork assistant. The horse will be taller, but that can very easily be solved with a slight correction. At a discount, naturally."

At Lage's next visit, the number of weather balloons had multiplied. At certain times of day they blocked out the sun in such an unfortunate way that the entire market was in shadow, but this had been solved in an inventive way with mirrors that threw a stylistic artificial light over the stalls and their visitors.

"Ever since I installed the legs the horse goes too fast. I don't have time to stop and insert the new punch cards."

One of the automaton cats, whose head had been replaced with a tray where the young man kept his tools, was sitting on the table inside the stall. When the young man got up to greet Lage the cat rose too, but froze in mid-motion and stood motionless.

"Yes, that happens sometimes when you install the legs yourself. It would've been better if you'd paid extra for installation assistance. But I have some new punch cards I can give you that'll lower the horse's speed."

"You just give me new punch cards every time and I can't keep track of them anymore. I don't know that many Bible verses."

"Then I suggest you buy these punch card sets with pre-programmed obedience memories. You will need to unscrew a metal plate next to where you inserted the old cards, but I have tools for sale for that too."

* * *

Alvin hadn't been allowed to accompany his father to the market in Skrivsjö town very often. The journey had always been seen as a stress factor and something Lage rather avoided and to bring the children along as well would have been too big a hassle. However, Alvin had accompanied his father in secret a few times and, even though Skrivsjö seemed large and scary, he had thought it was beautiful at the same time. The metal rods on the roof tops reminded him of dragonflies and the balloons resembled exotic fruits.

Now Alvin was grown up and could go when he wanted to. But you never did want to in Småland, you only went when you had to.

It took quite a while for him to find the stall where his father had always gone. Alvin had only ever seen it at a distance and he went the wrong way at first. More and more people had started buying automaton horses and other beasts, and so the man who had sold the horse to Lage long ago was no longer alone in offering his goods.

The man who managed the stall was much older than Alvin and wore highly unusual clothes – fancy gentleman's clothes covered by work wear, which had become fancier and dirtier over the years, respectively. At first the older man didn't react when Alvin arrived, he was far away, staring at the other stalls with their more advanced creations.

"Oh, excuse me." The older man adjusted his overalls. "How can I be of service?"

"Hello, my name is Alvin. I'm the son of Lage who used to buy parts from you."

"Are you Lage's son? How nice to finally meet you. Shame that you don't have your old man with you, he's a very good customer."

"He won't be coming anymore. He passed away yesterday."

For a moment, the older man turned even older. Once again, he threw a glance at the other stalls. Then he put a hand on Alvin's shoulder.

"I'm sorry for your loss. Your father was a good man, and it means a lot to me that you came here to the market to inform me. Is it too much to ask how it happened?"

"He fell off our horse and broke his neck when he went riding to the neighbor's farm."

"He rode on an automaton horse with spider's legs installed?" The older man looked genuinely surprised.

They both stood silent for a while. Then the older man went and fetched them both a cup of tea.

"The reason why I am here is that we children never learned how to control the automaton horse."

Alvin fidgeted and looked uncomfortable while he drank his steaming tea. "I've been standing for hours trying to make heads or tails of the punch cards, but I can't."

"Yes, they can be challenging for the untrained."

"I came here to get help with the horse and I thought that maybe you could come with me to the farm and show me how to use it? I also would need to buy new punch cards because I think there are many that have been misplaced."

The older man sighed.

"I would love to accompany you and show you, but if it is as you say and some punch cards are missing there isn't a lot I can do. Besides, the more recent automaton animals have switched over to smaller and more manageable cards, so I can't sell you any new ones that'll work with your horse."

Despite the fact that they were finished with their business Alvin did not get up to leave. The same thoughts that Lage had held were now floating around in his son's head and he wondered if it wouldn't be easier to just get an old horse made of flesh and blood. But such horses weren't sold here anymore. Besides, it felt as a big waste to just leave the old automaton horse standing there to rust – in Småland, you made use of what you had.

"When did you say your father passed away?"

"Yesterday."

"Wait here."

The older man came back with a big box out of which he began to pull saw-like tools. Lastly, he produced a glass container with a greenish-blue liquid inside. It was about as big as a man's head and its bottom was filled with rods, similar to those on Skrivsjö's rooftops.

"I think that I, thanks to your father, can give you a whole new control system that is far superior to the old punch cards. Normally this comes at a small cost, but I liked your father so much that this one is on me."

Since people from Småland never let anything go to waste Alvin agreed to let the older man accompany him back to the farm. Alvin's mother was against the entire procedure at first but, after a little persuasion, she came around. "God helps those who help themselves," she said.

The older man had brought a shovel out of sheer eagerness but it turned out to be unnecessary as Lage's body still lay under a blanket in one of the outbuildings. The older man asked if Alvin wanted to join in with the sawing but he declined.

Unfortunately, the new control device, which was placed between the automaton horse's ears, was not pretty to look at. Some of the younger children were afraid of it, so Alvin quickly made sure that it was always covered by a black piece of cloth.

But early in the morning, at the beginning of the work day, Alvin always left the glass container uncovered. He imagined that Lage would have wanted it that way. He had always loved sunrises, these majestic wonders of nature.

The Philosopher's Stone

Tora Greve

The row of horseless vehicles moved slowly along Kensington High Street. The green translucent leaves of Kensington Garden were colored red by the setting sun. The day had been unusually hot for this time of the year. Workers headed homewards now that the diminishing daylight no longer made it sensible to continue working.

The row of horseless vehicles had come to a standstill.

Dr. Isaac Barrow didn't curse the evening rush. He was on time for his appointment. Sir Robert Boyle had made a great discovery which he wanted to introduce to the most distinguished scientists of England.

Barrow repented that he had chosen the open vehicle for his trip to London. The smoke from the other vehicles was annoying and made him cough. His running eyes stared at the barrel at the back of the vehicle in front of him. He turned his head to look at something more pleasant.

Many female workers were hurrying home to take care of their families. Some of them had an appearance worth resting an eye on. Since queen Elizabeth had forced through women's equal rights with men, many women worked outside home and earned their own money.

One young woman didn't seem to be in a hurry. She walked slowly and confidently, looking like she owned the world.

Barrow leaned out of his vehicle: "Need a ride?"

She stared him up and down with peculiar green eyes and then turned away.

The row of vehicles suddenly moved forward some yards. It stood still again when the girl passed him once more. "Sure you're not changing your mind?"

"I will reach my destination faster by walking." When she spoke, he understood she was probably Scandinavian or German, although she didn't look like it. She had black curly hair and a tanned complexion. In addition, she wore long golden earrings. He would have guessed North African.

However, he didn't see her the next time the row of vehicles got into motion. Besides, he had reached his destination in Holland Park and turned up a quiet side street. He wondered whether his timid companion from Cambridge had found Sir Robert's address. The young man insisted on sightseeing alone that day.

Barrow had picked up young Isaac Newton when he failed to pass his first examination in mathematics and had to try again. The student had found Euclid "a dreary task". Newton was a shy and reserved boy from Lincolnshire having to pay for his tuition and board by being a servant to his teacher. When Barrow became his tutor, he soon discovered that young Newton did his duties as a servant without being asked. Barrow sometimes got the feeling that the boy was able to read his mind. Newton's ambition was to study history and chronology. But his interest in the subject was rather queer, Barrow thought. He had read Thomas Norton too thoroughly before he came to the university. Oh yes, he had read a lot, both sane and unhealthy literature. Unfortunately he was more inclined to the mystics. He firmly believed that pharao Sesostris the third had known the secret of the Philosopher's Stone, and kept on insisting that only *the body* of Sesostris had died. Isaac Barrow believed Newton might gain outstanding ability in geometry if he only learned the most fundamental theorems and definitions. Luckily he succeeded in turning his mind towards that subject instead. In addition, Newton absorbed the new geometry remarkably quickly. When Barrow had taught him all he knew of mathematics, he resigned his last lecturer's place to his pupil.

Barrow handed his card to Sir Robert's servant. It was so hot outside that he didn't have any coat. The servant showed him into the living room. "The others have arrived, sir."

"Dr. Newton too?"

"Yes, sir."

Barrow went inside. Six persons were present, sitting by the fireplace, which was lit, in spite of the heat outside. However, Sir Robert's living room was quite gloomy with its leaden windowpanes and heavy velvet curtains. One couldn't decide which season it was when sitting inside his house.

Sir Robert Boyle dominated the conversation. The subject was obviously alchemy. Officially the scientists didn't bother in regards to such ancient sorcery and scientific witch-craft. In private, though, several of them were attracted to the irrational element which called upon the mystic in them. Boyle was very eagerly talking, perhaps a little loud and breathless. His face had grown almost as red as his hair.

They all turned when Barrow arrived. He knew most of the faces. Robert Hooke was, of course, present. The irritable and cynical cripple who criticized everybody and insinuated that they had stolen the fruits of his labor was Sir Robert's assistant. John Locke, the philosopher, had placed himself in a chair near the fireplace, so that the fancy colors of his suit were revealed. He smoked a pipe and regarded the flames. Sometimes he nodded, confirming. "I admit that I'm an amateur in the natural sciences," he said and, chuckling, emptied his pipe into the fireplace. "I had to ask Dr. Hyugens whether the mathematics in Dr. Newton's *Principia* was sane before I would accept its philosophical parts." He cast a glance at the young man sitting beside him.

Newton sat as far away from Hooke as possible.

The two others Barrow had never met before.

Sir Robert rose, greeted him and led his new guest to a chair by the fireplace. Then Barrow was introduced to the two strangers. "Captain Edmond Halley, just come home from his travel to the southern hemisphere," Sir Robert said.

"Congratulations. I read about your discovery in the *National Geographic*," Barrow said. "Was it a common comet?"

A humorous hint to the unidentified flying objects was always welcome among the alchemists. The handsome face of Captain Halley stiffened. He probably had no sense of humor.

"Humanity will soon enough conquer the air, too," Sir Robert broke in. "I'm also expecting our impressive sailing ships to be replaced by ships driven by steam, like our horseless vehicles on the ground."

"God forbid," Captain Halley said and laughed.

"My consolations. I'm sorry for your father's accident. A pity. We used to go out together," Barrow said.

Halley just murmured some polite remarks. Barrow thought he had changed for the better since he was a child. His red, curly hair had straightened and become almost black, and his freckled complexion now had a tanned, even color probably due to his visit in a warmer climate. Amazing that a person could alter his appearance that much only by growing up, Barrow thought.

The second stranger sat on a pillow in front of the fireplace. She wore long golden earrings like women from North Africa. Barrow recognized the girl he had tried to invite into his vehicle.

"Dr. Fredrika Wilhelmina von Leibniz, the famous German mathematician," Sir Robert said. "I guess you two have much in common."

Barrow didn't blush. During their correspondence he had never fallen upon the idea that Dr. F. W. von Leibniz might be a lady. Germany had not yet given women equal rights to men. However, she lived mostly in Paris.

Barrow, who sat between her and Newton, lit his pipe. Newton had been annoyed when Leibniz invented a mathematical method similar to his own. Barrow bellowed out a big cloud of smoke which made Leibniz cough and turn away. He knew Leibniz was the elder child of a noble family in Germany, famous for its many scientists and philosophers. The present Dr. F. W. von Leibniz had a reputation for being a greater genius than any of the ancestors. Barrow had always admired Leibniz's abilities in mathematics, language and arts. But he had thought her to be a man and much older than she looked.

At dinner Barrow managed to sit beside her. Truly, she interested him even more than before. "You must come to Cambridge and give some lectures in your new mathematical method," he said. As a master of Trinity College he might invite whom he wanted as a guest lecturer, although the university still hadn't allowed any female students or tutors. It was a matter of housing, proctor used to say.

Her translucent green eyes met his. For a moment he felt being emptied of all thoughts below those eyes. "I accept," she finally said.

He didn't reveal that she had to live in his flat during her stay, due to lack of housing regarding female visitors.

After dinner they continued discussing alchemy. Barrow yawned in secret behind his hand. He comprehended that Sir Robert tried to tell them something important, but he used a very long time to come to the point. Sir Robert raised his brows. "Am I exhausting you, my friends?"

"Not at all, your theories are very interesting," the always polite John Locke assured and put away his pipe.

"As you certainly know, my friends, we can't divide or change a basic element into another," Sir Robert continued. "Therefor it is my firm conviction that we can't make gold out of mercury the chemical way. We must find the Philosopher's Stone. I have been scrutinizing Arabian manuscripts lately to try and find a hint."

"It's an old rumor I won't trust," Locke remarked.

"It's the only solution I can see. While I was trying to make gold out of mercury the ordinary way, I found the secret of the basic elements. There are not only four, but many, which can't be divided or changed into others, and both gold and mercury are among them."

"I read your theory last year." Locke nodded.

"Then we might perhaps give up trying to make gold out of mercury?" Barrow snarled with the pipe between his teeth.

"It is possible to transform mercury into gold," Newton suddenly exclaimed. He hadn't said a word the whole afternoon, so they all turned and stared at him. There was a glimpse of determination in his eyes.

"Since you seem to know so much, why aren't you rich?" Hooke said.

"I don't practice alchemy to become wealthy. I see alchemy as a way of living, a kind of philosophy. A true alchemist must resolve himself up wholly to it, and the prosecution of the same, next to the service of God. He must join prayer to God, with serious meditation, and diligent industry, this is the way to attain true knowledge."

Barrow was amazed by Newton talking so much. The man must have used a lot of time contemplating the subject to have reached such a conclusion, he thought. Newton was secretive, but Barrow still hadn't expected him to delve so deeply into alchemy. "True knowledge, is that another word for the Philosopher's Stone?" he said.

"They who search after the Philosopher's Stone by their own rules are obliged to a strict and religious life. They may be granted the discovery of the Stone as a gift from God, and must solemnly engage not to use the knowledge revealed to them for selfish ends or betray the secret to the wicked."

"This sounds more like an immaterial Stone than an actual physical one," Locke said.

"If you by accident reveal the secret to the wicked, of course unintentionally, what happens?" Barrow said.

"Then the Stone will revenge itself," Newton said.

"Nonsense, a dead stone can't perform any actions," Hooke said.

"The Philosopher's Stone isn't an ordinary stone. It's a living thing, it leads its own life, independent of all other forms of life in the universe. It is, you may say, the true spirit of God."

Newton had never before been that informative. Barrow decided to take care of the rare situation. Religion was his area of knowledge. "You are talking about God. What kind of a God do you worship? What kind of being is He, according to your opinion?"

"The true God is a living, intelligent and powerful Being, and, from His other perfections, He is supreme, or most perfect. He is eternal and infinite, omnipotent and omniscient, that is, His duration reaches from eternity to eternity, His presence from infinity to infinity, He governs all things, and knows all things that are or can be done. He is not eternity and infinity, but eternal and infinite, He is not duration or space, but endures and is present. He endures forever, and is everywhere present, and, by existing always and everywhere, He constitutes duration and space."

Locke nodded. "Much knowledge disappeared during the centuries. But we've still got some clues. The Rosicrucians claim to have their knowledge from such ancient societies."

"I'm a skeptic," Barrow said. "I fear that most of it has been drowned in mysteries and rites based upon several religions during the millennia. You can't be sure of what is pure religion and what was true science."

"The base was always science," Newton said. "The ancients believed in only one omnipotent and omniscient God, and therefore the other gods had only a symbolic meaning."

"How can you be so sure?" Barrow was amazed. Was Newton's mind completely screwed up? The poor fellow had been working hard for such a long time, and in addition had probably read some unhealthy literature.

"The Roman king Numa Pompilius erected a round temple in honor of Vesta, and ordained perpetual fire to be kept in the middle of it, as a symbol of the figure of the world with the sun in the center," Newton said. "In the Vestal ceremonies we may yet trace the ancient spirit of the Egyptians, for it was their way to deliver their mysteries, that is, their philosophy of things above the common way of thinking, under the veil of religious rites and hieroglyphic symbols."

"Are you being serious?" Locke said. "Do you mean to tell us that the mysteries of the ancient Egyptian religion were nothing more than a display of their natural philosophy? What about their many gods? Are they literally celestial bodies moving according to mathematical laws?"

"Since you are talking of the Vesta temple, do you believe the one omniscient God is a female?" Barrow said.

Locke chuckled, but Newton didn't seem offended. "The word God usually signifies *Lord*, but every Lord is not a god," he said. "I am convinced that the ancient gods of Egypt were divinized kings. In the case of Osiris, he is in reality the divinized Sesostris. Just look at the resemblance of the names."

"We all know that Egyptian kings were named after gods," Barrow said. "A slight resemblance in names doesn't prove anything. And where does Jesus Christ fit into this system? Is he crushed between the gravitating bodies of your mathematically treated system? Do you mean God is a mathematician?"

"As a blind man has no idea of colors, so have we no idea of the manner by which the all-wise God perceives and understands all things," Newton replied. "He is in a manner not at all human, in a manner not at all corporeal, in a manner utterly unknown to us."

"I thought the human being was made in His image. We must resemble him in at least one way," Barrow said. He knew he was regarded as the most learned clergyman of his time. He had been beneficent enough to free Newton from his duty to hold sermons, since he knew the young man felt awkward about it. "After all you have said, that resemblance must be grounded in our ability as mathematicians, is that what you mean?"

"Then the conclusion should be that the most powerful prophets are those who have the greatest understanding in mathematics," Locke concluded. Barrow glanced at him. Newton had no sense of humor so the point was wasted upon him, he thought.

"What if it really is so?" Leibniz broke in. "What if God only reveals Himself through mathematical coincidences in the universe as a whole, coincidences which can't be mistaken and not discovered before a civilization reaches the technology necessary to detect them?"

"Where does the Philosopher's Stone fit into this?" Halley said. "I mean, you said you started out as an alchemist."

"Honestly, I don't believe in that Stone," Barrow remarked. "I will classify it in the same category as the unidentified flying objects people have claimed seeing lately. After the ingenious Dr. Newton here introduced his theory of gravity and wrote that famous article in *Time Magazine* about artificial satellites, combined with the appearance of Halley's comet, people have been seeing things flying in the air. We haven't got one proof of the existence of the Stone yet."

"Would you believe in it if you saw it?" Sir Robert suddenly said.

"Many persons have claimed that they found it. They all showed a remarkable ability in hiding it from others under the pretext of secrecy," Barrow said.

"Then I suggest we go to my laboratory." Sir Robert rose and turned in the opened door.

They went through some dark damp corridors to a secret room below the rest of the house. Sir Robert went ahead of the group with a torch, and Leibniz followed next to him. When they reached the innermost door Sir Robert gave the torch to his assistant Hooke, put an old ornamented iron key into the lock and turned it round.

"Please enter, my friends." Sir Robert let Hooke wait outside until they all had gone in.

The laboratory lay in darkness. However, at the far end of it, they discovered four sparkling spots. This was a secret Sir Robert hadn't revealed to anyone, not even to his assistant Hooke.

"The Philosopher's Stone," Sir Robert announced proudly.

"But there are four," Locke exclaimed.

Sir Robert's assistant came in and hung the torch on the wall. Then they noticed that the laboratory was almost completely filled with a red rock.

"What purpose serves this rock?" Barrow enquired. "I suppose it isn't the Philosopher's Stone smashed to pieces because it was too big to get into the room?"

"It was during my experiments with mercury and grains of dust from this red rock I discovered the Philosopher's Stone. It hides in small portions within it, my friends."

Newton took up a piece of rock and examined it carefully before he threw it back.

"I have extracted everything of importance, this is only the leftovers."

Barrow stood behind Leibniz and divided his interest between her warm body, smelling of roses, close to him and the Philosopher's Stone.

"Feel how odd the Stone is to touch," Sir Robert suggested. "It's necessary to store it in four parts, its powers are so great."

The others progressed carefully. Newton was the first to stretch out his hand to get the smallest of the four pieces. He held it in his hand for a while, then slipped it back into the test tube. The scientists stumbled over each other in eagerness. Newton was standing in the corner washing his hands carefully. Leibniz withdrew and refused to touch the Stone.

The Philosopher's Stone was very remarkable, Barrow thought. It was warm and heavy, and yet it shone with a cool alien light, like an evil eye.

"Have you ever tried to make gold with the Philosopher's Stone?" Newton enquired from his corner.

"No, I will investigate it further before I try its powers. It is an element, but it seems unstable."

Locke held one of the pieces up to the light, carefully, between two fingers. "It is really glowing with its own light."

Barrow took two pieces and tried to bring them together. Leibniz had turned her back to him. When she noticed Newton staring, agitated, in that direction, she turned and peeped over the shoulder of Barrow. He felt her breath on his neck. Both pieces of the Stone were glowing more intensely. "They are getting hotter," Barrow remarked.

Suddenly Newton did something unexpected. He grasped the hand of Leibniz and ran out of the room. Captain Halley followed.

Barrow laughed. "I've always challenged the Devil, but I've never lost yet." He threw the two pieces back into the test tubes. "As a matter of fact, the Devil and I are very good companions, although I deny him the many victims Calvin offers him." Barrow went to the basin in the corner and washed his hands. "I must get rid of this devilish stuff. Are you never afraid when you experiment on it?"

"Now and then, perhaps," Sir Robert said.

"Alchemy is the science of the demon and of sorcerers and witches. Therefore no alchemist can be careful enough." Barrow went to the door. "Was I seeing Drs. Leibniz and Newton fleeing upstairs hand in hand?"

"Captain Halley went after them. They won't have a chance of being alone and causing embarrassment," Locke said.

The three others were still standing in the living room when the rest of the party came up. They turned their pale faces towards Barrow.

"Did you feel the cold touch of the Devil?" he enquired.

"No, rather the heat of Hell," Newton replied.

Barrow laid a hand on one shoulder of each of Newton and Leibniz. "I'm glad you two are becoming friends." His grip hardened. "I suggest both of you come with me back to Cambridge."

"I will stay in London over the summer," Leibniz said and brushed off his hand. "But I promise to visit your university this autumn."

Halley's dark eyes flashed. "Keep away from her. She is not what she pretends," he wheezed.

Barrow looked astonished. "I'm a grownup man. I don't need any advice from youngsters like you, Captain Halley."

"This is not advice. It's a warning." The handsome face before him twitched.

A terrible temper, Barrow thought. Terrible enough to commit murder? He shuddered. He felt the warning was seriously meant. Did old Halley too get one before he walked himself down into the river? Barrow began to comprehend that he was being mixed up in something he didn't quite understand.

The summer became very hot.

Barrow went to the Continent to visit John Locke in Paris. There he met a lot of other scientists, among them Dr. Christiaan Hyugens. The usually popular Barrow found that the other behaved rather suspiciously towards him. Barrow wondered if he had heard something unfavorable about him. He invited Hyugens to a coffee shop to become better acquainted.

Perhaps Hyugens too wanted to settle any misunderstanding between them. "Mr. Locke told me that you met Dr. von Leibniz in London."

So, that was the problem. "Quite briefly at Sir Robert Boyle's. She's doing some work in chemistry at Gresham College this summer. Do you know her well?"

"I was one of her father's students. I was around twenty the first time we met. She was six, a lovely child, very intelligent. Her father said she had a slow development in the beginning. As a four year old he was afraid she was retarded."

"May I ask a personal question: Are you in love with her?"

Hyugens concentrated on his chocolate. He got a mustache of crème on his upper lip when he sipped on the warm liquid. "Yes, you're right. We better settle this. I love her. But I promised her father to protect her. She lived in my house while she was a student. I taught her mathematics for two years. But I never touched her in any indecent way. I kept my promise. God knows I wanted her. I even proposed to her. But she's not the marrying kind. She's only interested in science."

They changed the subject. Now that they had settled the problem, the conversation ran more freely. They began discussing the solar system and the latest versions of telescopes. Barrow mentioned the unidentified flying objects seen over England the previous spring. He admitted that he hadn't seen them himself.

"We watched some over Paris, too. I actually saw them myself," Hyugens said. "I wonder if they are space ships from Venus or Mars or even from the other planets. Swedenborg mentions inhabitants from other planets in his book. Our Earth too is a planet, and it is inhabited. Why shouldn't the others be? And if we can conceive of artificial satellites and spaceships, why shouldn't the others?"

"The idea seems farfetched to me. It is one thing to speculate about space ships. It is another to build them. I guess the sightings are the result of a hysterical concept after Dr. Newton's theory of gravitation and its interpretations were published. However, is it of any concern to us?"

"Of course, if *the others* come as conquerors to Earth, it is the concern of all mankind. I remember Dr. von Leibniz was attracted to the problem even before Dr. Newton's theory was published."

"So? I find the speculations a bit naive. Mr. Locke always says that new ideas are more disastrous to a fixed society than are advanced weapons. If *the others* want to destroy us, it is sufficient to plant a couple of their own philosophers in our society to alter its structure to their benefit."

"So that we will destroy ourselves in due time? Honestly, Dr. Barrow, isn't that a rather slow method?"

"Well, the question of time may be different to people from other planets. Besides, it will save them from using any heavy artillery in a direct confrontation of which the outcome is uncertain." Barrow rose. "You are welcome to visit me at Cambridge if you wish. Dr. von Leibniz will be holding lectures in combinatorial analysis for us this autumn."

Middle of August.

Sir Robert Boyle and his assistant Robert Hooke died within a few weeks interval. Barrow came too late to Hooke's funeral, but he reached Sir Robert's.

The large family Boyle was present, and a rather pale and timid looking Leibniz. After the funeral Barrow ate lunch with Sir Robert's eldest brother, John. He grieved the sudden death of a brother and good friend. "He didn't die a natural death," John Boyle said. "He just dwindled away, lost his hair and bled from many small bruises. I guess his experiments with the Philosopher's Stone took his life. There ought to be a law against alchemists. As a matter of fact, I will pose that in the Parliament."

The following day Barrow fetched Leibniz and her belongings in Sir Robert's house. He used his biggest horseless vehicle with a roof, having learned from smoggy London last time. They went to Sir Robert's lawyer, another one of the numerous Boyle brothers, to listen to the will being read aloud. It turned out that Sir Robert had given the four pieces of the Philosopher's Stone to Locke, Barrow, Newton and Leibniz. In addition, Locke got his scientific writings.

The weather was still warm when Barrow and his female companion set out for Cambridge. Leibniz sat silently looking at the English landscape passing. The vehicle got very warm inside. Barrow opened a window.

"Were they killed by the Philosopher's Stone?" Barrow finally asked.

"I think so."

"Dr. Newton often talked about the Stone. He, in fact, foresaw how it would affect those who came into too close a connection with it. He tried to warn Sir Robert."

"I read those letters." She sniffed. "I'm sorry I didn't do more to make him stop doing those experiments. But I was occupied with my lectures at Gresham's."

"You couldn't have stopped him. He was obsessed." Barrow laid his hand over hers.

Barrow parked the vehicle outside a countryside inn. "Come on, let's have some food. We have been busy the whole morning."

She nodded and followed him inside. She looked timid and defenseless. He ordered food for them both and discovered that he liked to have her beside him at the table.

After the meal Barrow fired the vehicle up again and they climbed into it. He tried to concentrate on the driving, but got distracted by his passenger. Every time he cast a glance at her, he noticed that she was studying him with her peculiar green eyes. He moved uneasily in his seat.

A thunderstorm was threatening on the horizon when they reached Cambridge. Barrow parked his vehicle at Trinity College and led Leibniz across the Great Court to Master's Lodge. It was already raining. Well inside, he placed her in front of the fireplace which was lit by a servant. She took off her wet sandals. Barrow settled in a chair halfway in front of her. He wanted to look at her. She was the most attractive woman he had ever met.

"I have invited Dr. Newton for tea in Master's Lodge this afternoon," he said.

Leibniz nodded.

Just then the servant showed in the young mathematician. Suddenly it felt as if the electricity of the thunderstorm filled the room. Barrow could literally feel the connection between the two youngsters. It was almost supernatural. The servant brought tea and scones. Newton put butter on a scone and devoured it. Barrow thought the young man had probably forgotten to eat the whole day. Only the slurping of tea and the thunderbolts outside could be heard. Nobody wished to start a conversation. The air was electrical. The silence became unbearable. If nobody talks, this tenseness will cause an explosion, Barrow thought. It was up to him to start the conversation. He began talking about Sir Robert's funeral and mentioned the pieces of the Philosopher's Stone the three of them had inherited. "I hope you won't try to make any gold with it," he finally said.

They just nodded silently.

It struck Barrow that their adversity against each other had ceased the moment they met.

Leibniz looked uneasy when Newton left. She clasped her hands in her lap, shuddered and moved closer to the fireplace. Barrow put his arm around her and felt it was too intimate for her comfort. "You're shivering. Is it too cold in here?" He let go of her. "The servants have made up a good room for you upstairs during your stay in Cambridge."

Barrow noticed that the students, at first, were uncomfortable with a female teacher. Soon they accepted her, especially when her method of calculus turned out to be easier to use than Newton's. The young man didn't mind. He had moved on to another subject, the study of light and colors. Barrow had decided that Leibniz was to take her meals in the Great Hall together with the other tutors. Some of the old fashioned clergy expressed their dislike. However, Barrow was Master of Trinity College and had the final decision.

Soon after Newton's experiments on light and color began to leak out, Barrow got a letter from Huygens that he wanted to visit Trinity College. Barrow suspected Leibniz was the true attraction. He consented. A discussion between Newton and Huygens might be good for the scientific climate at the university. Barrow was tired of the old clergy working against the younger scientists. He comprehended their dislike really originated in Leibniz living in his house. However, everything was correct between them. He hadn't tried touching her since that first attempt, although he admitted that he wanted to. Besides, he needed to talk to an outsider about certain suspicions having popped up in his mind lately.

Huygens arrived before dinner on a crisp autumn day. Barrow had offered to fetch him in London, but Huygens declined. Since he came in a carriage behind two horses, Barrow suspected that Huygens didn't like the noisy ride in a horseless vehicle.

They all ate in the Great Hall. Afterwards Barrow invited Hyugens, Newton and Leibniz to his home for a nightcap.

Hyugens enquired about the latest results obtained in optics in England.

"I admit that I wasn't very lucky with my hypothesis of colors when I tried to explain, for example, yellow as a different degree of red and white intermingled." Barrow looked at Newton. He was pleased that Huygens himself brought forward the subject.

"I am more interested in Dr. Newton's peculiar theory," Huygens said.

"Why is it peculiar?" Leibniz asked.

"Although he obviously believes in corpuscles, he doesn't seem to be able to make a final choice between the two theories."

"I prefer to speak of light in general terms," Newton remarked. "And I consider your theory geometrical rather than mechanical. It contradicts physical principles, because of lack of periodicity. There's no use in producing a beautiful mathematical theory if it isn't confirmed by experiments."

"I didn't say that light waves don't have periodicity. I believe that light is longitudinal waves crossing each other without in any way interfering with one another."

"Such waves can't account for colors," Newton said. "If I were to believe in light waves at all, they must be transverse rather than longitudinal."

"Do you suggest transverse light waves when using those rather obscure phrases *fits* and *sides*?" Barrow interpreted.

"Really, I haven't investigated the problem thoroughly yet," Newton said. "I'm sorry certain undigested parts of my theory have leaked out."

The party broke up. Leibniz withdrew to her own room, and Newton went home. Huygens was lodged in a guestroom at Trinity College.

"What about a walk around the quadrangle before we go to bed?" Barrow suggested.

They walked the quadrangle twice before talking.

"I would like to talk more with Dr. Newton about his curious theory of light, but that'll wait until his book is published," Hyugens finally said. "I understand he's rather sore as regards undigested material."

Barrow nodded absentmindedly. "Have you ever thought upon the possibility of producing death rays?" he suddenly asked. "Just think of the trumpets of Jericho. The walls were destroyed by sound waves. When you were working on your theory of light waves, didn't the similarity of the two in your own theory occur to you?"

"Really, Dr. Barrow, I don't believe in the trumpets of Jericho, I mean, that it happened exactly that way, literally."

"I don't intend to scorn your brainchild, but suppose the corpuscular theory of light turns out to be the right one?"

"That can't be. I've performed a lot of experiments proving that light is propagated in waves. Therefore some of Dr. Newton's experimental results baffle me. They indicate light to be of both natures, and that's impossible. Plain logic shows that one thing can't be of two such fundamentally different origins."

"If it really turns out to be so?"

"Then such a discovery is abnormal for our age and lies in the future, because the conceiving of a totally dualistic nature requires a logic wholly different from the one we are used to."

"I want to show you something." Barrow turned and went across the quadrangle to his home. He removed a thick Bible from its place on the shelf. There he kept his piece of the Philosopher's Stone. It was glowing in the dark. Huygens reached eagerly for it. "Be careful," Barrow said. "It killed Sir Robert Boyle and his assistant. I think it emits death rays." He might as well tell Huygens of the meeting in London. If the man was into the science of light and color, maybe he could explain how an element could shed out light by itself. "Captain Halley was frightened of it."

"Captain Halley," Huygens said. "He was mixed up in an unpleasant story lately. Grave robbing in Egypt."

"Pharao Sesostris the third's grave, perhaps?"

"How did you know?"

"He was interested in the real Philosopher's Stone. I don't think he believed the glowing element in Sir Robert's laboratory was the true Philosopher's Stone. I have been suspecting Captain Halley all the time. You see, when I went to Oxford to visit a friend some years ago, I met the real Edmond Halley. As a child, he had red hair and freckles. A grownup man can't change that completely. I was puzzled when I met him at Boyle's. I know his father was murdered. He didn't walk himself into the river Thames when drunk. His heart was penetrated by some kind of ray, very hot and very fast."

"And who is the present Captain Halley?"

"I suspect he might come from Venus or Mars. You remember all those lights in the air last summer? They may be their vehicles."

"Why should they be interested in pharao Sesostris?"

"Maybe they believe a precious item is buried in his grave."

Huygens shook his head. "It seems too farfetched to me. A pity I have to leave for London tomorrow. I had hoped to discuss more on light and colors with Dr. Newton."

"I don't think he will talk about it anymore. He feels that his theory isn't ripe yet."

The day after Barrow didn't meet Leibniz before she came back from her lecture. He and Huygens had been sitting up the previous evening talking about Barrow's travels and consuming a lot of wine. Barrow had slept in and didn't come down to breakfast with her.

The autumn afternoon was chilly. Newton didn't show up. Perhaps he was afraid of being embroiled in another discussion with Huygens. Barrow was alone with Leibniz. They were silently regarding each other. He sat in a chair before the fireplace, she on a pillow below him. Physically he was attracted to her. He had never before wanted a woman that much. At the same time she repelled him, as if his instincts told him she wasn't quite human. This was a new situation. He had learnt to rely on his innermost feelings and warnings of danger during his stay in the East.

"Who are you?" he finally said. "What's really going on?"

"It's about the future of the Earth and our own civilization. It begins with the presentation of the true son of God. Firstly, he signs his secret alchemical writings *Isaacus Neuutonus*, which can be transcribed into *Jeova sanctus unus*. As the only son of God he thinks that he alone has access to the true knowledge. His method of describing the system of the world will, in a few generations, be regarded as the only method, even in fields where it doesn't fit. The true God of our beliefs will be crushed in mechanistic philosophies, based upon artificial mathematical systems. The sciences based upon mathematics will eventually replace religion. The mathematicians and scientists will be looked upon as mystics and high priests by the common people not learned in the art. Civilization will reach a point where the sum of its advances in different fields will supersede the ability of perception of a single human being."

"Are Dr. Newton and Captain Halley too mixed up in this?"

"Captain Halley is captain of a fleet of spaceships coming from a civilization which has been trying to steal the Philosopher's Stone. He revealed himself by breaking into pharao Sesostris the third's grave. Now that we know his identity, he will be properly taken care of." She laughed. "For a while I thought you were that interstellar spy."

"Where do you come from? Venus? Mars?"

"Venus – Mars! You know nothing of the universe. I might tell you secrets which would make your mind twist itself into insanity forever. Captain Halley flies around in his impressive spaceships, but my people don't need such primitive vehicles. Unfortunately, he spotted us at Sir Robert's when we fled out of the laboratory. He was, however, distracted by Newton's writings about pharao Sesostris and thought we had hidden the Stone in his grave."

Barrow listened attentively. He could feel the cold from outer space settling in the room. He suddenly conceived there might exist other solar systems outside the path of Saturn. And yet, he would be able to hold this attractive female being in a firm grip because she had chosen such a weak shell to hide in on Earth. "So, where do you come from?"

She rose and beckoned him over to the table.

"Sit down. I'll show you." Leibniz took a paper and drew a square on it, then some figures indicating openings. Barrow recognized an architectural drawing when shown it, and comprehended it was the room they were sitting in. She also drew two circles, one inside the room and one outside. "They are two-dimensional beings. If the being inside wants the one outside to come in, he must open the door. Agreed?"

Barrow nodded. He had many questions, but understood he wouldn't have to ask.

"However, we are sitting up here in the third dimension looking down into the room of the drawing. We can enter it from above without opening the door. If you let a globe pass through the room, the two-dimensional beings would comprehend it as several different circles passing through their world. It is not just the room which is open to us. Even the inside of the bodies of the two beings would be open. Now, try and comprehend a being of four dimensions. A three-dimensional house cannot keep him out. He can even enter a three-dimensional body without doing any damage to it. And that's what we intend to do." She produced a beautiful item looking like a sparkling blue delicate egg. "This is what we really look like. However, to function in this crude world, we need a human body. We are not individuals like you are, we are all one. But we can put parts of ourselves into different human beings and yet stay undivided."

"Where did you hide that thing?"

"I didn't hide it. I can produce it out of my being and take it back whenever I want." She made a small gesture, then showed her empty hand.

"Why are you showing me this egg or whatever it is?

"We will put it behind your forehead, between your brain halves. It will make you omniscient."

"Why me?"

"We need a person like you. You are one of the greatest scientists of your time. You have done important work both in mathematics and language. You are looked upon as the most learned man in England. You are well traveled. Besides, you are Master of Trinity College and an influential man people look up to."

This was the same situation as Jesus Christ experienced when he was tempted by the Devil in the desert, Barrow thought.

She rose to go upstairs and change for dinner. "Think it over until tomorrow."

Sunday morning.

Barrow was going to preach in Trinity College Chapel. He had hardly slept. He was reminded of a philosophical saying: "If God was standing before you holding the truth of everything in his left hand and the yearning for knowing the truth in his right hand, which hand would you choose?" He realized that he himself would choose God's right hand. Barrow didn't wish to become omniscient.

He was standing before the shelf putting on his gown, and then took his personal Bible to bring to the chapel. The test tube containing Sir Robert's stone was revealed. Suddenly it was in his hand. Barrow felt its warmth towards his skin. "It will certainly bring me luck in my last sermon of my Judgment day," he thought and put the hot little thing into his breast pocket, near the heart. In a glimpse in the corner of his eye he noticed Leibniz coming down the stairs behind him.

They walked across the Great Court, the short way from Mastern's Lodge to Trinity College Chapel. He already felt the deadly rays from the stone in his pocket penetrating him. Sweat began running down his body. He wondered whether he would be able to reach the Chapel before he collapsed. Barrow more felt than saw Newton coming up on his other side. They wouldn't let him chose. He already knew too much about them.

Barrow entered the pulpit. His sermons usually lasted for three hours. He intended to keep on talking until the stone had done its work, even if he had to collapse before the crowd. His eyes ran across the front row. Leibniz and Newton sat alone together.

Barrow knew the end was coming fast now. He laid his hand to his heart, uttered some well chosen words from the gospel, then stumbled and fell. Professors and students screamed. Some of the elder teachers and proctor rose, but Newton and Leibniz came first to the spot. Leibniz flung herself across the dying Barrow's body searching his pockets. How he had wished to have her that close all the time he had known her. She smelled of lavender and something he remembered from his mother when he was a child.

Then he lost consciousness.

A Sense of Foul Play

Andrew Coulthard

"Life dull? Need to spice things up? Join the Norsborg Players – you might even be good enough to go pro!

The Vellu-Beetles are almost through the door, their breath a combination of flame and oxygen. Their cutters fizz and hiss as they lance into the virtual foam-stone of the atrium, carving their way toward you. Glancing over your shoulder you reappraise your surroundings one final time: sheer walls, tiny armor-glass window, solid floor. Definitely no other way out. What do you do?

… she ran a hasty opportunity search through her internal tool forms inventory. No good. She'd already used every charge for every tool other than the most basic and they'd be no use against Vellu-Beetles. Worse, after three hours of solid combat the only alternative form she could still acquire was of a limbless aquatic creature, even that in need of major repairs. No. There was only one chance left, an all or nothing gamble.

She cracked open the steel cone in the center of the room to reveal the chamber command console and with a grunt plugged the interface links into her eye sockets. At once her in-tournament integrated visual sense-set collapsed.

She could no longer experience the game environment like the other players; conventional sight was out for the rest of the tournament. But games exist on more than one cognitive level and she was searching for a latent equipment cache or, better still, a local sector dashboard that would give her control over the whole sector.

A landscape of colored stacks and geometric forms opened out before her, leaving physical traces in her mind. She switched awareness from one to the other, attempting to intuit the patterns she knew must be there.

Distant popping echoes and a trace-odor of burning concrete warned her the Vellu-Beetles were almost through. Then it bloomed before her, beautiful, complex and intricately linked. Reaching into the array she modified the shapes, accentuating the core pattern. A shiver of excitement passed through her, the gamble had paid off better than she could have hoped. She'd found the god-console!

The entire tournament world emerged before her and she enveloped it, becoming one with the system. A single figurative blink sent the Vellu-Beetles packing. Then it was the turn of the other players:

Voices crackled over the message channel:

– *What just happened?*

– *Someone's found it!*

– *Found what?*

– *The Deus Console.*

– *Who? Player 9?*

– *No, I'm still ... argh!*

Scouring the halls, tunnels, chambers and mansions, she cleansed the tournament world of players with a wall of blue fire.

To the applause of her net-link audience Player 1 disconnected from the game trembling and dripping with sweat. Her head was aching. She felt faint. Her Body-Status-Display showed low blood sugar, high pulse and elevated blood pressure. But she'd done it – she was the Champion and destined to be Club Secretary!"

Extract taken from Norsborg General Gaming Club promotional audio brochure.

Norsborg Gaming Club Open Chat Channel – 8 December 7.37pm

PLAYER 3: Hi, U R new on here Rn't U? Club member?

NOOB: New here. Not member.

PLAYER 3: U shld join, can B lot of fun.

NOOB: OK, mayB. Have U had good day?

PLAYER 3: No. Work = dull. Not much happening IRL. As usual.

NOOB: No? Plenty if you believe the news.

PLAYER 3: Don't often follow bulletins tbh.

NOOB: Y?

PLAYER 3: C'mon, no point. Did U C main hub this morning? Full of l8test crazy conspiracy theory. Total BS.

NOOB: Hah. They just get worse. Did U hear about Govt security trying 2 infiltrate PVCs? Ministers afraid they're full of subversives.

PLAYER 3: No. Missed that. PVCs, do U mean Private Virtual Communities? Like gaming clubs?

NOOB: What's Ur real name?

PLAYER 3: I'm Player 3.

NOOB: Not a real name.

PLAYER 3: Club moniker. No names on here. Channel's multi-encrypted for a reason, surely U understand that ... unless U really R a Noob?

NOOB: Just wondering if U were real. Heard lots about how clever investigative probe-minds R nowadays.

PLAYER 3: Haha! U think me = Probe Mind? We don't use names in the Club. Use Club Seeding instead. Secretary won last year = Player 1, me 2nd runner up, = Player 3.

NOOB: Impressive.

PLAYER 3: Nope. But this year I'm going 2 win.

NOOB: Y U want 2?

PLAYER 3: RU serious? Winner = Club Secretary for 12 months. Full perks = able to quit my day job (at last). Go fulltime.

NOOB: Hmm, I spose.

PLAYER 3: Blimey, Y are you on this channel if U don't like games?

NOOB: Bit lonely.

PLAYER3: Oh. U2.

NOOB: If I join what will my name B?

PLAYER 3: Player X. Unseeded Players = Player X during 1st year.

NOOB: So is spending UR whole life in virtual land, really so gr8t?

PLAYER 3: There R real-life benefits, U know. I'm global top 5% gamer, but in real world low-budget. Bad results. My kid has medical condition, needs treatments – implants. Club Secretary = many advantages and connections.

NOOB: Illegal connections?

PLAYER 3: Course not.

NOOB: R U sure?

PLAYER 3: Look, need to go. Nice chatting. Will U B here again 2morrow?

NOOB: MayB.

Player 3 log 08 December

Dear log, I met somebody new on the Open Channel tonight. Asked odd questions, but it was nice having somebody real to talk with ... things have been lonely since Zrian left. Called themselves Noob. Didn't understand why I'd want to win the championship – sheesh, some people!

Only one round left now and three still in: Player 1, Player 2 and myself. The other two are good, but I'm younger. I have my determination.

PLAYER 3: Hi, how's U today?

NOOB: Yep, fine. U?

PLAYER 3: OK.

NOOB: Gonna tell me more about games?

PLAYER 3: Sure.

NOOB: I heard something about sense-sets before. Whatz that?

PLAYER 3: Most games are virtual, yeah? Hardware connects with us directly + uses our full sensory range to create game environment. It exists in the Club Mind + in our heads 2 via connection.

NOOB: So when U play UR really *seeing* unreal sights, *hearing* unreal sounds?

PLAYER 3: Mostly. But there R other types of game 2. Any sort allowed in principal, but virtual-world = most common.

Noob: Interesting. Didn't know.

PLAYER: What's allowed depends on UR Club charter. Ours = old club. So old charter. Includes all different games, even monopoly. XD

NOOB: Riiiight. You told me yesterday you were defo gonna win this year. How R U gonna do it? Other players must B better than U, right?

PLAYER 3: Lot depends on actual game. Top 10 Club seeds R all brill gamers, multi skill-sets etc. But not even greatest gamers master every category.

NOOB: Oh. So mayB if game is *bad* for U, U'll mess up? Do you know what style final will B?

PLAYER 3: No. Secretary told me this year is gonna B different.

NOOB: How?

PLAYER 3: She doesn't know yet. They've gone and bought new Club Mind. Given it the job of designing finale.

NOOB: Mind? Like a *probe* mind you mean?

PLAYER 3: Sort of. Minds = MINDS. U know about them? R U tech trained?

NOOB: Nope.

PLAYER 3: Manageable, Intelligent, Neural, Design, Systems. Programmable command units, cell-based, synth made. Intelligent apps. One application = design and run games.

NOOB: Okay. Is that good thing?

PLAYER 3: Don't know. This one = top end model. Ex-military sim + training system.

NOOB: Ex-military? Sounds dangerous.

PLAYER 3: Probably been factory reconditioned + adapted to civil safety standards.

NOOB: OK. What do U think about it?

PLAYER 3: Dunno. Call me Luddite (or worse, *conservative*), but don't really like Minds. They've come long way, but bugs and glitches still happen.

NOOB: Hahaha – "or worse, a *conservative*"? Look out for Govt. probes, Player 3!

PLAYER 3: I'm serious. I was a Mind sub-unit designer then they automated my level of production.

NOOB: What happened?

PLAYER 3: Usual story: design went fully automatic, me and few million others got laid off.

NOOB: Okay, I get it – down with Minds!

PLAYER 3: No, not really. Newer Minds = very sophisticated. Some do v. important work.

NOOB: But?

PLAYER 3: But most customization done manually at sub-system level = mistakes are made.

NOOB: And?

PLAYER 3: And I don't really like this tournament plan much.

Player 3 log 10 December

Dear Log,

Had coffee with the Secretary today. She told me what the Mind had so far let on about the finale: the game is going to be physical, nothing abstract or network – real space, real sense, full body presence, though possibly with some fantastical elements. Wonder what that means?

Real space is unusual, but actually fine with me. I wonder what skill-sets though? I need to know, because I *have* to get practicing if I'm going to win. Sam's been really poorly again.

Secretary's always nice to me, but there was something about her that bothered me a bit today. I mean she was friendly and everything, but ... I can't quite put my finger on it. Was she holding something back?

I drank too much coffee and was so focused on what she had to say that afterwards I came over a bit funny, like I almost blacked out for a moment. Only I'm not sure I actually did.

Ran some medi-tests on myself when I got home and everything was fine.

Got to stay well for the game.

Dear Log,

Haven't been able to connect with my friend *Noob* for a couple of days. Guess we weren't really friends.

Dreamt a lot last night. Can't remember any details, but I don't think they were good. Left me feeling low, like a shadow was over me all day. Sam's sick which doesn't help. She needed a couple of extra dosages. Her medicines aren't going to last this month.

Some official game details came up this morning on the Club Bulletin Channel, straight from the Mind. Game title is *2-sense*. Definitely real space, it says, but we're apparently going to be modified or restricted in some way and there'll be a pre-game medical. Beyond that nothing else is yet known. No mention of anything fantastical either.

Wonder how the other two are feeling. Secretary was fine yesterday, confident as always. I'm getting pretty edgy. Why don't they just publish the full details? The game is only a few weeks away now. Maybe not-knowing is part of it. That would be a bit over-subtle though, wouldn't it?

Player 3 log 12 December

Okay, got all the details at last. It's to be a sort of gladiatorial event. Elimination; search and destroy. Tag with electro-stunners. It sounds pretty basic, but there's a catch – we're only allowed two operational senses each. And we can't choose which. They're somehow going to be allotted randomly.

This is a really weird idea and by the way, where's the skill?!!

Apparently the arena is randomly generated from a pre-set number of possible parameters too. If it's all down to random chance, there *is* no skill.

That's disgraceful for a championship finale! See what happens when you leave game design to an unproven Mind?

I'm going to complain.

Player 3 log 13 December

Spoke to the Club Secretary today. There *is* skill involved. We get two senses each, then we have a fortnight to learn to use those senses to the best effect in various virtual training environments. The arena itself will be randomly generated but in such a way that at least one of the senses we each receive will be of use to us. So we get a couple of weeks to become proficient "electro-stunner fighters" using our allotted senses ...

Well, I suppose so, but I still don't like it. And what senses? Imagine if I get smell or taste as my only viable sense, what am I supposed to do, sniff or lick my way around the arena in search of the other two players? That's stupid. I think I need to take this up with the Secretary again, see if we can do something.

Player 3 log 14 December

Secretary says I'm overreacting, that the Mind is one of the most sophisticated ever made, that for all we know the game might already have started. I asked her what the hell that was supposed to mean, but she didn't answer. Instead she assured me that it *will* be possible for each of us to win regardless of which senses we're allotted.

But how can she be certain of that? She'd need privileged information and that's strictly prohibited.

If they're going to let a Mind take sole responsibility for game design it should be one with a proven track record as a game system. Nobody knows what this Mind is capable of.

And I have to be sure.

Sam was worse today.

Player 3 log 14 December

Can't sleep. I keep thinking about the game. I'm so concerned that the Mind is messing things up. But the only way of being absolutely certain would be to have a peek inside at what it's actually up to. I could do that, I've got the skills. Risky though. I'd have to manipulate the logs and other records or my intervention would come to light.

If I could get in as Administrator I might be able to have a look, wipe my footprints and then reset Administrator Access so that nobody else can get in after me. If I did that the only way for somebody else to enter the system would be by means of a full default-reformat. Only the manufacturer can perform those and there's an added advantage, in a full default-reformat everything that's ever happened in the Mind is erased because the system is reset to absolute zero.

Hmmm. But if anything went wrong, discovery would mean more than just disqualification. I'd be expelled from the Club without references, and if that happened no other club would touch me.

No, it's too risky.

But I keep wondering – what if the game *is* faulty? All I want is a fair chance at advancement ... and to help Sam.

The sense draw is in two days. I guess I could wait and see what I get.

Player 3 log 15 December

Situation's really getting to me. Bad dreams last night. Club Secretary kept banging on my apartment door telling me to wake up. Felt so real I actually got up to check. Then just after I went back to sleep the same thing happened again, only this time it was Player 2.

Player 3 log 16 December

I got sight and taste. Sight I'm okay with, given certain preconditions it will prove useful, but *taste*? Exactly what I was afraid of. What do I do if the arena turns out to be dark? I asked the Secretary about night vision goggles, sonar enhancements etc. but we're not allowed equipment like that. This really won't do. I have to know more about what to expect or else how can I prepare? And what about the others? What did they get? Turns out we're not allowed to find that out either, at least not until the event itself. Very convenient!

There's something fundamentally flawed about this whole thing, not to mention suspicious. I mean, think about it: there are three players each getting two senses, but there are only five senses ... how does that work? Does one of us only get one sense? Or are there doubles, so that maybe both me and another gamer get taste?

Neither scenario is fair. Depending on the nature of the arena one player might get an arbitrary advantage over the other two or perhaps be at a severe disadvantage. I made this point to the Secretary of course, but she just smiled at me and shook her head.

It wasn't a nice smile.

Objections noted, she said recording my comments in the Club log. Then: *No action taken*. She actually hinted that all this uncertainty might be part of the game. I asked her how she knew that but she just gave me another nasty, crooked smile.

She seemed pretty happy after the draw, I wonder what senses she was allotted. She's won three years in a row and as Club Secretary she's the one who ordered the new Mind.

What if she's cheating?

I did it. Can't believe I had the nerve, but I actually did it – I broke into the Club Mind! It was easy too, but now I'm even more troubled, though not so much about the game itself.

I waited behind at the Club premises until everyone had gone and found all of the Administrator details on an old-time data-pass in the Secretary's room. It wasn't even bio-coded, anyone could use it! You'd think in this day and age that even a child would have more sense than that. Our Secretary might be a champion gamer, but in matters of data security she doesn't have a clue.

So I went in as Mind-Admin using her pass and even though I don't feel good about cheating, I certainly did the right thing.

I discovered three very important and disturbing facts:

1. Somebody else has definitely been in there manipulating the Mind i.e. cheating. And I think there can only be one person – the Secretary.

2. The game is NOT real world as the Secretary claimed – it's completely virtual and allows for any kind of physics-defying tools or abilities in-game. Apparently we were to be connected up under the auspices of the pre-game medical examination. One minute we'd be laid out on a bed awaiting test results, the next we'd be physically sedated and mentally connected to our in-game avatars.

3. Most shocking – the virtual stun guns have been set for deadly force! That means a hit from the in-game electro-stunner would manifest as a fatal electric shock via the linkup interface, killing the real world player instantly. In plain speak: *murder!*

I have so many questions, so many doubts. I can't believe she was planning to kill us. Why? What would she gain from it and how would she explain it away? Would she try blaming our deaths on a faulty Mind? Does winning really mean that much to her? I wonder if it could ever mean that much to me. I don't think so, not even for Sam.

I ought to contact the police, but Minds can be destroyed even without Administrator access. If she knows I'm onto her she might choose that course. Even supposing the Mind survives it will be hard to prove beyond a reasonable doubt that she is the author of the game's deadly parameters.

Going public brings other potential disadvantages with it too. If I report my findings everyone will know that I looked into the Mind; in effect that I cheated. And if the Secretary is acquitted I'll be facing expulsion and dishonor.

I'm going to sleep on it.

Player 3 log 21 December

Strange night. Lots of dreams. The Secretary was in them and Player 2. I kept waking up, but I couldn't remember anything else. One thing though, I do feel much better today. After seeing what she's been up to I guess I understand her comment about the game already having started. I've made up my mind I'm going to play her at her own game.

I'll go back into the Mind today and make a few little changes of my own.

Player 3 log 21 December

Done it and there's no way anybody will be able to find out either!

Couldn't discover what senses the other players got, the info has been wiped. Too bad, but thanks to what I've just done that doesn't matter.

Remember I said the arena was going to be randomly generated on the morning of the contest? Lies. It was already fully realized with some very specific attributes; no doubt to favor one player's senses over the others – I wonder whose? Madam Secretary perhaps?

There were twisting passageways connecting vast empty spaces, zero illumination, intense high-volume white noise, and an overwhelming odor of necrosis throughout – there's no way I could have hoped to move around and find the other two in such an environment!

If her arena design neutralizes sight, hearing and smell I wondered how she'd be able to get around in a place like that with only touch. Then I realized I was being stupid – if she's designed the arena she can pre-program any other tools and aids she needs as well and for her use only. We'd be completely helpless.

I searched high and low for such hidden tools or augmentations but didn't find any, which was a bit odd. But that doesn't mean they're not there somewhere.

So what was my solution? Well, it's pretty clever, even if I say so myself. First I reset the virtual electro-stunners to eject the player from the game *without* causing physical harm. Secondly, I redesigned the arena parameters so that they work better with my senses – primarily sight. Thirdly, if any player tries to use tools or enhancements they will automatically lose the game. And to make sure she doesn't just undo my handiwork, I've programmed the Mind not to permit *any* further changes until after the game takes place *and* changed all Administrator passwords so my instructions can't be overridden. Sorted!

Hah! I'd like to see her face when she arrives in-game and discovers what I've done. And thanks to my intervention, I *will* see it too.

It's time at last. Bit nervous, but okay.

I look in on Sam before leaving and then catch the public transport carriage that will take me to the Club House for my pre-game "medical". I'm the only passenger.

I didn't sleep well last night. Had the same dream over and over. The Club Secretary kept breaking into my room, yelling: *"Get up, get up, the game started weeks ago!"* She was in terrible shape: bruised and unkempt, eyes wild and darkly shadowed. I had to force her out each time.

Disturbing. Perhaps I should have taken something, but I didn't want to do anything to interfere with my performance today.

I suppose I was anxious about sleeping in?

Never mind. Got to focus on the game now.

My body feels sort of numb and the sounds of the transport are muted. Lack of sleep I expect. I can still taste the dental-foam I used on my teeth after breakfast. It has a really overpowering mint flavor that's making me feel ill. I think I'll change brands.

Ah, there it is, the low streamlined dome just appearing on the horizon behind the storm-dikes. We'll be at the station in less than five minutes. Feeling really drowsy, but we're nearly there ...

The transport just stopped and woke me in the process. Can't believe I actually nodded off on game day! I was dreaming too; Club Secretary again. She was clinging to the outside of the transport, hammering on the windows shouting at me like last night, only I couldn't hear what she was saying. She looked mad.

The station is deserted, most of the lights dimmed. Really strange. I thought there'd be a delegation from the Committee to meet us.

Feeling slightly surreal as I alight from the transport and move to the lifts across a platform striped in shadows. My footsteps are dead in the dark like I'm walking on thick carpet. Behind me the transport door swishes shut, motors purring into life as the single carriage slips away. Everything seems too quiet and I remember that soon I won't be able to hear, feel or smell anything.

I press the lift button hardly aware of the texture of the up-symbol beneath my index finger. The lift arrives and the doors open silently.

Inside the Club House something feels wrong. There's still nobody around. I make my way to the medical bay, my footsteps so quiet they keep fading out altogether. One moment I can just about hear them then they're silent.

I put my hand out to the ident-pad by the medical bay door. It reads my palm-print and the status light flickers green, but I don't feel the usual electro-tingle. In fact I can't feel anything. Have the game parameters already kicked in? How can they? I haven't had my "medical" yet.

On a whim I lick the tip of my index finger and wince at the near overpowering taste of salt and grime.

Taste and sight – has it started early?

The medical bay is in shadow. The only illumination comes from dimmed night lights set low in the walls. Just inside the doorway I stop and listen. I can't hear anything, like my ears have been plugged. I sniff. Can't smell anything either or hear myself inhale. I run my fingers over the surface of the wall and feel nothing.

Yes it's started.

This isn't what I programmed into the Club Mind. Has somebody else has been in there? I just don't get it, that shouldn't be possible. I should be feeling anxiety in the pit of my stomach or fear constricting my chest, but my body simply doesn't register anymore, disquiet has become a purely cerebral matter.

Suddenly the Club Secretary is there before me, her face pale and drawn. Her eyes are wide, but staring blindly ahead and she's saying something I can't hear.

I shout back, but have no idea if I'm making any sound because I can't hear myself. There's no guarantee she can hear me anyway. Then I remember the electro-stunners and glance down at my hands. They're empty.

Is she armed?!

My head snaps up. I'm expecting to see a stun pistol pointing at me, but she's gone. Vanished.

None of this makes any sense and where's Player 2? I realize I haven't actually seen him since before the game details first started to come out.

I'm having some very discomforting thoughts.

There's a bed on the far side of the medical bay. Maybe I should go and lie on it, but I really don't want to. On the other hand if I do, things might start working the way they're supposed to.

I lie down. Close my eyes. When I open them again the medical bay is gone. I'm in a bright corridor with regular lines and perfectly smooth white surfaces. Relief. This is my arena.

If I could hear there would be the constant static of white noise. If I could smell there would be the overpowering odor of necrosis. If I could feel to touch, then the floors, walls and ceilings would be as smooth and featureless as glass.

I can *see* and I can *taste*.

I glance down at my hands. In the right hand I'm clutching a pistol-formed device; my electro-stunner. Okay. Now I need to find the others, take them down and win this game.

Not feeling your body is very strange. I'm reduced to a disembodied field of vision connected to a free floating tongue. I set off, aware of motion only thanks to the visible passage of my surroundings. The taste of my own mouth is overpowering. I have to keep looking to reassure myself that my body is still there and realize that when I see the others and fire I won't know if the signal has gone from brain to hand until I see them fall.

I reach a bend in the corridor and peek around the edge. Another perfectly white corridor stretches away before me. It's empty. I proceed, glancing down every so often to make sure the electro-stunner is grasped the way I want. It is.

Another corner and another furtive peek. Somebody's there in a quilted Club jacket, hood up with their back to me. Without thinking I shoot. The darts flash into my field of vision and strike the wall to spin past the person.

Missed!

Panic seizes me – but the person doesn't react. They just continue to stand perfectly still with their back to me as if they haven't noticed. I realize that I haven't even checked to see if my weapon is single or multi-shot. Idiot!!! I might have blown my chances already! I glance at the gun. There's a magazine protruding from the underside with the words *six-charges* printed on the side. Good.

I raise the weapon again, glancing from the pistol to the target several times to make sure it is pointing where it should be. Then the person turns round. It's the Club Secretary, her sightless eyes staring straight at and through me. One of her hands is on the wall, perhaps to steady her. I suppose that means she has touch sense. Her other hand is clutching a pistol like mine but it's not even pointing in my direction.

I don't wait to find out what other sense she was given. The electro darts punch through the fabric of her jacket and she goes down, her back arching as her body is wracked with spasms.

I approach her, crouching over her prone form. She looks dead, *really* dead and I become afraid. What if my intervention hasn't worked and I've killed her? I put a hand to her throat before remembering I can't feel anything, let alone her pulse. And anyway she isn't real.

It's just an avatar, stupid!

I keep telling myself that, but I'm not fully convinced. Other doubts start to surface. Why is she even here? According to my theory she designed the arena to cripple Player 2 and myself. But if that were the case she would have needed to employ tools or augmentations resulting in her elimination.

Yet here she is, obviously unable to navigate through the arena in anything like an effective manner. In other words no enhancements.

If I'd been able to feel more than just my taste buds firing off, my mouth would no doubt have been dry. I search her body and take her pistol, the weirdness of not being able to feel disorienting me further. I have to follow my every movement visually to make sure I've done it right.

I find a piece of folded paper in one of her pockets. When I unfold it I discover that it contains a note.

22 December
Fellow Player,
If you're reading this then I am probably out, perhaps worse. Something is very wrong with this game.
Somebody interfered with the Club-Mind. I don't know who, how or even when. I can no longer gain Admin access. But I realized yesterday that I was, in some way, already in-game and now suspect that I might have been for some time. Perhaps we all have? Not sure but I've tried to warn you both. Couldn't reach either of you.
Beware and good luck.
Player 1
Club Secretary.

How long have we been in-game? My thoughts are out of control for a while. The note is dated nine days ago. I'm reminded again that the capacity for fear remains when your body is completely numb.

I sit down next to her, an electro-stunner in each hand, glancing first one way along the corridor and then the other while trying to make sense of the situation.

I got sight, so if Player 2 appears he won't be able to see me, and whichever way he approaches, I'll be ready for him. Right? But maybe not. Maybe Player 2 is behind the manipulations? Could be he has any senses he wants ... I can't be certain of anything.

How long have we been in-game?

What if we've been playing since before I went into the Mind? That might mean I didn't actually manipulate the Mind at all; I'd have been interacting with some sort of game feature *posing* as the Mind and everything since would simply be part of the game. Perhaps my weird dreams and even the Secretary's note are all just ingenious gambits?

How long?

A memory surfaces. I was drinking coffee with the Secretary. Afterwards I came over strange, almost like I blacked out for a moment, only I'm not sure I actually did. At the time I didn't know what caused it.

It happened before we were allotted our senses.

That long?

So what's the point and how do you win? When I programmed the Mind ... but it wasn't the Mind or was it?

I decide to find Player 2. It's all I've got left.

One featureless smooth white corridor follows another, all of them empty. Before long I'm weary as well as afraid. The monotony of my surroundings makes me feel worse. I've only myself to blame of course, this is my design.

Just as I'm beginning to give up hope I find him. Player 2 is sitting mid corridor with his back to me, slumped against a wall. And I just know he's dead. None of the subtle signs of animation that we take for granted are present; total stillness. Like a dummy. His pistol is beside him on the floor, blue-white sparks arcing in a wriggling line from one dart to the other.

I approach slowly, dreading what I am going to find but compelled to investigate. His shoulders are slumped, head forward on his chest, legs at an odd angle. I place a hand on his shoulder, still clutching my stun pistol. I can't feel anything of course, but there's no reaction to me. Then I grasp hold of the cloth of his Club jacket and tug gently until he falls over backwards.

His face is creamy white mottled with dark blue patches where blood has pooled beneath the skin. He's been dead hours, maybe longer.

Just an avatar, I tell myself, but the knowledge doesn't help.

There's a note pinned to the front of his jacket. I snatch it up, open it.

Hello Player 3 Are you enjoying my game?
Player 1 got Smell and Touch.
Player 2 got Touch and Hearing.
Player 3 got Sight and Taste.
But what did Player X get?

Player X? There is no Player X this year, all our members are seeded. There've been no newbies in the last 18 months ... apart from the Mind.

Newbies. Player X. *Noob* ... the Mind!

My thoughts go into freefall as new words materialize on the paper:

Player X got omniscience and a sense of foul play.
Happy gaming!
Yours,
Noob

I drop the paper and ready my pistols, glancing first ahead and then behind me.

What form will it take? It could be anywhere or anything, the very walls, maybe. The lights flicker and go out and my world becomes one of thought, fear and taste; rank and unpleasant.

Nothing left to do but wait.

Waste of Time

Alexandra Nero

"This is a waste of time," M said as we poured the buckets of timewaste from the Entertainment Center into the large wastebins out back. The truck would be here any moment to take the bins to the Drain and we still had several buckets to empty, so I hurried back.

I bent down and grabbed the handle of a rusty bucket. As I straightened my legs I felt that familiar stretch at the bottom of my back, where the syntheti-skin had hardened. I shouldn't have skipped that last service.

The handle slipped from my grip. The timewaste sloshed about in the bucket as I lost my balance and fell. I hit the ground, the bucket landing beside me with a heavy thud. Thick oily liquid swooshed into the air and cascaded down my face.

Reality flickered.

Darkness, then a series of sharp, white flashes followed by darkness. I took a deep breath.

I was a ray of white light.

I was split into a rainbow of colors.

I was a prism.

Their lost time, their memories, rushed through me. I saw small fingers held tight within large hands. I saw fits of rage being calmed. I heard arguments that flared up and were settled. I saw bruised knees and heard cries comforted by soft voices. I saw tears being wiped from sticky red cheeks. I heard muffled complaints and saw smiles that curled at the edges of mouths. I saw a bed, sheets tangled, and a chest rising and falling with the steady breaths of deep sleep. I felt warm fingers squeezing at the nape of my neck, my lips kissing a sweaty forehead.

All those moments of love. All those irreplaceable moments of life. Lost.

Once the effect wore off I opened my eyes and gasped for air, my fingers clawing the ground. The syntheti-skin was worn down to the metal bone. I tried to sit up, but my chest was tight and my head jammed with images.

M handed me a bottle of refreshener, but I couldn't grab hold of it. M bent down and held the faucet to my lips. The salty liquid ran down my throat and my muscles relaxed.

"Such a waste of time," M said. "Such a waste."

M looked toward the Entertainment Center.

"For what? There they are. Connected to the web and to each other. Casual relationships, shallow affairs. And all the while their children are in the Care Centers, herded around by the likes of us."

I closed my eyes. Waste of all kinds – paper, plastic, metal – would go through the process of being returned to raw materials in order to shape new things. Their time would not.

"You'd better be careful now," M said.

"I know."

"Almost looked like you dropped that bucket on purpose."

"I didn't," I said.

"Sure."

"I mean it."

"I'm just saying. We both know what happens if you're exposed to too much timewaste."

I pulled my legs up to my chin and turned my head. The bucket lay empty beside me. Pools of timewaste reflected the light from the Entertainment Center in shades of yellow and blue.

I know it's not good for me. I know.

But still.

Still.

The Damien Factor

Johannes Pinter

"The mind is a treacherous and dangerous place, you don't visit it if you don't know exactly what you're there for."

Dr. Kirkegaard shuts the door to the separation room while he glances through his thick glasses at the two-heads-taller Lucas who is standing next to him. With a sharp hissing sound, like vacuum pressure, the door closes tight and shuts the world out.

Lucas takes a deep breath when the room's muted atmosphere over-whelms him, and he hears Kirkegaard do the same – the difference to the corridor they just left is distinct. The room is completely silent.

Kirkegaard smiles. "I do it too, every time: take that extra breath. It's as if you need to confirm that you're alive."

Lucas looks around in the small room, his right eye squinting slightly because of a scar running through the eyebrow down the eyelid. The sepa-ration room they stand in is about two by three meters, with three meters to the ceilings, all surfaces covered with a dull, rubber-like material. The room is empty, just two simple hangers on one wall. In addition to the door they just passed through there's a similar door on the opposite wall, both are covered with the same dull rubber material as the walls. The only light source is a spotlight in the ceiling, casting flat shadows down the men's faces.

The doctor claps his hands. Lucas watches in fascination: the sharp sound stays between the doctor's hands – nothing fills the atmosphere or bounces back from the walls.

"All sounds disappear into the walls," says the doctor. He reaches out and runs his wrinkled fingers over the gray rubber wall. The fingertips leave a trail that slowly closes up again. "It consists of ridges with sound-absorbing channels between."

"Why's that?"

"So that you'll get used to it."

"To what?"

"To the atmosphere inside."

Lucas waves a finger to his temple. "Inside the ..."

"Yes."

The doctor takes his overall off and hangs it on one of the hangers. He is short and skinny when he stands in only his briefs, and his head seems somewhat too big for his body because of the bushy gray halo of hair that surrounds his half-bald head. But he seems vigorous for his sixty-nine years, which suggests that he's not only been hunched over books and test tubes his whole life.

Lucas follows the doctor's example, and soon he also stands in just his underwear. He is the old man's opposite physically: nearly two meters tall with a muscular body that doesn't have much subcutaneous fat. On the left shoulder and upper arm, and under the ribs on his left side, long pink scars from knife cuts are visible.

Kirkegaard reaches out and touches one of the scars with his fingertip. Lucas jerks when touched and takes a step back.

"Sorry," Kirkegaard says. "But you've obviously been through a lot, *and* you're standing here. I just got a little more convinced that I made the right choice."

He turns towards the inner door. "Okay, Christine," he says loudly, "you can open the next one."

With a mechanical clicking sound from three different spots in the door frame the inner door slides open.

The next room is smaller than the first. It is equally dimly lit, but with a white sterile feel. The walls, floor and ceiling are covered in a shiny material, and a number of holes are placed at different heights on the two side walls. This room also has a door opposite the first one.

"Will you close, please?" Kirkegaard asks. Lucas pulls the door shut behind him.

The doctor claps a few times. Here the sound bounces back with a normal echo.

"No sound dampening effect?" Lucas asks.

"No."

"Why not?"

Kirkegaard doesn't respond. Instead, he talks straight into the air again. "Christine. Shower! "He glances at Lucas. "Better close your eyes!"

Lucas wants to ask something, when the room turns into an inferno of spouting hot steam that hits their bodies from the holes in the walls. The shower lasts for five very long seconds. Then it stops as suddenly as it started. A couple of dull puffs of white steam residue seeps from some of the holes in the walls. The air has a slightly milky whiteness to it.

Lucas looks around in confusion while taking a few deep breaths. "Oh, g-god *damn* ..."

He looks down, and finds that his underwear is not wet at all. In fact, none of the two are the least bit moist.

"Dry, saturated steam," Kirkegaard explains, as if he read Lucas thoughts. He looks at him through glasses that don't have a shred of mist. "You've probably never been as clean as you are right now, not even as a baby."

He turns to the next door and clears his throat. "Christine, next please."

With three synchronized clicks the inner door opens.

They enter a room that is almost twice as large as the steam shower. It has the same dim lighting, gray rubberized walls and silent atmosphere as the first separation room. Lucas discovers that he no longer finds the dead silence unpleasant.

There's a bench with a rubberized top along one wall. On the opposite wall there are hangers with white clothes. Below stands two pairs of white boots – one pair bigger, one slightly smaller.

"That's yours." Kirkegaard points at one hanger while taking down the clothes from the other and sits on the bench. Lucas feels the clothes; they are very light, the fabric is thin and elastic with a nylon structure.

"Sisal," Kirkegaard says.

"Huh?"

"Sisal. A natural fiber. Where we're going it's important to use organic materials as far as possible."

Lucas sticks one foot in the trouser leg, which proves to be a panty hose. He sits down to turn the heel of the leg right.

"It will just be the two of us?"

"Yes. But in the operating room with the girl, there are more people: the mother, a police officer, a lawyer, an additional therapist and a man from the prosecutor's office. And Christine, of course, in the control room next door."

"Why all these people?"

"Whatever comes up during the session, it must be heard first-hand by all parties. A recording would not be enough. The losing party could argue that the recording was manipulated afterwards."

Lucas gets his other leg into the trousers and twists the heel right. Sees that Kirkegaard is already pulling the shirt over his head.

"We are going to look for evidence of abuse?" Lucas says.

"Something like that. A brief recap might be in order." Kirkegaard fixates the hood over his head. "The case is this: we got a five-year old girl, Anne-lise, who has been sexually abused. Her vagina has been penetrated."

"There was no DNA?"

"Not from another person, no. If there was semen or other traces of an offender, they would not have had to remit the girl to us. The medical examination shows that the penetration was made with some kind of tool. It is suspected that the girl's uncle, the mother's brother, performed the deed when he was babysitting the girl in the girl's home. But he denies it completely."

Lucas takes down his shirt from the hook. Feels the elastic fabric.

"Can anyone else have done it?"

"There's no indication that anyone else was in the house."

"Can the girl have done it to herself?"

Kirkegaard stops what he is doing and looks at Lucas. "I hope Christine didn't have the intercom on, so that the mother heard that."

Lucas looks apologetically at Kirkegaard. "Sorry. It's probably still in my blood."

Kirkegaard nods slowly. "You were a damn good cop, that's why you got the job. However, you're not here to think like a cop, but to make sure that I get in and out again in one piece."

Lucas pulls the shirt over his head. Sticks one arm in, then the other.

"Okay. I will try to remember that."

"Good." Kirkegaard puts his feet into the boots and starts to tie them on. "And to answer your question – because it's not irrelevant – the tool that penetrated Annelise's vagina was too thick. A little girl, or any normal person for that matter, would have fainted from less pain than that. It is simply highly unlikely that it could have happened in any other way than by a perpetrator. The uncle is the prime suspect, and we will find evidence of that. Ready?"

Lucas corrects the rubber hood on his head. Then presses his feet into the boots.

"Yes."

The two men look like smooth white mannequins with human faces.

"Christine," Kirkegaard says. "Open the last door."

With a heavy mechanical rattle the door swings open before them, and they walk in.

The next room is the biggest so far, about four times five meters. The same kind of dull walls and super quiet atmosphere, and it is sparsely lit by spotlights. On the opposite wall sits a perfectly round metal door. The opening behind it cannot be more than one meter in diameter, and it sits about half a meter above the floor. A week ago Lucas would have guessed that it led to a bank vault. Now he knows better.

"The PSIscanner?"

"Yes."

Lucas looks around the room. On the right wall is a one meter high metal cabinet with closed doors. On the left wall sits three black monitors, one above the other, at eye level and next to them a large keypad. Kirkegaard walks over and turns on the monitors. Then he presses a combination on the keypad. On the screens different angles of a sterile white room appear. On one a gurney is seen with a small unconscious girl whose head is resting inside a cat-scan-like apparatus – the PSIscanners other end.

"Annelise?" asks Lucas.

"Yes. And there's the mother and the others." Kirkegaard points to the next screen. There, a group of people are seated behind a white wall with a glass window through which they can see Annelise and the PSIscanner.

"There's Christine." On the third screen they see a middle-aged woman in white clothes. Christine waves to the screen. Apparently she can hear them.

"And there we are." Kirkegaard points to a small screen on the control table in front of Christine where tiny images of Kirkegaard and Lucas are seen.

"Is everyone in place?" Kirkegaard asks.

"We are waiting for the prosecutor," Christine replies. *"He'll be here in ten minutes."*

"Okay. We'll prepare."

Kirkegaard walks over and opens the wall cabinet. Lucas stands behind him and looks at the things on the cabinet shelves.

"This one's for you." Kirkegaard lifts down a two decimeter long tubular container with two claw grips and a hole at one end. "Are you right or left handed?"

Lucas holds out his right arm. The doctor places the container on the upper side of the forearm with the muzzle pointing away from Lucas and fixes it with the gripping claws. He opens a hatch at the rear end of the container and finds three small cords. At the ends of the cords are tiny needles. Kirkegaard feels with his thumb along the muscles of Lucas upper arm until he finds what he is looking for.

"This may sting a little," Kirkegaard says and runs the first needle into the arm, followed by the second and the third. Then he activates the container by flipping a switch under a protective cover. A number of red lights lit up along the tubular body and turns green one by one. Lucas feels a warm pulse spreading along his forearm toward the shoulder.

"It's a –"

"A stunslinger. I know," says Lucas. "It fires energy bursts. I control it with my nervous system. Been there, done that."

"At the riots?"

"Yes."

"This one is a little different. Weaker. Unlike your previous job you probably won't be using it."

"Okay."

"This produces energy bursts ranging up to about four hundred volts. The same strength as in electric shocks. We just want to numb temporarily, not eliminate. This, on the other hand ..."

Kirkegaard takes down a bag and opens the lid. There are three compartments, each one containing something that looks like small spotlights with feet. Lucas takes one up, finding that it's unusually heavy for its size.

"The batteries are extremely compact," says Kirkegaard. "Lasts one hundred years. And they are more powerful than your stunslinger: six hundred volts. If we have to eliminate something in there we just place these around it and heat them up."

Lucas nods.

"They will last 'til the girl turns a hundred?"

"Exactly. Then we have these little lighthouses." Kirkegaard picks up a lamp the size of a hockey puck. "They are placed at the starting point. So that we find our way back."

Kirkegaard straps the bag to his back and fixates it with a second strap across the chest. Then he takes down two small wireless intercom transmitters. Puts one behind his ear and pulls out a cord that he squeezes into the ear canal. He hands over the other to Lucas.

"Let's test them. Christine ..."

"Loud and clear." Christine's voice sounds in the ears of the two men. *"Lucas?"*

"One two, one two ..."

"Thank you."

Kirkegaard walks over to the monitors. Looks at the one with the gathered people.

"Has the prosecutor arrived yet?"

"Five more minutes," replies Christine. *"You'll have to be patient. And, eh – doctor ..."*

"Yes?"

"Have you told him about the Damien factor?"

Lucas looks from the screen over at Kirkegaard. "The Damien factor?" Kirkegaard does not meet his gaze.

"Apparently not," says Christine.

"I want to stick to the facts at this point," the doctor replies shortly.

"I think you should tell him anyway."

"In due time. Now, please check if the prosecutor has arrived. Get back to me when we shall proceed."

"Will do." Christine turns her microphone off. On the screen they see her reach for the telephone.

Lucas lets his gaze drift to the monitor with the unconscious Annelise. She looks so small where she is lying under the thin sheet, halfway into the huge PSIscanner. Now he notices that the front part of her head is shaved, and a number of wires are connected to different points on her forehead.

"How's the loneliness?" asks Kirkegaard.

Lucas jerks. "Loneliness?"

"Are you lonely?"

Lucas gives the doctor a questioning look. "I'm afraid I don't understand the question."

Kirkegaard looks at Lucas; behind the coke-bottle glasses his eyes contain something that Lucas cannot place.

"I'm asking because we are about to enter something that can be a bit stressful ..." Kirkegaard explains. "Not everyone is able to literally be inside another person's psyche. The *host mind* becomes, for obvious reasons, extremely dominant: it permeates the place because it *is* the place. The *guest mind*, the one that is temporarily present within it, may experience the stay as overwhelming in a negative way – almost abusive – if it has an aptitude for weaknesses. Like loneliness. The loneliness becomes unbearable."

The loneliness becomes unbearable.

Lucas looks at little Annelise in the big machine. Unconscious, victim of a horrible crime.

There will always be evil acts – those exposed to them, those who perform them, and they who fight against them. Lucas has always seen himself as the latter. That was why he became a cop in the first place. But to enforce the law and to obey the law doesn't always go hand in hand, as Lucas slowly came to realize during his twelve years in the force.

The breaking point came at the election in 2026, when Ossian Hammarskjöld became prime minister. His reforms meant less funding for police and judiciary, and that killed the spirit in the force a little and, with it, the moral compass of many of Lucas's colleagues broke. Instead of living by the law they had sworn to follow, more and more colleagues fell into the criminals' behavior. The general attitude became: if we can't have the resources to defeat them with our methods, we'll crack them with theirs. As Lucas saw more and more colleagues and friends turn into criminals he made a choice: I let them go on, as long as I don't have to behave in the same way myself. He refused to be corrupted.

But one day – he should have realized that it would come sooner or later – he found himself standing at the crossroads.

It started when his colleagues got wind of a major drug deal: a courier would switch a bag of money for fifteen kilos of pure cocaine. The location was a parking garage in downtown Stockholm. The money courier and two men arrived with the drugs. When both the drugs and money were in sight Lucas's colleagues advanced and took the criminals out with their stunslingers. So far everything had gone according to plan.

Then things took an unexpected turn. Lucas's colleagues had made up an alternative plan without Lucas's knowledge: they simply left the criminals behind in the garage, taking the money and drugs for themselves. With all that Lucas had seen in the force, it was something he could live with, as long as he didn't have to take his share of the haul.

Then things got really crazy. One of the drug dealers, a burly, one hundred and fifty kilos Romanian, had not been knocked out by the stunslinger burst. When his disoriented mind realized that the bastard cops were taking all the goods he pulled his automatic weapon and started shooting. That's something that cops are always prepared for, business as usual. Lucas's colleagues dived for shelter, weapons drawn, returning fire the second the first burst echoed in the garage.

The mother with her three daughters in tow, however, did not. Appearing out of nowhere they were caught in the crossfire on their way to their car. Two of the girls died instantly, the third passed away later at the hospital. The mother miraculously survived without being hit by a single bullet.

Lucas's moral crossroad appeared as a result of this event, in the court of law. Was the death of the three children caused when the criminals opened fire on the police officers that where there to stop criminal business? Or did they die as a result of criminals opening fire on the thieving police?

Lucas had to choose between loyalty and morale. Become a dirty cop, or remain clean. He chose the latter.

From that moment on his existence in the station was a total vacuum. No one spoke to him, no one wanted to work with him, nobody saw to his interests. He was relegated to internal services where he sat in a room all by himself, pushing papers that meant nothing to nobody.

The loneliness eventually became unbearable. So he quit.

He stares silently at the monitor with little Annelise, weighing his words. Then he glances at Kirkegaard. "I have no wife, if that's what you mean."

Kirkegaard smiles. "You be grateful. I have one, and it's a never-ending nagging. I often say that I wouldn't have been so successful at what I do if I didn't have a wife – I've been here to avoid being at home."

Lucas smiles.

"Doctor." Christine's voice sounds from the speaker.

"Yes?"

"The prosecutor is here now."

"Thank you, Christine! Then we can proceed."

Kirkegaard walks up to the PSIscanners' round metal gate. Picks up two pairs of thin glasses with yellow plastic lenses and hands one to Lucas.

"Ready?"

Lucas puts on the glasses. They follow the shape of his head smoothly and make the room around him appear yellow.

"I think so."

"Good." Kirkegaard gives the surveillance camera a thumbs up.

A set of magnetic locks around the PSIscanner port unlocks with a muffled bang that makes the floor vibrate. The round door extends an inch, then smoothly swings open on well-oiled hinges.

The two men stare into a magnificent luminous *nothing*.

"Well then." Kirkegaard crouches and enters the round opening. Lucas closes his eyes for a few seconds before he follows.

First it's just a gray-white haze without reference points around them. Not even the ground is visible (or is it a floor? Lucas doesn't know, it feels solid but sags slightly). Around their feet a mist seems to transpire right out of the ground, creating a milky atmosphere.

Kirkegaard walks a few steps in front of Lucas and gets a lamp out of the bag. He puts it down in front of him and stomps on it. Immediately a bright light illuminates the area with periodic flashes.

The place is completely free of odors. The faint haze feels slightly oil-smooth on the palate but has no flavor.

It takes about a minute, and then the first apparitions appear. Literally appear, straight out of nowhere; from being invisible they suddenly fade into view, take shape right in front of their eyes. Adults, children and occasionally animals appear for a shorter or longer moment before they fade back into nothing. The visible apparitions roam aimlessly by themselves, never together, and they don't seem to notice the two men or each other. Even in their most solid state they are still slightly transparent and shine with a subdued glow in different colors, as if they had lanterns inside their chests.

Kirkegaard comes up to Lucas and talks in a low voice. "You know where we are, huh?"

"In Annelise's pre-conscious."

"Exactly. The people we see are Annelise's conscious – the people that the girl is actively thinking about. They fade away when she stops thinking about them."

"And the lights inside them?"

"The warmer the light, the warmer feelings Annelise has for that person."

Lucas recognizes one of them: Annelise's mother. She looks just like she did when she sat in the visiting part of the operating room. But her expression is calmer here, it doesn't reflect the concerns she clearly felt in the real world. She is faintly transparent, and her figure is lit from inside with a warm golden tone.

"That's the memory of her mother, right?"

"Yes and no. In a way, you could call it a cache memory, but it is correct to say that she is a part of the girls conscious. The warm color indicates that the girl has great love for her mother."

The mother fades away.

Lucas looks around at the glowing apparitions. It is like strolling around in a big, misty square on a summer day and to see other people appear and disappear in the fog. Everything is very harmonic and tranquil and doesn't at all reflect the traumatic state the girl must be in.

"Where are we going?" asks Lucas.

"To find a door."

"The door that leads to the girl's sub-conscious?"

"Exactly. Come on."

They cruise between fading apparitions. Lucas wonders what would happen if he touched any of them.

Then Kirkegaard stops. "That's strange."

In front of them is the shining ghost figure of a man. The light he spreads is warmly yellow – obviously love.

"Someone she likes?" asks Lucas.

Kirkegaard picks out a photography of his overall pocket. "Look here." he says.

Lucas sees that the man in the photo and the ghost figure is the same.

"Who is it?"

"Her uncle. The man accused of abusing her. He shouldn't be seen out here in her conscious. And certainly not have such a loving aura."

Lucas and Kirkegaard look at the figure passing right in front of them.

"Could she have two different impression of him?" Lucas asks. "A good one seen out here and a hidden bad one?"

Kirkegaard considers this. "I've never heard of it. However, the brain is an inscrutable place. We might have discovered something unknown."

Lucas looks at the doctor. "Maybe you'll be giving name to a new theory?"

"Maybe. It happens from time to time."

They watch Annelise's uncle till he fades away and is gone. Then they start walking. Lucas looks around. Thinks he sees outlines in the mist that he did not discern before; his perception has increased. Maybe he has a future in this profession. He just has to do this first job as well as he can, then the rest will follow.

"Hey, Kirkegaard," he says. "What was that thing Christine mentioned earlier? Some factor?"

Kirkegaard glances at him. "You mean the Damien Factor?"

"That's the one."

Kirkegaard is silent for a while.

"It was nothing really," he says. "A work accident."

"Were you involved?"

"No." Kirkegaard shakes his head. "It was seven years ago. Happened to a colleague of mine. *Former* colleague. PSIscanning had only been in practice for a couple of years. It was before they found out that there has to be two people doing a scan."

Kirkegaard stops and stares into the mist for a moment, then shakes his head. Lucas watches the glowing figures around them. No one sees them – it's as if the two men are invisible. They continue walking.

"A boy had been referred to the clinic," says Kirkegaard. "I don't remember his condition. Like Annelise he was unconscious when he came in. A PSIchologist, my colleague, got the assignment to him. That's all anyone knows – as the man went in by himself, the information about what happened next is limited and not very reliable."

The doctor falls silent. He looks around, beyond the apparitions, searching for the target door.

"What happened?" Lucas finally asks.

"Huh? Yes. Somewhere inside the labyrinth of the boy's mind, the PSIchologist encountered something."

"Something what?"

"Evil. Something purely evil. A primordial evil force, lying in wait deep in the darkest recesses of the mind. Or that's what they say. It attacked the PSIchologist. What it was, or how the man managed to find his way back, we don't know – he slit his own throat the moment he stepped out of the PSIscanner. The boy never woke up, and we never got to know what his trauma was."

Lucas absentmindedly watches the few apparitions in the mist around him. They shine with a colder blue light. "The boy's name was Damien?" he asks.

Kirkegaard nods grimly. "As I said: no one knows for certain. The doctor may as well have been an unstable person who snapped. You know, I wouldn't have told you if Christine hadn't brought it up. What we are doing here is science. Fairytales have no place here."

Lucas is about to say something when suddenly a large dog materializes in front of them. It looks around with jerky movements and barks with drooling mouth and sharp teeth. The barks come rolling from the deep of the dog's throat in hard blasts, but not like the echoing thunder claps of the police dogs Lucas are used to from work – no, they figuratively fall to the ground like stones. Lucas understands why they have made the PSIscanner rooms so sound proof – the sound dampening atmosphere here is very unpleasant. Lucas backs off a few steps, but Kirkegaard remains.

"It can't harm us," he says. "Dogs are often found in people's sub-conscious as untreated phobias. But Annelise does not seem to have any traumatic experience of this animal, as it's here inside her conscious."

"It must've been a terrible experience for a small child to meet a monster like that!"

"She probably met it in a controlled situation. But I do believe we are close to our goal. Scary parts of the conscious usually dwell near the door to the sub-conscious."

They stop and shade their eyes with their hands.

Lucas sees it first. The door. It is colorless and does not consist of anything but a rectangle. But in the undefined shape of the mist its lines and corners are as clear as lines drawn in the sand of an untouched beach.

They approach the door. Lucas tries to get his fingertips into one of the joints, when Kirkegaard stops him.

"Lucas. Before we go any further: we know nothing about what we will face in there. We might see terrible images. But you must remember that nothing we meet will be able to harm us."

"Okay."

The doctor's voice has a slight tremor. It could be fear, if it wasn't for his gaze being so clear, almost enthusiastic.

"We will be entering little Annelise's sub-conscious and work our way through a labyrinth that has no map, since all sub-conscious content is unique. We'll find the answers to her trauma. Once we've done that we will immediately turn and go back. The place may seem scary, but it cannot hurt us because we will not see our own images, but Annelise's. Do you understand?"

Lucas nods, then gets his fingertips into a crevice and pulls the door open.

Annelise's sub-conscious is a dark and immense place. Labyrinths usually are.

Kirkegaard and Lucas stand like two crouching white mannequins in a passageway that's about a meter wide and which disappears in both directions with slight curves and no ends. There's no ceiling above them; the walls disappear into a vast darkness that Lucas finds almost physical. If he reached up, maybe he would feel it against his skin.

Kirkegaard produces a new lamp that he puts on the ground and stomps on. It immediately begins to pulse with the same brief flashes as the one at the starting point of the pre-conscious. Lucas looks around.

"Which way?"

"The sub-conscious is shaped like a Trojaborg labyrinth," says Kirke-gaard. "There are no crossroads, it just winds around itself in coils that first gets wider and then narrower and narrower the closer it gets to the center." He looks both ways while he adjusts the bag on his back. Then he starts walking to the right. "Stay close behind me."

"Okay."

"And keep that ready." He nods at the stunslinger at Lucas's arm.

Lucas estimates that they have walked for almost fifteen minutes when Kir-kegaard signals for a halt.

The passage they are standing in looks very similar to the place where they started from, except that it curves in another direction. It is claustrophobic and bleak and colorless, and there's no smell or flavor to the air.

"Something's fishy," says the doctor, absentmindedly rubbing his lips. "We have not come across a single repression."

"Repression?"

"A buried image. We have not seen anything that Annelise has displaced to her sub-conscious."

"Should we have?"

"Yes. The girl is unconscious, that means that the activity in here is significantly lower than when she is awake. It was noticeable in the pre-conscious too. But like there, we should at least have encountered *something*."

Lucas nods. Pondering the basic psychology he learned at the police academy, the sub-conscious should be quite populated. He doesn't know *how* populated, but everybody has their fair share of things they don't want or have the strength to remember.

Kirkegaard leads the way deeper into the labyrinth. From walking through passages with large, subtle curves, the labyrinth now makes sharper bends and more abrupt curves that constantly turn left and right.

"We are approaching the center," Kirkegaard states. "The coils are more extreme, and it's getting darker."

The light is indeed more sparse in the deeper domains of the sub-conscious. They don't see further than a few meters forward or backward, and the darkness makes them instinctively stick closer together than before. The atmosphere is taxing for both the mind and psyche. Lucas understands Kirkegaard's reference to the unbearable loneliness: he didn't feel it before, but now it's like a black balloon has inflated in his chest – or more like an inverted balloon, full of echoing emptiness. And the lack of sound: their steps are silent, and the sound of Kirkegaard's breathing fades away before it reaches Lucas's ears. He cannot hear his own heartbeat or blood flow inside the head, like he usually would in such oppressive silence. It's as if he no longer exists, except for the empty shell of his body that mechanically moves forward.

"Lucas. Look!"

Beyond the next curve, the darkness seems dispelled by a faint light, but they cannot detect its source.

"You want me to go first?" Lucas asks.

Kirkegaard holds him back. "No. I'll go first. We don't know what it is."

They take the curve slowly, one hesitant step at a time. Then they see it: a small body of water, or rather a puddle, on the labyrinth floor. Stretching from wall to wall, about a meter wide. The puddle shines. Or it seems to shine *from out* of it, emitting the light.

"What is that?" Lucas asks.

"Don't know. Looks like water. A repression anyhow. Do you see what's wrong with it?"

Lucas shakes his head.

"It doesn't reflect the wall behind. The only thing we see is what's inside the puddle."

"Could it be a hole?"

"Maybe. But a hole that leads to where?"

To that Lucas has no answer.

When they are two meters from the puddle they note that it is completely symmetrical, with a perfect oval shape.

And it has a pink frame.

Lucas has witnessed horrible things in his life, but never anything that filled him with such a terrifying emptiness.

A feeling overwhelms him. An ice-cold pulsing helplessness as if his soul released all moorings and floated into space with no way back home. Lucas just wants to turn and run. Run as fast as he can, climb out of the labyrinth, and then keep running past all the glowing apparitions toward the flashing light and the exit of Annelise's psyche. But he cannot do that. He needs the job. And he's never been a quitter, one who leaves the ship when it gets windy. He's always stood up for what's right. Never let his soul become corrupt. It's all about keeping it steady. Not run. Keep steady.

It's like Kirkegaard feels Lucas's doubts because he turns and takes Lucas's hand and squeezes it hard. It makes Lucas stay.

They go closer to the puddle, hand in hand. Closer. Until they are so close that they can see that it's not a puddle.

It's the surface of a mirror. The leaking light comes from a lamp that is not in the labyrinth but only exists on the other side of the mirror's surface. They glimpse a pink wall with painted white clouds. On the wall a coat hanger with small clothes in white and pink, probably belonging to a girl.

"It looks like the wall of a nursery," Kirkegaard says and wipes his fingers over his glasses to rub out a stain.

"Why a mirror image of a nursery?" asks Lucas.

"It's the image of a repressed memory. Annelise must have looked in a mirror. And because the mirror image is here, in her sub-conscious, it must contain something that she for some reason repressed."

"But what is it?"

"Can't see. Must get closer."

Kirkegaard takes another step. Lucas follows.

If only there was any sound or smell or anything that could dilute the impressions he now takes in. But there is nothing besides the visuals. Lucas gets closer, and now he sees human skin. And that the skin is a person's leg. The scary stuff Lucas has seen before has always been accompanied by sirens and dogs barking and people screaming.

Here is only cold, dark, oppressive silence, like in the deepest trench of the ocean.

What Kirkegaard and Lucas see in the mirror – what Annelise also must have seen, as everything in her sub-conscious is based on her own visual stimuli – is the image of five-year old Annelise's exposed genitalia.

The two men see Annelise's small hands appear in the mirror, holding a wine bottle.

They see how Annelise places the bottle neck at the opening of her vagina, and then how her hands, with a sudden thrust, forces the bottle inside, stretching and tearing the sensitive tissue. When the two men understand what they see, they turn away in panic and disgust, unable to stand the sight of it.

They stand facing away, refusing to look each other in the eyes, too ashamed for watching the self-harming act for as long as they did.

"God damn it!" Lucas mutters, eyes tightly shut. "What kind of sick shit *is* this?"

"One cannot turn away from the horror. You have to face it with open eyes to fight it. But this ..." Kirkegaard shakes his head weakly.

"So she did do it to herself?"

"The sub-conscious doesn't lie," says Kirkegaard. "Now we know: her uncle was telling the truth, he is innocent. And I now understand why we have not seen other repressed images in here; this horrible repression has wiped out all other images."

Lucas gestures towards the mirror without looking at it.

"But how is that possible? You said she couldn't have made it without fainting from pain."

Kirkegaard straightens up with a thoughtful look, still turned away. "Her hand obviously did it. But was it her own will? Or could it have been something else that compelled her?"

Lucas looks at the old doctor. "Something else? What could have made a little girl to do such a thing to herself?"

"Another will. Another conscious. Something inside her that manipulated her like a puppet."

"But why?"

Kirkegaard looks at Lucas. "That, my friend, I do not know yet. But, if we continue further into the labyrinth, we are likely to find the answer."

They get past the mirror without looking into it. A narrow curve later, the light from inside the mirror is dampened, and after the next curve the place is as dark as before. Or even darker – their eyes miss the light from the mirror, even though they wish that they could forget its contents.

"Can't we use a flashlight?" asks Lucas. He keeps one hand on Kirkegaard's shoulder to keep up with him in the massive darkness.

"No. One should not risk illuminating particular things in the subconscious. It can lead to severe consequences for the host mind. I'll tell you about it later when we ..." Kirkegaard stops so abruptly that Lucas bumps into his back. For a few seconds Kirkegaard says nothing.

"What is it?" Lucas finally whispers, unwilling to break the compact silence around them.

"I don't know."

Lucas peers into the darkness. He can see the walls to the right and left of them disappear into the darkness in sharp turns. After the mirror, he is prepared for anything. But at the same time he wants Kirkegaard to say that there is nothing in the dark. That they have completed their mission. They got their answer. They know that the uncle didn't do it. They can both testify to that. Surely, it ought to be enough to call this mission a success?

Then he feels it too. What Kirkegaard must have reacted to.

Not seeing, as everything is dark.

Not hearing, as everything is silent.

Not tasting or smelling, as this damned place lacks all characteristics.

Feeling. A presence of something just ahead of them.

Kirkegaard takes a step back so that he comes close to Lucas.

"The id ..." he whispers.

Lucas leans close to the doctor's ear. "Have we reached the center?"

Kirkegaard gives a small nod. Then he starts walking, slowly, one tiny step at a time, into the dark.

Lucas hesitates. It's not funny anymore. When they get out of here he'll resign. There are other jobs, this is not worth it. He's been afraid before. At the force, there were times he feared for his life. But that feeling was not nearly as draining as what he feels right now. There's a vacuum within him that sucks all the strength out of him. Could this be the loneliness that Kirkegaard talked about? Was this how he felt, the one who went insane, just before all the fuses blew in his head?

"Lucas!" Kirkegaard hisses in front of him.

Lucas takes a few steps and catches up with the doctor. "Yes?"

"Do you see that?"

Up front, just past the last curve, something's approaching. Lucas stares into the darkness. There is no light, yet he sees it clearly. And he can't believe his eyes.

Kirkegaard takes a deep breath. *"Oh my God,"* he says in a voice full of fear, backing until he bumps into Lucas. "What do you see, Lucas? *What do you see?"*

Lucas shakes his head. It's not possible. But still, here he is, in the depth of little Annelise's sub-conscious.

"Father?" he whispers to the figure standing in the center of the labyrinth.

"You see your *father*?" Kirkegaard asks.

Lucas barely has enough strength to nod. It's his father, alright. He would recognize those hate-filled eyes and the big-knuckled ham hands anywhere. Father wears the same shirt and oil-stained jeans that he wore the last time Lucas saw him. The draining black hole inside grows even more, and now Lucas feels what he has not felt since he was five years old. When his father was still alive. Before someone up there finally heard Lucas's prayers and saw to it that his father got a knife between his ribs, in the alley behind the bar where he always hung out during his periods.

"How is it possible?" he whispers. "How can he be here?"

Kirkegaard shakes his head. *"Damn it!* It tricked us."

"What?"

Kirkegaard begins to walk backwards through the labyrinth. *"Run!* We might be able to escape before it –"

"What *is* it?" Lucas follows, but he keeps his eyes glued to his father. He never took his eyes off him then, and he wouldn't think of doing it now either. The chance to avoid the worst blows were better if he saw them coming.

Kirkegaard moves backwards through the passage as he thinks out loud. "It made the girl hurt herself to draw someone in," he says. "It needs a way out."

"Does my dad need a ..."

"No! You don't understand! *I* don't see your father."

"But he's right there in front of ..."

"*No*, I see something completely different. It appears as each person's worst fear."

Lucas wants to say something. But his father is closer now, just a few meters away, big hands reaching for him. Lucas knows what to expect if he gets hold of him: a couple of slaps won't do it this time, not by a long shot.

Kirkegaard groans. Lucas senses the old man's fear.

"Now I understand why he cut his throat." Kirkegaard whispers, then raises his voice. "Lucas, if you get out, promise to do what you can to stop it. It must not ..."

The old man's voice turns into a scream of terror when whatever he sees knocks him to the ground. For a moment Lucas thinks that he should use the stunslinger; he should help Kirkegaard, that's why he's here. Then his father's upon him, and he is petrified with fear. The big hands grab the front of his overall and throw him to the labyrinth floor. Lucas wants to scream and pray as he did when he was a little boy. But he knows that it is useless. Evil does not listen to prayers.

It never listens to prayers.

The small speaker above Christine's desk gives a metallic chime. Kirkegaard and that new big guy, Lucas, probably stand outside the gate and want to get in. Christine adjusts a blonde curl behind her ear and activates her intercom device.

"Doctor?" she asks.

First there's no answer, only silence. Almost like that dead silence that Christine could never endure if her life depended on it. She's been in one of those separation rooms just to test it – it was enough to know that she does not want to work as a PSIchologist. The small desk in the tiny secretarial room next to the operating room with the PSIscanner is a perfectly fine world for her.

"Doctor?" she asks again. "You coming in?"

"He cannot talk." She hears a voice that is not the doctor.

"Is that you, Lucas?"

"Yes. Could you please open the door, Christine?"

Christine smiles. The doctor is exhausted. Of course. It's amazing that he can continue doing what he does at his age.

"Certainly." She presses a button. On one of the small screens from the entrance room, she can see how the PSIscanner's round door slowly opens.

On another monitor, she sees that Annelise is still asleep in the operating room. A nurse stands next to her sleeping form, checking the girl's values on the PSIscanners side panel. But there seems to be something wrong – the nurse leaves the panel and returns with a stethoscope.

In the entrance room she sees the big guy, Lucas, come crawling out of the machine. But he seems to be alone.

"Lucas, where is Kirkegaard?" she asks in the intercom.

The big guy doesn't respond. He just stands up, staring into the camera, straight at Christine. And smiles. A strong feeling of discomfort spreads in Christine. She senses a presence, as if the guy was inside the room with her.

And there's something with his eyes.

On the second monitor, she sees that the nurse has dropped the stethoscope and is backing away from the sleeping girl. She *is* asleep, isn't she?

Christine looks at the monitor of the entrance room. Sees how the big guy takes a couple of steps toward the camera *(what is it with his eyes?)* and raises a hand. The next moment the reception is cut off, and the screen is filled with static. And not only that – all five screens in front of her suddenly display static.

The lights in the room go out. For a moment it's pitch black, then the red emergency lights turn on. *What is going on?*

Christine presses the intercom button, but all she hears is dead silence. When it's clear that she no longer has contact with the outside world she pushes back the chair and gets up. She looks around the room that is drenched in blood red light and on the static monitors. She wants to get out of here now, find someone who can tell her what the hell is going on.

A couple of muffled thumps followed by a low rumble is heard on the other side of the wall. From the entrance room. Where the big guy is. It sounds as if something breaks, and not just random things. *Everything*. The walls vibrate from it.

It's like the whole world is about to crumble and fall.

Wishmaster

Andrea Grave-Müller

Marcus was on his way to work, rush hour speed, when he spotted the goblin clinging to the back of a garbage truck in front of him.

Nothing unusual so far.

The goblin climbed up and down the back of the garbage truck, scrawny and greenish, wearing a tattered dress that once might have been pink. It looked to the left and to the right, over the solemn parade of cars slowly working its way along the road. It looked through the front window of Marcus's car and right at him with eyes that were big, red and frightened.

For a moment they stared at each other, man and goblin. Then the goblin dropped from the truck and was gone.

Marcus tried to catch a glimpse of it. A fear that it might have been hurt made him stir uncomfortably in his seat, but the goblin had disappeared without a trace, and he couldn't very well stop and get out of the car in the middle of the hour traffic.

He didn't tell anyone at work about it, even though it was never far away from his thoughts during the day. It even made him think a little less about *her* than usual.

That night, after another uninspiring dinner consisting of pasta, meatballs and ketchup, Marcus decided to take a walk.

He had always been quite a slender man. In his younger days, days he with horror realized were about twenty years past, sports and exercise had kept his belly flat and shoulders broad, but married life and a full-time job had put an end to most physical activity. Recently he had discovered that the past years had not only given him some quite flattering wrinkles around the eyes, but also a slight roundness around the belly. Maybe it was some sort of post-divorce vanity, but he wanted to get rid of this annoyance. He admitted to himself that his vanity also might be caused by the fact that he had a chance to run into *her* about once or twice a week. Not that *she* would ever be interested in him, she was way out of his league, but still – he told himself that it didn't hurt to look as good as possible.

If only it wasn't so hard to find new, healthy habits! Less junk food, more jogging, and a trip to the gym at least a couple of times a week, how hard could it be? A walk this fine spring evening was a good enough start, Marcus told himself as he put on comfortable shoes, a fleece sweater and pulled a knitted cap over his blond hair.

He hurried down the stairs from his apartment, stepped out the front door and nearly tripped over a scrawny creature with red dreadlocks and a dirty pink dress.

"Oh God!" Marcus exclaimed as he jumped back and slammed his elbow into the front door. The goblin was just as startled. It squeaked and hurried away a few meters. When it stopped, turned and scowled at him, he recognized it from the garbage truck.

"Don't *do* that!" it said in a high-pitched voice, a girl's voice.

Of course the goblin was a girl, Marcus thought. The dress and long dreadlocks were hints, but for a human, a goblin's gender wasn't always easy to determine.

"You were right outside my door," he said, rubbing his elbow. "I had no chance."

The goblin snorted. She certainly didn't look afraid now. She put her hands on her narrow hips, still scowling.

"Why were you staring at me this morning?" she said.

"Was I staring? Sorry," Marcus started, but then he became a bit annoyed. Who was this goblin to question him? "You were clinging to the back of a garbage truck, I was sitting in my car right behind you, where was I supposed to look? You were right in front of me."

"Oh," she said. "I thought you recognized me. I was worried ... oh, never mind."

"Recognized you? Sorry, should I?"

"Well, you know, you might have seen me at work. There's usually not many people left when I come in to clean, you're one of the few who always work late it seems. You're one of the IT guys, aren't you?"

Marcus knew the cleaners at the company were goblins, but he had never paid much attention to them. They just were there, doing their job in the evenings, looking pretty much the same. This one should have stood out, with those long, fiery dreads, but he couldn't recall her either.

"Oh, yes, now I recognize you," he lied. "Sorry. You know, sometimes, when you see someone you don't really know someplace where you don't expect them to be ..."

She hugged her own arms and peered at him, and Marcus realized that this goblin was very young, maybe still a child. He thought about the fear he had seen in her eyes this morning.

"You were afraid of something, weren't you?" he said in a softer voice.

She nodded.

"I think ..." she started, then fell silent for a few moments before starting again. "I think I might need help. Maybe you can help me? If you want to?"

Marcus hesitated. Help with *what*? a suspicious voice said inside him. Don't meddle in the affairs of goblin, it added. He opened his mouth to tell the goblin to go away and hide somewhere else.

"Sure," he heard himself say.

What?! the voice inside him exclaimed. *No!* Wrong answer!

"Great!" the goblin said, grinning with sharp teeth. "My name's Ella. What's yours?"

So much for taking a walk, Marcus thought about ten minutes later. Ella sat in his kitchen, eating his chips and drinking his Coke. She had kicked off her sneakers in the hallway and was now resting her big, greenish feet on his kitchen table, as if she owned the place.

Well, Marcus thought, goblins weren't exactly known for their fine manners, were they? They were called garbage-eaters and sewer-dwellers, known as thieves and fences, always ready to do the dirty work for the humans, if you paid their price.

If you didn't pay their price, everyone knew you would likely end up with their pointed teeth in your throat.

"So," Marcus said to the goblin, "what can I help you with?"

Ella swallowed the last of the Coke and threw the can into the kitchen sink with careless accuracy.

"I found something," she said. "And now I need to hide."

"So you want me to hide you? Here? In my apartment?" The idea didn't sound very appealing.

"Well ..." Ella tilted her head slightly from side to side while she seemed to study Marcus's kitchen lamp very carefully. "Not exactly. I mean, come on. You're human. You know basically nothing about hiding."

Her eyes met Marcus's. They are really red, he thought. Not bloodshot, but a pure, deep red.

"So what is it you want?" he asked.

"That thing I found – I need it to be returned to, uhm, to the rightful owner."

"Oh."

"And that's where you come in," Ella went on. "If you'll help me."

"So you want me to get this thing you, ehum, 'found', and give it back to its owner? Is that it? That doesn't sound too hard."

The moment he said it, he knew he was wrong.

"Well …" Ella said again, this time inspecting her dirty fingernails. "It's not really that simple."

The woman with steel colored hair brushed something from the sleeve of her likewise steel colored suit.

"You should do something about that leaking roof," she said. "There's a puddle on the floor."

Her remark made the other woman snort.

"Not your problem." Her voice was deeper and hoarser than most human women's. Her face was half hidden behind tangled black hair. Only one eye was visible, and it stared the human woman down. "Who are you to have opinions, by the way? I thought you were here to do business, not complain about my home."

"Indeed." The woman in the suit crossed her arms, but she didn't quite manage to look comfortable. Maybe the rat sniffing around her designer ankle boots had something to do with that. It was the biggest rat she had ever seen, and the way it looked at her made her shudder. Rats might be clever animals, but this one looked far too intelligent.

"So." The goblin woman sat down in what once must have been quite an expensive armchair. She tossed some of her hair away from her face, which made her look even more hideous, with a complexion in desperate need of some skin care. "You said you needed help finding something, eh? I suppose it's something you don't want everyone to know about, then, since you're here. We can do the job – as long as you pay the price."

"Yes, I'm aware of that," the human woman said in a dry voice. "I'm willing to discuss the price. Then I can give you the details."

"Oh no," the goblin chuckled. "The other way around. First you give me the details. Then I'll give you a price. I need to know what I'm dealing with, see. Come here, sweetie."

The last was directed to the rat. It scurried over to her and climbed into her lap. She scratched its chin while she continued:

"Is it illegal? Could my people get hurt? Do they need to hurt someone? Even kill? Are you the only one seeking this thing, or do we have competitors? What expenses are involved? I can't give you a price without knowing what I'm selling."

"All you need to do is to find a little girl," the human woman said. "A tiny, harmless little girl who happens to have in her possession an item that belongs to me. Find the girl, scare her a little, get the item back and deliver it to me. Discreetly, of course. A piece of cake."

"And the girl doesn't have angry parents or any other protectors? Or just happens to be the daughter of the police chief? That item we're talking about, it won't explode if it's touched the wrong way? What are you not telling me?"

"The girl's a goblin. That's the prime reason I'm here and not at the police station. You might even know her. Her name is Ella."

The goblin woman raised an eyebrow but shook her head.

"Nope, doesn't ring any bells. And the item?"

"A wrist-watch. A very, *very* expensive wrist-watch. This Ella girl stole it while cleaning my office."

"I see." The goblin woman nodded. "Well, you're right. It doesn't sound too complicated. I think we should be able to agree on a price."

About five minutes later, the human woman in the gray suit did her best to avoid getting sewer nastiness on her Jimmy Choos while making her way back to daylight and fresh air. Back in her sewer home, the goblin woman patted her rat on the head.

"Now be a good boy and hurry off to find Ella. Grandma needs to see her."

Friday morning. A bittersweet day for Marcus.

Sweet, because another workweek was over and the weekend shimmered within sight, full of promises of mornings without the alarm bell and time to do whatever he wanted (at least, that was what he told himself).

Bitter, because it meant two days without any chance of seeing *her*. Two days without knowing how *she* spent her weekend. Probably hanging out with her cool girlfriends and handsome boyfriend. He knew about the boyfriend, at least he assumed that the guy who picked her up after work every now and then was her boyfriend. Technically, he could of course be her brother or just a friend who used to accompany her to the gym, but Marcus tried not to be too optimistic. They were a pretty couple, both dark, both looking like models.

This Friday morning, however, Marcus found his mind occupied by other things. Like little goblin girls with stolen wrist-watches.

"I can't go back there!" she had exclaimed when he had tried to convince her to return it to the rightful owner herself. "Everyone will assume I stole it!"

"Well, you did."

"That's not the point! The point is that I don't want to be arrested, or worse. I might even get killed, who knows? It's not an ordinary watch! It's – it's – very special."

He had tried to ask her what was so special about it, but that had made her even more upset, and then she had marched off to his living room and refused to talk to him about it.

"No point if you won't help me," she had said. "And I'm going to sleep here tonight, just so you know."

Great, Marcus thought as he fetched the day's first cup of almost drinkable coffee. There's a smelly goblin sleeping on my couch and eating all my food, and I don't have the heart to throw her out. I'm too nice to people. Goblins included.

He sighed and went back to his office, making the usual little prayer directed at whoever wanted to listen, that there would be something to install or fix on *her* computer today, and that she would be in a mood for small talk, and that their small talk would lead to her discovering what a great person he was.

By lunchtime, he seemed to be out of luck. No reason to visit *her* office had presented itself. Just before Marcus went to lunch, his job phone rang. A deep, yet female voice growled a heartily "hello dear" in the other end of the line. Marcus frowned.

"Who is this?" he asked, convinced that the old lady had dialed the wrong number.

"Oh, you don't know me, dear," the coarse voice said with something between a laughter and a cough. "Name's Marilla. I do believe that you know my granddaughter, though. Ella."

Marcus almost dropped the receiver in his knee.

"What?" he gasped.

"Ella," Marilla repeated. "Skinny little redhead in her teens. Works as a cleaner. A tendency to get herself in trouble. Has she been trying to sell you something of value recently?"

"Uhm ... no. I'm sorry, but why do you think I know this granddaughter of yours?"

"Because she was seen through your window last night, of course. You're *that* Marcus Jensen, right? Had no idea she socializes with humans, but I suppose you can't always keep the young ones away from bad company."

"Excuse me? Bad company?" Marcus might have his flaws, but hardly enough to earn *that* label.

Of course, in the eyes of a goblin, any human probably was bad company, he thought. He needed to figure out what was going on, and getting upset with this Marilla person would hardly help. With a sigh, he admitted that Ella had shown up at his place yesterday.

"But I can't say I know her," he added. "We've only met briefly. For some reason, she asked me to help her. Have no idea why she picked me, really. Maybe she thought I looked kind."

The elderly goblin laughed.

"Yeah, right," she said. "So, she didn't try to sell you anything, but needed your help, then. With what?"

Marcus almost cursed aloud. I knew I should've kept my mouth shut the moment I realized I had a goblin on the line, he thought.

"She was hungry," he said, "and she said she didn't have anywhere to stay. I got the impression she had argued with someone, but she wouldn't give me any details. Her parents, maybe?"

He sucked his lip, hoping Marilla would swallow the lie.

"Her parents are dead," she said.

"Oh. Well, someone else, then."

"She lives with me. And we haven't argued."

"Well, I don't know! Ask her yourself. I'm terribly sorry, but I have work to do. You obviously know where Ella is, so please, by all means, go and get her."

"Ah, but that's the problem," Marilla said. "She's not there. And no one knows where she went. Hence this call."

Marcus rolled his eyes for himself.

"Well, I have no idea. As I said, I don't really know her. I gave her a place to stay and some food, and if she has left, that's fine with me. I don't mean to be rude, but now I've really have to go. Good bye."

He hung up before Marilla had any chance to object, quickly set the phone message to "out of office" and went for lunch.

So Ella had left his apartment. Good. He decided that he would assume that her grandmother would find her pretty soon and convince her to return the wrist-watch. Not his problem anymore. Now he could spend the rest of his day daydreaming of *her* instead, wallowing in his unrequited love.

Much better.

Marilla lit her pipe, sucking in air and breathing it out in short bursts. Small clouds of smoke emerged in a steady pace from her mouth until she decided the pipe had the proper glow and let out a happy sigh filled with smoke that slowly curled its way up against the ceiling.

Her pet rat squeaked.

"Yes, yes, I know, sweetie." She glanced at the phone on the table. "He wasn't very helpful, was he? And I have no idea where Ella has gone. Here I thought that stupid girl would consider herself safe with the human. Turns out the girl isn't so stupid after all. One might even think she inherited some wit from me! Ha!"

The rat squeaked again.

"There must be some trace," Marilla continued. "A scent – you must have picked something up."

The rat tilted its head and peered at its mistress with peppercorn eyes.

"You did pick something up, didn't you? Well, go then. Hurry, see what you can find, and report back to me when you know something." She raised her voice. "Gorm!"

A young goblin with bleached hair stepped into the room.

"You go with Rat. We need to find Ella before she gets herself into even deeper trouble. Don't hurt her, or I'll kill you myself."

Gorm crossed his arms.

"You know I wouldn't," he said. "Come on, Rat. Let's go."

A few floors above the office where Marcus spent his weekdays, dreaming hopeless dreams of a beautiful brunette he basically only knew by name, there was another office. This office looked very different. It had designer furniture, a large piece of trendy photo art on the wall and a young, pretty assistant, who fetched lattes, answered the phone and always made sure there were fresh flowers in the vase on the table.

Behind the large desk sat the woman with steel colored hair in her tailor-made suit. The facelift she had had a couple of years ago was so well-done it was hardly noticeable, and her forehead was Botox smooth. Her mouth, however, grew more and more tense while she was staring at the computer screen in front of her without really seeing it.

She lifted her cup, only to realize it was empty.

"Emilia!" she yelled. The assistant took her outstretched cup. She didn't need to ask to know that her boss wanted another latte (with triple shots of espresso). Besides, she knew better than to ask anything at all when Christina Lorentz was in this mood.

Christina leaned her head into her hands. That the goblin girl had stolen the watch was beyond question. But what the cameras hadn't shown was how the girl had managed to open the safe.

That safe was among the most advanced on the market. Absolutely no one except Christina was supposed to be able to open it.

Unless someone had found a way to fool the system with her DNA.

That "someone" could hardly be a goblin teenager, Christina thought. Which meant the girl must have been working for someone. Someone who somehow knew what Christina kept in her safe.

Question was, were they after the watch, or did they know the truth?

Christina rose from her chair and started to pace back and forth while waiting for her latte.

Her DNA. It wasn't too hard to get a sample of DNA. A stray hair from her suit. Or some lipstick scraped off her coffee cup.

I need to get out of here, Christina thought.

"Cancel my meetings for today," she said when Emilia returned. "I'm out of office for the rest of the day. I have something very important to do."

"Okay," Emilia said, with a quiet relief. With her boss out of the office she would get more work done, and probably be able to leave a little earlier than usual as well. As Christina put on her coat, Emilia was already canceling all meetings for the afternoon. No explanations were needed – everybody would assume Christina needed to attend some even more important meeting.

Marcus placed the pizza box on the kitchen table with a sigh. Ella was gone, but she had left his kitchen a mess. She must have gone through everything edible in the kitchen. She had eaten some, left opened boxes and trash on the floor and table, and even spilt milk all over the kitchen sink without wiping it up. He cleaned up after her while the pizza grew cold.

When he had finished his pizza, Marcus opened his second beer and actually found something on TV almost worth watching. When he leaned back, he noticed something odd with one of the pillows in the couch. He recalled having felt something small and hard against his back when he first sat down, but since he immediately had leaned forward to eat the pizza he hadn't paid attention to it until now.

The line between his eyebrows deepened as he found the zipper that kept the pillow cover closed, and unzipped it. He put his hand inside and felt his fingers close around – a wrist-watch.

"What in Oblivion?" he mumbled.

It looked terribly expensive, shining like gold and glittering of gems that Marcus feared actually were real diamonds. The words "Patek Philippe Geneve" on the dial didn't exactly calm him down, either. Ella had told him the watch was valuable, but not *that* valuable.

Hopefully, it was a fake. It has to be, he told himself.

He carefully put the watch on the table, where it looked out of place next to the empty pizza box and the two beer bottles.

Going to the police was out of the question. Who would believe him if he said that a thief had left something instead of stealing? And if he admitted that he had invited Ella to stay, he would probably be a suspect, too.

Ella had wanted him to help her return the watch, but since she had left it in his home without telling him who actually owned it, that left him with only one option: he needed to find Ella. But he had absolutely no idea where to look for her.

Her grandmother had called from an unlisted number, but at least he knew her name. That was a start. The goblins lived in the sewers, didn't they? People said they had whole systems of tunnels down there, and underground houses. It would be like looking for the famous needle, but it was the only clue he had. He turned off the TV and emptied his beer to be a little more courageous.

Just as he put on his shoes and jacket, he was startled by the doorbell. He opened the door, for a moment hoping it was Ella.

It wasn't.

"Hi," the young goblin outside the door said. Marcus was almost completely sure it was a boy. His bleached hair fell down into his eyes, creating a quite striking look against with his red eyes and grayish skin. "I'm looking for Ella. Is she here?"

"Seems like everyone is looking for Ella," Marcus muttered. "No, she isn't. And no, I have no idea where she is."

"Too bad. Her smell is all over the place, Rat says."

"Sorry?"

The goblin nodded in the direction of a Dachshound sized creature in the corner.

"Oh dear God," Marcus exclaimed without thinking. "That's a *rat*?"

The rat rose on its hind legs, and to his horror, he could have sworn that it nodded.

Since the goblin stood right in Marcus's doorway and didn't show any signs of moving, Marcus felt obliged to keep talking to him.

"You're a friend of Ella's?"

"Yeah," the goblin said. "I am. So you don't know where she is?"

"No, I don't," Marcus answered with a feeling of already having had this discussion. The goblin, however, still didn't move.

An idea formed in Marcus's head.

"Did by any chance Ella's grandmother ask you to come here?"

The red eyes narrowed.

"Maybe," the goblin said. "Did she contact you?"

"She called me today, actually. Was quite concerned. I think. You know what ... What's your name, by the way?"

"Gorm."

How very goblinish, Marcus thought.

"You know what, Gorm? This might be a long shot, but thing is, I'm also looking for Ella. She's barely more than a child, and she's missing. Maybe we could, you know, join forces, so to speak?"

"A human concerned for a goblin?" The boy seemed genuinely surprised. "Okay. Okay, fine. If you think you can help, yeah, why not. Did she say anything before she left?"

"She left while I was at work," Marcus explained. "She seems to have had a good meal before she left, but that's all I know."

No need to mention the watch. Not until he knew more about Gorm and what this business really was all about. He had it in his inner pocket. He wasn't sure if that was a good idea, but he didn't want to leave it in the apartment, either. God only knew who might break in looking for it.

She stirred in her cage as she felt it move, noticed the shifting lights and new voices. She was excited. After ages of darkness, she saw opportunities.

She had always been good at seizing them.

At least the rat keeps itself out of sight, Marcus thought as he followed Gorm through city streets filled with people going for gentle strolls, and crowded cafés and restaurants. The young goblin with his almost white hair and motorcycle jacket and the human man in jeans and fleece sweater formed an odd enough couple, in Marcus's opinion.

Gorm seemed to know exactly where the rat had gone. Without hesitation, he turned left and right and eventually took another turn into a small park. Marcus followed, hoping the goblin knew what he was doing.

He hesitated when Gorm was about to leave the lit main path and enter a narrow, dark path that winded in between the oak trees. Maybe the goblin had let him tag along only to rob him? He didn't think Gorm could possibly know that he was carrying a watch that might very well be worth more than any of them would earn in a lifetime, but he could still make an educated guess that Marcus had his cell phone and wallet, and not to mention, the keys to the apartment.

"Are we really going in there?" he said, probably sounding just as nervous as he felt.

"That's where Rat went," Gorm said. He didn't stop to discuss it further, but jogged up the path. "Come on," he shouted over his shoulder. "We'd better hurry!"

With a feeling that he was about to do something immensely stupid, Marcus followed the goblin.

That was when he felt something stir in his inner pocket. A quick check confirmed that he had his phone in the pocket of his jeans, just as he had thought, and besides, it didn't really feel like a phone vibrating. The only thing he had in his inner pocket, maybe apart from an old receipt or shopping list, was the watch. When he clearly felt it stir again, he had to stop and take it out, discreetly, trying to hide it in his hand.

The dial was glowing mildly in the darkness. As it vibrated again in his hand, something flickered on the dial. Marcus squinted. It looked like a shape – a tiny, humanlike shape.

Then it was gone, and the dial went dark. Marcus frowned and was just about to put the watch away, when it moved again. He almost dropped the watch. It wasn't just a stir this time. It felt more like holding a thin paper box with a small animal trapped inside, desperately trying to get out.

Come on, Marcus, he said to himself as he squeezed the watch tighter in his hand. You're imagining things. A watch can't move. Nothing can be trapped inside.

By now, Gorm had begun to wonder why Marcus had stopped, and before Marcus had a chance to put the watch away, the goblin stood there, asking what he was doing.

"Is that a watch?" he said. "Looks expensive."

"It's a fake," Marcus said, maybe a little too quick, as he put the watch away. "Well, not really a fake, more of a toy."

Gorm raised his eyebrows.

"An expensive toy, then."

"No, no, I ... uhm ..."

A squeak and a rustling in the vegetation further up the slope followed by the voice of a girl cursing interrupted them.

"Ella!" Gorm shouted and started running. "Stop there!"

A small shape emerged from the bushes and started to run. Gorm ran after. So did Marcus, even though he lagged hopelessly behind.

Ella was quick as a mouse, but Gorm turned out to be an explosive kind of runner. Within a couple of seconds, he was close enough to throw himself forward and knock her to the ground. He pinned her down.

"Did I hurt you?" Marcus heard him ask in an anxious voice. "Sorry."

"No, you didn't," Ella grumbled. "Just let me go, I have trouble enough as it is."

"Sorry, I can't," Gorm began, but when he paused, Marcus added:

"That's why we're here. We want to help you solve your problems."

"That's very nice of you, human, but I don't think that's why Gorm's here," Ella said. "You can let me go, I won't run," she added.

Gorm got up, allowing her off the ground, but he didn't let go of her arm. It looked brittle in his hand.

"Your granny wants to see you," Gorm said and was rewarded with a glare.

"No kidding," Ella muttered under her breath. She glanced at Marcus, a sly glance. He bet she wondered if he had found the watch.

Suddenly, she quickly turned around, making an elegant movement with the arm Gorm held that caused his own arm to twist in an awkward angle. As he lost his grip, she pulled away, slightly crouched, ready to attack. Her right leg whipped out to kick him in the groin, and as he bent over with a moan, another, lower kick swept him off his feet. Ella hurried to Marcus.

"You've got it?" she hissed.

He nodded, a bit shocked by the sudden display of martial arts training.

"Mrs. Lorentz owns it," Ella whispered. "And please don't let her out."

She walked back to Gorm with an innocent smile.

"I'll kill you!" he groaned.

"No, you won't," she said. "Come. Let's go see granny."

Marcus watched them go, confused by Ella's last words. Mrs. Lorentz was his boss, and he understood that the watch belonged to her, but why wasn't he supposed to let her out? And from where?

He supposed he had to figure out a way to return it without getting arrested for theft. Maybe he could send it by mail? Or simply throw it in the river instead? That might in fact be an excellent idea, he thought.

Since her husband had left the house in the afternoon for a golf weekend down the coast, Christina figured it was safe to call Emilia after work.

"I need to see you," she said. "Can we meet at the usual place?"

"No, I, uhm, have plans," Emilia tried, sounding reluctant, but as usual she agreed anyway. Christina was never sure if Emilia only came to their secret rendezvous out of fear of losing her job. She never took the initiative herself, and always let Christina convince her. On the other hand she seemed to enjoy their meetings once they took place, making love with great enthusiasm and creativity. Christina didn't care, as long as she got what she wanted. She bought Emilia expensive gifts every now and then, had even helped her with buying an apartment, and the girl certainly couldn't complain about her salary.

This time, however, sex wasn't Christina's top priority. When Emilia wrapped her bronzed arms around Christina's neck and began to kiss her, Christina gently pulled her away.

"We need to talk about something," she said.

"Can't we do that later?" Emilia whispered, pressing her body against Christina's. "I want you. Here, come."

She tried to guide Christina's hand towards her breast, but Christina resisted (with some reluctance).

"No, we'll talk first," she said. "Have a seat."

Emilia sighed and flung herself down on an old couch that looked like it was overdue for a one-way trip to the city dump.

The apartment they met in belonged to one of Emilia's friends, who currently was abroad and probably had no idea Emilia used it as a love nest. Christina had never met Emilia's friend, but judging from the interior of the apartment, the friend had little money and horrible taste. A bad combination. However, the apartment did have a bed. And a couch. And a kitchen table. And a bath tub. And a rather soft carpet on the floor.

It sufficed.

"Someone stole something from my office," Christina began.

"What?" Emilia's eyes grew wide. "Today?"

"No, Wednesday."

"Really? No! How could I not have noticed? Why hasn't the police been there?"

"The thief knew exactly what she was after."

"Sounds like you know who it is." Emilia got a little wrinkle between her perfectly angled brows, a wrinkle that soon would be gone again, without the help of Botox.

"I do. One of the cleaning goblins. The surveillance cameras got her."

"So I suppose the police is onto her. Why are you telling me this?"

Christina thought about telling her about Marilla, but decided that she might just as well let Emilia believe that the police was involved. The police would probably frighten her more than a goblin, even a goblin gangster boss.

"She must have had help," Christina said. "She broke into the safe in my office. You know that I'm the only one who can open it. But this goblin somehow got it open, something that should be impossible as far as I can tell. You have any ideas?"

Emilia shook her head, still with that little wrinkle between her brows. She chewed her lip, twisted a strain of dark brown hair around her finger.

"There was this guy asking about the security last week," she said. "He called from some security company, said he wanted to know more about our surveillance solutions since he might have something better to offer us. I didn't tell him anything of course, I transferred him back to the switch-board and told them to direct him to the security manager instead. You did check with him, right?"

"Of course I did," Christina said. "I told you about the surveillance cameras, didn't I?"

"Oh, right."

Her security manager hadn't mentioned anything about someone calling about surveillance solutions. On the other hand, it was possible he didn't think it was important. Maybe he was familiar with whatever company the man had called from and found nothing strange about it. Emilia, on the other, wouldn't normally receive such calls. Of course she had found it unusual.

Unless she was making it all up to avoid suspicion. If anyone at work had plenty of opportunities to get a sample of her DNA, it was Emilia.

"So, will you find this thief?" Emilia said and got up from the couch. "What did she take?"

"A watch I was intending to give my husband as a birthday gift," Christina said. "A very expensive watch."

She watched Emilia as she said it, but Emilia only shrugged and came closer.

"Too bad," she said. "Are we done talking now?"

This time, Christina didn't pull Emilia's arms away.

"Yes, we are," she whispered as Emilia began to kiss her neck again.

Marcus woke up and pulled away the sweaty bedcover from his chest. He ran his fingers through his hair. More sweat. He sighed, tossed and turned, warm and freezing at the same time.

He sat up in his bed and looked at his phone. 02.36 a.m. Marcus sighed again and tried to get back to sleep, unsuccessfully. He wasn't sure what he had been dreaming, but the dream had definitely had goblins in it. And rats.

Rats the size of horses. Was it even a dream? He recalled a talking watch – no wait, that was in his dreams. In reality, it had only been glowing. The rat had been big, but not *that* big. And the hot part about *her* had definitely not happened.

"In my dreams," Marcus said to himself, sounding more bitter than he ever would want anyone to know.

Your dreams could come true.

What was that? Just his wishful thinking, probably. Some dreams just didn't come true, that was a fact.

Wishful thinking, wishful wishes, wish upon a star my darling, wish what you want and it shall be yours.

He actually heard the voice, faint, female, seductive.

Okay, Marcus told himself, now I know that I'm not awake. Or I'm losing it completely.

He shook his head and got up, had a glass of water, went to the bathroom, went back to bed. His efforts to go back to sleep were severely disturbed by thoughts of *her*, innocent fantasies about casual conversations with her, mixed with still fairly innocent thoughts of romancing her, mixed with far from innocent thoughts of other things he could do with her.

She could be yours. You want her in your bed? You want her hands touching you, her lips kissing you, you want her to beg you to …

"Stop it!" Marcus sat up again, holding his head. The fantasies were one thing, but this voice or whatever it was didn't even feel like it came from his own mind. Yet it had to. He was one hundred percent sure that he was alone in his apartment, and that his neighbors weren't talking to him through the walls.

Think about it. I can offer all you want, and you don't have to do a thing in return. Just make a wish.

And the voice was gone. He knew it.

With a sigh, Marcus lay down in his bed again.

The memories would be there for eternity. There was nothing she could do about that. She embraced them instead, let them linger in her mind, even though they made her feel like she was suffocating again and again. She sometimes wondered if they had been right after all, when they captured her and imprisoned her, accused her of defying gods and angels, of being a danger to everyone, herself included.

Back then, she had known that it was all just a game, a way to get rid of her, the rebellious one, the one who they thought threatened their power and position with her fire and joy of living.

Ages later, she wasn't so sure.

Fire.

Fire needs air to burn. Put a blanket over fire, and you will kill it. But pull it away just before the fire dies, and you make the pain last longer. Do it again, and again.

She went through her memories again until she could not breathe anymore. Then, she simply floated in her cage, feeling empty. She had no idea for how long. Time didn't matter much to her. She knew she had been imprisoned for a very, very long time. This cage was only the latest in a row.

Sometimes, she tried to grow, even though she knew it was futile. None of her cages had ever broken to her attempts. She had tried until every part of her body made her want to scream with pain, but trapped she was and trapped she would be, unless she could find a way.

He made the coffee stronger than usual, especially for a Saturday morning, when he normally would sleep long and wake up reasonably rested.

Being haunted by mysterious voices might have had something to do with it.

After the first cup of coffee, Marcus rose from his chair and went back to the bedroom. A thought had hit him, and when he saw the Patek Philippe watch there on his bedside table, he began to suspect that he might be on to something.

The thing was, the more he thought about it, the more certain he was that the voice had come from somewhere next to his bed. Like his bedside table, for example.

Marcus took a close look at the watch. That tiny shape he had seen last night ... He was sure it wasn't an imagination. And the way the watch had – well, moved. It had in fact moved. He shook it gently, tapping the glass on the dial.

"Hello?" he whispered, feeling like an idiot.

Hello.

He dropped the watch on the floor.

Okay, he said to himself. So I've got myself a talking watch. Maybe that's completely normal. It is one of the world's most expensive brands, after all.

He picked it up again. There was the shape again, tiny, female, the color of glowing ember.

"You're in the watch," he breathed.

Stating the obvious, the voice answered. The shape made a gesture with what probably was one of her hands. *Trapped. Will you free me?*

"And you will grant me a wish? What are you? A genie?"

The voice chuckled.

Maybe that is what you call it. A jiniri I am, of the jinn. And you can have a wish. In fact, I need you to make a wish. If you agree to my offer, make your wish, and get the thing you desire most in the whole world, no matter the cost. And I will be free. What say you?

I'm having a fairy tale conversation with a watch, Marcus thought. For a moment, he almost said "sure, why not" to the genie, then he stopped himself.

"What's the catch?" he said.

The genie was silent for a second.

No catch, she said. *Only the woman you desire by your side, forever, loving you. If that is what you wish. Maybe you want fame instead? Fortune? A different appearance? Eternal youth and health? Say what you will, and it shall be done.*

"I'll think about it," Marcus said and put the watch down. No doubt about it, there was definitely a catch. "No matter the cost," the genie had said. Being loved by *her* surely sounded like the perfect dream, but what if it meant manipulating her into loving him when she wouldn't have otherwise? Could they really be happy then? And what if the cost was that one of them became crippled, or died young, or something like that? "Eternal youth and health," did the genie mean that literally? Live forever, long after all his friends and family were dead and buried?

On the other hand, maybe he was overthinking it. Maybe he could word the wish in a way that wouldn't hurt anyone. Add that it had to be for the best of everyone involved, and no one was allowed to get hurt. Maybe that would work. He still needed to think about it, though.

Seemed like the tales were wrong, he thought. Didn't Aladdin have to rub the lamp and the let the genie out *first*, before he could get his wishes?

She smiled. Her experience with lovestruck humans was that they were easily manipulated. Desire seemed to do that to them, make them forget about consequences, as long as they could mate with the object of their desire. She shuddered, having had the misfortune to see that happen on a couple of occasions. Creatures of flesh and blood were so disgusting.

This one might seem a bit reluctant, but it would come around. Better than the last one, who had had a strong mind and a plan, tricking her into that agreement, locking her cage away in darkness.

In her mind, she toyed with ideas how to get back at that human. She had had plenty of time to figure out fun and creative ways to torture it. Take away everything she had granted it, and then take away all that was left. Keep it captive somewhere. Cause pain to its mind and body.

It would be fun.

And when she was done with that human, she would find the other ones. The ones who had captured her in the first place, who had decided that it was best if she was kept away from the world, their precious plants and animals and humans. It would be harder to take revenge on them. They were of her own kind, after all.

But she had a few ideas. She had had plenty of time to plan that as well.

Marilla shook her head. She pulled a strand of black hair away from her face and looked Ella in the eye. Ella did her best to keep her back straight and not look away.

"What were you thinking, girl?" Marilla said, and so it started. She didn't raise her voice, but she made it very clear that Ella had been a stupid, stupid girl.

She went on for quite a while. Ella nodded every now and then, looked regretful, even lowered her glance. Finally Marilla stopped and asked the girl what she had to say to her defense.

"Nothing, really," Ella admitted. "But I think I can explain."

"Well, explain, then." Marilla crossed her arms.

"I was in the office building," Ella said. "I was cleaning the fifth floor, where the top management has their offices. So I was in the VP's office, about to vacuum the floor ..."

"You don't need to bore me with all the details." Marilla waved her hand. "The VP, you mean that woman? Lorentz?"

"Yeah, that's her. Anyway, she usually has this large framed photo on the wall, but someone had taken it down and leaned it against the wall instead, and I noticed there was a safe behind it."

"Sweet demons, humans are so predictable, aren't they?" Marilla rolled her eyes.

"I know!" Ella exclaimed, feeling more confident thinking she was getting Marilla on her side. "And the safe was open. So I went over there to look. I mean, who wouldn't? I wasn't planning on taking anything. But then I heard this voice. It was such a strange voice, it didn't sound like a human or a goblin, and it sort of whispered inside my head and told me that if I took it out of its prison it would grant me a wish."

She looked at Marilla and realized that she had lost.

"Okay, that was about the stupidest thing I've ever heard," Marilla said. "Next you're telling me that the voice came from the watch and that the watch ordered you to take it, right? Seriously, girl, I'm not that daft. Now tell me: who paid you to get the watch?"

"No one did!" Ella clenched her fists. "I swear, gran, I wasn't planning on taking it! And I have no idea why someone would leave the safe open! I just couldn't resist it, it asked me to help it!"

"A watch asked you to help it?"

Ella sighed.

"I give up," she said. "Believe me or not, but that's what happened. No one paid me, no one helped me. And I *know* I did a stupid thing, but I'll set things straight, I promise. Please just don't let her get to me."

"Christina Lorentz? Don't worry, she won't get her hands on my flesh and blood, even though you have proven more foolish than I would have imagined. Just give back the watch."

"I can't."

"You can't?"

"No, I've ... I got rid of it."

"Oh? And how do you plan on settings things straight if you don't have the watch anymore?"

"I have help."

Marilla sighed.

"Let me guess – that human? Marcus Jensen? Did you know he's Lorentz' employee?"

"I know. I asked him to give it back. He's not in trouble, is he?"

"He shouldn't be since she knows you're the one who stole it. She might wonder how it ended up in his possession, though. She might even threaten to frame him if he doesn't help her find you. Am I scaring you, child? I'm just pointing out possibilities. Besides, does he know that Christina Lorentz knows you took it? Maybe he's not in trouble, but he might think he is – and then Mrs. Lorentz might never get her watch back."

"You think so? Yeah, I suppose." Ella chewed her lip, staring at her feet.

"Maybe we should make him an offer," Marilla said. She rose. "Come, Ella. Let's go see him."

Marcus was visibly nervous. Ella watched him with interest as he rubbed his hands, offered Marilla coffee (which she declined) and then a beer (which she accepted). Marilla sat at the kitchen table, beer bottle in hand while Ella checked the cupboard and helped herself to some cookies before sitting down as well. Marcus didn't protest. He stood by the kitchen sink, arms wrapped around himself, watching Marilla like a bird in a cage might watch a cat, wondering how long it would take before the cat figured out how to open the cage.

"So," Marilla said after swallowing a mouthful of beer, "I have good reason to believe you have a certain watch in your possession. And I also have good reason to believe you want to get rid of it. Am I right?"

Marcus sighed.

"I never intended to be involved in this," he said.

"I know, I know, dear." Marilla seemed to have decided to go for the "understanding-old-granny" approach, Ella noticed. "I can help you with that, see. If you just hand over the watch to me, I'll make sure it gets back to its rightful owner. No questions asked, no accusations – no police."

Marcus's eyes narrowed slightly.

"Can I trust you?" he said. "No offense, but ..."

"But everyone knows you can't trust a goblin, eh?" Marilla laughed.

"No, no, I mean, I just – don't know you."

"Well, Ella didn't know you either, still she trusted you to help her." Marilla's voice grew serious.

"That's true," Marcus admitted. He was silent for a few moments, looking down while thinking. Then he told them to wait and left the room. When he came back, he put the Patek Philippe wrist-watch on the table in front of Marilla. She whistled.

"Well, well, look at this little baby!" She began to examine it closely. "Now, I'm no expert, but I have some knowledge, and it certainly looks like the real thing to me. Not that it matters to me. As long as the owner thinks it real and is willing to pay me the agreed fee to get it back, I'm happy."

She emptied the last of the beer and rose from the chair.

"Gran? Can I see?" Ella said.

Marilla handed her the watch. The moment Ella felt it in her hand, she knew something was wrong. Something was missing.

She looked at Marcus, but he wouldn't look back.

This time, Christina Lorentz had chosen an outfit straight out of a Harris Tweed ad, complete with rubber boots. She wouldn't risk ruin another pair of Jimmy Choos. She was greeted by a young goblin in leather jacket, who showed her to Marilla. The goblin woman was sitting in her armchair, smoking her pipe and petting her mutant rat. The young goblin placed himself by the door, arms crossed. Two other male goblins were in the room as well, both grim-looking, both carrying guns.

"Nice to have you back here, Mrs. Lorentz," Marilla said. "Please. Have a seat."

"No, thanks," Christina said, after a glance at the offered chair. She could swear it had lichen growing on it. "Do you have it?"

"Straight to the point this time, I see." Marilla chuckled. "Yes, I have it. But payment first."

"No, I want to see it first."

"You know what, Mrs. Lorentz, I have a feeling that under other circumstances we could be good friends. We think alike, you and me. Or maybe we would be mortal enemies, hah! Here it is." Marilla dug in her pocket and presented the watch.

Christina nodded.

"Can I have it? I want to make sure everything is – alright."

"No, you can't."

"Do you expect me to run away with it?" Christina nodded towards the armed goblins.

Marilla sighed and handed her the watch. Christina looked at it, weighed it in her hand, shook it slightly, and when she realized what was wrong, she closed her eyes for a moment, pressing her lips together.

"Damn," she cursed under her breath. She opened her eyes and looked at Marilla, her voice rising. "What have you done? You let it out! Have you any idea what you've done!"

"What are you talking about?" Marilla was genuinely confused. One of the male goblins started to raise his gun, but she waved at him and he relaxed.

"There was something in the watch," Christina said. "Something that's gone. Someone has let is out. You didn't know? Damn! Then it must have been the girl."

"Exactly *what* was in the watch?" Marilla asked.

"It's too late anyway," Christina sighed. "I might just as well tell you. A jinni – a genie. I have no idea how it ended up in there. It was there when I obtained the watch a few years ago."

"Obtained?"

"It was a gift. Now, I could probably afford a Patek Philippe, at least the less expensive ones, but definitely not back then. But it doesn't matter. What matters is that a very dangerous creature has escaped."

Marilla stared a Christina for a moment. Then she raised her voice.

"Ella! Come on in, I know you're listening!"

The door opened and a familiar-looking goblin girl in a dirty pink dress sneaked inside and stopped beside the goblin in the leather jacket. He immediately straightened and put his hands on his hips, protectively trying to look bigger and broader than he was.

"Yes, gran?" the girl said, and Christina understood that the old woman had fooled her from the start.

"Ella," Marilla said, "this lady here has something very interesting to say, as you probably heard when you were eavesdropping. What was it you were telling me about the watch, Ella? Why you took it?"

"It ... it asked me to. I'm so sorry about this, Mrs. Lorentz, I know I did something wrong, and I shouldn't have taken it, but it begged me to take it. I know it sounds insane, but ..."

"Actually, it makes perfect sense," Christina sighed. "But how did you open the safe?"

"I didn't," Ella said. "It was open."

"What? No, that's impossible."

"Well, I didn't open it!" Ella protested. "I have no idea how to open a safe without knowing the combination!"

"So the safe was open when you entered the office? And the watch was still there, obviously. The jinni saw its chance to find someone new to manipulate. And then you made a wish."

"No no," Ella said. "Come on, Mrs. Lorentz. Everyone knows you can't trust genies, especially not trapped ones. Don't humans have fairy tales?"

"Actually, in our tales you have to let the genie out before you can make the wish," Christina said. "It was sheer luck that made me realize that it might be trapped in there for a reason. And when it tried to bargain with me I figured I could – alright, I admit it, I took advantage of the situation. Made it agree to grant a certain number of wishes before it would go free. And when the number was almost up ..."

"You locked it away." Marilla nodded in approval.

"I did," Christina said. "Now I have pretty much everything someone could ever wish for. And I did some research as well. It seems that being trapped in a device made of humans and forced to grant wishes is an ancient method of punishment practiced among the jinn. Experts of jinn lore think the idea was that jinn deemed as dangerous to mortals should be humbled by serving them. This jinni – jiniri, actually, it's a female – has probably been trapped for hundreds or even thousands of years."

"In a modern wrist-watch?" Marilla raised her eyebrow.

"Not all the time. It might very well have started out in a lamp, like in the old tales. I have no idea how the transitions are made, and why it's not freed if an old item breaks, but it's likely that the jinni has been trapped in several cages before ending up in this watch."

"Well," Marilla said, "even though this little lecture in jinn lore and history is very interesting, I think the time for this business meeting is running out. You've got your watch back, with or without the genie. The genie was never part of our agreement, so I consider my job done. Payment, please."

Christina produced an envelope from the inner pocket of her tweed jacket.

"Please don't insult me by counting the money," she said. "Now excuse me, but I have to figure out how to escape the revenge of an angry genie."

She turned to leave, but stopped and looked at Ella.

"If you didn't let it out, who did?"

"No idea." The girl shrugged. "Maybe Rat wished he could have some extra food, I don't know."

"Or maybe your human friend did," Marilla said. "Marcus Jensen."

"Gran!"

"Marcus Jensen?" Christina frowned. "That name sounds familiar."

"He works at your company," Marilla said. "Some sort of system administrator, I believe."

"Oh yes, now I know," Christina said. "Rather nice-looking guy in his late thirties? He drops by my office every now and then to install something on my PC. How did he become involved in all this?"

Marilla stared at Ella until she began to explain that she had contacted Marcus since she figured he might have an opportunity to give the watch back unnoticed. Christina interrupted her before she was done.

"Do you know where I can find him? Good. Let's go there right away."

The result came quicker than he could ever have imagined. Frankly, he hadn't even expected it to work. But less than an hour after the genie had stretched out in her full glory and disappeared in a cloud of yellow and white sparks through the window – which was closed, by the way – Marcus's phone rang. The display showed a number, not a name.

"Hello?" he answered.

"Hello?" a female voice said, a voice he would have recognized anywhere. "Marcus? Is that you? This is Emilia, from work."

"Hi, Emilia!" Marcus said, probably sounding far too happy. Part of him wanted to jump up and down with excitement, while another part of him tried to reason that this probably was a work call. Maybe she worked overtime and her computer wouldn't connect to the system correctly. Not that anyone at work would or even should call him on a Saturday about something work-related.

"Hi!" Emilia said. "I bet you wonder why I'm calling, but thing is ... Well, I was wondering, can I come over? I'd really really like to see you. We've never really *talked*, you know? You seem to be such an interesting person, and I want to get to know you better. Are you at home?"

"Yes, I ... uhm ..." He wanted to ask her why she wanted to see him, but the excited part of him told him to shut up, tell her she was welcome, then clean up the worst mess in the apartment as fast as possible, have a really quick shower and maybe even have time to run down to the convenience store and buy condoms.

The less excited part tried to point out that Emilia's behavior was a bit odd, and maybe Marcus should be careful, but he chose to ignore it and began cleaning up instead.

Half an hour later, the doorbell rang, and there she was, with her big brown eyes and copper skin and dark hair curling over her shoulders. She gave Marcus the kind of smile he had dreamed of so many times.

"Hi!" she said. "Here, look, I brought wine!"

She stuck the wine bottle in his hand while she took off her jacket and revealed a tight pink top that made it very clear that she didn't wear a bra. When Marcus finally was able to remember to look at her eyes and not further down, he saw that she still was smiling.

"You're so handsome!" she exclaimed. "Why haven't we spent more time together? Come, where do you keep the wine glasses?"

There was still a reluctant, more logical part of his brain that tried to point out that Emilia seemed a bit unbalanced, hardly acted according to normal social codes, and possibly, maybe, just *might* be under a spell.

Shut up, Marcus said to the logical part of his brain as he followed Emilia's swaying hips towards the living room. If there was a problem, he could worry about it later.

A short while later, Emilia had nearly emptied her glass of wine while talking eagerly about how much she hated celery (which Marcus quite liked), that she liked to play tennis (which Marcus found boring), that her favorite author was one of most popular (and in Marcus's opinion least interesting) crime authors, that she just loved house music (which Marcus hated) and that she had seen some celebrity at some trendy club last weekend (Marcus couldn't care less). She asked Marcus what he liked to do in the evenings, and when he replied that he enjoyed RPGs, her face got a blank look for a moment before she told him that "I love RPG too, those movies always make me laugh!"

Marcus was just figuring out how to tell her that he was talking about role-playing games and nothing else without making her feel stupid, when the doorbell rang for the second time that evening.

To be honest, he didn't mind.

Waiting outside were Ella and Gorm, which was a bit surprising but not completely unlikely. The woman in their company, however, was none less than Christina Lorentz herself. Having her show up on his doorstep was about as unimaginable as Emilia sitting on his couch, placing her hand on his thigh every time she mentioned another completely uninteresting fact about herself.

On the other hand, that was just happening, right?

"Good evening, Marcus," Christina Lorentz said. "Do you have a moment? There's something very urgent we need to discuss."

"Come in," Marcus said. "Anyone want a glass of wine?"

Christina Lorentz' eyes switched back and forth between Marcus and Emilia, clearly surprised and also clearly dissatisfied with what she saw. Marcus reminded himself that the company didn't have any policy against romantic relationships between the employees as far as he knew, so if he and Emilia wanted to spend an evening together, it was really none of the VP's business.

Nevertheless, Christina's dislike hung thick and heavy in the room.

Emilia didn't look happy either, but for completely different reasons.

"Make sure they leave quickly," she whispered to Marcus, leaning herself heavily against his arm (definitely no bra). "We're having such a good time, don't you think? It can only get better, you know."

She winked and smiled, and Marcus was once again torn between the more logical part of his brain, that told him that he unfortunately had absolutely nothing in common with the girl of his dreams, and the part of him that was more concerned with the fact that he hadn't had time to buy those condoms.

"So, Marcus," Christina said. "I think you might guess why I'm here, so let's get to the point. I got the watch back, you see. The only problem is that something's missing. And I think you know perfectly well what that might be. Or maybe I should say – who?"

She knew about the genie. *Of course* she knew about the genie.

Please don't let her out.

Ella had known as well. The pieces began to come together in Marcus's mind.

"Shit," Marcus said, leaning his head in his hands. "I think I've made a terrible mistake."

"You made a wish, didn't you?" Christina smiled a wry little smile. "The last wish of the hundred wishes she was to grant before being set free. I made the first ninety-eight. I was a bit sloppy at first, didn't keep track, wished for insignificant things. Then I learned to think at least twice before uttering the words 'I wish'."

"How could you be sure you made ninety-eight wishes if you didn't keep track?" Ella asked.

"I asked the jinni. *She* kept track, believe me! I never trusted her, though. I suspected she might try to fool me by saying that I had more wishes left than I had. That's why I locked her away when my records said ninety-eight."

"I only made one wish," Marcus said.

"Turns out my ninety-eight wishes were in fact ninety-nine, then," Christina said. "I was right, she did try to trick me. And in the end, I guess she did."

"I thought genies were good," Marcus said.

"I suppose some might be," Christina said. "But this one struck me as wicked – actually, I think she's a bit insane."

"If she's been locked up for hundreds of years, that's no wonder," Ella said.

Christina nodded.

"I think I'm done here," she said. "Unless someone has more information on how my safe was broken into?"

The question sounded innocent enough, but Christina's eyes were sharp and mean as she looked at them all in order.

Gorm looked blank. Emilia frowned.

"I still don't understand that," she said.

"I've already told you, the safe was already open when I came there," Ella said. "But okay. I admit that I did take the photo down. It was hanging askew, so I thought I should straighten it up, and then, you know, there's always a safe behind paintings, at least in films. So I had a look, and there it was, and it was open, and – you know the rest."

Christina looked at her, and after a few moments, Ella noticed how she had a worried look in her eyes, as if she just had remembered something troubling.

"I actually believe you," Christina said. She cleared her throat. "Thank you all for taking the time. And Marcus and Emilia – don't be surprised if the company will find itself under new management very soon. I think I have to take a long vacation, some place where genies don't go."

Marcus followed her out in the hallway.

"Mrs. Lorentz," he said, "you don't happen to know if those wishes are reversible, do you?"

"Not as far as I know," she answered. "I suppose you could use another wish to undo one – but in this case, there are no wishes left. You have regrets, don't you?" She shook her head with a knowing smile. "Yes, I've been there, too. I suppose you have to figure out a way to solve the situation on your own."

"I suppose I have to," Marcus said as Christina Lorentz closed the door behind her. "I suppose I have to."

I wish Emilia would fall in love with me, even though we might not have much in common.

That was what he had said, first.

And I wish that this is for everyone's best, that no one is hurt because of it, and that we both can be happy together.

He hadn't really made one wish. Of thoughtlessness, he had made two. But since the first one had freed her, the genie hadn't bothered with the second.

Humans. What was so special about them? Filthy creatures of flesh and blood, created by dirty clay. The jiniri stretched out in a way that she had been prevented from for centuries. She looked at her limbs glowing and sparkling, created by pure, smokeless fire.

It felt good to be perfect.

She laughed aloud as she recalled how she finally had managed to play with the human woman's mind, made her forget to lock the safe, to leave the door open. And then the goblin girl! An easy victim, the jiniri had thought, but even though she was quick enough to grab the cage, the jiniri hadn't been able to persuade her to make a wish. Lucky for her, the girl had left her with the human man – and now, here she was, flying high in the heavens again.

She knew exactly where her last prison keeper was. Boarding one of the machines the humans had created in an attempt to fly like jinn and angels.

The jiniri chuckled.

An accident was about to happen.

Quadrillennium

A.R. Yngve

The family has gathered at the northern habitat on the bloodline's home planet, as tradition commands.

Winter Solstice is imminent. We land our ships near the foot of the mountain range, and get dressed in suitable winter bodies.

The reunion with distant members of our family becomes unusually emotional. We pass around joyful greetings and comments.

"Young Klallapar! How cute you are! Let us hug you and take a few cell samples."

"Mojniham! Such a long time since we saw you in bodily form! How's life on Neptune?"

"Nothing new, dear relatives. We look forward to our brains bonding tighter to make a stronger We."

"A happy Winter Solstice to you all!"

"Where's the mother unit?"

"In the kitchen."

"Mmm, it smells great!"

"How we missed the traditional smells on Ganymede ..."

We exchange pheromones and move our fleshy, fur-clad winter bodies to the kitchen, under the merry shouts from the mother unit: "Come and see! The Savior is baked and ready!"

The Savior slides out of the oven: an adult man of our forefathers' breed, dressed in an arcane manner, without implants, unmodified.

But he is not completely baked; his brain is like a newborn, devoid of experience.

We swiftly put him into a sleep and feed the brain with the stored Savior memories, as tradition commands.

Listen to how his growing memory curves, translated into sound, sing as in the days of old. Ah, this is going to be an old-fashioned holiday!

The little ones gather expectantly in the kitchen where we prepare the Savior: Ertoj, Klallapar, and our favorite Inrawdack who soon will be joined with the family We.

Inrawdack, triple-sexed to mirror a complex structure, helps our oldest family members lift the Savior out of the oven mold.

He rises unsteadily and looks about himself in confusion.

Instead of thought transmission he uses a mixture of lisping, clicking and howling sounds which are shaped by tongue and larynx.

The voice is deep yet mild and pleasant.

Our mother unit sets a bright, warm illumination so that the unfamiliar environment won't frighten the Savior unnecessarily.

"Where am I? Is this the land of the dead? Are you angels?"

We chuckle and exchange transmitted smiles. He gets just as surprised every time! But he must not remember the previous holiday; it would have broken the commands of tradition.

We call for the droids, traditionally dressed up as Roman soldiers, and they quietly drag him out of the house, to the holiday hill. He makes lame protests, but soon gives up and goes quiet. We follow slowly.

The smallest units watch wide-eyed from the foot of the hill. We let Inrawdack sit on the lap of Our oldest winter body.

The Savior sees the awaiting cross. He seems to understand it is meant for him, and resists. It is of course futile; the droids are ten times stronger than his flesh body. He is dragged up the hillside and dust stirs where his sandaled feet scrape and stomp the ground.

And so they arrive. The site is starkly illuminated, to mimic the weather and temperature of the Savior's own era. The cross is lowered into a horizontal position, and the Savior is pushed on his back against the beam. The droids tie the terrified Savior to the traditional wooden cross, and now his implanted memories awake: Jerusalem, the disciples, the trial, the sermons.

He yells the names of his disciples. They were not recreated; last year he did not call for them. We discuss his unexpected behavior, and wonder whether it is a supernatural phenomenon or coincidence.

Inrawdack sends Us a quick question: "Is it true that the Savior knew he would die, and could prevent it, and still chose to die this way?"

And how else can We answer, but with the truth that tradition commands?

"Yes, child," We send.

"But why?"

"The meaning of the Savior's sacrifice has been interpreted many times since the very first time. But in all times the forefathers have agreed on one thing: the Savior would die, and then be resurrected. And each year we show that the forefathers were right. Each year we create him again."

"But what would happen if we just stopped awakening him?"

We shudder inwardly. "Child, you don't know what you're saying. Do you want the Savior to really die, one last and final time? It would make a mockery of the Savior's sacrifice. We honor his prophecy and make him immortal, from his first death to the end of time. Behold the man up there, child, and marvel."

Our favorite child watches the hilltop in silence, where the droids have begun to hammer in the nails. We watch the blood that flows from the wounds in his hands and feet.

The Savior cries out loudly in anguish and pain, as We have witnessed at least a hundred times before. We are overcome with emotion, and sob solemnly before the sacrificial scene.

The cross is raised, and the Savior continues to scream; it looks like he is going to live a little longer than last time.

When he ceases to live we shall keep the body in the kitchen, cleanse its brain of memories ... and freeze it until next time.

Tradition is not as strong as it once were, but We know many families who also recreate their Savior to celebrate Winter Solstice in the traditional way. With them we exchange transmissions and sensory recordings of our respective holiday celebrations.

Some families, We hear, have begun to question the manner in which We celebrate. They think that the story of the Savior's Last Meal should be interpreted as cooking and eating the Savior's body and blood after his death – or possibly while the Savior is alive and offered a meal himself.

But we have no plans to do such things. Tradition binds the family's We together, and We stand by it.

After six hours of feasting, noise-making and play around the hill, the Savior finally gives up the ghost. His head hangs limply against his thin chest. We cheer, hug each other's units and the mood in the habitat is filled with love and friendship. The droids take down the Savior's pale, bled-out body and We already look forward to next year's Winter Solstice.

Blessed holiday!

Mission Accomplished

My Bergström

Sound slowly crept into her awareness – electric blips and longer wavelike sounds – like drops of water falling into the ocean.

It took a while before she could move, but eventually she managed to open her eyes. Her eyelids felt stiff and dry, as if they hadn't been used for a long time. She could practically feel them creaking as she forced her eyes open. It was an unpleasant feeling. Something was floating in front of her – something vaguely familiar – she felt that she should recognize it. A shape, round and colorful. White. Green. Brown. More than anything – blue.

This ... is ... Earth ...

She nodded to herself. Earth. That sounded right. Earth was beautiful and filled her field of vision almost completely – a globe of light floating in the darkness around her. As her eyes adjusted, she noticed stars around the edges as well, faintly visible through the glowing circumference. Her eyes were drawn back to Earth. Looking at the familiar patterns of the continents helped focus her clouded mind.

Lieutenant, do you copy? This is the Earth coalition, stationed at Luna base.

Sudden realization that it wasn't her own thoughts that she kept hearing – someone else was calling for her attention. A radio? She tried to keep her thoughts together, but they kept floating away from her, like afternoon clouds in a warm breeze across the sea.

After a moment of disorientation, it dawned on her that she couldn't feel her body. Panic crippled her thoughts. Where was she? How did she get here? She felt trapped. Fear made her field of vision narrow down to almost nothing.

Lt. Berger, do you copy? Please confirm. A short silence. *Please, signal me if you can hear me.*

The voice sounded concerned. Listening to it and focusing on what the words meant calmed her down. Her mouth was too dry for her to talk, so she spent a while trying to work up some spit, but all she managed to do was chafe her parched tongue on her teeth. She made a sound of dismay in her throat.

Lieutenant, is that you? Has the transfer gone well? Can you speak? Remember your training. Please indicate one for no, two for yes and three if you don't understand the situation.

She moaned three times in a row, after which the voice in the radio disappeared for a while. When it returned, it began to explain.

Lt. Berger, your mind has been transferred wirelessly into a semi-organic body, but something seems to have gone awry in the process. Hang on; we're attempting to shock your nervous system online as we speak.

A moment later pain spread through her entire body and she screamed, soundlessly at first, until her voice came back. She screamed again. The radio voice disappeared and didn't return for several minutes. By the time it did, she was able move her body, while receiving input from the suit's systems that gradually came online. The exhilaration of not being locked inside her head didn't last long, though. Moving her arms, legs and head had brought another realization to her: she was trapped in a space suit, floating in vacuum.

She found the mobile camera lens on top of the suit and pointed it, with some effort, away from where she was facing. Behind her was the lunar surface, but far enough away that, even at full zoom, she couldn't make out any detail. Earth's relative size actually made it look closer to her than the moon, but her calculations placed her approximately three kilometers above the lunar surface. All that separated her artificial body from being exposed to hard vacuum was the space suit. Why had they put her out here, and not on the surface?

As if it could read her thoughts, the voice in the radio came back. *Lt. Berger, are you all right? Awaiting status report, over.*

"I'm a'right," she slurred, glad to finally have a voice. "What am I doing out here?"

Glad to hear your voice, Lieutenant. We're concerned though; how much of your initial orders do you remember?

"Nothing. I remember waking up here. Other than that, nothing." She tried to turn around in order to face the moon, but without anything to push off from, not even air, she was as helpless as a tortoise turned upside-down.

Nothing as in you don't remember your orders, Lieutenant?

"Nothing as in nothing at all. I don't remember why I'm here or even who I am. You called me 'Lt. Berger,' but I have no recollection of that name or anything connected to it."

Hold on, Lieutenant, we'll get back to you in a moment.

The voice went quiet for several minutes, long enough for her to start wondering if it was ever coming back. To pass time, she examined her body through the space suit. If she hadn't been told, she probably wouldn't have noticed that it was artificial. She could feel touch, register what position she put her body in, and it seemed to her that her limbs had full flexibility.

"I wonder how I know all the basic stuff about being alive, despite having no memory of anything else?" she wondered aloud. "Shouldn't it all be gone?"

We're working on that, but the general assumption is that your personality data file suffered an unexpected corruption during transfer. We knew that it was risky when we decided to make the attempt, but hopefully we'll manage anyway. Your body is equipped with kinetic memory functions as well as a basic memory core that fills in all details needed to help you with basic necessities, like movements and operative actions. Fortunately, they both seem intact. Other than that, you'll have to adapt to what you encounter.

"I didn't know you were listening. I was just thinking out loud."

Sorry. We've decided to do a quick debrief on your way down to the Luna base. First, you will need to use your suit's ion thrusters in order to descend to the surface. Most of your systems are controlled locally, so you'll have to do it yourself. We'll walk you through it.

The voice then proceeded to tell her how to activate the interface and link her body to the suit, in order to synchronize the suit settings with her particular thought pattern. Blink once for confirm, squint for marking options, double blink for opening sub-menus, sift through panels by looking right or left, zoom by looking up or down. The menu wasn't visualized outside of her body, she realized, but was still visible to her. It looked like it hovered in front of her face, but that was probably just design flair. Blink, slide to the left, double blink, squint, confirm. Repeat.

Finally, the voice told her to execute the sequence of settings they'd helped her set up. *It'll take you down close enough to help you get to your mission objective within our window of opportunity, while still far enough away from enemy fire for you to be able to get your bearings before executing your orders.*

"So, what is my mission? Where am I heading?"

We need to evacuate all non-military personnel from the Luna facilities that are currently under enemy control. They launched a sneak attack at 0500 hours this morning and we've been under heavy fire here at the Luna headquarters ever since. We haven't been able to activate our emergency pro-

tocols properly. What we need you to do is infiltrate the peripheral areas of the main base and get as many civilians out as possible. A short pause, as if the speaker was bracing for what was to come, then: *Without an official count it's impossible to say how many people are trapped behind enemy lines, but an early estimate puts the number at almost a hundred.*

The ion thrusters had finally turned her around while she was being briefed, and now started pushing her towards the surface below. She was eventually able to make out a cluster of buildings and other facilities, faintly visible even from her altitude. "Has it been ascertained that the people down there are still alive?"

No, which is why we need you. Risking a whole troop by sending them into enemy territory, with our defenses crippled, would be a waste of lives. There's also a concern from our side that the enemy will start taking hostages, if they realize that we're preparing to abandon the station. But the odds for a single agent to sneak unnoticed through their defenses have been deemed favorable. Your body is equipped with stealth technology and should provide enough cover for you to make it inside the base unnoticed.

"How come you're only sending me in?" She was close enough to be visible from the ground now. As a security precaution, she manually altered the ion thrusters towards a crater, which she hoped would place her in a blind spot of the hot zone. "Wouldn't a small tactical team be able to produce better results? Seems like there's a lot hanging on my mission. Also, why was I floating in space? Was there a problem with launching me from somewhere?"

The first thing the enemy did was to bomb our orbital defenses, including the weapon storage where our artificial soldiers were kept. They were all destroyed, except the one you currently inhabit. It seems to have been flung into space by the impact blast, mostly unharmed. We discovered it a few hours ago, through a general vicinity scan. You volunteered for the mission.

"Copy that. By the way, I'm less than ten minutes away from the surface," she pointed out. "Final check: All systems clear. Standing by for deployment. Please repeat and confirm my orders." The ion thrusters slowed down and eventually flickered out, leaving only the momentum propelling her forward. Less than a kilometer left until she'd reach the surface. She'd have to get her act together quickly. "Also, I need a time line. Over."

Copy that. Lt. Berger. Stand by for your final information burst, based on data collected less than three minutes ago. We'll update if we receive more information. Your orders are to enable the evacuation of as many civilians as possible. You will secure each zone before alerting us of evacuation pickups. We can only give you limited air support, so use the opportunity for air strikes and evacuation conservatively. No repercussions will be given for eventual losses, but we expect you to do your utmost to rescue as many people as possible. Your time limit is ten hours.

Maps and blueprints of the Luna structures below her were being transferred directly into her mind, together with blurry heat scans, providing clues as to where she could expect to find people who were still alive. The data transfer felt vaguely unsettling, but as soon as the discomfort lifted, her mind began breaking down the information in order to plot different courses and strategies. It felt natural; as if this was something she'd done many times before.

"Why only ten hours?" She couldn't help asking.

That's how long we estimate that our ground forces can hold out, before we're forced to pull out and detonate the whole Luna base.

"Understood. I'm on it."

The landing went badly. She lost control of her suit temporarily a hundred meters above the surface and once it came online again, it was too late to reverse the thrusters in time for a smooth takedown. Her body slammed down into the crater at a steep angle and continued to slide forward for several meters until the friction made her stop. She winced mentally with embarrassment, but reminded herself that no one was around to see her disgraceful landing. After confirming that all systems were still online and her artificial limbs undamaged, she picked herself up from the ground and began running toward the base.

From now on, you'll be on your own. Only contact us once you've secured a zone. We can't risk alerting the enemy to your position while you're in the middle of a hot zone. Your suit will also collect and analyze necessary data between debriefs. Good luck, Lieutenant.

At first, following her orders was easy. The buildings on the outskirts of the base were easily evacuated and most personnel were in the process of heading to safety with or without her help. But as she continued deeper into the base, enemy presence became more prominent, keeping her constantly on her toes. Instead of just disabling a hacked gun turret or shooting down enemy lookouts, she was forced to plan further ahead as well as quickly solve unforeseen problems as they appeared.

Scanning the vicinity using the short-range heat monitor imbedded in the helmet visor, she plotted a course for her next target: three dots on the screen, one of them smaller than the others. A child? She quickened her pace. Time was precious enough as it was.

She reached the building, realizing with a stab of dismay that it was under siege. Bright lights of deadly fire smattered against the walls, causing flakes of superheated metal to fly through the vacuum. The flares looked like strange fireworks in the dim, gaseous light. They left trails on her artificial retinas. Would the metal alloy in the walls hold much longer? Someone inside the building was returning fire in long bursts, but judging by the way the bullets impacted the ground the shooter was using low-grade ammunition, probably from an automatic handgun or army-training rifle. A weapon like that wouldn't do them much good once the enemy breached the walls.

She sneaked past the enemy by activating her suit's stealth field. The field generator was resource-heavy and could only be used for a few minutes at the time, after which it would need to be repowered by solar energy or an external power source. Keeping it up for too long would also risk draining her shields. She currently only had access to the pale sunlight reflected by Earth – it would take longer to repower her suit than she could afford. The seconds were ticking down on the internal display, visible to the lower left on her eye screen. She hoped that she wouldn't lose her stealth field, or shields for that matter, before she reached the roof.

Once she made it onto the roof, she found cover behind a sealed maintenance shaft and flattened herself against the cold metal for a few seconds, before judging by the lack of commotion that she'd made it without raising any alarms. She checked her shields – only a few percent of their power supply left. Among the information received during the briefing, she found blueprints for the building – it was a generic living unit for personnel stationed long-term at the base. The maintenance shaft seemed to be the best way in. She immediately started working on the hatch sealing the narrow shaft, opening it up by short-circuiting the lock. She quickly crept inside and closed the hatch manually behind her. A shimmering force field, gleaming faintly blue, crept across the metallic walls in the cramped space around her. Instead of the dead silence of vacuum, sounds from an air pump reached her ears, as the vent filled up with air. She groped around and found a ladder, leading down into the apartment.

The maintenance shaft ended in a small kitchen. When she peeked through the door on the other side of the room, she could see that there was only one more room in the apartment. The building lacked advanced defenses as well as warning systems, so she managed to make it into the main room without alerting those trapped inside.

A woman dressed in off-duty military clothes stood by the side of the open window, force field faintly visible just outside. She was aiming an army-training rifle at the enemy outside in a stream of bullets. After spending so much time in the complete stillness of the vacuum outside, the sound was overpowering. Lt. Berger stepped closer to get a better view of the situation. Beside the woman sat a man in an environmental suit with his back against the wall. There was a hastily applied bandage wrapped around his chest and waist area. It was drenched in blood. He was reloading a spare rifle, handing it to the woman as she ran out of ammunition. In the middle of a room, behind improvised protective walls, lay a baby in a crib.

It was dressed in a baby-sized environmental suit. The couple must have been preparing for evacuation when they were attacked.

"Don't shoot. I'm here to help." She managed to raise what little was left of her shields just in time, sinking into a crouch in the same motion, as the woman by the window turned around and fired at her. A burst of radioactive slugs sputtered against her shields, then fell harmlessly to the floor. "No need to shoot."

"Who are you?" The woman didn't lower her weapon, but at least she didn't fire at her again. The man looked at her warily, with the gun he'd been reloading aimed firmly at her, but said nothing. Perhaps he couldn't. The severity of the wound in his stomach and the amount of blood on the floor around him suggested that he wouldn't last much longer.

"I'm here to get you guys out." She crept up to the window and took a quick glance at the enemy outside. They were dug in so deep that she knew she'd never be able to disable them in time to safely transport the wounded man out of the area. She'd have to come up with a plan. In the lower left of her visual field, the seconds kept ticking away. How to prioritize? Leave the wounded man and try her luck with other people? But she would have to sacrifice more than one person if she did. Looking at the woman, who was back at the window, firing, she knew she'd never abandon her partner.

"You have to get our baby out," the man finally said to his partner, his voice hardly more than a whisper. "There's only one intact survival suit left. It's too late for me. Leave me here."

"Never." The woman didn't take her eyes from the enemy, but her stance was stiff. She was tired. How long had she been keeping this up, in the hope of defending her family? The blood around her husband had started to coagulate at the edges. The bandages hardly seemed to stop the inevitable trickle. He must have been bleeding out for quite a while. Stomach wounds were slow. Slow and painful.

Lt. Berger evaluated her options, but no perfect solutions leapt to mind. Looking down at the wounded man, she met his eyes. He knew.

"Do it," he whispered. "Please. Save them." He seemed to be at peace with his fate.

"I'm sorry," she said and shot him in the head. Blood and brain matter splattered against the wall with a sickening noise.

The woman at the window turned around, screaming wordlessly. The baby started screaming too, its wailing muffled by the environmental suit. Lt. Berger, if that was indeed who she really was, had no other choice but to knock the mother out. "I'm so sorry," she murmured, while hauling the unconscious body toward the back of the building.

She searched the place until she found a military storage box containing the remaining environmental suit, which she put on the woman. She then went back to get the baby and put it close to the mother. It took her almost ten minutes to build a blast shelter around herself and the others, but when she opened the emergency com-channel from the house and called in an orbital strike, the building shook and the vacuum field collapsed, taking away all sound once again, but the shelter held. She checked the mother and the child – both seemed unharmed, though the mother was still unconscious. Perhaps that was for the best. Pearls of blood from the dead husband had spread through the room when the vacuum field collapsed, glittering like frozen rubies around them. Lt. Berger swept the blood aside and stepped out of the demolished building.

Outside, she tentatively checked the charred bodies of the enemy. It seemed like they were all dead, but just to be sure, she stayed by the blast shelter until the pick-up team arrived and didn't leave until she knew that the mother and her baby would be safe.

Good job, Lieutenant. It was the voice again. *The headquarters are impressed with the way you handled that last rescue.*

"Just doing my job," she answered. After a moment of consideration, she added, "Can I ask you a favor?"

The voice paused for a moment. *Within certain limits, yes.*

Was it just her imagination, or did the voice sound more reserved than before? "Remind me to check in on the mother and the baby afterwards, in case the mind transfer back to my real body goes as bad as when you put me in here."

We'll be sure to do that, Lieutenant.

She nodded to herself. "Good. Remind me to tell her that ..." She hesitated. "Just remind me to tell her I'm sorry."

Acknowledged.

The following rescues became increasingly messy. She lost five persons after that in a quick succession; the worst of them a technician who made a desperate suicide run, trying to take as many enemies as possible with her but ultimately failing to kill anyone beside herself. Lt. Berger couldn't mourn them, couldn't afford to do more than confirm that their life signs had gone completely dark before moving on to the next target.

"I'm a soldier. A tool. There will be plenty of time to mourn later." Unsure of whether there even was a later to be had, she nevertheless repeated the mantra while moving from hot zone to hot zone. Her failures burned inside her.

At last, there were no more red dots left on her visor scanner. All personnel in the area were either rescued or dead. Some of the dots she hadn't reached in time. They had just flickered and disappeared, subtracting a digit from the counter indicating possible survivors from time to time.

She tried to stay focused on her task, but it was hard to avoid speculating about who those people had been and how they had died. Had they been in pain? Could she have rescued them if she'd plotted another course, rescued people in a different order? She'd never know; for all she knew, she might have failed them all. And in any case, she couldn't travel back in time – couldn't do anything different.

She opened her com-channel, reaching out across the vacuum surrounding her one last time. They must have anticipated her contact, because before she could say anything, the by now familiar voice crackled through the speakers.

Good job, Lt. Berger. You've exceeded our expectations.

"That's great, really," she muttered. "When and where will you pick me up?"

It took a while before she got a reply. *There have been some complications. Unfortunately, we're unable to retrieve you.*

"Okay, so just copy my memories and merge them with my original." That was standard procedure for cyborg personality implants, of that she was sure.

We're sorry, but we can't do that either. We've been analyzing the corrupted fragments of your code from the failed transfer to your suit earlier, and we've come to the conclusion that you're a honeypot.

"What do you mean?" She frowned.

We believe that the enemy infected your suit with a virus and left it in orbit on purpose for us to find. The attack on Luna base is possibly no more than an elaborate ruse in order to infiltrate and disable Earth's cyber defenses. We're sorry, but we won't be able to extract and merge your imprint with your original personality. The risks are just too high.

She searched her memory files for an adequate response. "The Cyborg Treaties from 2268 states clearly that all cyborgs must, in case of corruption, be put in temporary isolation – possibly forced into dormancy if necessary – in order to preserve their minds, same as the Universal Health Treaty condemns medical negligence against all members of humanity," she reminded them. "Destruction should be a last measure, after all other attempts to restore the mind has failed."

As we said, we're sorry. We can't help you. Our forces will pull out in approximately seven minutes. After that, you're on your own. Unless you want us to …

"… deactivate me." She finished the sentence herself. "No thanks, I'd rather not."

Lt. Berger.

"Yes?" Annoyed, she snapped at the emotionless voice.

We're … I'm sorry.

"Yeah, well, you should be," she muttered indignantly, then disconnected the com before the voice on the other side could answer.

She tried to clear her thoughts, walking around the charred ruins of the moon base. She could see a couple of evacuation transporters moving further and further away from the moon, escorted by smaller aircraft and civilian mid-range shuttles tailing them. She felt a moment of pride that she'd been able to save at least some of the civilians. Then she started running towards the nearest crater.

Earth was still visible as a huge, blue sphere far above the horizon. As she was running towards it, she started wondering about her life before this. She'd been too busy for any soul-searching, but now the questions overwhelmed her with their intensity. Had she ever been to Earth? She knew that some people, called Spacers, spent their entire life in space. Had she been one of them? If so, where did her intense longing for the blue world stem from? She wondered what she looked like in real life. Was she short and stocky, like most gravity-influenced Eartheners, or a thin and waiflike Spacer? Did she have brown hair? Black? Did she use artificial gene therapy in order to change the color? Come to think of it, did she have hair at all? Most of the people she'd encountered on Luna base during the rescue operation had been bald, due to the mild but constant radiation that bombarded the moon.

As she gained momentum, running toward the edge of the crater and traversing several meters with each step, she could feel the pressure in her chest growing stronger, making it hard to breathe. Then she realized that she had neither lungs, nor heart or even a real mouth and that made her ache even more. *How can I ache when I have no body? How can they rationalize leaving me here, when I don't even know who I am?*

But she knew who she was; she was an entity that had been born facing Earth from her solitary orbit around the moon.

Her suit had been slowly powering up as she ran, absorbing the pale light reflected by Earth, but as she reached the top of the crater, the sunlight hit her at full strength. Electricity ran through her like a drug, filling her with more energy than her electric body could handle. Using the energy surge caused by her systems nearly overloading, she pushed off from the edge of the crater and propelled herself into the sky, towards Earth. She initiated the suit's ion thrusters immediately and let them carry her forward. She knew that she probably wouldn't last the whole way, not even with constant access to solar power. Her handlers wouldn't let her reach the beautiful, blue orb in front of her, and her suit ion thrusters were far too weak to stay ahead of any vehicle pursuing her.

And still, she knew that it would be worth it. A shiver ran through her body. Eventually, she'd have to power down her awareness system or risk data corruption from too long exposure of the unshielded electromagnetic radiation from the sun, but for now, she just wanted to stay awake. She let her eyes focus on the beautiful, blue planet in front of her, took a deep, imaginary breath, and sighed contentedly.

Mission accomplished.

The Road

Anders Blixt

A river running the wrong way – that's what the Road is to me. My first impression was a long time ago when I arrived at the Port Kad coastal terminus. Standing on the observation deck of an ocean liner, I looked beyond the city through binoculars and saw a broad dark line wind towards the hills, alive with tiny people, carts, and motors. The Road seemed to flow away from the coast, feeding the adjacent lands all the way to the Ariana Highlands and the Makir Plateau. Lots of narrower tributaries stretched out to towns and villages, mining camps and forts, connecting them to the rest of the Rim.

I was born far from the Rim, but the Hinterlands are my adopted home. Most of the time I speak a native tongue and I always follow the local custom of revering the Road by using the pronoun "she," even when I use the Oceanic language.

Trade, law and administration tie the Hinterland provinces together, using the Road as a conduit. The Road Council, a stateless administrative entity flying the old Imperial flag as a sign of its strict neutrality, is charged with keeping the lanes open to everyone all the time. And I had been recruited to serve as a cog in its abstract machinery.

When patrolling the Road, I ride. I want to move among people, to be a part of the bustle of wagons and carts, to stop wherever I wish and to speak to whomever I wish. That is the road marshal's job and I cannot do it properly from a motor. Some colleagues call my method old-fashioned, but I call it effective. I touch the Road, and she touches me – the best way of forming a bond.

The day grace brushed my life, the air above the Road shimmered from the heat. The repair crew in front of me, a mix of dark brown locals and light brown Oceanic immigrants, had stripped down to pants and boots. They had fenced off a long section of the outer of the three rim-bound lanes to do their work safely. I had no objection to that. But their vehicles and equipment were parked carelessly and obstructed movement in the adjacent middle lane. Pedestrians were not affected, but people pulling handcarts had a hard time moving through and animal-drawn wagons were forced to shift yet another lane to the left. A rim-bound motor, passing at a good speed, avoided the hassle by crossing into the coast-bound lanes. I didn't like that at all – if the flow of vehicles increased, there would be serious congestion.

I told my deputy to deal with the immediate disruption and rode up to the foreman. My steed growled. The fumes from the cauldron with boiling tar irritated his sensitive nose. I scratched his furry neck to calm him.

"Good day, workmaster," I said.

"Good day, marshal." The foreman did not look at me as he spoke, watching his men instead. My broken face tended to unsettle people so I was used to such behavior.

"I'm not happy with how the traffic flows here," I said.

"I've got a priority rush job. If you want to complain, speak to the planning bureau," he said.

"I see two infractions here. Your men are handling hot liquids without the protective clothing listed in the Road Safety Office's work safety code. And your equipment is obstructing lane two." I pulled my official notebook out of the saddle pocket as a threat. "Are you willing to take some advice?"

"All right, marshal, I'll listen."

Some men just don't want to take instructions from a woman, but right now he had no choice – he had to look at me as my right hand showed him what I wanted. "They say that an Ariana convoy will be going this way later today and you don't want the army provosts to get pissed off, do you? Put those things over there."

He grunted and issued new orders to his men.

A coast-bound coachman waved at me. I urged my steed across the six lanes of the Road to his wagon. He pointed over his shoulder. "Marshal, there's a broken-down half-track beyond that ridge, about a league away. I think they need assistance."

"Thanks, wheelmaster."

I summoned my deputy and moved along.

The blue half-track stood halfway out on the shoulder, causing minimal traffic problems. The travelers had hung a tarp from the right side of the vehicle to protect them from the burning sun while they waited for help – good, roadwise people. The trailer was an extended cargo-fuel combo, so they must be on a really long haul.

"Good day, travelers. We're here to help you." My greeting summoned four people out of the shadows: an Oceanic young man in an expensive beige traveling suit, a middle-aged local driver in blue shorts, shirt and cap, and two Oceanic friars, one tall and thin, one short and chubby. I pitied them having to wear woolen clerical habits in the hot weather. The short one seemed to fear the sun – big dark glasses and the habit's hood covered most of the head.

I dismounted next to them.

"Greetings," said the man in beige and bowed. His eyes darted from my face to the name-tag and the marshal's badge on my shirt. "I'm Mattir Toglas, master of Blackrock Manor, and these are the friars Brod and Klim."

I removed my hat and bowed to the clerics. Brod, the tall one, nodded and looked away. His hair was thin and his scalp was exposed to the sun. Klim, who looked a bit too young for going to the Rim, bowed back.

Mattir said: "We're rim-bound out of Port Kad. My vehicle has suffered an engine failure and I'd appreciate your help."

"The Road Marshalcy will assist you, sir," I said as custom dictated. "Deputy Thakarrian will inspect the engine with your driver and then ride to our post to get a salvage crew. Meanwhile, I'll commandeer help from a wheelmaster heading that way. You'll get a ride to the post and should expect to spend at least one night at its caravansary."

"Thanks," said Mattir.

The commandeered wagon was loaded with smelly hides. To keep my steed at ease I rode on the upwind side. Mattir and Brod sat with the driver up front, whereas Klim had found a comfortable spot on top of the cargo.

Our two-league journey would take most of the afternoon. Boredom is a traveler's companion and is most easily dispelled by conversation. "Friar, what's your destination?" I said.

"The Ekklesia has appointed Brod shrine-shepherd in Teritha and I'm his acolyte."

"That must be pretty far up the Road, because I have never heard of it."

"It's a mining town. After Big Fork, it's a few days' rim-bound journey towards Makir."

"Well, that's unknown land to me. How come you're traveling with Mattir Toglas?"

"We met him on the ocean liner and he offered us to come along in his vehicle up to Big Fork. He said he has inherited an estate there." The hooded round face was turned towards me all the time. The implied scrutiny unsettled me, even though I did not know what those covered eyes really looked at. I saw that the cheeks were greasy.

A skin affliction? I thought and said: "Keep on drinking. Newcomers don't realize how much they sweat in this weather."

"You're right." Klim opened another water bottle and emptied half of it in a few gulps. "Pardon me for asking, but what happened to your face?"

I chose my words carefully not to reveal my feelings: "Well, no offense. I served in Ariana. Working with security in the multilateral operation. It was an infernal device. I survived the blast, some of my colleagues didn't. My face and chest were badly burned. But both of my eyes still see and I can hear with one ear. I have enough teeth left to eat. And one can live without a nose. So I manage."

"You should be home with a veteran's pension!" Klim's outburst affected the voice in a strange manner.

Suddenly professionally wary I gave an appropriate response while assessing the situation: "And waste away in idle loneliness? I'm no cripple. And if a marshal looks hideous, it's a small matter. People still have to deal with me." I watched Klim's face closely: the chin was round and small with no sign of fuzz.

"I understand. Please tell me what a road marshal does."

I started explaining the minutiae of my job while checking Klim's mannerisms and speech as taught by our manual of investigation. "The Road is shared by all states with a presence in the Hinterlands. She is like the sea, too important to be controlled by any one government. The Road Co-dominion administers her as neutral ground, open to everyone all the time. That's why we even use the old Imperial flag. The marshals serve as the Road's police force." The more I observed, the stronger my suspicions became that Klim was not an adult man.

I stood in front of the commandant's desk. "Sir, I'm a bit concerned about the two friars who arrived with me today."

"I heard of them. Quiet fellows. Please tell me what's troubling you."

I reported my observations.

"Well, I trust your detective skills, but investigating the Ekklesia, that's sensitive."

"I know, sir."

"Any suggestions what to do?"

"Well, sir, if you ask them to carry out a divine service at the post chapel, they could hardly refuse. After all, we don't have any resident cleric right now. And that would give me a chance to study how well they carry out their duties."

"Clever. We'll do that."

The trilling cadences of a silver flute filled the chapel. Klim was a master musician, but certainly not a friar – so much clumsiness, so much obvious lack of experience during the service. Brod, on the other hand, had performed the liturgy convincingly. I therefore believed I knew what was going on.

The service ended with Brod giving the blessing of the One God, his right hand holding a candle and making the Circle of Light in front of us as he chanted the benediction.

The friars left the hall for the sacristy and the participants exited through the main door. I went to my favorite icon: the Divine Whisper. On my knees I lit a candle and meditated on the abstract depiction with red and black symbols on gold. *What next?* I opened my heart to the silence of the stone and the light. Some words of the Heavenly Sage rose from my memory. *So be it.* My right index finger made the circle over my heart and I got up.

A knock on the door and I entered the sacristy. The friars had put away their liturgical vestments and were relaxing in armchairs among the bookshelves. A pair of brown eyes and a set of dark glasses looked towards me.

"Greetings, marshal," said Brod and looked away.

"Greetings," I said and pulled a chair to me with the foot. "You two are in trouble. We are going to straighten it out right now." I slid into the chair and assumed the law officer's know-it-all attitude. "You're an impostor," I said and pointed at the covered eyes. "I've watched you carefully and you've done a poor job at being a cleric. You're an adolescent woman and you're pregnant. Your way of moving tells me that."

The girl sighed.

"So you're Brod's mistress and you're carrying his child. The breach of his celibacy vow is a disciplinary matter for the Ekklesia and of no concern to me. But deceitfully pretending to be a practitioner of a licensed occupation is a crime according to the laws I enforce. Explain yourself."

"Brod is an honorable man," she said. "I don't carry his child. It's his brother's. Brod has done all these things to save me and the baby."

"Why?" I said.

"Because my brother is a bad man," said Brod.

"It's more complicated than you think," said the girl, as she flipped down the hood and removed her dark glasses. She looked at my mutilated face without flinching while the glasses trembled slightly in her hand.

I stared into a pair of light blue eyes nested between pinkish eyelids. *Ah, she is using skin-darkening lotion*, I realized. "Have you dyed your body brown? Are you one of the Forsaken?"

"Yes, and I'm fleeing for my life. We're from Akrovâl."

Many times I had read in the newspapers what maltreatment the Forsaken suffered in that country. "I understand," I said and slumped in the chair. In that instant, something shattered inside me – the concrete around my heart. "I will help you."

"Why?" she said. "You are not one of us."

My voice cracked. "Look at my face! I know what it's like to be an outcast. People call me 'monster' and they call you 'vermin', right?"

Tears appeared in those horizon-colored eyes. She got up and extended a hand towards me.

I shivered. "Don't touch me, please."

Her face stiffened.

"No, it's not you. I can't stand touching. Not by anyone," I said. "The scars run deep in my mind."

Her face relaxed and she sat down.

"How will you help us?" said Brod.

"There's a Refugium for distressed women in a nearby town," I said. "Miss, I'll drive you there straight away. I know the matron and your background won't trouble her. You can stay there until you give birth and meanwhile figure out what you want to do with your future. As for the locals you'll meet there – for them you're just another weird foreigner. Their prejudices are different from ours."

"Thanks," she said and wiped her face.

"I'd like to know your real name, please," I said.

"Nëavoira."

"Brod, while Nëavoira and I are getting out of here, you'll have to talk to Mattir."

"I'll take care of it," he said. "By the way, I never expected a public official to do what you just have done."

There are some decisions that are surprisingly easy to make and surprisingly difficult to explain. "Well, life is the way it is. You can't run it according to regulations all the time."

This was not the first time I had escorted a woman to the Refugium. But this case turned out to be different: I could not let go of Nëavoira. She had touched my heart and my memory of her would not fade. So I requested to have my Road-patrolling schedule changed to take me to the town where she resided as often as possible. Every time I also went to the Refugium, pretending to have some legitimate reason.

After my second visit to Nëavoira, I stood in the Refugium's stable and groomed my steed before putting on the saddle. He growled in that particular approving way.

A child burst through the open door like a dust devil veering off the

Road. She wore a boy's off-white breeches and nothing else. Her skin was light brown like mine, not the dark brown of the locals.

"Greetings," I said.

"Hi." A long braid danced along the child's back as she skipped and darted around me.

"Why don't you wear a skirt like the other girls?" I said.

"I'm no girl, I'm a chepard." Her face contorted and her hands moved liked clawed paws while she growled like a feline.

"Then I should call you Chep," I said.

"Yes, yes, please. And what's your name?"

"Kitu," I said.

"That's a strange name."

"Not where I come from," I said. "I'm from the islands in the middle of the ocean."

"What's your job?"

"I'm a road marshal."

"So you capture bandits?"

"Sometimes." I smiled to the extent my stiff cheeks permitted.

"Why are you here?"

"To see a friend," I said.

"Why is your face so ugly?"

Trust a child to speak bluntly. "Bad people hurt me a long time ago. What are you doing here?"

"I live with the orphans. I came here to see your steed. The stable-lady says it's a beauty." She came closer. "Is it dangerous?"

"That's a 'he' and his name is Gale. And he is dangerous to anyone who threatens me. Look at his sharp teeth."

Chep bent to get a better look. Gale turned the head in her direction and sniffed. He was at ease; children make him curious.

I scratched his neck. "Try here. He likes it a lot."

Chep imitated my action carefully. Gale's growl made her back off.

"Don't be afraid," I said. "He likes it. His dangerous growl is different."

Once again, Chep scratched Gale. He licked her hand.

Friendship at first go, I thought.

At my next visit, I found Chep in the stable with Gale when I came back from the main building.

I was in a good mood, because I had seen how Nëavoira had started to adjust to her new life. She consorted with a group of pregnant locals of her age, picking up their language word by word and learning the traditional crafts. They treated her like an equal, despite – from their point of view – her sickly pale skin and ghostly eyes. She had told me that Brod had promised to come for her after the delivery. I usually get suspicious when people make big assurances, but I expected him to keep his word.

"Greetings," I said. "What have you fed him?"

"Nothing. I'm just scratching," said Chep.

"I see that Gale likes having you around." My words made her smile. I made a quick decision, once again breaking a Marshalcy regulation. "Do you want to learn how to take care of him? He'd love it."

"Yes, please."

"Then today's lesson will be food and water," I said.

I taught Chep every step of that task and she picked it up quickly.

A few visits later, Chep had learned so much that I could leave Gale in her care at my arrival without worries. At my return to the stable, the steed was clean and fresh.

"Do you want to become a marshal?" I said in jest.

"I want to be like you," said Chep.

"You can't be serious," I blurted without thinking, because why would anyone wish that?

"I am, I am, dungbag," she shouted and darted out of the stable.

Tantrums go with that age, I thought while tacking up Gale. *But what will she think of me tomorrow?* The uncertainty troubled me.

At my next visit, Chep came dashing to me as soon as I approached the Refugium. Her hair had been cut in the military style I used.

"I thought you'd never come back," she shouted.

"Why?" I said while dismounting.

"Because I was nasty to you."

I handed her Gale's reins. "It doesn't matter." Slowly I put my hand on her head and caressed the soft short hair. The cut suited her. "You're a chepard and they growl and fight, don't they?"

She hugged me before I could react. I stood still without flinching. Without hurting. Without shivering. *The touch of grace*, I thought.

"And you're an ursi," she said, "a big one prowling the hills and eating sweetberries and rivernewts. Ursis aren't afraid of anything, not even chepards."

I put my slouch hat on her head. "The ursi and the chepard are buddies, always."

In the middle of the wet season, Nëavoira gave birth to a healthy son. I was present to bless the baby. She had asked me to perform that task in the absence of relatives.

The dry weather arrived, Brod came back and the three departed rimward. I was there to wave goodbye together with the matron and Nëavoira's friends.

When I mounted Gale, ready to leave, Chep came running and looked up at me.

Now or never, I thought and bent down with my hand extended. "You can ride in front of me."

She grabbed my hand and clambered into the saddle. Then she looked at me over the shoulder. "Will you …?"

I saw the longing in the square face and understood. "Yes, Chep, call me mother."

She leaned back with the shoulders resting on my breasts,

"Yes, you are my daughter," I said and awkwardly kissed the top of her head. "I won't let go of you." Then I looked at the matron. "You set this up, didn't you?"

She smiled. "Of course. Are you unhappy?"

"No. We'll be back in two days for the adoption paperwork."

The matron moved her hand in the circular blessing of the One God. I saluted her and urged Gale into a canter. My daughter and I headed for the Road, going home.

"Is that the full story?" says Chep. "Really everything this time?"

I nod and hand over the box with the birthday gift. She tears it open: a brown and gray hunting dress for adults with a matching long dagger. Her first set of clothes for grown-ups. She is no child anymore.

"Thanks, mother." She kisses my scarred cheek. "For my next birthday, I would like to have a father."

I smile at her banter, caress her close-cropped hair and think: Well, who knows what the Road will bring?

Lost and Found

Maria Haskins

She was standing by the window, gazing out at the disappearing frost while sipping the last of the soup from the thermo-jar. The pain in her left foot was always worse just after waking, and she was leaning on the wall to take the weight off it until the pills kicked in.

She liked looking at the frost in the mornings. The ground was covered with a thick layer of sprawling ice crystals, and the windows were coated with swirls and intricate patterns, shimmering like glass prisms in the first sunlight. Soon it would all melt away, and trickle down the capsule's metal hull to be absorbed by the sand. Only in the deeper, shaded valleys would the frost remain until afternoon, the sand there hard and frozen, shattering beneath the soles of her boots.

How long now? she wondered, instinctively checking her watch. It was flashing the same useless numbers over and over again. The same numbers the computer gave her, as if time had stood still since the crash.

How long?

But trying to remember was pointless. She had lost track of the days and nights sometime after the first two weeks. When she awoke she never knew how long she had been asleep, if it was days or just a couple of hours. Sometimes she would wake at the first light of dawn, but more often she woke up much earlier, laying there in the dark, waiting. In the darkness, sleep and wakefulness blended together, with the wind ever-present. Its high, lamenting, pitiless tone was always there, penetrating even the thick walls of the capsule, piercing every dream and thought.

Maybe one of the others had a watch that still worked.

The thought took her by surprise and made her throw the empty thermo-jar against the wall in sudden frustration.

Stupid, stupid, stupid. Why hadn't she thought of that before?

I could go and get it, she mused, looking out the window at the steep rise, its shadow creeping slowly across the ground as the sun rose higher in the sky. It wasn't far. It would just take a couple of minutes to climb up the rocky bank, shuffle down the slope on the other side, and then she would be there, with them.

She felt the food turn inside her, the vomit burning in her throat.

No. She should have thought of that before she moved them. It was too late now. She couldn't go back, she couldn't face them again.

Two had died in the crash. The third had managed to stay alive the first night, but she hadn't been able to help him. When he too was dead, she had hauled out the bodies one by one, dragging them up the hill and then rolling them down into the hollow on the other side, out of sight. They had been much heavier than she had expected, so difficult to move, their cold skin resembling some kind of syntho-material when she touched them, their eyes still wide open, their mouths ajar as if they were about to speak.

What would you say? she had wondered as she watched them. But she knew it no longer mattered.

When the last one had been placed in the hollow, she had stretched out on the cold ground next to them to get some rest. She stayed there for a long time before recovering enough strength to go back. It had been so quiet, protected from the sand and the wind, and it would have been so easy to stay with them. But night had fallen and the cold had come with it, so in the end she had crawled back up the sandy incline. She had left her gloves behind, and her hands had been so stiff, numb fingers searching for something to hold on to, scratching and scraping.

How long ago now?

She studied the palms of her hands. On the crest of the ridge she had fallen, slamming her hands hard into rock and sand and gravel. The cuts had healed by now. How long did it take for a wound to heal? A week, two weeks, three? But it must have been longer than that, months probably.

The frost was melting, glistening drops running down the window. She followed one of them with the tip of her finger, saw it join other droplets, becoming larger, heavier, until it finally fell out of sight, into the dry sand.

Falling.

The screech of the emergency signal stabbing her eardrums.

She had always assumed that people would scream in situations like that, but nobody had screamed. The only voice had been the computer's voice, calmly repeating that the rescue capsule's emergency landing system had been activated. And then there had been the noise of the bodies slamming into each other.

The guidance system was defective, she thought, nodding to herself and wetting her chapped lips with the tip of her tongue.

She went over what had happened before, during, and after the crash quite often in her mind: memorizing the details, recapitulating the sequence of events, making sure that she remembered everything. Her report had to be complete and accurate when the rescue team arrived. She had tried to document it all, had even attempted to make a voice-record of it. It had been like reading a fairytale to herself at bedtime, but when she reviewed it the next morning she couldn't stand listening to it and had erased the file.

They had to know about the crash by now. The emergency signal must have reached the beacons. It wouldn't be long before someone came to get her.

There was so much to do until then. She had put most of the intact scientific equipment to use, setting up atmospheric and seismic testing stations in three different locations. The wireless relays were not working, and the stations were not situated as far apart as they ought to be, but all the stats she had gathered so far looked promising. She was already preparing several terraforming proposals as well as a preliminary resource plan, suggesting which transformation methods would be the most suitable. In ten years this planet would be ready for limited colonization and maybe then she could return here: apply for a settlement permit and get a place of her own. Ten years of service gave you top priority in the colonies, so they couldn't deny her that.

Her breath was fogging up the window and she wiped off the mist with her sleeve. A few drops on the outside of the glass were all that was left of the frost now, but tomorrow morning it would be back again.

It always came back.

Today she would take readings from the station she had set up by the cliffs. She was always hesitant about going outside and especially to that location, because it was so far away from the capsule. But by now the pills she had taken had numbed the pain: her foot hardly hurt at all when she pulled on the thermal suit and put on her boots, tightening the straps of the left boot to give her ankle enough support for the walk.

The inner airlock opened with a sharp hiss, then closed behind her before the outer hatch opened. Dust and grains of sand drifted in, sparkling in the sunlight, and she snapped the UV-shield down over her eyes so as not to be blinded.

When she stepped over the threshold, the wind immediately grabbed hold of her, pulling at her hair and clothes as she walked around the capsule to perform the mandatory, daily check of its exterior. The wind didn't seem

to have changed direction at all since they arrived, and the dunes surrounding the vessel built up higher every day. They almost covered the windows
by now. Soon she would have to remove some of the sand, or the capsule
would end up completely buried.

Halfway around she suddenly stumbled, causing her left ankle to bend
awkwardly underneath her. She banged the hull hard with her fist so that
her knuckles ached, sucking on the pain through clenched teeth.

They were back. The tracks were back.

They looked the same as before, and trailed across the sand in exactly
the same direction. She already knew that trying to follow them was futile:
a short distance from the capsule the ground turned stony for a stretch and
after that they didn't reappear.

Crouching down, she studied the tracks. There were more of them this
time, crisscrossing each other, coming and going, leaving and returning.
Ripples and marks in the sand. Nothing strange about that. Wind patterns.
Yes. The wind had made them, and now the wind was erasing them, and in
just a few hours they would be obliterated.

She squinted past the capsule, towards the crest of the ridge, but there
was nothing to see there, nobody could see her anymore. Turning around,
she stood up and kicked sand over the tracks, trampling them until the only
marks were the ones made by her own boots.

Afterwards she stood there, a little out of breath, rubbing her still
aching knuckles. The wind was pushing her very hard. It was inside her
hood, wailing in her ears, groping her neck with cold fingers. The shadow
of the ridge was shrinking already as the sun moved higher. Later in the day
the shadow would fall on the other side, where they were – in the hollow
where not even the wind could get to you, where all sounds were so muted
and so distant that it almost seemed like silence.

But she couldn't go back there.

Adjusting the UV-shield she turned around and began walking away
from the capsule, taking long, confident strides. With every step she put
her left foot down hard on the ground to test it. It barely hurt at all. As she
walked, she tried not to think of how far she had to go, and rattled off snippets of data in a loud voice to occupy her mind: atmospheric oxygen levels,
rotation times of other planets they had visited, details of planetary orbits,
the periodic table, anything would do. It wasn't like it mattered what she
said. The wind ripped the words out of her mouth and scattered them, leaving nothing but sand on her tongue. Still she kept on talking, putting her
head down, leaning into the gusts and striding onwards.

Even though the wind-rippled ground seemed level and unchanging,
she was soon unable to see the capsule when she turned around. Out
here the wind was all there was. It never left her alone: it screamed in her

ears, it whipped the sand against her face, and it blew in under the UV-shield, stinging her eyes. She tried to think of something else, something from before, something from back home, but she no longer had any such memories. They had been swept away by the wind, leaving only the high-pitched wail, the sand, and the shadows.

Finally the cliffs were there in front of her: their sandblasted silhouettes rising like twisted, crumbling towers out of the otherwise featureless landscape. She ran the last hundred meters, limping and panting, the sweat chilling her skin. The station was situated at the mouth of a small ravine, and even from a distance she could see that the instruments had been knocked over. As she got closer she saw the tracks, looping and circling around the scattered equipment.

For a moment she just stood there, trembling in the harsh wind, staring at the destruction. Then she kneeled down and started brushing sand off the instruments, but there was nothing left to salvage. Pieces of smashed plastic and fragments of twisted metal were strewn everywhere, the electronic innards pulled out and shredded. As best she could, she gathered up the pieces and put them in a small pile next to the cliff, then used her hands to smooth over the tracks.

When she had done all she could, she crawled further in between the walls of the ravine, scrambling in on all fours as far as she could until the gorge became so narrow that the rock walls touched her on either side. Between the cliffs, she was protected from the wind, but she could still hear it moan and wail through innumerable holes and crevices. Even though the wind couldn't touch her, the noise of it ripped through her: piercing her, shaking her thoughts and bones and flesh, and she wrapped her arms tightly around her body to hold it together. The wind howled ever louder, its howls sometimes resembling high pitched cries and voices, frayed and difficult to understand. Now and then she thought she could make out certain words, and after a while she could even recognize the voices. It was their voices, their words speaking to her out of the cliffs and the sand. They shouldn't be able to talk to her anymore, and yet she could hear them.

Nothing but the wind, she thought, banging her head against the rocks. That's all it is. There's nothing else. Just the wind. Making ripples in the sand.

The tracks had been there the very first morning, the very first time she headed out to check on the hull after the crash. She had covered them up immediately, but he had seen her. He had been watching. When she came back inside, he was sitting up in bed, leaning on one elbow, facing the window. She had been so certain that he would sleep longer than that.

"It's just the wind," she explained before he had a chance to say anything.

He just shook his head.

"I saw it," he said without looking at her. "During the night. It was there, outside the window. It was watching me."

Then he lay down, facing the wall.

"We should never have landed here. The probe would have given us info about it. Whatever it is."

She had tried to be understanding. After all, he had suffered from shock, confusion and amnesia after the crash. That made it difficult for him to remember what had really happened during the last few days on board. She had explained it all to him again, that the probe had been sent out and that the readings hadn't shown anything out of the ordinary. Then she had asked if he remembered the accident.

"We had no choice," she had told him, holding his hand to comfort him. "The guidance system was broken and we were forced to evacuate to the emergency capsule."

"It's too risky to land without probe info," he said stubbornly as if he hadn't heard a word, and he still refused to look at her.

"It was an emergency landing," she said, speaking slowly and clearly so he would understand. "We had no choice."

But it was as though he couldn't remember that.

"Where are the others?" he asked and she nodded towards the two bodies covered with blankets next to the exit.

"They died. The entry was rough. Don't you remember? Don't you remember that the probe didn't show anything unusual and that the systems malfunctioned and we had to get out of there?"

He had just looked at her then: eyes glazed, a trickle of dried blood in the corner of his mouth. Still she had tried to be patient. He was suffering from hallucinations. Nightmares. Just like she was.

"It was watching me," he told her again. "It was standing out there, looking right at me. Even with the insulation, the capsule must give off some heat. Maybe that's what lures them. It must be so cold out there at night."

There had been nothing more to say after that. She had given him his pills and then he went quiet and fell asleep. The next day she moved them. His eyes were still shut when she dragged him across the sand, and finally put him to rest on the other side of the ridge with the others. She had put the memory clip with the ship's log on his chest, placing his hands on top of it. It just seemed like he ought to have something with him. She didn't know for certain whether he had made entries in the log since the crash, but he could have done it while she was asleep, and there seemed to be no way to crack his encryption.

The bodies had looked so lonely laying there on the ground. She had put the first two face-down so that they wouldn't be able see her, but his eyes were closed, so she had left him on his back. There was nothing to see anyway. Not now. Not anymore.

Nothing to see, she thought as the cold, rough surface of the cliff scraped her forehead.

The UV-shield was cracked. She pulled off her gloves, removed the shield and threw it away, then rubbed her eyes to get rid of the sand but now the tears came, stinging her nostrils, spreading their salty taste in the back of her mouth.

The wind grabbed hold of her when she stood up to leave, it shoved her in the back, almost toppling her while the cliffs kept howling behind her, calling out tattered words she couldn't escape and didn't want to understand. She tried to get away, didn't want to listen, but the sand was soft and deep and her boots sank into it, it was like treading water. In the end you always sink no matter how you fight, you're pulled down and under until you can't breathe. The pills were wearing off and the pain in her foot had returned, but she couldn't stay here, she had to get back. So she went on, every step another stab of pain.

When she dared to turn around the cliffs were gone. The storm was blowing harder now, whipping up swirls and clouds of dust that filled the air and sky, making the landscape look exactly the same in all directions. She could feel the world turning, tumbling and spinning around her until she had no idea where she had come from or where she was going. Standing there, assaulted by the wind, she hesitated, squinting up at the sun until her unprotected eyes burned, vainly trying to remember the position it had been in before.

It seemed to her that there were other shapes surrounding her in the storm, but she couldn't see clearly and they always seemed to stay right at the edges of her field of vision, flitting in and out, uncertain and unseen. They flickered in the wind and the light, then disappeared completely when she turned to face them. Shadows. Sand. Wind.

Maybe it's the search party, she thought. Sent out to find me. Maybe they just landed and found the empty capsule. She shouldn't have thrown away the UV-shield. It was so difficult to see in the shimmering sand and sunlight.

She screamed, but the sound of her own voice being devoured by the wind was so strange that she immediately fell silent again. After a while the shapes around her disappeared and the air seemed to clear. She was alone and started moving again, more slowly than before, dragging that left foot. The fatigue overcame her then, it entered her mind and her body like a familiar, almost welcome warmth in the chest, spreading slowly into her arms and legs.

It was like it had been when she dragged the others across the ridge.

The fatigue had been like an inviting, seductive heaviness – making it difficult to move and even more difficult to think.

Soon, she thought and struggled on, they'll be here soon. Maybe they're already here.

When she finally reached the capsule, she collapsed inside as the airlock closed, and lay there for a while with her flushed, wind-burned face resting on the floor, listening to the wind howling through the holes and cracks inside her, just as it had howled through the cliffs.

There was nobody there. Nobody had come for her.

She took two pills before sitting down at the work-desk. It was difficult to get the boot off because of the swelling, and the searing reddish blue bruise had spread halfway up her calf and shin. Carefully, she wrapped her ankle with a cooling bandage and felt the throbbing subside. She pulled up the diagrams and graphs on-screen, all the data she had previously collected from the test sites, and she sat there staring at the screen, trying to make sense of it all. It was so difficult to concentrate, so difficult to see, as if the sparkling sand and sunlight were still in her eyes. The report was incomplete, but maybe it would still be enough for a terraforming license. It would have looked better with the info from the probe, but it was too late to do anything about that.

I can't do it all by myself, she thought angrily. They'll understand that. They have to understand that.

She felt her lacerated forehead and saw blood on her fingers.

The damn probe.

If they had just listened to her it would have been so much easier, but she had done the best she could under the circumstances. She had done what had to be done.

It had been roughly six months into their trip, barely halfway through their mission.

When she had accepted the position with the research team, she had thought that analyzing and classifying the planets in the sector they had been assigned would challenge her terraforming knowledge. After only a month on board she had realized that it was going to be very different than she had imagined. The work was monotonous and repetitive and mostly consisted of evaluating long-distance sensor info, not analyzing environments on-site like she wanted to do. The others always found something that ruled out surface expeditions, and soon every new planet became just another source of disappointment.

Scanning the first long-distance data for this planet, she had immediately realized that it was ideal, near perfect for terraforming, and she had wanted to get down there immediately. It was true that they had lost contact with the first probe, but that was just a technical mishap, and the others ought to have given in when she reported the impressive info from the second probe. Instead, they had requested access to the raw data feed. She had refused because it was unnecessary, but the others remained obsessed with seeing that raw feed. In spite of her expertise, in spite of the well-written reports and the excellent stats she provided, they did not want to listen to her.

She ate even though she wasn't hungry. The whole time she could hear the wind outside – the sand hissing as it drifted over the dunes and rocks. She could feel it on her face, hear its mournful whine through the crevices and crannies of the cliffs. Voices. Their voices. She shook her head when she heard what they were saying. No, she said, no, it wasn't like that. But that didn't silence them.

She didn't go to bed when darkness fell. It was impossible to see the sunset from inside the capsule, but you could see the sky shift from dark blue to black and then the night sky was split in half by the galaxy's wide spiral arm, its brilliant white starlight casting shadows on the ground. She turned off all the lights until just the screen on the desk remained lit behind her: a cold, pale light fueled by statistics, data, numbers, plans. More distant than starlight.

It was very cold out there at night. Ice and frozen sand, frost and cold fingers curled as though they were still trying to grab hold of something. Other hands stretched out as if to protect, or fend off. The wind was picking up, she heard the sand scraping against the windows and the hull, and she covered her face with her hands so that it wouldn't get into her eyes.

If it drifts up against the door, she thought and the wind was screaming in her ears now, could not be shut out. If it drifts over the top and buries me.

The screams and the voices rushed at her, the words clearer now, more distinct, but she shook her head because they didn't know, they didn't see, they couldn't know, they couldn't see.

How long now?

She looked at the useless watch that kept flashing the same numbers, the same moment again and again and again.

They would find her. It was just a question of time.

When they finally did come she didn't dare to move at first, hardly dared to breathe so as not to scare them, but they seemed completely unafraid.

I knew they'd come, she thought, leaning closer to see better – just the glass separating her from them now. She raised her hand in greeting, placing it on the window, fingers spread.

After a while they disappeared from sight and she stood up. The thermal suit was hanging in the closet but she didn't need it.

They finally came. I knew they would. I knew they would come for me.

The door closed behind her as the outer hatch opened. She ventured into the darkness, into the cold, where they were waiting for her.

* * *

The capsule was almost completely buried when they reached it, and he thought to himself that it resembled a rock or a cliff formation, a part of the planet itself.

"Get going," he said, pulling irritably at his tight silver collar adorned with the black leadership pin. "Looks like we'll have to dig our way in."

The wind pulled at his hood and the sand lashed his face when he turned around, squinting up at the ridge further away.

A noise. Distant.

He tried to catch it again but it was difficult to hear with the hood pulled up over his head.

It took less than ten minutes for the team to dig their way down to the outer hatch. When they were done they stood silent for a moment, leaning on their shovels. In their black outfits with silver click-seams they resembled nothing so much as a gathering of mourners.

The corpse patrol, he thought, brushing the sand off his shoulders. A well-deserved nickname perhaps, but they could at least have given us suits that look a little more cheerful.

"Perhaps their comm-system has been damaged," he said in a loud voice to make himself heard over the wind. "We can't know for sure. They may still be alive."

When he closed his mouth grains of sand cracked between his teeth.

The hatch opened and they looked at each other but didn't need to speak: they had all done this before. When they stepped inside they prepared themselves for the smell and sight of death.

"Light," he said and the capsule was illuminated.

Empty.

The tension eased slightly around his shoulders and neck. Most of the interior seemed intact. Only one computer unit appeared to be damaged, its interface panel black and cracked but the screen on the work-desk seemed active. In a corner they found bloodstained clothing and empty packs of painkillers.

"Somebody's been working here, after the crash," one of his crew said after checking the work-desk.

"Working on what?"

"Looks like observation stats. They must have set up a couple of stations judging by this. But nothing from the probe as far as I can tell, neither the first nor the second one."

"Not surprising considering that we haven't found any traces of them either. Not even a positioning blip."

"Crew of four, right?"

"Two men, two women, the usual. One terraformer, a couple of engineers, a ship's specialist."

"Somebody must have been injured. Almost half the pain pills are gone from the medical supply."

"Okay," he said. "A search party. You three. One k radius to start. Maybe they've collapsed close by. Look for tracks."

"With this wind it'll be difficult to find any kind of tracks. Anything older than a few hours, maybe even less, will be gone."

"I know. But look anyway."

"If they've spent the night outside they must be dead by now. It's pure desert and tundra out there."

When the others had left, he haphazardly went through the furnishings, the bedding and toolboxes.

"I don't think they've been here for quite a while," said his second in command who was still going through the work-desk entries. "The last info is a few weeks old already. Before that it seems to have been used almost daily."

"So where are they?" he asked testily. "The life-support systems are intact and as far as I can tell the hull is intact as well. The rest of it is no worse than that they should've been able to fix it in a couple of days. The food and water supplies have hardly been touched, the solar panels are working. Why aren't they here? Try to find the ship's log. It must be here somewhere."

"Maybe they snapped. Wouldn't be the first time that happened. You and I have been on enough expeditions to know that. The psych problems in these teams are rampant. Even worse than our own."

He was standing by the window, peering out into the sunlight.

Nothing but sand and wind out there, he thought. Sand and wind. Finally he said:

"Out there, when we approached. Did you hear something?"

"Hear something? Like what?"

In the light he could make out a palm print on the window.

"I don't know," he said. "Kind of a yell, or howl."

"Human?"

"Perhaps."

"I didn't hear anything. Could've been just the wind. This place is not too inviting. Blustery to say the least. That sand gets everywhere and it's as cold as a deep freeze at night."

"No worse than many other places they've terraformed."

"We've found them."

The sudden sound from the comm-link in his ear gave him a start even though he'd been expecting it. He adjusted the volume behind his earlobe: it was always set too loud.

"What shape are they in?" he asked.

"Dead. Have been dead for quite a while. Since the crash is my guess. Frozen solid by now. But there are only three of them here. One of the women is missing."

"Cause of death?"

"Two of them have skull fractures and some serious lacerations. Death was probably caused by a sharp object to the head. Almost identical injuries on both. Could've happened during the emergency landing I guess, but I don't want to speculate. The third has some broken bones and signs of internal injuries. We've found the ship's log but it's useless. Looks like somebody tried to erase it. Not a professional job, but there are only bits and pieces left."

"Erased it? And no sign of the fourth?"

"Nothing so far."

To hell with it, he thought and held up his hand to shield his eyes from the light. To hell with all of it.

When they left four days later he was standing by the round observation window in the gathering hall, watching as the planet's illuminated crescent disappeared beneath them. The three bodies were resting in the cargo hold, sealed in shiny metal containers.

"Seems perfect for terraforming," his second in command remarked.

"But without complete stats they can't begin. And they don't know when the next science team can be sent out here. They're pretty busy elsewhere."

That elicited a derisive snort.

"Busy. Right. If they'd start terraforming now, it could be ready for colonization within the next decade. Instead we have to wait for another expedition before the process can begin. Sending out another ship could take several years considering how slowly Search and Science works."

"The regulations are there for a reason."

"But following them is occasionally a waste of time. We both know that. As if we have all the time in the world. As if we can afford to be picky. You know my opinion. These manned expeditions are a waste of resources. A couple of robot teams could make evaluations on flyby, maybe not all that precise but good enough. We don't have to be so thorough."

He said nothing, just blew on the hot cup of tea he had just poured, watching the steam fog up the window.

"They're running an analysis on the remains of the ship in Tech-lab right now," the other man continued. "But with the crumbs they have to work with, it'll be difficult to determine what really took place."

"What do you think happened to her?"

"Anything could have happened to her. Most likely an accident on the way to one of those useless monitoring stations she set up."

"But no body."

A shrug.

"No body. Maybe she overdosed on pain pills like the ship's specialist. Maybe she committed suicide out there in the sand somewhere. We'd never find her."

"And the probes? Two of them gone and not a trace. And the monitoring stations? Every instrument smashed."

"She must have done it before she killed herself or got herself lost. Psychosis. How many times have we seen that before? A couple of months down there all alone would drive anybody crazy. It was a stupid idea to set up those stations, but I guess it gave her something to do anyway."

The stars were dense here in the inner spiral arms of the galaxy, and they stood silent side by side looking at scraps of white starlight while the ship kept going.

Cold, he thought. It must have been so very cold.

"Long shifts for those teams," his second in command mused. "Enormous psychological pressure. I don't envy them. Hey. Are you listening?"

He felt the tug at his sleeve and turned, but instead of the other man's face he saw the ridge and its shadow and the shimmering ice crystals that had shattered beneath the soles of his boots when they had gone down into the hollow to pack up the bodies.

If it wasn't so cold.

He closed his eyes so the sand would not get into his eyes.

"The wind," he said finally. "Almost like voices sometimes even though you can't understand what they're saying."

"What are you talking about?"

But he turned away, staring out the window again.

I wonder what she saw, he thought, placing his palm on the window, fingers sprawled on the glass as if in a greeting, but all he could feel was the cold outside.

The Publisher's Reader

Patrik Centerwall

"How was your holiday?" The manager put down his cup on the desk.

Helga shrugged. "It was quite okay. I stayed at home most of the time, but spent one week in Paris."

"Paris? How was it?"

"A lot has happened since my last visit. Guess the Parisians have become accustomed to the fact that the Eiffel Tower is gone, but for me it was a bit odd."

"I can imagine that."

"How was your holiday then?" Helga knew that she had to ask, even though she wasn't interested at all. When her boss told her how amazing it was in New Crete she barely listened and let her eyes wander along all the awards on the wall.

Awards received by The Publishing House for bestsellers edited and marketed by her boss.

"Well, well," the manager said at last. "Let's get to the point. I have two authors who have just begun writing their books and who might suit you."

"Do I get to choose?"

"Given that you stopped that filthy creep before your vacation, you might say that The Publishing House is very pleased with you."

"Okay, what do we have?"

"Well, you can choose between Thomas Kladesky, who I think you are familiar with, and a young aspiring woman who just got her license to write."

Helga did indeed know Kladesky. She had been responsible for one of his books before. He was boring. He wrote uninteresting stories and his prose was at best miserable. But they sold like hot cakes.

New authors who had recently received their license were mostly enjoyable, even if they didn't always finish their stories. Besides, a lot of them were of course often forced to terminate their novels, and sometimes even have their license revoked, since they didn't fully understand or want to abide by all the rules.

"I'll take the debutante," she said.

The manager smiled. "I guessed you would say that. She has already written six to seven pages so you can start immediately."

Helga returned to her station, logged on to her terminal and opened up the newcomer's pages. It had been a long time since she had stopped hoping that she would read anything really good, but she still felt a special thrill to work with a new and fresh author.

Her job was to read the pages just hours after they were written, make some corrections, come up with amendments and hopefully approve the writing so that the author could continue the next day. All steps part of the process to make sure that the book was finished as soon as possible and could enter into circulation and be downloaded to the audience's e-readers.

It was stimulating work, but she had to admit to herself that it was not often that she read something that really grabbed her, made her think, or caused her remember why she loved literature.

The Publishing House had strict guidelines for the appropriate content of a book, and it was up to her and the other publisher's readers to stop whatever didn't work. For example if it was too peculiar and would be too difficult to sell on the market. Or if it was obscene and did not meet the moral requirements.

Now and then a few more literary works were published, but it was mainly the more experienced readers who worked on those.

Sometimes she toyed with the idea of applying for a year's leave to get a higher degree, but she never got around to it.

Occasionally, in her spare time of course, she read works from one of the smaller publishers. That was not looked upon favorably by her employer, but when her boss confronted her about it, he had to admit that it was good to keep an ear to the ground. If she found something that could become a bestseller they would buy the author. Or prevent further releases.

In any case she harbored no high hopes when she opened the aspiring author's pages – even though she knew it would at least be a little more stimulating than Thomas Kladesky.

Two hours later she was not sure what she had read.

It was the strangest and most disjointed first chapter she had ever seen. But it was also one of the best she had read. It was absolutely wonderful.

The prose sang, the language was clear as well as sweet and the story was mysterious, dreamy and playful.

But it was also something The Publishing House would consider completely unsellable. And some parts were even a little bit obscene.

How this author had been able to get her writing license was totally incomprehensible. Helga knew the rules well enough and she knew what she had to do.

But before she entered the code that would stop the author from continuing, she read a few paragraphs over again. Could she really end this? She started from scratch, read everything again and sighed. It was too good. It was too beautiful.

The story was like a fragile bird that was learning to fly. She simply couldn't stop it. She wanted to see the bird fly. She wanted to read more. Just a few days. Then she could terminate the script. She could come up with a lie that the whole thing started well but deteriorated after a while.

Without further hesitation she approved the text with some changes. She couldn't remember the last time she had longed to return to work with such zeal the next day.

After a few weeks her colleagues began to ask her questions since they had noticed that she didn't talk about her project when they were on break.

"Come on, Helga, what are you hiding from us?" Marianne asked when they had lunch at the usual place.

"Nothing ... I just like to listen to what you're talking about."

"But you could at least tell us what genre the new book is?" Thomas said. Just then the waiter arrived with their food. It looked pretty good, even though it was almost completely odorless.

"You could say that it's fantasy," Helga said.

"You could say? My God, if we don't know what genre it is, the readers will never be able to tell. And then you can't sell it." Tomas picked up his knife and fork but didn't seem to be ready to start eating until he received a satisfactory answer.

"Of course I can say what it is. It's fantasy."

"With elves and dragons?"

"No, no dragons."

"But elves?"

Helga nodded in response. She didn't want to go into details. For the characters were not really elves, at least not in the classical sense, and definitely not according to The Publishing House's standards. This was something completely new. She cut up a bit of her lunch and stuffed it into her mouth so that she, at least for the moment, could avoid her colleagues' questions.

"I once worked with a fantasy novel," said Marianne. "But I had to terminate it about halfway through."

"What was wrong with it?"

"The author went too far. Suddenly there was a lot of unmotivated violence, and then there was some kind of ritual where everybody had to be naked. I do not remember all the details."

"Everyone knows that it is impossible to have any nudity in fantasy!" Thomas said. "I mean, I could understand it if someone thought they could get away with it if they wrote crime, but fantasy? Come on!"

"I don't recall if she described very much nudity. But they were about to undress anyway. She filled in Form 26B and it became quite clear that she would not be able to finish writing the book. She was suspended for six months, but then filed an application for writing a young adult book which she managed quite well. Without any nudity of course."

"I assume that no one takes their clothes off in your book?" Thomas asked. Helga looked up.

"No, not yet anyway."

And it was actually true. For the pixie-like creatures that a large part of the book revolved around did not even wear clothes in the first place. During the morning she had read an almost dreamlike passage were they danced naked in the moonlight. The author had described how the rain fell and how beautiful it looked on their naked wet bodies, how the dance and the joy just increased the more it rained. It was a hopeless passage. It did not carry the plot forward and was too sensual to be approved.

But the scene was so incredibly beautiful. When Helga had finished reading it, she had gone to get a cup of coffee, but had first taken an extra lap through the office just to calm down and think about something else. She just had to close her eyes to see the dance in the forest glade, feel the rain drops on her skin and hear the music from the handmade instruments.

This was the best book she had read in a long while, and she knew that it could not be published. She knew she eventually had to terminate it, tell the author that it was impossible for her to continue, and then delete the entire text.

She was quiet during the rest of lunch while thinking about it. The novel would vanish from the world. There would be no copies left, no trace of it all. The text on the network would be removed, and only exist in her and the author's memory.

She was so incredibly sad that something so beautiful should disappear.

The story grew, and one day Helga was even more surprised when the author broke another rule and sent a message to her. At the end of the text, she found a sentence that obviously did not belong to the novel:

"Why can't I write more? Ten pages a day is not enough. Is it possible to increase the amount of pages? "

Helga had never seen anything like it. She had to turn around to make sure that no one was standing nearby and could read over her shoulder. Ten pages a day was the maximum limit for writers who were not yet published and authors who didn't make a living from their writing. There were few who could deliver that much in one day, and Helga could not imagine that anyone would be able to write more. Moreover, it would of course mean that the author neglected her life in general. To cope with a daily job, maybe a family, and write ten pages a day was a big challenge. Trying to write more was just stupid.

But on the other hand, if the author wrote more Helga would get to read more. And what if the author didn't have a family and managed her regular job no matter how much she wrote? There were many good reasons for the rule, but if the author herself felt that she could write more, then why should Helga be the one to decide how many pages were allowed?

The argument would not hold if she was discovered, so if that happened Helga had to come up with some excuse, maybe a technical glitch. But that was a later problem. She doubled the number of pages and hoped that no one in the IT department would notice anything.

When she sent back the changes that needed to be made in the text she also included a small message.

"You now have twenty pages a day. And I think we have to meet."

The next day, she began with the last page where she indeed found an answer to her question.

"Sure. When and where? And why?"

Helga knew the perfect place.

"Every Wednesday at noon I will sit in the Botanical Garden. You'll find me by a bench a hundred meters down the trail in the rose garden. Come and see me there."

After three weeks and huge amounts of text she finally met the author. Helga used to occasionally eat lunch in the peace and quiet of the Botanical Garden, and loved to sit in the heat and light under the glass dome in the midst of the beautiful plants.

Every time someone came walking towards her, she looked up, but by the time the author finally arrived, she had almost stopped believing that she would show up.

Helga was sitting, eating her sandwich and observing the vegetation when she noticed a young woman, or rather a girl who could not be more than eighteen, standing in front of her and looking at her.

Neither of them said anything while studying each other in silence for what seemed like several minutes.

The girl was wearing a pair of pants that had been fashionable many years ago, and a red blouse, and she had an alert, clever gaze.

"You want to sit down?" Helga said at last.

"Sure." The girl sat down on the bench.

"How old are you?"

"I'll be seventeen in a month."

"Seventeen? Then you cannot possibly have been licensed! How can you write?"

"It's my sister's account."

"Your sister? You pretend to be your sister? Don't you understand? You're ruining her chances of ever writing! If she has taken the course and is licensed ..."

"She'll never write!" The girl stood up, crossed her arms and looked down at the ground.

"You don't know that!"

"My sister is in a coma. She will never wake up. The doctors talk about ending ..."

"Oh." Helga was silent. She put aside her sandwich and laid her hands on her knees. "What is your name?"

"Sophia," said the girl without looking up.

"Sophia ... I'm truly sorry about your sister. How ... how long do you think she will remain in the coma?"

"They have started talking about pulling the plug!" Sophia looked up and met Helga's eyes. This was truly an extraordinary young lady. But she did not understand what she was doing when she wrote using her sister's account. They were both silent for a moment.

"It's a great novel you're writing," said Helga. "I'm impressed."

"Thank you. You really like it?"

"I love it. It is one of the best I've read. Besides the classics. But the problem is that it is not okay to write this kind of novel. It is too strange and not commercial enough. I should have terminated it a long time ago, but I haven't been able to do it, because it is so good. I really want to finish reading it."

"All new books are so boring," said Sophie. "They're all the same. I want to write one like the classics. Like Lord of the Rings, The Flowers of Evil or Brimstone Sleep."

"Have you read them? But you're not old enough to borrow or buy classics."

"Dad works at the university library."

Helga nodded.

"I understand. I will not tell anyone."

"Thank you."

"You really have talent. I have worked all my life as a reader for The

Publishing House. Most of what I read is actually quite boring. Skillful but boring. Every now and then I have the good fortune to read some good stuff. Your text really stands out. It does not follow any rules. It is funny, sad and exciting. And your language is wonderful."

"I just write what I like to read."

"That's a good principle. You could really be a great writer. Even some original writers who write different from the rest are occasionally licensed to write. At least if they have talent. And you have talent. But there is a problem ..."

"What?"

"If it ever becomes known that you have used your sister's account you will be banned for life. Then you will never write again."

"Oh. I didn't realize that."

"It's a long process to get permission to write and a lot of people are turned down for various reasons. Last year a guy who was suspended tried to bypass the rules and ... let's just say that you don't want to know what happened to him."

"Does anyone know what I have done?"

"Just me. And I have loved reading your book. I would do anything to see you finish it."

Helga thought about what she had just said. And she realized how right she was. It was about time that there was a book that would shake the foundations of the literary world. A beloved book that broke the rules. An impressive and groundbreaking book. A book that would break the boredom of modern day storytelling.

"Forgive me for asking," said Helga, "but how long will it be before the doctors turn off your sister's life support system?"

"I don't know. They just started talking about it. Mom and dad haven't decided yet."

Helga knew a little about the process since she had a cousin who was an anesthesiologist. If they just had started talking, it meant that after the parents had consulted the physician it would take at least a month before the decision was approved by the administrators.

"How long do you need to finish?"

"I don't know. A month. Maybe two."

"Okay. Then I know what we should do. And I do not want you to argue with me. Not under any circumstances. Do you understand?"

Sophia looked back at her with her wise, clever eyes.

"Yes I do."

Helga enjoyed her coffee at the favorite spot in the Botanical Garden. Two days after Sophia had finished the novel, they had turned off her sister's life support systems. As soon as she had been pronounced dead the account was automatically disabled.

But Helga had the novel. A book that made her smile just by thinking about it. A daring and unusual book. A book she had longed for without knowing it.

Normally, someone at a level above her should read a book before publication, but Helga had ignored that rule. She had made sure that it would be published anyway. She had worked for so long that she knew exactly what to do.

"Her actions would cost her more than her job, but she was at peace with her decision. In any case she did not have much to look forward to. Read boring books and go on holidays to cities that were like museums. Celebrate Christmas with cousins she never saw otherwise.

But now she could say to herself that she had done something that mattered. Something that was real.

As soon as the management discovered the book, they would begin the process of withdrawing it, but at that point it would have reached enough readers, and above all enough reviewers, that it would be difficult for them to stop it completely.

At least if the book received the attention she hoped it would get. To be on the safe side she had made sure to send the novel to some literary scholars and critics who she thought would agree with her opinion. Who in not so many words used to call for books that were a bit different, that did not follow The Publishing House's common template and standard.

But she also knew that even if they couldn't do anything about the book, they would certainly do something about her.

She had just had time to drink up her coffee when she heard the boots. There were many, far too many, to arrest a middle-aged lady who worked in culture.

It wasn't long before she was surrounded by uniformed men and women who all turned their guns on her. She smiled and was about to stand up when one of the soldiers shouted at her not to move and to raise her hands.

She found such contradictory orders rather amusing, but realized that it was best not to say anything, and she simply raised her hands.

It was beautiful here in the enclosed garden, and she had done something she believed in.

Not even an anti-terror squad could ruin her day.

Stories from the Box

Björn Engström

He didn't know how long he had been without food. He didn't even know how long he had been in the box.

The first few days had been easy to keep track of, but after a while, distinguishing each individual day had become impossible. The days seemed to merge, to create a new entity, a new time unit. Not days or weeks, but simply chunks. He'd been in here for countless chunks. He'd even been without food for a few chunks.

He sucked water out of the damp walls. The last food he ate was some tasteless gray paste which he scraped out of a small plastic package. The package had been thrown to him – no one ever gave him anything here, they threw or thrust things at him – by what he assumed had been a guard. Normally, he was given one plate of food every day, and when he had finished eating, they opened the door again and removed the plate. This repetition gave his life at least some kind of rhythm. But then they stopped bringing the plate. He had already lost count of the days by then, but without the plate, his life changed from "one plate a day" to simply "one". One man. One box. Until the door was opened and someone threw him the package.

He had made the package last. For some reason, he had assumed that it would take a long time before someone threw anything at him again. And he had been right. He had only eaten a thumbnail-sized piece of paste when the hunger pains in his stomach had become unbearable. Given the size of the package, that meant a lot of days had gone by. Maybe even chunks. And in all that time, the door had not been opened once.

Sounds confused him. Before, back in the days when they used to bring him the plate, there were sounds of metal against metal, creaks of wheels, the occasional distant scream. Now, there was nothing. Only once in a while the roar of thunder or the howl of a strong wind whipping his box. Something had changed on the outside.

His box was small. He could only sit or crouch, he could not stand up and he could not take a single step. All the walls were rough concrete. He spent his days leaning against the door, enjoying the smooth softness of its rusty iron against his back. When he felt more stiff than usual, he forced his ass into a corner and stretched his legs towards the opposite corner. This was still not nearly enough, and he wondered if he would ever be able to fully straighten his legs again. Or his back.

He tried to remember his life before the box. When he could actually do things, when he could go to real places instead of only letting his mind wander. Didn't he once read books? Didn't he sometimes travel to faraway places? Didn't he actually meet other people? Didn't some of those people accuse him of something he didn't do and try to beat him into confessing?

All those things seemed so distant. They were like fairytales, buried deep inside him, not real memories but made-up stories he could tell if he ever got out of here. He leaned against the iron door and let his mind drift into those stories, living his life through other characters. Time passed in the company of women he had always wanted to meet and men who all looked like him.

He felt his body giving up, starting to eat itself from within.

His thoughts dissolved into small fragments that quickly lost track of each other. He was still in the box, he was sure of it. He was almost certainly still alive. Everything around him was in all likelihood very quiet, unnaturally quiet.

Until suddenly, a metallic clicking noise cut through the silence – and he fell out the door.

Complete darkness surrounded him.

He tried to remember how to move his body. Slowly, he managed to pull his legs out of the box. Gravel outside the door scraped his skin, sending lightning bolts of remembrance into his brain: this was what it felt like!

He took a deep breath and his eyes nearly popped out of their sockets as the fresh air shot into his lungs and propelled his blood into his skull.

He was sure his eyes were open, but the darkness was impenetrable. He seemed to remember a story about something called stars and how they ought to be in the sky. And another story called City Lights, about how the world is never dark but always lit by man-made technologies.

It was dark, though. It was as if the world had never heard those stories.

He didn't mind. He could just lie here, enjoying every breath of air and the barely audible sound of the breeze moving over the ground. He could lie here for a very long time, and still be happy.

At first he thought someone was coming. But then he realized it was only the sun, far beyond the horizon, its faint light starting to lift the darkness. Still, he was not disappointed. It would be nice to meet the sun again after all this time. Probably a lot nicer than meeting the people who were guarding him and the box.

But where were they? He had been lying here for hours – not chunks, just a few hours, he was sure of it – and he had seen or heard no one. Shouldn't they be here after opening the box? Weren't they supposed to guard him? Beat him? Something?

He stood up. Had anyone seen him, they would have thought he was crawling. But to him, this was walking, this was happily skipping along, this was sprinting to the cheers of a large audience. His muscles slowly took charge, forcing his joints to unbend from their box limits, pulling him up, up.

The sun had not yet climbed over the edge of the world, and still the light was so bright he had to shield his eyes. He looked around, beginning to notice his surroundings. The box was just one in a long row of boxes, surrounded by a barbed-wire fence. On the other side of the fence: low buildings, trucks, a road leading across a flatland of dust and rocks.

And something else, hidden in the shadows of the trucks.

He walked to the next box in the row. On the front of its door was an electronically controlled lock, powered down, unbolted. He eased the door open, peered inside. For a moment he saw himself, curled up into a ball. Then he understood that the man was not him, did not look like the men in his story memories – nor was the man alive. The skin had dried up around the bones.

He went to the next box and found another corpse.

His crouched body took a few aimless steps, and he stared at the long row of boxes. Dead. They were all dead. He was the only one alive.

Then he remembered the things in the shadows.

His eyes watering from the strong sunlight, he looked again at the world outside the fence. In the shrinking shadows of the parked trucks, there were things on the ground. He could not quite see them yet, but he knew what they were: corpses. They had been his guards, before they also died.

His stomach suddenly screamed with hunger, and the pain made him fall to his knees. He looked around, then crawled – really crawled this time – to the nearest box and felt inside. He found a package. It seemed empty at first, but his eager fingers unfolded every crumpled seam in the stiffened plastic and finally found a tiny piece of gray something. He eagerly put it in his mouth.

He looked through more boxes of the dead, and found enough to eat to ease the pain in his gut. Something chewy. Something insubstantial. Something tasteless yet disgusting. All of it kind of pointless. Most of it invigorating.

He stood up straight and took a deep breath, careful not to let the sunlight blind him.

Time to get out of here.

As he reached the top of the mountain, he turned and looked back down towards the prison camp. What had happened there? What had killed all those people?

He had found a gate in the barbed-wire fence, its electronic lock open just like the ones on the boxes. Ignoring the bodies of the guards, he had searched through the buildings, and had found food and drink in a fridge and clothes in a wardrobe. Dressed in a guards' uniform and with a backpack full of food packages and water, he had started one of the trucks. That he even remembered how was proof that he was really alive. The stories in his head had filled him with knowledge that he had forgotten he had.

The truck had brought him as far as the foot of the mountain. Then the engine had simply stopped, and he had been out of ideas on how to make it run again. Maybe he could have found a story in the back of his mind that could have told him what to do, but it felt so good to be able to move that he didn't mind walking.

So he had climbed the mountain, or hill as someone more acquainted with mountains might have called it, pausing only to soothe his aching stomach a little. Not too much, a story had reminded him, eat slowly. Yet he had still eaten more than he should, and had lost some of it a while later.

Now he turned away from the dry valley with all the boxes of the dead, and started down the other side. Into the world.

A world that was strangely quiet.

It was impossible to understand.

Was it his mind that was weak after all those chunks in the box? Or was it just such an impossible thing, such an improbability, that no one would have been able to make his mind believe what his eyes saw?

The first sign had been the gas station. He remembered – he knew now that the stories in his head were mostly memories – that this was the kind of place where he should have been able to fix the truck after it stopped. "Fillerup" was a sound he heard in his head and didn't quite understand.

The place was abandoned. No cars, no trucks, no people. Nothing was working. The screens on the gas pumps were blank. He pressed the buttons, but nothing happened.

Then there was the village of the dead.

He had approached it slowly, remembering stories about how some people took their guns out to greet strangers. But here, no one had come out to greet him. No man, woman or child. No dog. No chicken. Not even a chirping little bird.

In fact, he had not heard a single bird since he came out of the box. He had not seen a single animal. There in the village of a few small houses, in the middle of a flat landscape, he had realized how strange it was that there were no animals.

He had found human bodies. Corpses, sitting on chairs or lying in beds. Skin dried to the bones. There were no flies around them, as he had seen in his story memories. Death was accompanied by flies. Death was rotten. Yet here, this was not true.

His feet had moved faster then. He had walked for days – with the sun as a guide, he was able to count the days again – to reach small towns and even cities. He ignored the abandoned cars he passed, choosing to explore the world on foot. When he found shops, he changed his shoes and socks, and when he sat down to rest in the evening, he made sure to give his sore feet plenty of air and to wash them lovingly when he had water to spare. His feet carried him for countless miles, giving him strength.

He drank all the water he could find – from lakes and streams, from rusty jugs and muddy puddles. Food was scarce, as store shelves seemed to have been emptied long ago. He found mostly freeze-dried reserves in the basements of dead people's houses. Tasteless, it still gave him the energy to continue his journey.

He didn't meet anyone anywhere. There was no life. The world was full of dead, dried-up remains of people and animals. Nothing on the planet seemed to be alive. He thought at first that the trees and the grass would also die when there were no insects to help spread pollen or seeds, but as time passed and the world stayed green, he realized that many plants would probably survive.

For a long time, he held on to the hope that what had transformed the world he remembered into this lifeless silent shell was a local phenomenon, and that as long as he continued walking, he would eventually find people who were still alive. That somehow this plague or contagion or whatever it was had only affected a limited area. But then he reached the shores of a Great Ocean, the end of the continent, and still there was only death.

Crossing the ocean seemed impossible, but maybe he could communicate with the other continents? He tried radios he found, phones, computers. Nothing worked. Electricity had died with the people. Batteries had been depleted. Carrying a heavy shortwave radio on his back for weeks, he eventually found a house with solar panels on the roof. But even with power, the radio stayed silent.

So he had taken command of a ship. Not too small, not too big. Fully prepared for a journey across the ocean, before its crew had all died. He set out across the calm waters and found the weeks on the ocean a largely pleasant experience. The air was fresh, the sun warm, and his feet could rest from the endless wandering.

He reached the shores of another continent, hoping to find people waving at him as he approached. He wanted to see their smiles, hear their voices calling him, shake their hands.

But there were no people. There was only death. Endless masses of dried-to-the-bone corpses.

This place was even worse than his own continent, its ancient cities stacked so close together that death was always present, always close. He could not stay here. He put on the best walking shoes he could find and started to walk away from the ocean, further inland, to search for life.

But hope had already left him.

He had lived for many years. Years outside the box. Years in the land of the dead.

Bushes and other undergrowth covered more and more of the remains of the dead world. Houses were covered in thickening moss. Roads were buried under decaying plants turning to soil, and concrete buildings were broken apart by unstoppable roots. The creations of man were slowly returning to nature. The world was turning green again.

For a few years, he had tried to settle down, to live off the land and make himself a home. He had found a good spot, cleared it of the all-devouring undergrowth and built himself a house. He had planted seeds and learned everything there was to know about taking care of the plants. He had felt good growing his own food instead of scavenging the remains of the world that once was. Pollinating the fruit trees with his own hands had made him feel a part of creating a new balance, a new existence.

But after a while, sitting in a comfortable chair in his own house reading books had felt too much like sitting in the box, remembering stories. He had to move, had to see things.

Had to get out of the box.

Things were all there was.

Its.

There were no yous, no hes, no shes. Only its.

And the I.

The I had wandered aimlessly, seeing every corner of the world.

From time to time, the I had wondered about the box, and about how the I was the only thing that had stayed alive in the world. What the box had done to protect the I from the death. What the I had done to deserve the box. The I seemed to remember a story about a man being punished for something he didn't do, punished for being in the wrong place at the wrong time. But that was only a story, like all memories.

As the I became older, it found it moved around less. Its life slowed down. It saw less of the world, cared less.

Finally it stopped.

Sat down.

Its thoughts, once filled with all the wonders it saw in the dead world, started filling with stories from the past. Those kinds of stories that are memories, or could be memories.

Stories of a life with family and friends.

Stories of laughter and tears.

Stories of love, of loved ones. Of the betrayal of a loved one.

Stories of adventures. Of a great adventure gone bad.

Stories of a world gone mad.

Stories of brutal violence and of incarceration.

Stories of hope fading.

As it curled up into a ball, the I realized it had heard those stories before.

They were the stories from the box.

The Membranes in the Centering Horn

KG Johansson

There is a club in London, not far from Baker Street, just a few hundred yards from Tussaud's, where time has stopped. I happened to visit this sanctuary once, in the nineties, with my friend S.; casual visitors were usually not popular, but S. had some kind of hold on the *maître d'* and just needed a few words with this gentleman to get us in. Darkish and dusty rooms, chandeliers, of course no ladies, towering bookshelfs with volumes in French leather binding – you know. As did I.

What I didn't know was that S. was a gambling addict. He'd urged me to join him by holding out prospects of relaxing with a nice Scotch, see his friends, maybe talk to some of the celebrities that could be glimpsed through the pipe smoke – this was back when smoking was permitted. I believed my friend but nothing worked out that way. S. placed me in a sagging old armchair, right across from a white-haired old man who seemed covered by spider webs and who to all appearances was sleeping heavily. S. provided me with the promised whisky, said he'd be right back. And disappeared.

As said, I didn't understand that he had gone to the gambling tables. No doubt with the best possible intentions: just one or two hands, at the very most a round. But things worked out as they usually do in such circumstances. I was alone.

After a while, I started looking around. Before long I bas bored and worried. This was my first visit in London, my English was hardly perfect, and I didn't know anybody at all. I turned around, over and over, trying to hide my desperate search for my companion. When I turned back to the table for the third time the white-haired man had opened his eyes and was watching me.

"New member?" he said, in a voice that was as dusty and dark as the premises.

"Guest," I managed to stutter after a few moments. "But he, well, disappeared."

The eyes below his white hair were sharper than I would have thought. "You're not from this country. Dutch?"

"Swedish."

"Don't worry, he'll be back." Shaggy eyebrows went up just a little.

"Hope so."

The old man seemed to wake up. He huffed and puffed and worked his way up to a reclining position.

"You can talk to me for the time being."

What could I do? Instead of saying this was the last thing I wanted, I nodded and mumbled some commonplace phrase. And S. was nowhere to be seen. I reached across the table, shook hands with the old fogey and immediately forgot his name.

"You remind me of myself," he said. "When I was your age. In a strange land. Getting ready for life."

"So," I said. Well, he could work his mouth while S. was gone. And I was slightly amused by the idea of someone calling a 35-year old "getting ready for life." I said: "And which country were you in?"

"It all began in Egypt," he said in a tone that suggested this story had been told many times before. "You know the Aswan Dam?"

I nodded again.

"This was when it was planned. During the war. I was in Luxor when I heard of an expedition – they were going to study animal and plant life at the sources of the Nile. The usual stuff, you know. Documenting nature before the dam would change it. I was young and naive, hardly forty; I didn't know much of biology but I immediately accepted coming along as an assistant."

I made some quick calculations. The old man was definitely lying, or misremembering. It wasn't just that his statements would make him more than a hundred years old. In addition to that, his facts were wrong ... In short: I braced myself to listen to a cock-and-bull story.

Still, I had no inkling.

The beginning was traditional. The old boy himself and the three scientists, along with twelve black porters, had walked from Wadi Halfa and into the Sudan. They had passed between Al-Fashir and Al-Ubayyid, refusing to be oppressed by a more and more unbearable climate.

"But then," said the oldster, seemingly more and more livened by his own story, "we could notice the darkies getting worried."

I almost raised an eyebrow at his choice of words but managed to check myself. Instead I said, "Worried?"

He straightened just a little bit more. "There was an interpreter among them, and old man, over seventy no doubt. He spoke of a place that was supposed to be nearby, the mythical city of Nuzi. For some reason this was out of bounds and now the porters thought we were heading there."

He paused. I looked around again: no S.

"Well," the old man resumed. "To cut to the chase, as they say. I was going to bed that night, crawling into my tent, when everything went black. Woke up next morning. I'd had a nasty knock, nasty enough that the darkies left me for dead. But I was lucky. Thick skull, I guess. The scientists, two tenured professors and an emeritus, had thinner skulls, or else they got banged even worse. They were dead. And all the supplies and weapons, all lost, quite lost ..." His gaze disappeared into the crevasses of time for a moment. "The only ones left were the old interpreter, Mwunga, and I. Me surviving was a mistake, and Mwunga insisted that he himself was alive because the porters didn't trust him, but refused to kill somebody of their own kind. Well, I'll believe that as much as I want – I never saw such discernment among that race. But that was what he said: 'Darkie no hit darkie, boss'."

A waiter, also gray as spider web, passed and noticed my glass, which somehow had become empty. I nodded and gestured at the old man. "Two fingers," he said thankfully, "well, you know, Edmund."

Edmund obviously knew.

"So what Mwunga and I had to do was to reach some kind of civilization. We didn't even have a compass. Mwunga mentioned villages near Al-Fashir, so we went that way. But we must have gotten lost.

We crossed a mountain range that I've never seen on a map. Found a little stream right when we really needed water. Lovely water. Best I've ever had. Well, best water anyway," he elucidated as Edmund put two glasses on the table.

Edmund gave me an ambiguous look. I smiled and nodded. Edmund raised his eyebrows and silently vanished. The oldster drank deeply.

"The next day we were in much better shape. We kept following the stream. That water made you strangely exhilarated. In fact, the darkie and I were singing songs as we went. Can you imagine!"

I was close to asking which was more strange – singing although they were lost in the wilderness, or that the racist opposite me had sung with a "darkie" who unhesitatingly called him "boss". But I held my peace.

The old man put down his glass. "It's about here that things get weird," he said. "You may have had some difficulty believing me. But I swear it happened."

I looked as neutrally friendly as I could.

"We probably followed that stream for a week," he went on. "And after that week – well, I'll be darned if Mwunga didn't look a lot younger than when I got to know him! And me, I felt like I was eighteen all over again. Seventeen. Younger and younger, day by day. And the craziest of all ..."

He fell silent. I didn't urge him on. No need.

"The crazy thing," he said, "was that we suddenly realized – after a week! A week! – that we'd been following the stream the wrong way. Of course, you're more likely to find villages and towns downstream. That little stream might very well have been a headwater of the Nile, for all I know; we may have walked right back to Wadi Halfa. But no. We didn't. We followed the water upstream, right into the mountains. Why? Just don't know. And then, you may not believe this, but then the land changed. We saw flowers reaching twenty feet up, lovely orchids growing higher than trees, mushrooms big as houses, and it all was beautiful. Strange birds and butterflies ... unbelievable. Just so wonderful. And those last days –" his eyes went dreamy again – "those last days we were like kids. Younger and younger. We sang and laughed. We'd been chewing roots and berries for a week but now we found giant bananas and tamarind and all you can imagine. Life was lovely.

And then we arrived at the forbidden city of Nuzi."

By now, I must admit, I was getting interested. Although I didn't care for the old man, his story was getting to me.

"The city was a necropolis," the old man said. "Do you know the ruins in Meroe? The capital of old Kush?" I shook my head. "Not very different. Same steep pyramids. And not a single live person – but still everything seemed new, clean and sparkling, and there were parks and gardens and those beautiful birds singing. But there was no human being there. There was one living being, but I don't think she was human. Depending on how you define ..."

He interrupted himself and looked straight at me. "Do you believe me?"

I shrugged and mumbled.

"She looked like a woman. She did. Her skin was whitish, but her features were those of a black woman – broad, flat nose, full lips. And she was unspeakably old. She called us her little boys. Oh, I'm sorry," he suddenly remembered, "I should tell you that she spoke the same language as Mwunga – a variant of *Lango*, more or less extinct now. I didn't understand a word and had to communicate with her through Mwunga." He let out a long and trembling sigh. "Well," he went on, "to get to the point: she claimed to be four thousand years old."

This time I couldn't help raising my eyebrows.

"I know," the oldster said. He wagged his finger at me. "That was my reaction, too. The woman jabbered at Mwunga. Then she took me to a small spring nearby. I thought she wanted me to drink. But what she wanted was that I should look.

You see, I'd watched Mwunga change during an entire week. I'd gotten used to it. And many of his wrinkles still were there – it takes some time for such things to disappear. So I'd kind of accepted his change. But seeing myself ... I couldn't believe it.

All my small wrinkles were gone.

I really was twenty years younger. Believe it or not."

He looked almost aggressive. I made a gesture meaning: I'm listening. Keep talking.

He did so.

"I began listening in a quite different way. Asking questions. Trying to understand. And within a couple of days, I'd pieced her story together.

She wasn't quite a human being. Those were her own words. She was of a race that had used the Earth for one of many research projects. Not quite unrelated to our own mapping of flora and fauna by the sources of the Nile, but millions of times bigger. And her people, they didn't stop at documenting. They'd been traveling around the universe, manipulating genetic materials. She was of an ancient race, she said, and our planet had been grafted many times – for instance at the Cambrian explosion, and as late as fifty thousand years ago, when her people had helped defeating the Neanderthals ..." He raised his hands as in defence. "I'm just trying to repeat what she said, you see? I can tell you don't believe me. But if you'd been there. If you'd felt twenty years younger, and looked it, and heard all the details she told – then I think ..."

His voice shuddered; he drained the last of his whisky and sat very still for a long moment, actually long enough to make me think he'd fallen asleep again. Just when I was going to get up and look for S. he spoke again.

"Please forgive an old man. I promise not to get emotional ... Anyway, I believed her. And I still do. Is it so impossible that life on earth may be engineered? I don't think so."

He looked into his past again.

"Of course we spoke by way of Mwunga. But he and she also spoke when I wasn't there. I asked the darkie what she said to him. He just shrugged and said 'More same, boss, more same-same.' But it didn't quite feel that way to me.

By now, Mwunga looked like a thirty-year old. I also felt a lot younger, but when I asked the woman she said you didn't really get younger. The potion, or whatever it was, that she added to the water only put you in absolute mint condition. Wrinkles and whatnot disappeared, hardening of arteries too, and so on ... I'd give a lot to drink that water again.

But anyhow. The old girl said that the water only was part of what she intended to give our world. 'My time is up,' she said, 'and your world is ready to accept what I have to give you.' At first, I didn't think very much about that. But I could see he and Mwunga exchange glances. That was when I started thinking.

She died the next day.

I didn't see her die. I had been bathing in that wonderful water and came back, almost naked, letting Africa's sun caress my body. My young body. Can you imagine ... I remember it as yesterday ..." He made an obvious effort, shook his feelings off and sat up straight. "I saw her sitting in her usual place, in front of those steep pyramids, while Mwunga stood in front of her. I saw her offering something to him. Saw him accept it. She closed her eyes. And then – I was maybe a hundred feet away – then a kind of wave seemed to sort of undulate through her. And she fell, very still, so slowly that the Negro in front of her had time to catch her and lay her down on the ground ..."

His language made me want to get up and walk away. But I stayed. Just a few minutes more ...

He went on. "I called out to Mwunga. He turned around. I immediately saw guilt in his face.

'What happened?' I said.

'Granny' – he called her that – 'granny, she die.'

'How do you know?' I said. 'You're no doctor? Maybe she just fainted?'

'I know, boss.'

And he was right. She was dead. And somehow she had died by her own volition. I could tell. Sometimes one just knows. I said:

'What was that she gave you?'

You see, I already knew. But I asked anyway. Courtesy, you know.

'Nothing, boss,' the Negro said.

'Don't push me,' I said. 'Now get it out.'

He only wore a loincloth. I could just have ripped that off him. But I rather wouldn't. One has some decency in one, isn't that right? So instead I bored my eyes into him. He gave up in two seconds. Started fumbling in his loincloth.

'But it mine, boss,' he said. 'She say it mine ...'

He gave me something that looked like a folded piece of paper. I accepted it very carefully – knowing where he'd kept it – and tried to unfold it. Which was impossible. Instead, it fell apart. Or rather it divided. Divided into hundreds of pages, maybe thousands. Every impossibly thin page was covered in writing. I tried to flip quickly, which wasn't that easy – every page seemed to divide over and over again, as if they were infinitely thin. The letters were Latin but I couldn't understand a single word.

'Is Lango,' he said. 'My language. But boss, his letters.'

Of course, his tribe had no written language.

'What does it say?' I asked. I was fascinated by that material. Have you read Moby Dick? Melville's book? When they cut blubber in slices and the mates cry 'Bible leaves, Bible leaves?' I stood there and let the pages split under my fingers. Thousands, maybe tens of thousands. Bible leaves.

Mwunga hadn't answered my question. 'What does it say?' I asked again. He hesitated.

'Come on, out with it.'

He opened his mouth. Gaped like a fish.

'Eh ... it be ...'

'Well?' I raised my hand, just a little. That made him decide.

'She say, it be answers to all questions. Water we drink here. Never be sick. She say, go to other Earths. Boss, she say great witchcraft.' His eyes were wide. Round.

'I'll take care of it.'

'No!' He almost attacked me. Immediately changed his mind. 'Boss, she say it mine.'

'Yours?' I said. 'Why the hell should it be yours?'

He hesitated again. I could see him steeling himself. 'Boss, she say my people be the real people. She say, first people. She say boss people be ...' he hesitated over again ... 'lower race.'

I couldn't help laughing. 'Lower race?'

'I just say what she say, boss!' His eyes rolled in his black face.

'I'll take care of it,' I said. I put all those pages together and they promptly melted together, becoming a single folded paper again.

'But boss ...'

'Be quiet,' I said. I held my hand up and the darkie was silent. I said: 'Bury her.'

You see, I'd already started thinking about possibilities. I needed a Lango interpreter whose English was better than Mwunga's. If I could find that interpreter, and if just a tenth of what the Negro said was true ... I could be a millionaire. A dollar millionaire.

We left the next day. Followed the water downstream this time.

You can already guess what happened. The darkie was the person he was. During the third night he went for me, on a ledge above a waterfall. He tried to grab that strange paper. I punched his stomach but he already had hold of it. He yanked and I punched. The paper unfolded. Mwunga yanked till I almost lost my grip. I tried to get a better grip and the weird paper divided again; we were right above the abyss, fighting desperately, I tried to get a new grip but only caught a piece, a little corner of inconceivably thin leaves. A corner!

And in that same moment Mwunga lost his footing. There was a ripping sound when the thin material tore. The only thing that had kept him on the cliff was my holding on to the paper.

He fell.

I shouted out 'No!' since he was falling with almost the entire document. Mwunga screamed an unintelligible word, probably something similar, in his own language. He and the document disappeared into the raging waters a hundred feet below.

I made it to civilization. The effect of the water wore off and I caught malaria – I arrived as a gibbering fool. Spent six weeks in a hospital at Wadi Halfa. Refused to let go of the fragment. Still held it when I woke."

The old man fell silent. I realized that I'd been spellbound by his tall story. I shook my head to clear my thoughts.

"You don't believe me?" he said. He groped in his pocket. "I still have it ..."

He reached over with something. I took it. It actually looked as paper, a corner of a page, and it was actually full of unintelligible words. I frowned when it parted under my fingers and the torn page became many.

"Same writing everywhere ..." I said in surprise.

"You don't believe me," he said. "Of course you don't believe me."

"Wait," I said. "You mean to say ... you mean you let humanity lose a document that could have changed the entire world? Just to prevent it from ending up with a black man?"

He looked at me as if I was an idiot.

"Well, what would Mwunga have done with it?" he said. "Showed it to a medicine man? Danced around a fire, chanting prayers to his ancestors? No, young man, that belongs to Europe. Not to a bunch of naked savages."

I shook my head again.

"So what does it say?" I asked presently, trying to relieve the atmosphere.

He looked wistful. "I found an interpreter. In Wadi Halfa. He translated the fragment for me. I still know it by heart." He cleared his throat, thinking, and then said: "It says: 'From world to world in the intensity of light across the membranes in the centering horn.'"

I stared.

"I know," he said apologetically. "But it's impossible even to know which lines are complete. By the way, you're right – every page has the same words. When I saw it that first time, it wasn't like that. Every page was different. But with the pages torn ... it's as if the document was a hologram or something, and this fragment just repeats that one phrase until it's connected to the whole ... And the words might as well mean 'Intense light from other worlds against the cornea.' I've thought about this for years and years." He gestured. "'Sharp spear of blinding light from another celestial body through the fabric of space.'"

I tried to remember. "'From world to world in the intensity of light across the membranes in the centering horn?'"

"Right." He shrugged. "That interpreter was a darkie and knew nothing of physics. Or maybe he thought of it as poetry. I still think there's something in that phrase. Something fascinating. But you don't believe me and it doesn't matter."

"I don't believe you," I agreed. "You've been lying from the start. You are a liar and a racist, and I –"

At that moment I was interrupted, when there was a commotion from the next room. The oldster followed my glance. The butler Edmund came walking towards our table, a little too fast for his dignity.

I could hear S's agitated voice over the din.

The butler bowed quickly to me. He tried to conceal a certain shortness of breath. "Sir," he said, "your friend, he is leaving now ..."

I tried to protest but quickly fell silent when a man of quite another type appeared from nowhere: under his tails he was a very modern bodybuilder, full of steroids up to his ears. He grabbed my arm and pushed me toward the exit. The old man didn't call after me, which surprised me a little.

I guessed what had happened and S. confirmed the whole thing, out in the street a moment later: Big stakes, a lost hand, trouble. Thrown out.

I told the old man's story in a few sentences. S. laughed heartily, unperturbed, as far as I could tell, by the intermezzo in the club.

"So," he said, "how did you know he was lying?"

"I barely got the chance to tell him," I said. "He claimed to have been in Africa during the war. But the Aswan dam wasn't planned until the fifties."

S. made an impressed face. "Well, did he confess?"

"No," I said. "Brace yourself. He was quite unperturbed. He said, 'Oh, I am sorry. I was talking about the *Assuan* dam. The first one, the lower dam. Those names are easy to mix up. I wasn't there during World War II. I was there during the Boer war.'"

"The Boer war? When was that?"

I met his gaze. "Around 1900."

S. stared at me. Then he laughed again. "So he claimed to be a hundred and fifty years old. 'From world to world in the intensity' ... what was that?"

"'From world to world in the intensity of light across the membranes in the centering horn.'"

"What a wonderful cock-and-bull story."

"Yes ..." I said. "Really. An inspired liar."

"Did he try to have that weird paper analysed?"

I shrugged. "No idea. Never thought to ask."

My hand closed around the paper in my pocket.

That's almost all. We went to my hotel and parted after a quick hug. The next morning, the paper was gone. I immediately suspected S., called him for days but got no answer.

He was then found dead. He had starved to death at his kitchen table with two pieces of paper – two thin but almost infinite stacks – in front of him. Nobody seemed to care and I took the stacks. Saw them melt into one.

I counted the pages. This took me a few weeks. I may have been slightly off but I counted to 1 327 653 corners of pages. All had the same text – except one. I'm sure I saw a different page. But I didn't want to stop counting at that time and when I backed up the page was gone. I know I saw it. Never found it again.

The old man in the club didn't call for me when I left. I think he wanted to get rid of the paper. But S. was a fanatic gambler. He must have felt the kick for every infinitely thin Bible leaf he lifted.

I still have the stack. Somewhere is that other page, a page with some important words. A clue. Maybe something that might work as a key and suffice to display the entire hologram. Something that may reveal the gift that the old woman wanted to give to Mwunga. I can't count the nights I've stared at that stack, quietly cursing the old fool who was so sure of his superiority that he stole the gift and ruined it.

I've found a Lango teacher and begun my studies. The language is difficult. But I have to. Those fragments could change the world. Maybe they've just become jumbled. Maybe, when I have a sense for the language, my teacher and I will try rearranging the pages. Just a few tries. See what happens.

The membranes in the centering horn.

One Last Kiss Goodbye

Oskar Källner

She walked the last stretch through the woods. The birds were singing and the wind played in her hair. The driver had protested when she left the car, but she wanted to feel the sun on her face and hear the road gravel crunch beneath her shoes. Also, it would give her some more time.

Time.

She laughed and nervously fiddled with the glasses in her blouse pocket. A lump grew in her stomach. At one time she had loved to walk here. Those memories were now just shadows from a distant past.

The road passed over a crest and she glimpsed the cottage, traditionally painted in red with white trim. Everything felt smaller, the cottage, the garden and the lake. Suddenly the trees leaned over her. She couldn't breathe. She took some quick steps backward and touched the earpiece.

"Who would you like to call?" said a synthetic voice.

With a tug she tore the earpiece from her ear and pushed it deep into her pocket.

What am I thinking? she thought, and clenched her fists. *I must do this. Otherwise, I will always wonder ...*

She walked slowly toward the house, one foot in front of the other. She tasted the words which she had prepared; let them dance over her tongue again and again. She was good with words. At the holo interviews before the trip, she had quickly become the journalists' darling. There was not a magazine whose cover she had not graced, not a major talk show where she had not been a guest. After the return the media people had been even more persistent. But she did not have patience with them anymore. Nor did she need the attention.

The forest parted and she stood in front of the cottage. It seemed to be in disrepair. The gray wood shone through in places and the roof was missing a few tiles. The garden was overgrown and in a corner a wheelbarrow and an old rake were rusting away. Around the corner the plot was cut short as it swiftly sloped towards the black lake. An old canoe lay in the grass, a life jacket slung beside.

There suddenly came the sound of splintering wood. She walked round the corner and found him swinging an axe against the chopping block. She stopped aghast. His hair was almost white. Fine wrinkles traced across the face. His bare arms had big, blue veins and wrinkled skin. She had always known he would be old when she returned. But it was one thing to know, quite another to see it with her own eyes. She cleared her throat.

"Hello."

He stopped mid-swing and stared at her. The axe fell from his hands. The look on his face went from shock to anger and finally settled on disgust. She would have preferred anger.

"What are you doing here?"

His eyes bored into her. They were as dark and intense as when they first met. She tried to speak, tried to bring out the rehearsed words, but they got stuck in her throat. Suddenly he turned his back to her, as if she was not there, and picked up the axe. A powerful swing and chips and splinters flew all around. He dropped the axe and leaned heavily against the block. His whole body shook. She took the final steps over to him and gently put a hand on his back. He spun around and pushed her away.

"Don't touch me!"

His face was red and eyes wide open. He stepped away from her, breathing heavily as if he had just run a marathon.

"I just wanted ..."

But he did not listen.

"How dare you come here?"

"I wanted to see you."

An animalistic growl rose from his throat.

"But I don't want see you." He pointed toward the road. "Get lost!"

"But I've already sent the car away. It will be dark in an hour. You're not going to send me back into the woods, alone, are you?"

"You can call it back in no time."

She picked the earpiece out of her pocket and threw it in the lake.

"Not now, I can't."

He stared at her with bloodshot eyes and, for a moment, she was almost afraid of him. Then he sighed and turned his head away.

"I could lend you my phone, but I know you. You'd probably just throw it in the lake as well. I'll drive you into town. Tomorrow." He yawned. "Now it's too late." He crossed his sinewy arms. "An old man needs his sleep."

Then he climbed the stone steps and disappeared into the house. She was still standing on the lawn. He did not return. After a few minutes of silence she plucked up her courage and followed suit.

Nothing seemed to have changed. Wooden bookcases filled with old-fashioned paper books lined the walls of the small living room. The floor was dominated by a brown couch and an old, brass floor lamp. In the hall-way outside the kitchen was a small round table with two wooden chairs. On the walls hung paintings of Nordic artists: Anders Zorn, Carl Larsson and John Bauer. A voice came through the kitchen door.

"Sit."

She did as she was told and sat on a chair. He came out with a steaming cup in each hand and a packet of cookies clamped under his arm.

"Coffee with a lot of milk," he said and sat it down in front of her.

He remembers how I like it.

"Thank you."

He pulled out a chair for himself and sat down.

"You can sleep on the couch tonight." His voice hardened. "But tomor-row, I want you out of here."

He held the cup tightly with both hands, as if he was afraid it would fall out of his grip. His fingers were wrinkled with blunt, chipped nails. Sud-denly she jolted.

He still has the wedding ring!

He followed her gaze. His face darkened.

"This is nothing," he said, and tapped the ring against the cup. "You made sure of that."

She looked down at her own hands. Her ring was long gone. She had thrown it into a sea of lava on Siponia. It had felt like final liberation back then. Now the gesture somehow felt paltry.

"Why did you do it?" He stared down at the tabletop. The words were strangled, as if he couldn't get air. "I've never understood it. I did everyth-ing for you! I took care of the house. I cooked and cleaned. I took care of everything. It didn't bother me that you were in the orbital shipyards for months on end because I knew that you would always come back. I was proud of you." He lifted his gaze. A lone tear found its way down his cheek. "Why did you abandon me?"

She tried desperately to find the words that she had planned to say. But they refused to come to her aid.

"When they asked me ..." she tried. "You have to understand. It was the first expedition to leave the solar system, and see other stars, other worlds. I simply couldn't say no."

"But what about me? Our life together? You didn't think it was enough to make you stay?"

"But we fought all the time."

"So what? All couples argue sometimes." He put the cup on the table and rubbed his temples. "Okay, it's true that it wasn't that good towards the end. But all relationships go through ups and downs. I thought we had it under control. I thought we could work it out."

"I gave up."

"We had even agreed to go to couples' therapy."

"I gave up."

"And we had begun to decorate the nursery. You were going to pick out the wallpaper."

"I gave up, I tell you!"

He stood up so quickly that the chair flew to the floor.

"Yes, you gave up! How could you? This wasn't some worthless piece of junk that you just throw away. It was our marriage! We promised to be faithful until death do us part. Did your vows mean nothing?"

She tried to speak, but her words caught in her throat.

"We were just kids," she said finally. "I was only twenty and you were twenty-three. We were too young to be making promises to last for the rest of our lives."

"Maybe you were a child," he sputtered. "But I meant every word of my wows. And then you show up forty years later, as beautiful now as when we were young and you think you can just ..." He took a deep breath and calmed himself. "Yes, you're still young I guess. Isn't that how relativity works?"

"Well yes. Relative to Earth, time slows on the ship when we travel. For me it has only been eight years." She dug into her blouse pocket and pulled out the glasses. "Here, take these. It is loaded with pictures and videos that I took on the planets we visited."

She put the glasses on the table. He stared at them as if though they were a poisonous snake.

"Why would I want to do that?" His eyes bored into her. "Have you any idea how painful it was to hear your reports? To see photos of you along with the rest of the crew? To see films of you from alien planets? Every time, I thought to myself that I should be proud. But I couldn't ..."

He began to cry. Soon his entire body was shaking. She walked around the table and gently put her arms around him. He did not reject her this time. She let him cry.

"I'm so sorry," she said. "I never meant to hurt you. But you must understand that I thought we were over." She looked up at the ceiling, trying to speak not just the right words, but the truth. "Every time I came home it was the same thing. You had always arranged absolutely everything. I felt completely superfluous. And then we fought all the time. Finally I couldn't breathe. So I fled."

He buried his wrinkled face in his hands and groaned. Then suddenly he stood up. Unsteady legs bore him toward the door. He flung it open. Light poured into the hall. Against the brilliance he became a black silhouette and for a moment the young man she had once lived with stood in the door-way. Without a word he went down the stairs and disappeared. Unsure, she sat still in his chair. *He may need a moment to himself,* she thought. *Or maybe, I don't have a moment to lose.* She got up from the table and hurried after him.

He had sat down on the boulder by the water. It was big enough for both of them. Like so many times before she sat down beside him. They were silent for a couple of minutes, looking at the setting sun over the lake. Small waves drifted slowly toward the shore. Some birds circled over the water at the cape. He was the one who broke the silence.

"Why did you really come here? You must be after something other than to show me images of your travels. I have followed the news reports. I know you are going back to ... Eta Proxima was it?"

"Yes, they want me on the board of the new colony."

"So what is this? A final farewell?"

"The colony ship has limited space and it is important, when starting the colony, to get as wide a genetic variation as possible."

"Yeah, so what?"

"So we're bringing an egg and sperm bank with us."

"And ..."

"We are free to choose the other parent of our children."

He sprang to his feet, his face a scarlet mask of rage.

"Go to hell!"

"I want to have your child. Our child."

He took a step backward, as if to get to safety.

"Over my dead body! You still just don't get it, do you? I wanted to have children with you! I wanted to have a family. But not this way. Never."

"I looked in the registry. We're still married."

"A mere formality. I never sent the papers."

"Why didn't you?"

"I just never got around to it."

She looked at his hand again.

"Then why are you still wearing your ring?"

He fingered the ring, pulled it off and put it back on.

"I don't know," he sighed. "It's hard to let go. I thought about taking it off, every now and then. Several times I made up my mind to do it. But then came another report on the holo about your adventures on a new world.

And there you were." He shrugged, all spent, and was silent for a moment. Then he said in a small voice: "I love you. I have always loved you. I loved you even when I hated you."

"So give me this child."

"Never. You've already taken everything else from me. You will not have my child."

She slept on the couch that night. She thought about entering his bedroom. Her body yearned for him, but she didn't know if he would push her away. So she stayed.

When she awoke the sun was high in the sky and the house was empty. She found him on the rock by the water. He was wearing the glasses. Silently, she sat down next to him. After a while, he took off the glasses and laid them gently in his lap.

"A beautiful place, Eta Proxima," he said. "Those forests are quite similar to our own."

"The planet also has rainforests and deserts closer to the equator. But the place we have chosen for the colony has a climate much like northern Europe, with forests, mountains and fjords."

He chewed for a while on a nail. Tried to say something but his voice cracked. She put an arm around him and waited.

"What would you tell our child about me?" he said.

She thought for a moment.

"That you always loved. Even when all hope was lost. That you wanted this child's life, even when you could not be there yourself to see it."

He wept quietly. Tears dripped down onto the tufts of grass on the shore. He sniffled and said:

"Eta Proxima looks like a fine place. A child could be happy there." He looked at her hands. "Where is your ring?"

"Lost. Years ago."

He pulled off his own ring and put it on her finger. It was a little big but not so big that it would fall off. She wasn't sure if she was the one that kissed him, or if he kissed her, but for a moment everything else disappeared. It was one last kiss goodbye.

The Mirror Talks

Sara Kopljar

November

I kept looking at the pictures, even though the psychologist said it was time I tried to think of other things. I drew a sharp breath in irritation and in my mind I asked her what other things could ever be more important! I kept that question to myself, and walked out. I decided that she could never understand how empty my life was. Now the only things I had were the pictures. Images I kept flicking through, video snippets of laughter and drawings drawing themselves on the screen. I remembered my child's fingers pushing across it, painting in changing colors and smudging the screen. It was clean now, and the lines forming themselves on it were an echo of my child's movements. The colors seemed duller.

I had been watching the news screen on the train when a notice came up explaining that a company had started selling androids for private use. There was a short text explaining that this was the next big step in android technology, but what my eyes really stayed fixed on was the video. It was just a demonstration video from the company, but it kept rolling in my head long after I stepped off the train. An android had been walking side by side with a real human, and I couldn't tell the difference. It was so lifelike. When I got home I looked up the company online, and even though I browsed their site quite thoroughly I knew I had already made up my mind when I saw their website. "To meet your deepest desires," the header said. I imagine they had something quite different in mind than a single mother wanting her beloved child back.

January

I had always had these desires. I kept these thoughts to myself, satisfied in knowing that I had them and that they were mine. Satisfied in knowing that they were forbidden, and that no one would know. When I was a child I was afraid that people would find out, afraid that someone would read my mind in class and rat me out. I was afraid of being shunned, even of being put in jail. Mostly I was afraid that my parents wouldn't love me anymore.

When I grew up that didn't matter. I realized no one loved me anyway, because I knew they couldn't read my mind and thus no one ever knew what they supposedly loved. Today I don't have friends, only neighbors, colleagues and acquaintances. I was fifteen when I found out you could watch children being tortured on the internet. I visited sites on the deep web frequently, but I always stayed quiet. I was just an observer.

Then, observing wasn't enough. I found myself longing for the real. I fantasized about using my own hands to force a small body down, cutting it slowly, smashing it up and seeing the panic in its eyes even as it lay perfectly, perfectly still. When my eyes glazed over at my desk at work that was what I was thinking about: Children.

They sold android companions. No questions asked, you paid and they delivered it discreetly to your door. What you did with it was your business – nothing was illegal, except taking it out in public. Their page said nothing about what the androids were actually for, but there were videos of customers with their new androids; customers who seemed to be mostly old and lonely men. One video even showed a man with his android on a leash, smiling happily. That video disturbed me, but I had already made up my mind without even realizing it.

June

The sofas outside the office were modern, but there was dust between the pillows. Something hummed inside my chest as I was sitting there, and sitting still simply wasn't an option. I worried that I had forgot my tablet and I nervously checked my bag. It was there. The man who appeared in the doorway was slightly chubby, smiling softly behind his beard. We shook hands rather stiffly. I didn't really want to touch him. His office was friendlier than the waiting room, but it still gave off a feeling of anonymity that made me uncomfortable. I took out my tablet and placed it on the coffee table between us. I had to lean down and I noticed him peeking at my cleavage, still smiling warmly as I showed him the video of my child.

He started flicking through the pictures, stopping at some and hardly looking at others. He paused for a moment, looking at one of the drawings that grew on the screen. I leaned back in my chair, disgusted by this man who was trying to evaluate whether or not he could make money from my loss. I had offered his company everything I had if I could have my child back, I had such a profound longing to love and be needed.

"You understand," he took a deep breath and made himself comfortable in his chair, "that this isn't what we normally do. We usually create companions from scratch, perhaps inspired by someone but never a precise copy."

I decided to pick at him where I knew he would be uncomfortable. "I've seen the promo videos. You've made children before."

He stopped smiling. "Not as someone's child," was the answer he finally decided on. I stared at him coldly. "We will do our best," he said, and took out a contract.

"So I will have everything I want then," I replied as I scrolled through the contract without really taking it in, "except my money back, it seems." I signed and put his tablet on the table, leaving in silence.

September

The doorbell rang and I knew it was them. Two anonymous looking men carried in the plastic capsule. It looked like a large, blue egg, flat at the bottom so that it would stand upright. I signed with a code I had been given at purchase, they scanned my ID with a satisfactory bleep and then the capsule opened. Inside was the little blond child, stepping out slowly as I beckoned, looking up at me with two scared eyes. It was so beautiful. I never dared take them seriously when they told me I could have my deepest desires. The men took the capsule with them as they left, and the android hid behind me until the door closed. Its head reached just above my waist and the golden curls fluttered a little as it smiled. I asked if it knew its name. It shook its head. "You are my child," I whispered, more to myself than to it, and it took my hand. The hand was warm and slightly sticky, smaller than mine. It felt perfectly real.

I forgot for a moment my child didn't know where to go, and I had to lead it to the room. All the toys were still there, I had cleaned but never put them away or really made the room look tidy. As I watched my child sit down on the floor and grow more and more excited with play I felt a happiness grow in me that hadn't been there for years. I was a mother again. I couldn't tell the difference after a while – if there even was a difference between this child and my lost child. Perhaps I just stopped thinking about it. Having my child back meant so much to me that I could omit the little things that weren't quite right: The shit wasn't really shit; it was just chewed food with water. At night, when I put my child to bed I didn't turn on the night light anymore, but I turned on the wireless charger. My child didn't remember the things it should have, but we looked a lot in photo albums and talked about friends and relatives and things eventually became normal. A new sort of normal.

The only thing that really bothered me was not being able to take it outside. I would have liked to be able to bring it to the park, take it along to the supermarket, have other people see it and acknowledge it as a real child. They definitely wouldn't be able to tell the difference, and it would make the experience so much sweeter for me. Only, someone might recognize it. Someone might ask questions about the hair, if they looked closely. Perhaps it would even say something. It wasn't predictable, but I wanted to take it outside. I wanted to be seen as a mother.

November

I was so scared. Of course I had thought about it before, even almost cherished the fact that my child wouldn't grow old, but lately it had come to gnaw at my mind. My child didn't change. Experiences left no mark on my child, the personality stayed the same and it didn't grow. I thought I would like that, but it frustrated me enormously now. I had tried to make the bond between us grow, but it stayed the same. In my mind I began to doubt that there even was a bond.

Sometimes I got chills up my spine when I looked at it eating. I had started feeding it from a bowl on the floor, like a dog. It sat down with its legs crossed and ate whatever I fed it. By now it hardly ever protested; my child started to learn. I had imagined that I would get some sort of satisfaction from that, but it just made me angry. I think I had started to love it, and I had a hard time leaving it during the days. I started staying home from work with it. We did the housework together, and sometimes I would just watch. A real child would have thought that was strange, would have acted up, but not my child. I started to reprimand it for no reason, punishing it. Once I hit it so hard the skin broke on its forehead, and a sticky liquid came out, brownish, but nothing like blood. That frightened me.

December

I felt so attached to my child by then. I refused to leave it alone. I really believed my child loved me. I still hadn't figured out if it could think, sometimes I looked into its eyes and all I saw was wet circuitry. Other times I still saw my child in there. Then I thought about that brown liquid whenever I looked at its head and I was so scared. I felt like it wasn't real. My love was fake, just like the child. It was driving me insane. Sometimes I would just walk past my own door, too frightened to go in, and when I looked up through the windows I saw it staring at me. It looked sad. I wonder if androids can feel sadness.

I stayed away from home for three days before coming back. The first thing it did when I got in was to hug me and say hi. It called me mum. I'm not a mother anymore. It's in a closet, locked in. I can hear it moaning when I pass. My child moans for me from the dark, and my love grows. It's been almost two days and I can't hold back any longer.

I took it out and threw it against the wall the first thing I did. Children are surprisingly light, when you get angry. It cried there, and for a while I felt a little sting inside me. Then it looked up and I remembered. A part of me wishes that it was a real child. It would have been so much more satisfactory to kill it then. It scares me that I have such thoughts, but I want to see blood, flesh and real tears when I kill it. I want to see real suffering, created by real love.

I don't think my child feels my abuse. My child loves me anyway. It's like a dog that pines for its owner even though it's starved and forgotten. I find I am taking things to the extreme. Last night I crushed one of its feet completely. It would have been satisfactory, but then I was reminded it's not real. My child can't walk now, my child crawls across the floor after me wherever I go. I don't know if I like that my child still loves me. It's not natural. By now my child should turn away from me.

I keep hurting it. I feel like I'm going insane. I was supposed to love this android; I was supposed to have my child back. I can't control myself any more. I hit it and hurt it and the worst part is, I think I like it.

I can't help but be moved by the way my child loves me. Through everything it loves me. It only has one eye now, but the remaining eye looks at me with such fondness. The more I hurt my child the more my child loves me.

It screams as I hold it down. It screams just like a real child. I feel the little drops of saliva against my skin as it coughs and twists underneath my arms. My elbow digs into its chest, it slips off the ribcage and suddenly all the pressure hits my child in the stomach. It stops screaming and I feel my own tears burning. My child lies perfectly still now. I can see my child's eyes yearning for me, pleading to me, but it's too frightened to make a sound. I am the only thing in my child's world; I am the only person to trust and to love. Here I am, smashing its frail body to bits with a steel pipe I picked up by the docks on my way from work. The dark brown goo splashes across me, but it's not enough to satisfy me. It's just a surface layer right below the skin. Inside my child there is a mash up of bones, plastic flesh and electric wiring, but no blood. There are no organs, no heart. Its eyes still blink at me before I smash the battery. In all my angst and excitement I remember that it is just an android, but in my heart I feel I have killed my own child. I feel content, relaxed and free, for the first time.

Keep Fighting Until the Machines Fall Asleep

Eva Holmquist

Kate held her breath and pressed her face against the glass dome. She was watching a falcon as it circled in the sky. Magnificent. How she longed to escape the city, and see the other animals that lived outside. The city was stifling – much too big for her taste, and then there were the machines – always watching and everywhere, except down in the culverts, below the streets.

"Do we have to spend our free day like this?" Erik complained with a sigh. "We haven't had a free day in a month. There are lots of exciting things to do."

Kate turned from the breath-taking view and leaned against the balcony railing. Below her Third Main Street dissected the city. If she could fly like the bird and view the dome from above, the city would look like a small circle within a larger, the four main streets passing from perimeter to perimeter through the center.

"We could take the elevator to the top floor and go for a swim," Erik suggested.

"I don't feel like swimming," she said.

Every balcony on each floor, as high as she could see, was filled with human figures. Some, she knew, were people, but an unknown number were androids, humanoid robots indistinguishable from their flesh and blood counterparts. She shuddered. Not being able to tell the difference disturbed her deeply. The bigger machines, the ones used for construction, and even the smaller ones were easier to cope with, because they didn't look like humans. She knew the androids were as much machines as the surveillance and construction workers, but they looked like her. And now there were as many androids as humans in every part of the city.

"Kate," Erik said, grabbing her hand. "I wanted to spend time with you, but it feels like you're not really here."

His blue eyes looked sad, and she felt a pang of guilt. She hadn't even been listening.

"Okay," she said, forcing a smile and trying to shake her feeling of gloom. Erik caressed her cheek.

"I know just the right place for you," he said. "I stumbled on it by accident last year. I think you'd love it."

"What is it?" she asked, her mood lifting. She loved surprises.

Erik grinned.

"You'll see," he said.

He took her hand, and led her along the balcony to the elevator at the edge of the dome. Outside viridian woods stretched south of the city to distant mountains that appeared blue in the sunshine. She kept looking out, forcing her gaze away from the city. The further they descended, the more of the ground came into view. Rabbits were leaping across the fields. A lone deer stood in the distance seeming to gaze back at her. Then they arrived at street level, and she had no choice but to plunge into city life again.

"Come on," Erik said dragging her onto the busy Third Main Street.

Hot air hit her like a wall. She gagged on the odors of warm, sweaty bodies. The street was packed, and it was difficult to move forward, but Erik had her in a firm grip, and wove as swiftly as he could between passers-by. Every fifty meters, a surveillance camera gazed at them, the eyes of the surveillance machine. She forced herself not to look, desperate to stay off the radar. The machines didn't know about the resistance, not yet. But she mustn't draw undue attention to herself.

She started the group soon after suffering a serious accident, an event that had robbed her of her memories and been a turning point for her in many ways. They called themselves the Pro Humans and so far numbered five, all dedicated to the cause of freeing the city from machine control.

Erik didn't know about the resistance. She watched his back, blue sportswear covering his lean body without a seam. It wasn't that she didn't want him to know, or didn't believe he would support her. She just didn't want to put him in danger.

They turned into a narrow alley. There were fewer people here, and Erik picked up the pace. Kate hurried after him, looking around. There were no balconies facing the alley, only windowless walls. High up, the sun shone in through the dome, but the alley was too narrow for its rays to reach all the way to street level and without the streetlights, they would be in darkness. There were fewer cameras here, and no permanent security detail.

Erik stopped at a door. There were no cameras nearby. He punched in a code, checked that no one was watching and then entered the building.

They passed through a narrow corridor into a larger room filled with shelves, each weighed down by large, old world books.

Books? Kate was confused. Why would Erik think she was interested in them?

"Not what we're used to, eh?" Erik said, smiling. "No thought implant with immediate access to the network. But I think you'll like it."

"Like it? What is it?" she asked and took a step over the threshold. The door closed behind her.

She couldn't see any cameras in the room, which was strange. She'd never been to a place without surveillance, except the culverts where no one was supposed to go.

"These are the rooms of Kavi Bhagat, the inventor of the Generation Next Machine."

"The first machine with the ability to learn," Kate whispered.

She had always thought that the ability to learn was the main machine feature that had enabled them to seize power all those years ago. Now she was in the very rooms of the man who was to blame.

"He predicted the machine take over," Erik said, a starstruck look on his face as he eyed the books.

"Did he *want* the machines to seize power?" Kate snapped. Erik looked at her, sad again.

"No of course not," he assured her. "But if he hadn't made the invention, somebody else would have. He tried to warn people, but no one listened. The inventor himself prepared these rooms, to store all knowledge about the machines. I thought you might be interested."

"Well ... I am," Kate said and began browsing the shelves. *The Power of Learning*, *The History of Generation Next Machine*, *Network Theory*, *The Machine as the Next Generation of Computers*, and *The Base Function of Generation Next Machine*.

"How did you find it?" she murmured.

"I didn't," Erik said. "Last year, I had to pick up an interrogation machine, from an old programmer. He showed me the place."

"Hmm. Khavi Baghat wrote a lot of books," she said, picking out *The Base Function of Generation Next Machine*.

Erik looked relieved.

"We can spend the rest of the day reading, if you want," he said.

Kate didn't answer. She was already immersed in the book.

Two hours later, Kate put the book back on the shelf. She couldn't help smiling. This had to be the best day ever. She'd spent so many nights exploring machine operating systems, but had never been able to find a way to beat the machines. Now, with the help of the information in the books, and her previous knowledge, she'd found the key to solving the problem. Erik had been instrumental, but now he sat, eyebrows arched and his back against the door.

"I thought you'd be interested," he said, "because you talk about the past a lot and work with the machines. But I hope you'll be responsible with this knowledge."

"Responsible?"

"Some might use it as a way to change things."

"What if I do that?" she said. "You know I want freedom."

"I'm not sure what you mean by freedom," he said getting to his feet. "There haven't been any attacks in years, and no protests. Most people like their lives. They haven't got any problem with the machines being in charge."

"I know," she said, "but I do. As long as they're at the helm, we can't do what we want. I've never been outside. At least not that I remember."

"The accident messed with your head," Erik said with a sigh. "Did you even object to the machines before you moved here?"

Her eyes stung. Did he think she was crazy? She'd thought he understood.

"I don't know," she said trying to hide her emotions. "Everything is a blur. I don't even remember living in the fourth inner quarter. Nor why I chose to move."

"What is freedom to you?"

"To be able to do what I want."

"Like what?"

"Be outside," she said, and took a step towards him. "No surveillance cameras, or surprise interrogations by the security detail. I want more free days than one a month. It's hard to get to know people when you work all the time."

Erik sighed again. "I'd hoped *my* company would be enough," he said.

"It is, mostly," she said, trying to make him understand. "But I want freedom for all of us. These books are truly amazing."

She left him by the door, picking up the book she'd been reading.

"This should be compulsory reading for all programmers," she stressed. "It gives a deeper understanding of what we do, programming their tasks into the new machines. Hypothetically, we could put all machines to sleep."

"To sleep?" Erik said and smiled at her eagerness. "You must be kidding."

"There are several base commands the machines are forced to obey."

"They're protected. You can't access them."

"I know," she said with as light tone of voice as she could muster, "but it's fun to speculate. Anyway, how about that swim? It's getting warm in here."

Erik smiled.

"Sure," he said, and opened the door.

A nice swim now, and then she'd make an excuse. There was no surveillance in the culverts. She could use an old terminal there, and write a virus to crack the protection, make the machine distribute the virus, destroy the *Wake up* command and then execute the base command *Sleep*. She'd have to construct some kind of mechanism to prevent all attempts to counteract the command. But it shouldn't be too hard.

While she'd been planning, they had arrived at the elevator by the Third Main Street.

"Thanks," Erik said, smiling as they stepped in.

"What for?"

"Spending your free day with me."

And he placed a swift kiss on her cheek.

"You're welcome," she said, but couldn't smile because she felt like a traitor.

Kate was pacing the small room, in the furthest corner of the culverts, waiting for the others. She just couldn't stay still. Had she found a way to beat the machines? The noise from the pipes above sounded like cogs and bolts moving in her brain. She had mulled over her plan for too long. It should be possible, even if the risk was high.

Her thoughts were interrupted by the arrival of Akim. Monifa was close behind and the thick steel door moved back into place with a thud.

"Why have you summoned us?" Akim asked, a crease forming between his brows and his lips pressed into a thin line. "A meeting is dangerous."

"Relax, Akim," Monifa said and gave Kate a hug. "There is no surveillance here. No eyes and ears in the culverts."

"But all the ways leading down to the culverts are monitored. Is your information worth the risk?"

"It is," Kate said, and couldn't help grinning.

She forced herself to stand still, concealing her nervousness. It was a great plan providing Pro Humans at last with a chance to bring the machines down. It was a slim chance, but it was possible. They had an opportunity to be free. She could feel it in her marrow. The only remaining question was if the others were going to accept the risks.

"Let's hear it," Monifa said leaning against the gray wall.

"Not until the others are here."

Kate paused, prepared to defend herself, but neither Akim nor Monifa protested. They stood waiting in silence. Kate's palms were sweaty and she wiped them discreetly against her pants. The room was an old maintenance area no longer in use and sparsely equipped. A terminal at the end furthest from the big steel door, the pipes running along the ceiling and concrete walls painted gray. It was chilly in here.

Fina stepped in dressed in a cerise outfit with black stripes. Her high heel boots were all black and her black curly hair flowed freely down to her waist. She looked like she was going to a party.

"We have to hurry," she said. "I am on my way to an important reception. The Director is going to be present."

"You're not going to learn about their plans," Latif said, stepping in.

"If I can gain his trust," Fina said with a sharp voice, "we'll have a chance to make a difference."

"None of that will matter after today," Kate interrupted.

Immediately she had their attention. She took a deep breath. This was it.

"I have a plan," she said.

Akim sighed.

"Another one? How many times have we been through this?" he protested. "There's no way to defeat them completely. There are too many machines and they control everything. Even humans do their dirty work for them now."

"But I have a plan," Kate repeated patiently. "I've discovered a way to defeat them."

Monifa clutched her hands, eyes wide with excitement. "How?" she asked eagerly.

Kate waited, regarding her team one by one. Akim glowered back at her, still sceptical, but the others were curious, excited. If she was going to convince them it was now or never, she decided.

"Listen," she said. "You need a history lesson to understand the plan. The era of the machines started when they seized power all over the world, simultaneously."

"Come on, we all know that," Akim interrupted.

"But you don't know why they succeeded," she snapped. She took a deep breath. She'd have to stay calm if she was going to convince them.

"They belong to the same network and synchronised the takeover," Latif said.

"I mean before that," Kate said glaring at Latif. "Nobody told them to seize power. It started when we gave them the ability to learn."

"Yeah, but that's ancient history," Latif said. "We don't need to know everything."

Kate continued, ignoring him.

"Some humans were afraid the machines would learn too quickly, but they were laughed at. Now we know what happened, and we think it's too late to change things. You can't unlearn what you've learnt. The machines have developed far beyond our expectations. Androids are impossible to distinguish from humans on the surface. They are fully integrated into the surveillance system, connected to all cameras. A lot of humans don't even care if the machines rule or us."

Now even Fina was becoming impatient. "We already know our cause is pretty much lost," Fina interrupted. "That's why this reception could be so important. I have to go."

She turned to leave and for a moment Kate didn't know what to do. She needed them all to succeed with her plan.

"Wait, please" she blurted. "I've discovered a backdoor."

Fina stopped, but didn't turn.

"The machines were programmed to follow certain base commands. And they've been automatically programmed into all new machines ever since."

"What's a base command?" Akim asked, a look on his face that told Kate he was interested at last.

"A base command is an instruction the machine *has* to obey. When a machine receives the command *Sleep*, for example, it shuts down. Because all of the machines belong to the same network, I can make them relay the command to the closest machine in the network, before they themselves shut down."

"How many machines?" Akim asked.

"All of them, even the androids."

Fina turned around, her eyes wide with surprise. Monifa drew in a sharp gasp while Akim, eyes shining, took a step forward. It was working, they were going to help her.

"So, what's the catch?" Latif said, breaking the spell. His voice was soft, but Kate was still nervous and almost jumped.

"Come on, Latif, if what Kate says is true there isn't one," Monifa said. "She knows everything about machines."

Kate clenched her fists. This was what she had been dreading.

"It sounds too easy to me," Latif continued.

Suddenly suspicious, Monifa spun round with such force her plaits struck her face. "Well?" she demanded. "Are you misleading us?"

"No," Kate assured them, raising her hands, "but there *is* a certain risk involved, otherwise someone would have tried it before. But the chance to regain power over our own destinies has to be worth it."

"What's this risk then?"

"Okay, we can issue the command from this terminal," Kate said, pointing to the grimy wall-mounted terminal. "It's old, but it *is* still connected to the rest of the network."

Latif was glaring at her now, arms crossed over his chest. "Come on, Kate. Spit it out!" he demanded.

"Well, there's another base command with the opposite effect," she answered. "Normally it works in a similar way. A machine can command the next to *Wake up* and once woken it transmits the same base command onwards to the nearest in its network."

"That's not a catch, " Akim muttered. "It's a fucking gaping hole."

Kate shook her head violently.

"No," she said. "I've taken care of it, more or less."

"More or less?" Latif again.

"I don't want to get too technical, but I've written some code that will go out with the sleep instruction. It interrupts and blocks all unwanted commands on the affected machines."

"So they can't wake each other up?" Fina said.

"Not easily. To counteract our command they'll have to broadcast new software to all machines, replacing the core code that my modified base command has affected."

"Well, they can do that, can't they?" Latif said, exchanging glances with Akim.

"Yes, but if they do, this terminal will activate immediately and I can re-issue the sleep command again. We just have to guard the terminal long enough for all machines to fall asleep."

Latif was watching her. "You're still jumpy. There has to be something else." He could always see her through.

"Yes ... the alarm goes off network wide the minute I access the terminal."

Shouting erupted immediately. Akim approached her and waved his clenched fist in her face.

"Are you crazy?" he screamed. "We'll never manage to knock them all out before security gets down here. You're going get us all killed!"

Kate raised her hands to stop him, backing away until she felt the terminal pressing into her and could go no further.

"This is our only chance," she screamed back. "I don't want to spend the rest of my life controlled by machines. Freedom is more important than being safe and we have to defeat the machines. You all said so."

The shouting died down.

"Do you really want us to risk our lives when there is no chance of success?" Akim asked.

"There is," she insisted. "A big one. Yes, they'll know I cracked the protection, and where I am. Their first priority will be to stop me. But the moment they broadcast new software, I'll know. Information travels the network far faster than an android can run, and probably all androids in the neighborhood are relatively close in the network. Even with the time my virus needs to crack the protection our command should travel fast enough to outpace their network response. If we can hold them off physically until all have been deactivated into sleep mode, we'll win."

Latif was silent for a time, then he nodded.

"Okay, what the hell," he said, "I'm in."

"Me too," Monifa agreed. "I'll rig up some explosives to slow them down."

Fina and Akim nodded as well.

Four hours later preparations were complete and Kate was once again back in the small room.

"I've set up a simple visual surveillance using only lenses and optical fibers in two locations," Akim said. "The first one is placed at the other end of the culvert leading here and the second at the bottom of the closest ladder from Third Main Street. The images aren't great, but we'll be able to see the androids approaching."

Kate nodded looking at the screens. Monifa and Latif were in the culvert. Fina was on the ladder. Akim had drilled holes through the concrete above the door to make room for the fiber and placed a screen on either side of the door. It would do.

The door opened and Monifa backed into the room dragging a cable and switch box. She used her back to keep the door open while Latif followed with a similar cable and device.

"We fixed the explosives," she said. "The blast is going to take out our surveillance system though."

"It doesn't matter," Akim said, holding the door for them. "We only need to see when to pull the trigger. When the first surveillance is gone, we'll still have the second so we can see when they enter the last culvert. If there are any still operational after the second blast we'll have to hold them off here."

He indicated a heap of antique laser carbines on the floor near the door.

"Not exactly top of the range, but they'll do the trick," he said.

Fina was last to arrive in an outfit the same gray hue as the walls. Akim released the door and it closed to with a soft thud. Monifa and Latif finished mounting the trigger switches on a wooden rack in the middle of the room.

"Okay," Kate said. "Let's go through the plan. I'm going to issue the command from the terminal. Akim, you're in charge of watching surveillance, and informing us about incoming androids. Latif, you're responsible for detonating the explosives by the ladder."

"And I'll take the second charge," Monifa said. "Latif is a better shot than me, so he needs to be ready with the laser gun from the word go."

"Yeah, and I'll help Latif shoot everything coming through the door," Fina said. "We know what to do, Kate. Instead of preaching make sure you're armed too. Once the charges have gone off, defending this place is going to require a team effort. We all need to be ready for them when they enter."

The room filled with nervous clatter as they armed themselves and readied weapons before assuming positions. Latif and Monifa remained close to the wooden rack. Fina was by the light switch to the right of the door. Kate was poised at the terminal, and Akim was on her left.

Kate placed her rifle on the floor. The moment she launched the virus, she'd grab it and defend the terminal with her life. Her heart was thudding in her chest. Would it work? Everything depended on how fast her virus progressed through the network. Sweat beaded her forehead and she wiped her clammy hands on her pants.

The countdown had started.

Normally she could interface directly via thought implant, but the terminal was so ancient she could only access the system via a keyboard. That meant slow work. She thought of Erik and wished he was beside her. But then she forced those thoughts away – she mustn't think about him now, had to concentrate.

She pressed the last key; the terminal blinked once and then went black. On the instant the alarm sounded, a shrill piercing wail that hurt her head. In a smooth movement the laser carbine was in her hands and she faced the door.

Fina flicked the light switch and the room became darker, a faint glow from the surveillance screens sending flickering shadows. Monifa was nearly invisible with her dark skin and black outfit and Kate couldn't see Akim, because he was turned towards the door. But Fina's face was a lighter oval in the gloom.

"They're coming," Akim whispered.

Kate could see the legs of an android dressed in the dark green uniform of the security detail stepping down the ladder. Suddenly the android fell.

"It's been deactivated, the plan's working," Kate murmured.

"No," Akim said. "They're still coming."

He was right. Android after android stepped down the ladder. Kate held her weapon tighter.

"Now, Latif," Akim said.

Latif reached towards the switch but then froze and collapsed over the rack.

"What the hell?!" Monifa shoved Latif aside and pressed the switch. The surveillance screen monitoring the ladder went black.

The culvert was still empty. Monifa turned Latif over examining him.

"What happened?" Fina asked. "Is he dead?"

"No." Monifa shook her head "He's ... it's like he's asleep."

Before Kate had time to ponder the information, Akim shouted: "They're still coming!"

The door into the culvert was open and the androids were pouring into the tunnel. As they watched, one froze, stumbled and collapsed. Then another. The remaining androids stepped over their fallen comrades and kept coming.

"Now," Akim said, then he too collapsed, his laser gun skidding over the floor and into the rack. Monifa pressed the switch and the last surveillance screen went black.

"What's happening to us," she said, her voice shrill with fear.

Kate swallowed. "I ... It's the command – Latif and Akim must have been androids." she said.

"We've been infiltrated, we're doomed," Monifa moaned, grabbing the laser and getting ready for action.

"Don't give up, we're so close," Kate yelled. "Keep fighting till the machines fall asleep!"

They could hear the androids' footsteps pounding towards the door, but also thud after thud as the command reached them and sent them to sleep.

The door burst open, an android in the gap. Fina fired into the culvert and the door closed again with a loud thud. One second passed, and the door swung open again. Kate saw a laser blast hit the wall beside Fina, before she even had time to shoot. Fina fired, but there were too many of them and one of them got inside.

"Aaargh!" Monifa bellowed, showering them in laser shots.

The android went down. The next one in the door collapsed, causing the one behind to trip. Kate's hands were shaking. She fired and missed, but Fina hit the stricken android with a burst, and it flattened against the floor, smoke trailing from its wounds. The next one collapsed before they had time to shoot it.

The door was wedged open by the heap of fallen androids, while beyond them the culvert was still teeming with their fellows. Fina fired into the culvert, hitting one of the androids in the chest.

"Yeah," she cried, and then collapsed.

Fina too? Kate was trembling so hard she could hardly aim.

"What the hell *is* this?" Monifa shouted, still firing. Then she stopped.

In a daze Kate watched her collapse. She fired at the next android and missed, but it didn't matter. The android collapsed before she had time to shoot again.

Then there was silence and stillness. The culvert was heaped with fallen androids. Nothing moved. No sounds to indicate more were coming.

She moved close to Monifa clutching tightly to her carbine. Monifa was asleep. Her chest moving slightly. Kate hurried to Fina, then Akim. Both the same. Latif was actually snoring. Her comrades were all androids. How? She didn't get it.

There was motion in the culvert. She rose, her carbine gripped firmly.

The door at the far end was moving slowly. She held her breath and tried to steady her hands.

Inch by inch, the door opened. She could see the dark green of a security detail uniform. She swallowed, her mouth dry. The android moved into sight and she pressed the trigger. Missed. The newcomer's barrel was pointed right at her. She threw herself to the floor. Pain exploded in her shoulder. She fired blindly, looked up, fired and missed again. Her heart was pounding like a drum. The android took a step forward, taking careful aim. There was nowhere for her to go. Then it collapsed.

Kate took a deep breath. There was a big smear of blood on the floor. Her blood! She was dizzy. The room seemed to swirl. She rose, her laser gun falling from limp hands. No strength left to pick it up. The strangest feeling.

It seemed they had succeeded, but her comrades weren't there to celebrate with her. And if her friends were androids, why hadn't they stopped the plans? Didn't they know what they were? How was it possible to be an android and not know?

At last the humans were free, but there were no fireworks, no music and nobody to celebrate with her. She needed Erik. He should have been here. She'd go up, find him and help him. People were so used to the machines there'd be chaos at first. But they were free at last. She felt herself smile.

Kate staggered towards the door. Something buzzed in her head, then the floor jumped up to hit her and everything went black ...

Outpost Eleven

Markus Sköld

"Commander, come take a look at this."

It takes a second before Marta realizes that Sing – the communications specialist – is talking to her. She's not used to the title. Not yet.

"What is it?"

"We have a priority message from Outpost Ten, to all outposts."

She's been in command for about thirty minutes. She tries to remember if there ever was a priority message before, when she was a mission specialist. She doesn't think so.

"What's the message?"

"They've detected changes in the cloud. They want us to check at our end."

The master cloud they call it. Before it was discovered, reports popped up from around the galaxy about a phenomenon people called *black clouds*, drifting between solar systems. Being impervious to scans, nobody knew what they were made of.

The ships that did travel through them were lucky to make it out on the other side. So when a deep space exploration vessel discovered the master cloud ten years ago, far away from the most remote settlements, Central Prime decided to build a series of outposts to keep watch.

The cloud hasn't moved at all since it was discovered. Nobody actually knows how large it is, but projections dictate that it could probably cover the entire region of space populated by man, save for a few really remote planets.

Marta looks around. Her role as station commander is new, but Outpost Eleven has been her home for the last five years – minus the year of training at Central Prime. She wonders if her crew knows that she used to be a missions specialist. That she used to sit where that young guy, Sandan, is sitting right now? How many times she's sat there, looking out the enormous panoramic window? There should be stars out there – in space. Instead, there is only the cloud.

Of course they know. They must have checked up on her before she arrived. That's what she would have done.

They all look at her, waiting for her to give an order. The outpost is technically a military station, but the chain of command has always been quite relaxed by tradition. They are all scientists after all, not military. But this is not an ordinary situation and they all look to her for leadership.

She clears her throat.

"Sandan, do we have a reading?"

He spins around in his chair and starts pushing buttons.

"Unclear," he says. "I'm detecting some type of disturbance, but I can't confirm that it's coming from the cloud."

"Computer, what is the status of the sensor array?"

The station's computer sounds like an old school teacher – nurturing, but stern.

"Sensor efficiency at thirty-four percent, commander. Manual calibration recommended."

"I'll go check the sensor tower," Warren says and starts towards the elevator. He is the only one of her crew that she's worked with before. She follows him with her eyes, hoping he'll turn around to glance at her before he leaves. He doesn't, and then he is gone.

Nothing has ever happened between them. A relationship on the outpost would be problematic at best, catastrophic at worst. Besides, he is fifteen years younger than her and can probably get any girl he wants with just a glance from those steely blue eyes. She puts her hand on top of her pocket, the one with the note in it, and feels the paper through the fabric.

"Let's see," Sandan says, interrupting her thoughts. "We have a reading," he says and points at a display showing the clouds position. "It's one kilometer closer now than it was a couple of minutes ago."

"Is it still moving?"

Sandan shakes his head.

"It's impossible to tell right now. We just have to wait and see."

Marta bites the flesh of her lip, unsure what she is supposed to do now.

"Where are Trinn and Grule?" she asks.

"In engineering," Sing says.

"Call them. Tell them to start a level one diagnostic. All systems. We need to be sure that all measurements are accurate. And call Warren and tell him to get back here as soon as he has calibrated the sensors."

"With pleasure," she says and smiles.

Marta wrings her hands together behind her back and takes a few steps towards her station.

"Oh, and call Outpost Ten. Tell them we have seen some changes, but that we need to verify our results."

"Should I send something to Central Prime?"

Marta shakes her head.

"No, not until we know for sure."

Marta sits down at her station and takes out the small piece of paper from her pocket. She found it in her cabin when she came aboard, just a few hours ago. It's a handwritten note from Warren with two words on it: "Welcome aboard". It's just like him. She can't read him, she never knows what he wants, what he actually thinks of her. He barely speaks to her around other people. And then he does things like this. The paper alone must have cost him a fortune. It's real paper, not the synthetic kind. And he has made the effort to write it by hand. She looks at the letters. He has beautiful penmanship. A bit straggly, but elegant in a masculine way. Marta sighs and puts the note back in her pocket.

"Commander," Sing says. "Trinn and Grule have started the level one diagnostic. But Warren hasn't responded."

"Computer, open a channel to the entire station."

There is a low beep.

"Warren, this is the commander. Where are you?"

No reply. Sing and Sandan turn in their chairs to look at her.

"Warren? It's Marta. Can you hear me?"

She glances at Sing, silently asking her if the communications system is working properly. Sing checks her console, then nods. The message is broadcasting throughout the station.

Marta steps off the elevator and turns left towards the ladder leading up to the sensor tower. Each step is both familiar and strange. So many times she has been here before, in another life. Why is now so different? It's like coming back to a house you once lived in that is now occupied by someone else. Familiar and strange at the same time.

It seems a little darker in the corridor than she remembers. The walls a bit dirtier. Maybe not all that strange. Cutbacks. That's why the outpost now runs with a skeleton crew. Why spend money watching a cloud that hasn't moved in ten years. Until now.

Two years ago, the crew was twice as big. Everything looked new back then, everything worked. The new engineers – Trinn and Grule – are highly competent and keep the station in good working order, but they can't perform miracles. She's read the reports. Little things – showers without hot water, automatic doors closing too fast. Their priorities are to keep the station operational. Who cares about cold showers?

She takes a deep breath and starts climbing up, into the sensor tower. Antennae and receivers crowding the rather large room with tubes of coolant snaking its way between the equipment. There is a constant hissing from air circling the tower, trying to keep the machines cool. The window in the sensor tower is nearly as big as the one in operations, but the view is the same: darkness. The master cloud has swallowed all the stars.

"Warren?"

There is no reply. She climbs the final few steps and walks over to the systems console. It's active, and shows the progress bar for sensor calibration nearly completed. That means he was just here. But where has he gone?

"Vera, are communications working in this section of the station?"

She calls the computer Vera sometimes, when nobody is around. The voice reminds her of her old nanny.

There is a slight delay, then she hears the old familiar voice.

"Yes, Marta."

"Was Warren here?"

"He logged keystrokes on the tower panel fifteen minutes ago."

"But where did he go?"

"Unknown."

She locks the panel. Warren should have done that when he left, but she's not going to report him.

She starts for the ladder when suddenly she feels the hairs on the back of her neck standing up. There is a presence there – watching her. She turns, slowly.

"Hello? Warren?"

Her heart is racing. Diodes blinking on panels, the hissing from the coolant. It's not healthy to spend too much time in the sensor tower. The radiation starts to affect you after a while. Marta has spent hours up there. In her other life, before someone else moved in. But there is nobody there. She's imagining things.

It feels a lot cooler at the bottom of the ladder. She shivers as she lets go of it and starts walking towards the elevator.

That feeling again. Stronger this time. She turns.

In the far end of the corridor, where it's a lot darker than she remembers, she sees a shape. No details, just shadows in a formation that her brain connects into the shape of something ... alive. For half a second she thinks it's Warren and opens her mouth to call out his name, but she stops herself. That's not Warren. It's something else.

Her hands feel cold, as if her blood is draining from her arm and legs. She licks her lips. They feel cold too.

Could it be Trinn or Grule over there in the shadows? No, it can't be Trinn. She's too small. Grule is a large man, but this thing is bigger than him too.

"Hello?"

Marta takes a few steps closer, wishing she had something to hold onto. Something to comfort her. Passing the ladder, there is a sound from above. She looks up. Nothing there. She quickly turns back to the shape in the shadows. It's gone.

She lets out a lung-full of air and shakes her head.

"Get a grip, Marta."

She turns around and hurries back to the elevator.

Marta's hands are still shaking when she gets out of the elevator and walks over to her station. Sing looks up and Marta shakes her head at her.

"Open a channel to engineering." For a second, nothing happens. "Computer?"

Finally, the beep.

"This is the commander," she says. "Trinn? Grule?"

"This is Trinn."

"Have either of you seen Warren?"

"No."

"Nope, me neither," Grule says.

Marta gives a nod to Sing to close the channel, then paces a few steps, her hands folded behind her back.

"Computer, when was the last time Warren logged any keystrokes? Anywhere on the station."

There is a strained sound from the speakers, like an electric motor that's stuck.

"Warren has not logged any keystrokes since the sensor tower," the computer says.

Marta twists her fingers, and slowly walks over to Sandan's station.

"Could we recalibrate a few of the sensors to scan the station for life signs?"

Sing and Sandan look at each other.

"Well, yes ... but shouldn't we be monitoring the cloud?"

"Just for a moment. Warren could be hurt. We need to find him."

Sandan shrugs, then nods and starts pushing buttons.

"It's done," he says, a couple of minutes later.

"Start the scan."

"Scanning ..."

Marta stares at the cloud though the window. Most of the sensors are still directed at it, but somehow she feels she needs to compensate for the sensors they're using to look for Warren.

The panel in front of Sandan beeps. Marta leans in close, peeking over his shoulder. He shakes his head.

"I can see Trinn and Grule on level two. And I see the three of us here in operations. Other than us, there is nothing alive on the station. Not even any anomalous heat signatures."

Marta pulls at her collar which is suddenly way too tight.

"Okay, reset the sensors. And get Grule and Trinn up here. We need to go find Warren."

"But he's not onboard, the sensors showed that."

"He must be somewhere out of reach of the sensors. Where else would he have gone to? He can't just have disappeared. Maybe something's interfering with the sensors. You said it yourself. There was a glitch a few minutes ago. Before Warren disappeared."

Sandan scratches his head.

"I don't know how. The instruments would have detected an interference. The reading would have been way off."

"A part of the cloud maybe?"

"I guess it's possible," he says. "But we should have detected it."

Marta looks the young man in the eyes.

"So where is he then?"

He opens his mouth to answer, but shakes his head instead. At the same time, Trinn and Grule step out of the elevator.

"What is it?" Grule mutters.

"We need to organize a search party to look for Warren. All of us. He is missing."

Grule looks Marta straight in the eyes. He is almost the same age as her, but looks at least twenty years older. Nobody pushes Grule around.

"We don't have time for this," he says. "If the cloud moves while we're out playing hide and seek, there'll be hell to pay. For all of us."

"We'll set the computer to monitor all systems. If anything happens we'll be notified immediately."

Grule scoffs.

"Computer. Monitor all systems, and report to me immediately if anything happens."

There is that strained beep again, even more tortured.

"Computer?"

Nothing. Trinn and Grule look at each other. As does Sandan and Sing.

"Computer, confirm monitoring of all systems, sensors and communications."

Still nothing. Not even the tortured beep.

"Vera? What's wrong?"

She ignores the looks from the rest of the crew. Finally, she hears the computers voice. It sounds sluggish.

"Comman– *click* Commande– *click*"

"Computer, self-diagnostic."

There is no response.

"Sandan, what's wrong with the computer?"

He pushes a couple of buttons.

"I don't know, commander."

"Commander," Sing says. "The canary signal from Outpost Ten just went silent."

Marta hurries over to Sing's station. All outposts transmit a continuous transponder signal – a way to let the other outposts know they're still there. A red light flashes on the panel.

"They're gone," Sing says. "Last recorded transponder timestamp reads one hour ago. Not long after they sent their priority message."

"What do you mean?" Trinn asks.

"It takes about an hour for the signal to reach us. Distance through space and all that," Sing says.

"I know that, but what do you mean gone? Couldn't it just be a malfunction?"

"No, that would show. There are two options: they have either been destroyed, or the cloud has swallowed them."

"Is there any difference?" Grule grumbles.

Nobody answers. They all know ships have flown through black clouds before, but it's a dangerous journey. Nothing works, instruments are dead – sensors, communication. You have to program the course before entering the cloud and hope your calculations are correct. For some reason it's impossible to travel faster than light through the cloud. The hyperdrive is knocked out immediately, and without instruments to navigate by, the risk of going around in circles until fuel runs out is very real. Survivors have spoken of that exact scenario, like there was something inside the cloud actively preventing ships from leaving. They say that only ten percent of ships entering a black cloud ever come out again.

"Commander," Sing says. "What should we do?"

Everyone turns towards her. Her heart bounces like a ship without inertial dampeners leaving hyperspace.

"Are we reading any changes in the cloud?"

Sandan checks his instruments.

"Only small fluctuations on the surface," he says.

"We must find Warren," she says, quietly, almost to herself.

Grule sighs and folds his arms.

"Something is wrong here," she says and stares at him. "Can't you see that? He can't have just disappeared."

"We know," Trinn says. "It's just hard to grasp. Somebody vanishing like that."

"That's exactly why we need to find him. Sandan, you keep an eye on the cloud, and try to see what's wrong with the computer.

"Sing, you stay here too. Monitor the communications. There is little chance, but just in case a last message from Ten should show up. And besides, nobody should be alone.

"Trinn, Grule, we'll go down to zero together and work ourselves up. Nobody is left alone at any time."

Grule and Trinn nod.

"Are we in agreement?" she asks before she can stop herself. She could – she should – just give them an order. This is no democracy. But right now she needs to have them on her side.

"Yes," Trinn says. "It's the right thing to do."

Marta breathes a sigh of relief.

"Okay then. Check all places that might be shielded from sensors in some way. We'll bring portable comlinks and lights, just to be safe. No unnecessary risks. We don't know what's happened."

While Grule finds the comlinks, Marta walks over to the window to look at the cloud. She thinks she can see the fluctuations on the surface, but it's probably her imagination. How could she see anything? Black on black hundreds of kilometers away.

"We're ready," Grule says.

Marta turns around. Trinn tests her light and nods when it appears to be working properly.

"Let's go."

Marta hasn't been at the bottom of the station in years. And neither has Trinn or Grule. It's the level nobody ever visits as long as nothing is broken down there. It's a basement, in every sense of the word. It's dark. The only sources of light come from the emergency beacons every ten meters along the corridor.

"Isn't there any more light?" Marta asks and sweeps from side to side with her portable lamp. Trinn shakes her head.

"There's no need. People aren't supposed to be down here. Only machinery."

Steam vents from a pipe further ahead, which makes Marta jump.

"I hate this," she mutters to herself and continues along the corridor. Grule and Trinn are close behind her.

Grule sweeps his light back for a second, then sighs and ducks under a pipe.

"What would Warren be doing down here? There's no reason for him to be here. There's no reason for anyone to be here."

Marta shakes her head.

"I don't know, but we need to check everywhere." They pass a large metal container. "What about this? This might block sensors, don't you think?"

"Not likely," Grule says. "We have the most advanced sensors available. Metal would never stop them. We're using them to monitor the master cloud – and that thing's immune to scans."

Marta sighs.

"So what do you think happened?"

Grule mumbles something she can't hear. But he doesn't argue any more.

"Wait!" Trinn says and turns around.

"What is it?"

"I think I saw something. Back there."

All three turn their lights to where Trinn is pointing.

"I don't see anything," Grule says.

"But I did see something, I'm sure of it."

"More steam?"

"No, it was something else."

A bang echoes through the corridor. Marta turns around. Then the emergency beacons flicker for a moment and die.

"What the hell was that?" Grule asks.

Marta can sense something approaching in the darkness, and for a moment it feels like it might be Warren. She touches the piece of paper in her pocket through the fabric. Then she sees the shape. It's not Warren. It's the same shape she saw before, below the sensor tower. And it isn't human.

"Run!"

Shuffling steps behind them. Not human, something else entirely, like each step is accompanied by several echoing footfalls. Panic erupts like a small fire inside her chest.

Up ahead, a ladder.

"Up, there!"

Trinn and Grule racing ahead of her. The shuffling steps behind.

"Up, up, up!"

Grule is climbing, way too slow. Trinn yells at him to hurry up. Marta shines her light – which now seems to have lost some of its power – back along the corridor. Long arms stretching out from behind a cluster of pipes.

She lunges at the ladder and starts climbing. Grule has his hand out and grabs hold of her, pulls her up. Trinn is ready and slams the hatch closed as soon as she is clear. Then she sits on the floor, panting.

"What was that?"

Grule shakes his head.

"I have no idea. I couldn't get a good look."

"How did it get on board?"

Marta shakes her head. "I don't know."

"And what's happened with the power?"

Marta looks around. Level one should have lights, but it's as dark as level zero.

She shines her light in Trinn's eyes and sees fear reflected there. What's worse, Grule, the bitter old engineer, is terrified. Dread threatens to suffocate her. She shakes her head to clear it and lifts the comlink to her mouth.

"Sing, what's happened with the power?"

There is no reply. Not even static from the comlink. She shakes it and tries again. Trinn tries hers, and then Grule. All the comlinks are dead.

"What's going on here?"

"That. Whatever it was. That's what must have killed Warren."

"Don't say that!" Marta blurts. She shuts her mouth, wishing she could take her words back. They sounded anxious, almost hysterical, which is exactly the way she feels. And she doesn't like it, but the thought that Warren might be dead ... she's just not ready for that.

"It's the only reasonable explanation," Grule says. "Something has gotten on board and Warren is missing. Put two and two together. We should evacuate immediately."

Marta swallows. *Give up?* Her body is shaking. She has never been more afraid, of anything. She doesn't want to die. But the thought of leaving on the rescue ship, not knowing if Warren is still back there somewhere. She has to know.

"It's still down there. We made it. That means maybe Warren did too. We continue upwards. We still need to go through all levels now that the elevator is out."

Trinn nods. "Okay, but we must hurry. There are other hatches leading up from level zero."

Marta stands. "Yes. Where is the next ladder?"

"At the other end of the level," Trinn says. "Right next to the other hatch coming up from level zero."

Marta looks at Grule. He nods. "It's our only chance," he says. "If we hurry, maybe it hasn't made it there yet."

They run through the corridor. Shadows seem to come alive around them, reaching for them with ghostly arms but never connecting. Marta scans their surroundings as she runs, checking every dark corner, but she almost trips over her own feet and has to focus on where she is going instead.

Trinn runs ahead of her, and she can hear Grule's heavy footsteps behind. Suddenly, Trinn stops, crouches down and sneaks forward.

"What is it?" Marta whispers.

"We're almost at the hatch."

"Can you see anything?"

Trinn shakes her head. Marta sees the hatch now too. She shakes her portable light to try to boost its power. It doesn't work. She points the weak beam at the darkness in the hatch.

"Let's close it."

Marta takes the first step. She looks at Grule who nods at her. He knows what he's supposed to do. He walks around the hatch, waiting for her signal. She slips closer to the edge of the hatch, her chin out ahead of her body, trying to peer into the darkness below.

There is nothing down there. Marta lets out a gasp of frustration. It would have felt a lot better to know that they'd trapped the thing on level zero. She leans in closer, angling the light to catch as much of the floor below as possible. Then there is sound. They all look around, then at each other.

"It came from down there!" Trinn shouts.

Grule pushes the hatch closed and spins the wheel to lock it.

"We got it," he says. "I'll be damned, we got it."

"Are you sure?"

"I saw something down there," Trinn says. "Something that moved."

"Was it the creature?"

"I don't know, it moved so fast. It must have been. Didn't you hear the sound it made?"

Marta nods.

"Is there any other way up?"

Grule shakes his head.

"Just those two hatches. It's trapped down there. Now, let's get the hell out of here."

"Lead the way."

Level two is familiar ground to Trinn and Grule – main engineering.

"Do you see anything out of the ordinary?"

Grule shakes his head.

"Nothing, except for that it's dark as hell."

They continue through the maze that is engineering. Marta's breath comes out as smoke and she starts to feel cold. The metal creaks and cracks as the coldness of space outside slowly starts to cool everything down.

Grule walks over to a panel and pushes a couple of buttons.

"That's strange. Everything has closed down. That's why it's getting colder. I can't get a reading from the engines, but if they've shut down too, we might start drifting."

"Do you think they have?"

Grule becomes silent and closes his eyes.

"What are you doing?"

"He's listening," Trinn whispers.

"Quiet, both of you."

Grule is silent for almost thirty seconds.

"I can't hear anything. As far as I can tell everything is dead."

"Dead? How?"

"Not dead exactly. More like sleeping. Look at this panel, how it's dimmed. That's what's happened to everything. It's online, but it doesn't work. Any of it. This must be what happens when a ship enters a black cloud."

"But we're not in the cloud."

"And you know that, do you?" Grule snaps.

Trinn puts her hand on his massive forearm.

"Grule, relax."

A loud creak echoes through the station.

Marta's voice carries no more than a whisper.

"What was that?"

"The hull setting," Grule says. "Or the hatch down to zero being forced open."

Trinn shines her light around her.

"In any case, we should hurry. Follow me."

Marta can see the ladder when she hears a hissing sound.

"It's right behind us. Hurry!"

Grule gets to the ladder first and starts climbing. Trinn is right behind him. Marta waits at the bottom of the ladder, shining the light at where they came from. The hiss is constant. She squints in the gloom and tries to see.

"Is that a gas leak? Steam venting?"

Nobody hears her, and her thoughts are interrupted by Trinn screaming. She drops from the ladder, frantically shaking her hands.

"What is it?!"

Marta turns her light on Trinn. She is red all over. Sticky red dripping from her face and hands.

"Oh no ..."

She looks up. Blood is trickling from the top of the hatch and Grule is gone.

"It took him! It took him!"

Trinn is hyperventilating and slumps to the floor. Marta pulls her up again.

"Trinn! Pull yourself together! Is there another ladder? *Trinn!*"

She just shakes her head, going "No, no, no, no ..."

Marta turns around, spots a narrow passage between some pipes and two large machines. She should know what they are but her memory isn't serving her right now. She grabs Trinn by the arm and pulls her along. Another corridor on the other side. Or is it the same? Everything is different in the dark, and she hasn't been down to engineering in years. She was a mission specialist, working in operations analyzing data from the sensors. Alongside Warren.

She bolts down the corridor, turns right around another large machine. There is a wheezing sound coming from behind it, like the labored breathing of a sleeping giant.

She stops. Behind some pipes there's a shape – like an extended shadow, vaguely human, but still monstrous. The arms appear to reach the floor and the head is elongated. She backs away, slowly. Turns left behind the machines and enters a dead end.

"Trinn, where do we go?"

Trinn stares at her, her eyes blank.

"It took him ..."

Marta draws a deep breath and puts her hands on Trinn's cheeks.

"Trinn, listen to me. Is there another ladder up?"

Trinn only shakes her head and starts to slump down again. She is about to faint. Marta feels her own hands starting to tingle and her head is spinning. She presses her forehead on the cold metal and closes her eyes.

Think.

Five years on this station. She knows this. She clenches her teeth. The answer lies there, somewhere in her brain.

A hissing. It's coming closer.

There is no more time. She grabs Trinn by the arm and starts running. Just running, away from the hissing, away from the thing that killed Grule. Killed Warren. The thought comes from nowhere, like an unexpected punch in the gut. She imagines him on his back, his beautiful eyes staring into space. Dead.

No. Push away all thoughts. She has responsibilities. For her crew, for the woman she's dragging behind her, for Sing and Sandan. For the station. She needs to get back to operations. Make a plan.

Suddenly, it all comes back to her. The layout of engineering. She just needs to go right after that cluster of wires. She turns to see if the creature is still behind them. She can't see it anymore. Rounding the air filtration unit, she spots the ladder.

"Trinn, climb!"

She's pushing the engineer up the ladder. Still sobbing, her panic seems to lessen and she starts climbing like a mad woman. Marta follows her up, slams the hatch behind them and locks it.

"Next ladder!" she shouts, at the same time realizing there must already be a creature on this floor as well. Or is it the same? They never closed the hatch where Grule died. No matter, she's not about to stay and find out.

Trinn starts up the ladder. Marta flies up behind her and locks the hatch behind them.

Trinn is coming back. Her blank stare is replaced by red eyes.

"Are there any more hatches on this level?"

Trinn shakes her head.

"Not on this level. This is the only one between third and fourth."

Marta lies down on the floor and draws a deep breath, but the air seems thin.

"I'm sorry," Trinn says. "I didn't think I was like that. Someone who loses it."

"Don't apologize." Marta reaches out and pats her leg. She tries to sit up, but can't. Her entire body is shaking, coming off the adrenaline. Trinn helps her up.

"We must get to operations, try to figure out a plan."

Trinn nods.

"The next ladder is over there."

"Show the way."

The hatch is heavy, but by joining forces they get it open. Marta sticks her head up.

"Sing? Sandan? Are you here?"

Quick steps approaching.

"Commander, is that you?"

"It's us."

Marta climbs up and turns to help Trinn.

"Where's Grule?" Sing asks and goes silent when she sees Trinn's blood spattered face.

"Grule is dead," Marta says.

"And Warren," Trinn says.

Marta wants to protest, but the realization aches in her chest.

"Why does nothing work?" Sandan asks.

"We don't know. Some sort of suppression field maybe."

Marta takes a few steps towards the console, but stops when she sees they are dim, just like the console in engineering.

"Any news about the cloud?"

Sandan shakes his head.

"Still nothing. But we lost sensors when the power went out, so I couldn't say for sure."

"It's starting to get cold in here," Sing says. "In a couple of hours it'll be freezing."

"Yes, we noticed. Is there any way we can send a message to Central Prime?"

Sing shakes her head.

"There isn't enough power to send a hyperspace message. Maybe a normal one, but that would take decades to arrive."

Trinn looks at Marta.

"We have bigger problems. There is something onboard."

"What?"

"We don't know. It's not human."

"From the cloud?"

They all know the stories. Half mad space captains saying that something lives inside the clouds. Something alien. Many want to believe it, given that no other intelligent life has been found in explored space. At the same time, so many theories exist that nobody knows fact from fiction.

"Where else would it come from?" Trinn asks, looking out the window.

"But how did it get here?"

"Maybe a part of the cloud has broken loose without us noticing it?"

Sandan shrugs.

"That's highly unlikely."

"But what should we do?"

"We evacuate," Marta says and looks at the floor. A few hours as commander, and she is giving the order to evacuate. "We don't have a choice. We need to warn Central Prime about what's happening. We have something on board that's killing us and we've seen changes in the cloud."

"You'll get no argument from me," Sandan says and lets out a chuckle which sounds very inappropriate.

She understands him. Part of her feels the relief as well. The other part wonders if Warren is still out there somewhere.

Every outpost has an escape ship. Sending for transport is out of the question, since it would take months for rescue to arrive. Outpost Eleven's escape ship is called Runner Eleven. Marta can see its outline as they walk across the bridge above the hangar, and at this moment she has never seen a more beautiful ship.

Sandan is on point, tightly followed by Sing.

Just as he takes the first step on the stairs leading down to the hangar deck, he is stopped by Trinn, whispering.

"It's there."

Marta strains her eyes and sweeps the hangar with her light, and then she sees it. A presence, moving in the shadows.

"Is it the same one?"

"I can't tell."

Their breath is fogging on the icy air, but Marta feels the cold worse than that, like the sweat on her back is freezing.

"What do we do?" Sing asks.

Marta bites the flesh of her lip.

"Somebody has to lure it away from the ship."

She looks around. Nobody meets her eyes.

"How?" Sing whispers.

"I'll do it," Trinn says, still looking at the floor.

Marta shakes her head.

"No, I will. The rest of you, get on board and get her ready for takeoff. I need you there, Trinn. In case something is wrong with the ship."

"Grule always made sure the runner was in top condition. He never talked about it, but I know how much pride he took in that part of the job. He always loved ships more than space stations."

"I still want you on board. If the suppression field is affecting the runner we might need a little engineering wizardry to get us going."

Marta takes the note from her pocket. She dares not fold it open to see his handwriting, but she needs to feel it under her fingers. For luck. And in case it's the last time. The paper feels warm against her cold fingers. She closes her eyes and draws a deep breath through her nose. The air is thin. It's becoming harder and harder to breathe and they are all out of breath.

Runner Eleven will have air. And heat. They just have to get inside.

"When you hear me whistle, head straight for the ship. Sandan, do you have the key for the access hatch by the landing gear? We can't expect the loading ramp to work right now."

"I have it."

Marta feels nauseous. She doesn't want to die, but she doesn't feel like she has a lot to live for either. And maybe in death she won't have this feeling of rusty screws slowly drilling into her heart.

She licks her lips and takes a couple of steps down the stairs. The steel creaks and all of a sudden she is on the hangar floor. Her heart is racing. She feels like a five horned gazelle on the savanna of Jabez 6. She can feel the presence of the predator, but she can't see it. She turns. Tries to bathe the hangar in light, but her light source isn't nearly powerful enough.

Maybe it's more cunning than they think. Maybe it expects them to behave this way, and is two steps ahead already. What if it doesn't work? Marta shakes her head. That is a forbidden thought. She can't think like that. Not now. Not ever. She must focus on the job at hand.

She treads towards the wall, where the hangar door's magnetic lock release is located. She breathes, but she can't get enough oxygen. The air is so thin. Is the outpost leaking oxygen into space? Is that why the reserves are depleting so quickly?

The lever is freezing and the cold hurts her hands. The metal creaks as she puts her entire weight on it and starts pushing it down. A crack, like ice breaking, and the lever gives. She pushes it all the way down.

A sound, from across the hangar. She flicks the light in the direction and sees something moving along the wall, very quickly.

"Here, you bastard! Come and get me!"

She whistles, and immediately hears the sounds of steps on the metal staircase. The creature hisses and she hears the sickening sound of its alien feet. The sound makes her skin crawl – underlining the fact that what they are dealing with is nowhere near human. Rather something from a nightmare – from everybody's nightmares. A collection of the most horrible things humanity has ever dreamed up, given physical form. Is that what the clouds are made of? Humanity's dark imagination? Of course not. She forgets she's a scientist. She feels light-headed.

She throws her light at the shadow and runs in the other direction. Angry hissing and the shuffling steps moving closer. Something behind her in the darkness, closing in. She sees Trinn's foot disappearing into the ship. Lights flickering from the opening in the ships abdomen. She is alone now, the monster right behind her. She screams. She wants to live. If she dies now, Warren's death has been in vain. Everything blurs except for the lights from the hatch. Hands reaching down to help her. The steps behind her, closing in. Alien hands tugging on her clothes. She screams.

"Help me! Pull me up, pull me up!"

She throws herself the last bit and tries to grab hold of the hands. She swings forward and feels fingers around her wrists, pulling her up. The wind is knocked out of her as her stomach hits the side of the hatch. The next moment, she is inside, panting.

"Close the hatch, close it!"

Sandan throws the hatch shut and turns the locking mechanism until the studs lock in from all sides.

The ship jars as the engines start up.

"Sandan, Sing. Stay here and keep a close eye on that hatch. Don't let that thing get in here."

Marta's legs are shaking as she finds her way through the ship. It's not very large. Just an engine room, a hypersleep chamber, a small galley and the captain's ready room – her ready room. She climbs the ladder into the cockpit. Trinn is in the pilots chair, going through checklists.

"Are we ready? Can we open the doors?" Marta asks.

"Extending twist beam now." Trinn pulls a lever and a metal shaft extends from the ship, towards the hexagonal lock by the hangar doors. The shaft locks into the socket and starts spinning. The electric humming is almost drowned under the roar of the engines, but slowly, the hangar doors are opening. Air seeping out as white mist into the icy vacuum of space.

"I hope the fucker chokes to death," Trinn says.

Marta says nothing. She's just staring out through the window with her jaw clenched.

"Ready to go, captain."

"Take us out."

"Aye, aye."

Marta stands besides Sandan and Sing, looking out through the back window in the cockpit. The lower half of Outpost Eleven is wrapped inside a portion of the master cloud, protruding like some sort of tentacle-like tongue.

"Ready for hyperspace, captain."

"Good."

"How did we miss that?" Sing says, staring at the cloud.

"The sensors," Sandan says. "Why didn't they detect it?"

"Maybe they didn't see it," Marta says. "Black clouds don't always show up on sensors."

"Not regular sensors. But ours were made to monitor the cloud."

"Maybe they weren't good enough."

A moment later the stars stretch into thin lines, surrounding them in a tunnel, leaving Outpost Eleven behind.

"Sing, would you go and prepare the hypersleep chamber. Me and Sandan will fix us something to eat before we go to sleep."

Sing nods, and climbs down the ladder.

"How is the ship?"

"Everything is running smoothly. The course for Central Prime was pre-programmed and everything is in good shape. He did a good job," she says, her voice trembling.

Grule's blood has dried into dark brown spots on her face. Marta is about to say something about it, but stops herself. Trinn will see them when it's time to wash up and she deserves a few minutes of peace without being reminded of what happened to her colleague.

Marta climbs down the ladder and walks towards the galley when she sees a shadow moving in the corner of her eye. Sandan comes down the ladder behind her.

"What's the matter? You look all pale."

"I thought I saw something."

Now Sandan's face turns white.

"Do you mean ... it?"

Marta shakes her head.

"There's nothing there now," she says and nods towards the corner. "I'm just jumpy, I guess. The ship is working fine. In a couple of months, we'll be home."

"I can tell you one thing," Sandan says. "I'll never work on an outpost again. It doesn't matter what they pay me."

"I'm with you there. Would you tell Sing to come eat something."

"Okay."

Sandan leaves, but he is back just a minute later.

"She's not there."

"What?"

"She's gone."

The lights in the ceiling blink. Then they go out.

Marta is crouched in the corner of the captain's ready room – the only lockable room on board.

Everything happened so fast. First Sing disappeared, then Sandan. In the end she was alone with Trinn – and the creatures. There is more than one.

She saw one of them once, when it came for Trinn. She can't remember what it looked like, except that it wasn't remotely human. But still, there was something familiar about it, something that made her think about Warren.

At least two weeks left until the outer colonies. That's what Trinn said. Before the thing took her. It came out of the shadows – out of nowhere – grabbed her, and then they were gone. But she could still hear her screams, and then that sickening gurgling sound when she became one of them, like she was drowning in her own blood.

She understands that now. That's what happens when you're taken. They do something to you, make you into one of their own. Her crew – raw material to breed new monsters.

They scratch the steel on the other side of the door.

Two weeks left. They changed the course, her and Trinn, before they took her. Or at least they tried to change the course. Nothing worked any more. Could be they're heading for the center of a star. Or, the course was locked – unchangeable – and she'll come tumbling out of hyperspace at Central Prime in a couple of months.

There are emergency rations in the room, so it's possible for her to survive. But the sounds. The scratching. They are taunting her, trying to crack her, luring her.

She hugs her legs and buries her head against her knees. She will never make it. Not two months. Not even two weeks of this, alone with the monsters outside the door.

Then she hears another sound.

"Mmmaaarrtaaaa ..."

Soft hissing. Like it's whispering into the door frame.

"Mmmmmmmaaaaaaaarrrttaaaaaaaaaa ..."

"Be quiet!"

It sounds like Warren. It can't be, but it sounds like him. He wants her. Marta shakes her head.

"Mmaaaaaarrtaaaa."

"Shut up!" she screams until her voice cracks.

She clamps her palms against her ears. Two weeks. Two. Weeks. She shakes her head. The scratching again. Claws against metal. Something out there, wanting to come in. Something that sounds like Warren, but isn't.

Not anymore.

* * *

Angesum Bard likes his job. He is space travel controller of sector four. The station, in permanent orbit around Eskwan 4 – one of the up and coming colonies in the sector – is comfortable. He likes to be alone at night. When the others go down to the surface to be with their families. Or try to create a family to be with.

Not Angesum Bard.

He loves the quiet, just looking at the stars. The odd ship passing by, automatically validated by their transponder signals. Nothing ever happens at night. Just like Angesum Bard likes it.

He leans back in his chair and puts his hands behind his head when a red light starts flashing on the console in front of him. He tilts forward, frowning. The message in front of him: "Hyperspace exit imminent."

"What the ...?"

No ships are supposed to arrive now. All traffic to and from Eskwan 4 is regulated. That is Central's way to take control of the pirate problem, and it has worked out pretty well so far.

Angesum Bard looks up from the console and sees space starting to fold in front of him. Then the ship is thrown out of the rift – sideways. Its engines cold, drifting.

A few quick clicks on the panel and all the station's sensors start prodding and prying at the ship. No transponder signal, but one sensor zooms in on the name printed on the side of the ship: "Runner Eleven", and a government seal. A government ship. Angesum Bard sits up in his chair as the sensor reports start listing in front of him. The ship is dead. No life signs on board and all systems offline. Practically a big piece of space junk. He licks his lips. He really should send a report immediately, but a government ship adrift ... It's tempting to take a look. It probably has a lot of valuable equipment on board.

It takes him a couple of seconds to decide, and then he punches the panel, activating the tractor beam. The station starts towing the ship as he stands, brushes a few crumbs off his jacket and heads down to the hangar deck.

There it is, right in front of him. It looks odd. Not at all as strict and well managed as he'd expect from a government ship. It seems almost like something is growing on the outside of it. Something organic. That's not right. Angesum Bard takes a step back.

He's been around for a long time and he likes to think the reason for that is that he trusts his gut. And now his gut is telling him something. He breathes heavily and releases a whiff of asthma suppressant into the suit's air supply.

No amount of salvage is worth being reckless. He turns around and punches a button on the control panel behind him. There is a hum in the air and a slight shiver around the ship as the stasis field is activated. He activates the comlink in his suit.

"Surface control, this is orbit station. Priority concern. I have towed a derelict, and I need some assistance."

"Copy that, orbit station. We'll send a team to take a look."

Angesum Bard signs off. The ship looks so peaceful now, inside that stasis field. He shakes his head and removes the helmet. He can't believe he was almost stupid enough to go into a derelict alone. He chuckles, and turns around to hang the helmet on the wall.

He considers for a while whether he should go back to his station or wait in the hangar for the team to arrive. It shouldn't take too long.

The lights in the ceiling flicker for a moment and he hears a thud behind him.

He spins around. The ship's loading ramp has opened and there is a soft glow coming from inside. The stasis field has been disabled. Angesum Bard reaches for his helmet, accidentally knocking it off its hook and it rolls away on the floor.

Something moves inside the ship. Shadows of some kind. Not completely dead after all. But why didn't they register on the sensors?

"Hello?"

He hears a hissing sound from within the ship as black smoke starts trickling out on both sides of the loading ramp. Then he sees another shadow, and another.

The lights flicker a final time and die out. A moment later Angesum Bard hears shuffling footsteps approaching in the darkness.

Messiah

Anna Jakobsson Lund

A pale sun rises as I make my way through the city. The air is thick with the smell of burning garbage. Fighting among the scavengers again, for the third night in a row.

Some say it will spread over the wall. That the people living off scraps at last have reached the point where they can't be stopped. I don't believe them. The demi-kings of human waste will have their fight. In two or three nights smoke will fill the air when the losers burn their dead. The winners will take a bigger piece of the enormous piles. Maybe a couple of kids from the losing groups. Then relative peace will once again settle in the outskirts of the city.

I cross the canal on the rickety bridge, careful not to step on the right side, where some of the wood is rotting away. It's a hot night and the planks feel slippery and moist. Like the bridge is covered in fungus.

The humidity clings to my skin, makes beads of sweat trickle down the back of my dress. Three more months of the hot season. I don't care. The chilly winds during the dark times are just as bad.

"Need a fix?"

The girl is skinny and at least half a head shorter than me. Young.

"What?" I give her a sharp glance. "Do I look it?"

"Yeah, kinda."

Her voice trembles. Not just young. New.

I clap the pocket on the side of my dress.

"I've got three days of sleep right here, darling. Maybe some other time."

With a nod she disappears into the shadows. I couldn't get anything else even if I wanted to. Maybe it shows.

Tonight I sold one of my very last dreams to the virtual pleasure joint on the shady side of the second hill. Cheap too.

My childhood was filled with dreams. Of wasteland. This city in ruins. Other cities that I know I must've made up, because I've never seen or heard about them. Always covered in dirt and dead bodies.

But in the dying cities there were other things. Love. Children playing. I would dream myself a man together with his lover. Or a beautiful woman sitting in the Council of leaders.

The dreams left me with the feeling that they were real and my waking life just a faded shadow of reality. The injections don't give me dreams like that, they just take away the feeling of strangeness in the world.

From the canal a web of narrow streets creep up the city's fourth hill. The second hill, with its bars and live-tattoo places and swingers-clubs, never sleeps. When I trek the steep slope I think that this is the part that never really wakens. It's stuck in the mad-man's deliria.

People I meet are not dressed for a night out. Some of them are barely dressed at all. They scratch their arms with dirty fingernails and mumble. This constant, confused mumble is the breathing of the fourth hill. Ever present. Sometimes heavy and strained. Sometimes light and fast.

A man breaks from a group of people standing around a small fire.

"Messiah!" He reaches for me, his arms thin as branches, his fingers dry as twigs. "The Armageddon is upon us. The truth will set you free. Take your responsibility. Messiah!"

The second coming crazies are spread around the city. I remember them from my childhood. The mumblers would sit in front of our whitewashed villa on the top of the first hill, if my mother's maid didn't get there first to shoo them off. They increased in number as I grew. Sometimes I would even meet them in the university corridors.

But never like this. On this hill they occupy the streets, live in every building and burn-out. They attack me at night. When I leave the apartment to eat every two or three days they sit around crying and begging.

My house is squeezed between two wide buildings, both of which were institutions when such things still existed. Orphanage to the left, asylum to the right.

A lady in rags leans into me as I pass her in the doorway, grabs hold of my arm. She reeks of piss and dirt. Her mumbling is fast, shaky.

"Take the rose. Do what's right. Take the rose. Do what's right."

She gives a little scream as I push her down.

I hate this hill.

The stairs smell of roast potatoes and cabbage, of sweat and red dust. There's the sound of madness tossing and turning. The constant mumbling.

Take the rose.

The ones that don't mumble about the second coming curse the sin of the fix. Always turning to the rose as the solution.

It's hardly more than a myth. The mother of drugs. One injection will flush your system. If you survive you're clean.

There are many ways the rose can kill you. If it stops your heart and leaves you for dead, you're lucky. Sometimes it just takes your sanity. Some say the mumblers are old junkies, obsessed with their failed way out of misery.

Dangerous or not, many people, and their families, still take the risk. The dealers know this, and the drug costs a fortune. I would have to sell myself into slavery to afford it. That is if I wanted it.

I lock the thin door behind me, head for the bathroom. My face looks more angular than last time I saw it, the eyes big and bloodshot. The gray scarring next to the brown iris has grown quite a bit. I should change the eye I'm injecting. But losing one of them seems like a better deal than damaging both.

Eventually I'll lose them both. There's no stopping me now.

Black hair sticks out from my skull in spikes. I shaved it when I spent a week chasing a high instead of studying for the pre-med finals. The feeling of true joy, of oblivion, escaped me and I couldn't help looking for it deeper and deeper. Eventually I crashed and slept through the test. They didn't find any substance on me but they kicked me out just the same.

There's no stopping me now.

I take the bottle from my dress pocket, shake out the contents. Three days of relative peace. I swallow two of the yellow pills and go lay down on the bed. Close my eyes.

The pills are dirty.

Instead of sleep I get the itch. It starts at the elbows and spreads. Like wriggling worms under the skin. I must get out and find the bastard that sold me these. Or at least work my way through the sellers until I find someone who will accept what I've got.

Fatigue shackles me to the bed. I scratch my arms like a mumbler and try to fall asleep. Just fall.

When the sound leaks through the wall I first think that I succeeded. That I'm in one of the pill-induced dreams that I used to love and now always want to escape. It's a wailing, half human half animal. Like the tree spirits that some people nowadays turn to for guidance.

It's a cello.

Mum used to play it, long into the nights after her shift at the War Memorial Hospital. Those hands that cut into people's hearts could make the cello cry like a child. She taught my brother. Not me. She knew by then that my restless brain could only take so many hours of memorizing.

School was never hard, but it ate at me. The teachers wanting me to conform, to be a good girl. My mother wanting me to be something else entirely. *There's no room in this world for good girls.*

The more I see of it, the more I think she was right.

I curl into a ball, my joints hot and aching, my mouth dry and the itching like wild fire under the skin. With my head between my arms I try to keep the music away. It's not the bittersweet sound of a child crying softly. The cello is just off pitch, and there is too much hurt in the notes.

Sleep runs in circles around me. Three nights without, I should drop like a stone into those deep, deep waters of rest.

I need clean pills. And if I can't have that, I need silence.

The door next to mine is cracked open. The room smells of something sweet. Incense? It's the smell of the small chapel at the far end of my childhood garden. A woman that cuts into hearts needs someone to curse. Somewhere to beg.

I visited her after I got kicked out of med school. When she cut the allowance. This time she wouldn't budge. Stood with her arms folded and didn't even let me in to see my brother. But I know her. There was fear in her eyes. Sorrow.

The cello player sits at the dirty window. Some of the reddish light hits her gray hair. When she hunches over the cello, with her eyes closed, she looks ancient. A hag. Then she straightens, meets my gaze. And it's a young girl. No cracks in her dark skin. Clear eyes that look black in the faint light.

"They said this'd work," she mumbles. "I thought I'd have to work harder."

What did I expect? A woman playing the cello in the thin house that is pressed between institutions. Of course she's a nutter.

"Could you keep it down? My ... shift just ended. I need my sleep."

"They said it'd be bad. But I see they lied." She shakes her head, the bow slides and makes a harsh, grating sound. "I wouldn't have come if I'd known the truth."

"Please? Could you put it away? Just for a couple hours?"

She lets the cello rest against the wall, stands at the window.

"Come."

I'm an idiot. So I take four strides across the floor and stand next to her. She nods to the low rooftops stretching beneath us, the blood red sky.

"The world's burning."

"The trash fire started a couple nights ago," I say. "It will pass."

Her gaze goes from the window to me. I can't hold it.

"No Gracie, this time it shall not pass. The world has gone too far."

"What did you call me?"

"I've been told you shed your name. I thought I'd try something from long ago. See if you remember."

Granny. The crazy lady that always fed the mumblers. Our afternoons in the garden. How I never knew why she called me that name.

"Who are you?"

"A nobody. You, on the other hand, are not."

My laugh is as grating as the bow missing the strings. I haven't heard it for months.

"This hill makes you good at spotting the nobodies," I say. "I think I know one when I see one."

"Self-pity's a bad color on you." Now it's the girl-hag who's laughing. A dry, short snort. "I wonder what went wrong this time. You've never lost it like this before."

I back from the window. There are other worms crawling now. My stomach's full of them.

"Why are you here?"

"For you of course." She chuckles. "We're a whole bunch. The trip got to some. Well ... most. Sometimes they're not that clear. But you must've heard them. The second coming crazies. Isn't that what you call them?"

"What?"

My back's against the wall, and I feel the ground slowly swaying beneath me. The woman takes a step towards me.

"Messiah? That's what they call you. The crazies. We just call you Grace."

There's my laugh again. It sounds scared. What will she do to me? It took me forever to find this place, what if I have to move?

"I think you got me mixed up with someone."

The door is full of splinters and it hurts my palm when I search for the handle.

She gives me a small nod, licks her lips.

"You know what they say about Band-Aids? That's crap. Sometimes it just hurts too much to take the whole damn thing at once." Her smile's sad. "But there's no other way to do this, I'm afraid."

"Do what?"

"We don't know what went wrong. The dreams, are our best guess. You never got them before. You never had the faintest about what had happened to you. But dreaming about places you never been, again and again, that must've felt so strange. Maybe that made you start to lose it."

"You know Granny."

She is the only one I've told. And just in the beginning. It made her eyes look too worried for me to keep telling her.

The woman laughs.

"Sometimes I think I *was* Granny. It's hard to tell."

"You're not making any sense."

The itching is slowly replaced by an ache behind my eyes. I need to sleep. I need my pills. I need to get out of here.

"The second coming crazies know what they're talking about," she says with a hint of a smile. "Armageddon isn't far. Mankind survives, of course. We're worse than roaches that way. But the world will never be the same. We saw all of this, and we knew we had to do something. You volunteered. Or at least, you did the first five times."

"I did what? This is crazy. I'm leaving."

She reaches for me as I turn. Her thumb presses into my skinny arm. I could easily break free. But there's something in that touch. Something I do remember. How the heat from her used to rush through me, make me crazy. Make me do whatever it took to be with her.

I let my arm sink and face her. She looks away, for the first time not seeking my gaze.

"You ran the Continuum Center. We were ... colleagues, sort of. In theory sending people back to be reborn wasn't a problem. But there were some practical issues. And moral. It worried the board. It was banned by the Council of leaders. You didn't care about that. Couldn't sit around when the world was burning. You went back and left notes for us to go after you if we didn't see the right changes."

"Changes?"

My head is a mix of stupid questions.

"You were convinced there's a chain of disaster. That if some of the first links could be broken, the world would never come to its end."

"Didn't work out, right?"

She shakes her head.

"Twelve times and we've come up with nothing. Then we fetch you. Sometimes it's easy. This time it was bad. We've lost hundreds to the travel. They stop believing in the mission."

"Fetch me?"

"You want to be in a position to make a difference when the shit hits the fan ten years from now. You mostly get there in time. But you end up making the same stupid mistakes. Keep letting the world burn."

"Why?"

Her laugh is lighter now, like that of a young girl.

"Who understands the minds of people in power?" She straightens, gives me a look. "This time you're not gonna get there. I've been told to get you home. They say they'll start over."

"Come with you? That means dying, right?"

"In a way you can't die. In another you can't truly be alive."

The bow makes a scratchy noise against the floor as she picks it up. Her index finger runs the length of its hair. I can feel the soft, sticky feeling on my own skin.

"What if I refuse?"

She lifts her head slightly.

"Would you? I'm offering a way out. Peace."

Everything goes red as I close my eyes. Rest. A chance to do it over. Do it right. Gain power and make a difference. Be a good girl.

There's no room in this world for good girls.

"How would you even do that? Take me back?"

"The chapel at the back of the garden. On the first hill. We'll go right away."

My legs feel like mud. Home.

"It's an hour's walk. I'm sorry, but I'll never make it."

A shadow falls over her face as she crosses the room to me, it looks like she's smiling, weakly. She hands me a small glass vial.

"This will take you as far as you need. But change your eye. The nerve is heavily damaged already."

What does it matter if I lose my sight if I'm dying today? I don't ask. I hold the drugs tight in my fist.

"Will they be there?"

"Your family? No. They will be kept away."

That should feel like a relief. But still. They will never know. Mum will think that she lost me. And my brother will never stop asking what happened.

"And when I get back? What then?"

"Maybe fourteenth time is a charm. There's talk of trying to get you into the financial sector. It should be possible to stop disaster from there."

"You think?"

I look out the window. The sun has let go of the towering structures of the fifth hill, but there's still a reddish glow as of a sunrise. The garbage fires. Maybe the world is really burning. And they think the bankers can save it? I shake my head.

"It won't work. You said it yourself. I'll get a taste for power. Lose purpose."

"Maybe." She's still a few steps behind me. "But what's the alternative?"

"I stay. I fight. I figure it out."

"You're just afraid. Death can do that to you."

"I'm not dying. Not today."

She clicks her tongue.

"How much time do you have? Six months at this rate. If you don't run into something dirty. That could be next week."

"I know. But I can't do this. I can't give up."

The sun hurts my eyes, I squint and make out the people moving in the streets. All the people suffering.

"I've been waiting for this," she says.

It sounds weak and I glance back. Then I turn on my heel. The room is empty.

I let out a sigh.

It never felt like a dream. But they never do, do they?

Something hurts my skin as I clench my fist. The vial. I turn it with my thumb, feel jagged edges of an engraving. It catches the red light from outside and I see what it is.

A rose.

The Authors

Hans Olsson

Hans Olsson is the author of one fantasy trilogy and two horror themed short story collections. Books are a big part of his life and he likes to read as much as possible. A few of the most inspiring authors, according to Hans, are Stephen King, Joe Abercrombie and Terry Brooks. In his own writing he is inspired by folklore as well as video and computer games, such as *Dark Souls* and *Final Fantasy*. He has studied computer science and, when not writing, works with software testing. Hans would like to thank Johan Olsson, Therese Karlsson, Stefan Nerby, Adam Steiger and Nickolas Reynolds for proofreading and helping with "Melody of the Yellow Bard".

hansolsson.net

Boel Bermann

Boel Bermann has a background as a reporter for several large newspapers in Sweden. On top of that she is a member of the Swedish writers' collective, *Fruktan* ("Fear"), which blogs and produces a podcast of science fiction, fantasy and horror short stories. Boel Bermann's debut novel *Den nya människan* ("The New Children") was published in Sweden in 2013. She has also contributed to several anthologies, such as *Stockholms undergång* ("The Downfall of Stockholm"). Besides writing, Boel works at a gaming company, and she has previously studied journalism, criminology, social science, film science and social anthropology at Stockholm University. She always closes her wardrobe before she falls asleep to stop the monsters from crawling out.

boelbermann.se

Erik Odeldahl

Erik Odeldahl is a writer and game developer who lives in Stockholm with his family. He is very interested in how ordinary people act in extraordinary circumstances, and finds science fiction and horror to be perfect venues to explore those themes. He has had short stories published in the science fiction anthology *Maskinblod 3* ("Machine Blood 3") and in the horror anthology *Stockholms undergång*, co-written with members of *Fruktan*, the writers' collective he is a proud member of. Erik spends a little too much of his income on comics, books and video games, and doesn't plan to stop doing that any time soon.

odeldahl.se

Ingrid Remvall

Ingrid Remvall is a writer and art director with degrees in psychology and communication. She mostly writes fiction where she is not restricted by the laws of reality. Thrilling adventures with a touch of humor and unexpected twists are her trademark. She has had three science fantasy novels and a couple of short stories published. Apart from storytelling she is also interested in new ways of using technology. In her latest novel she let her readers illustrate the characters and monsters, and in the e-book you bounce between the story and 647 images in a linked illustration index. Ingrid consumes loads of books, mostly in the fantastic area, and eagerly awaits the new episodes of *Twin Peaks* to hit the screen.

ingridremvall.se

Love Kölle

Love Kölle has been writing since childhood and cares as little for genre divisions as he does for the limits of realism. In 2013 he released his debut novel, followed by a bizarro short story collection in 2014. His short fiction has been published by indie presses such as Affront Publishing, Epok Publishing and Oneiros Books. He lives with his fiancée and two cats, prefers Dr. Pepper to any other soft drink, has a bachelor's degree in history and finds immense enjoyment in watching black and white movies of questionable quality. His first name isn't pronounced the way you think.

lovekolle.se

Lupina Ojala

Lupina Ojala is a freelance graphic designer and copywriter. She absolutely adores the long Nordic winters and finds them inspirational – dystopian and apocalyptic stories are best written in such a dark environment. Other favorite genres of hers are fantasy and steampunk. She has participated with short stories and poetry in a number of Swedish anthologies and her debut novel saw the light of day in the spring of 2015. When not reading or writing fantastic fiction she enjoys practicing Japanese martial arts and spending quality time playing MMO games with her teenager.

lupinaojala.se

Christina Nordlander

Christina Nordlander grew up in Kalmar, Sweden, but lives with her husband in the small town of Stalybridge near Manchester in the UK. She has a doctoral degree in classics and ancient history from the University of Manchester. Since graduating, she has held various office and freelance jobs. Christina has loved stories ever since she learnt how to read and started writing in order to give something back in return. In 2007, she became one of the semi-finalists in the Swedish televised writing competition "End of Story". She has published several fantasy and horror short stories and is one of the writers working on the Tempus Ren module for the tabletop RPG Pathfinder. She likes playing computer games, reading books of all kinds and walking in the hills.

ananke-adraste.livejournal.com

Pia Lindestrand

Pia Lindestrand has a a bachelor's degree in history and a master's in literary science. Her biggest guilty pleasure is horror stories – movies, books and TV shows. In her own writing she likes to combine horror with a working class perspective and a rather dystopian view of the future. So far some twenty or so of her short stories have been published in anthologies and magazines. Pia also writes reviews of new books and theater plays. Her favorite TV shows are *Supernatural* and *American Horror Story*.

Jonas Larsson

Jonas Larsson began his career as a professional author in 2014 when he had his first novel published, an urban fantasy story about subterranean viking pirates. He has also had a few short stories published, and written for the Swedish gaming magazine Fenix. When not writing, Jonas works as a librarian, which includes helping adventurers fight Eldritch horrors and reading aloud to children.

trevligascenarion.se

Tora Greve

Tora Greve is mainly a writer of science fiction, fantasy and steampunk or alternative history, based on scientific theories. For example, "The Philosopher's Stone" was inspired by Sir Isaac Newton's writings on alchemy. In Sweden, Tora has published three science fiction novels, one fantasy novel and numerous short stories, one of which appeared in a German anthology on rising Scandinavian authors. She is interested in traveling, mountaineering and astronomy, especially solar eclipses. The latter interest takes her to all parts of the world. She is the leading female solar eclipse hunter in Sweden.

toragreve.se

Andrew Coulthard

Andrew Coulthard first saw the light of day in the wind-lashed, eastern coast of Northumbria. He later spent much of his childhood in the westernmost shadow of Scotland's highland boundary fault. For the past twenty-four years, however, he has been living north of the land of the Geats where it can sometimes get very cold. A college lecturer and communication trainer, he enjoys exploring heroic landscapes and partaking of good food and drink in his spare time. His short stories have been published by Eibonvale, The Alchemy Press, Morbidbooks, Trevor Denyer's Hellfire Crossroads, Oneiros Books and in the Ironic Fantastic.

Alexandra Nero

Alexandra Nero lives with her husband and son in the countryside of western Sweden. She studied literature and English at college, where she found a passion for constructing stories rather than only reading them. She works in administration by day and writes science fiction and fantasy by night. When she is not working or writing she can be found haunting the shelves of second hand book stores, looking for the next book to read. She has published a portal fantasy novel and short fiction in Swedish.

myotherblogisatimemachine.wordpress.com

Johannes Pinter

Johannes Pinter lives in Stockholm with his wife and two teenage kids. He has been working in the Swedish film industry all his life as a director (two feature films), screenwriter and editor. He debuted in 2014 with the horror novel *Vackra kyrkor jag besökt* ("Beautiful churches of Sweden") from Eskapix Press and will be releasing his second novel, *1007*, in August from the same publisher. He has published eighteen short stories in various Swedish and American horror anthologies. He also teaches the writing class On Writing Horror.

johannespinter.se

Andrea Grave-Müller

When Andrea Grave-Müller was a little girl, she learned how to write. She started to write stories. She hasn't stopped so far. Now, several of her fantasy stories have been published in Swedish magazines and anthologies. Her first collection of short stories was published in 2014 and received excellent reviews. Andrea has a university degree in archaeology, works in administration and has two children. Her interests include literature, history, gaming, music, martial arts, yoga, crafting, and a whole bunch of other things. Apparently, she still hasn't realized that the day only has 24 hours.

vinterdotter.se

AR Yngve

AR Yngve is a writer, illustrator, cartoonist, satirist and computer game designer. He writes in both Swedish and English and his short fiction has been published in Sweden, Britain and China. In his native country, Yngve has published several novels, children's books and comic strips. He currently lives in Norway, where he has written a radio series (broadcast and podcast in 2009).

aryngve.com

My Bergström

My Bergström is a freelance writer and translator with a bachelor's degree in Japanese. Most of her stories are born when she travels. As a student, she spent three years in Tokyo, Japan, which became a major source of influence. Her writing often explores themes of identity, expanding horizons and Japanese folklore. She has previously published essays, articles and reviews in various magazines, but "Mission Accomplished" is her first short story to be published. When not writing, she's been known to enjoy reading, daydreaming and writing about comics.

Anders Blixt

Anders Blixt is a political scientist and a linguist. He has designed numerous role-playing games, worked as a science journalist, served as a civilian specialist in multinational nation-building operations, e.g. in Afghanistan, and written two non-fiction books about United Nations peacekeeping. In 2011, he published a science fiction novel and a fantasy novel. His fiction is characterized by carefully crafted social milieus and sand-in-the-boots storylines that draw on his experiences in the field. The protagonists often get entangled in turmoil beyond their control and thereby have to face tough moral decisions, such as "What constitutes decent behavior in the chaos of war?" or "When facing a Hobson's choice, how does one identify the lesser evil?" Anders enjoys role-playing games with his buddies and keeps an eye on the exploration of the solar system, in particular NASA's Mars rovers. He is also one of Sweden's most successful Jeopardy contestants.

gondica.wordpress.com

Maria Haskins

Maria Haskins is a writer and translator with a lifelong interest in, and passion for, science fiction. She was born and grew up in Sweden, but since the early 1990s she lives just outside Vancouver on Canada's west coast. She has had several books published in Sweden (as Maria Larsson), including three books of poetry, a novel, and a collection of short stories. Inspired by past and present science fiction masters like Ray Bradbury, Ursula K Le Guin, Arthur C Clarke and Isaac Asimov, she writes about the human condition in a future where space travel, cloning, genetic manipulation and other technological advances affect the world and every human being in it, allowing her to explore both outer space and the inner workings of the human mind.

mariahaskins.wordpress.com

Patrik Centerwall

Patrik Centerwall lives with his patient wife and lovely daughter and son on the rainy west coast of Sweden. He works with communication and public relations for the city of Gothenburg and holds a holds a bachelor's degree in philosophy from the University of Lund. His collection of short stories, *Skymningssång* ("The Twilight Song"), was released in 2013. He has also been published in various Swedish magazines and anthologies.

skymningssang.wordpress.com

Björn Engström

Björn Engström is a film director and writer with a background in applied physics and interactive media. His short films "This Glorious Life" and "Unanimous Decision" have competed and won at festivals all over the world. Obsessed with story structure and new technology, he strives to twist scientific theories into entertaining fiction. Movies are an endless inspiration, from *Star Wars* to Tati, from *Terminator* to Tarkovskij. He lives in a suburb of Stockholm with his wife and two children.

bluemarblestories.se

KG Johansson

KG Johansson was born at about the same time as rock music, which became an important part of his life. He obtained his doctorate with a thesis on playing music by ear in 2002; in 2005 he became Sweden's first tenured professor in rock and roll. Since 2006, he's been writing and playing full-time: young adult novels, fiction, film scripts, opera libretti, translations, music books. He seems unable to stop writing and playing. Which somehow brings to mind the story of how Edward Gibbon proudly presented yet another volume of his magnum opus *The History of the Decline and Fall of the Roman Empire* to Prince William Henry, Duke of Gloucester and Edinburgh, and the Duke tiredly said: "Another damned thick book! Always scribble, scribble, scribble! Eh, Mr. Gibbon?"

kgjohansson.se

Oskar Källner

Oskar Källner is a trained theologian and computer scientist. He is as fascinated by folk tales and mythology as by astrophysics. In his writing he often mixes speculative ideas with fast action and existential issues. He has had two fantasy novels published and is currently working on the third. He is also an award-winning short fiction writer and recently published his first collection of science fiction and horror stories. Oskar enjoys playing video games and watching anime. Favorite shows include *Game of Thrones* and *The Walking Dead*.

munin.kallner.com

Sara Kopljar

Sara Kopljar grew up in the academic circles of Lund, a Swedish university town. Inspired by the history and international culture of the academic world, her writing brings up the darkness below the surface of a seemingly perfect world, and explores human interactions from a new standpoint. Sara's engagement in feminism brings another dimension to her work, allowing her to bring out the voices of women and LGBTQ people and break with the male domination of the world of literature.

sarakopljar.se

Eva Holmquist

Eva Holmquist is an engineer with a master's degree in computer engineering. She works with test strategy and architecture. Everything about the human condition fascinates her and she uses science fiction, fantasy and horror to explore what it means to be human. So far she has had four novels published – three science fiction and one fantasy – as well as numerous short stories, both science fiction and horror. Eva loves to read; among her favorites authors are Cherie Priest and Kelley Armstrong. Cooking and dancing are two other activities she enjoys in her spare time.

evaholmquist.ordspiran.se

Markus Sköld

Markus Sköld has always been interested in the supernatural, strange phenomena and speculative fiction – interests reflected in his writing, which often contains elements of horror and a touch of the unknown. His debut novel, a horror story set in the deep, dark forests of northern Sweden, is no exception. His second novel, *Kalldrag* ("Cold Draft"), will be published in 2015. He has also written a number of short stories, lauded by several reviewers as fast-paced page-turners. Markus also likes superheroes, the concept of intelligent robots and watching documentaries.

markusskold.se

Anna Jakobsson Lund

Besides being a writer, Anna Jakobsson Lund also works doing policy analysis and with group processes. In her writing she explores humanity, ideology and relationships. Her stories focus on human interaction in the midst of oppression or chaos and she often writes characters that break the norms of society. She has previously published two novels, the most recent a dystopian young adult story of friendship and resistance in a future Europe. The novels, along with two short stories published in 2014, have been well received. Anna seeks inspiration in science fiction and fantasy novels and is a big fan of TV series such as *Fringe*, *Game of Thrones*, *Top of the Lake* and *Marco Polo*.

annaskriverunder.se

Waiting for the Machines to Fall Asleep

Edited by Peter Öberg

Cover illustration by Andreas Raninger

Proofreading and additional copy editing by
Karlie DeMarse, Katarina Öberg, Andrew Coulthard,
Jeannie Matthews, Emily Moser and Melissa Manes

© The authors

Affront Publishing, 2015

ISBN 978-91-87585-31-9